Diamonds <u>are</u> forever!

"Suzanne Enoch's sparkling
talent makes each book witty,
romantic, and always an eagerly
anticipated pleasure."
Christina Dodd

"One of my very favorite authors."
Julia Quinn

"Suzanne Enoch just
keeps getting better and better.
Her books are witty, intelligent,
and—oh, my!—quite deliciously sexy!"
Kasey Michaels

"Indulge and be delighted."
Stephanie Laurens

To Whom It May Concern,

You may not believe in curses; I didn't. I do now. Look at the diamond, hold it in your hand, and then put it back. It's brought the Addison family good luck for nearly two hundred years, and I expect that that luck will have lasted up until the moment you made this discovery. Put it back, and the luck will continue.

Regards,
Marquis of Rawley

By Suzanne Enoch

Coming October 2007

A TOUCH OF MINX

SUZANNE ENOCH

Twice the Temptation

AVON

An Imprint of HarperCollinsPublishers

This is a work of fiction. Names, characters, places, and incidents are products of the author's imagination or are used fictitiously and are not to be construed as real. Any resemblance to actual events, locales, organizations, or persons, living or dead, is entirely coincidental.

AVON BOOKS
An Imprint of HarperCollins*Publishers*
10 East 53rd Street
New York, New York 10022-5299

Copyright © 2007 by Suzanne Enoch
Not Quite A Lady copyright © 2007 by Loretta Chekani; *Sins of a Duke* copyright © 2007 by Suzanne Enoch; *Sleepless at Midnight* copyright © 2007 by Jacquie D'Alessandro; *Twice the Temptation* copyright © 2007 by Suzanne Enoch
ISBN: 978-0-06-123147-6
ISBN-10: 0-06-123147-9
www.avonromance.com

First Avon Books paperback printing: August 2007

Avon Trademark Reg. U.S. Pat. Off. and in Other Countries, Marca Registrada, Hecho en U.S.A.
HarperCollins® is a registered trademark of HarperCollins Publishers.

Printed in the U.S.A.

10 9 8 7 6 5 4 3 2 1

*For the ladies of the reading group
at Sunshine Books in Cypress, California—
not only are you warm and funny and insightful,
but you always have chocolate.
Thank you.*

A Diamond or Forever

Chapter 1

June 1814

"Aunt Rachel, you are not on the verge of being put to bed with a shovel," Evangeline Munroe said primly, her hands folded on her lap. "I daresay you're more likely to be dancing with that nice Lord Geary at the next assembly."

"That's not so, child," her aunt said, giving a dramatic cough. "I've been slipping for days. I'm only glad you arrived to pay your last respects before I'm gone to kingdom come."

"I'm not paying my last respects; I'm paying my ordinary ones." Evangeline frowned briefly, then smoothed the expression. Her face would be chasmed with wrinkles if she didn't take care. "Which is not to say that my ordinary respects are not sincerely meant."

"Oh, Gilly, Gilly, Gilly. Such a dear one, you are. Would you hand me one of those chocolate biscuits? I think I could possibly manage a nibble of one of those."

Evangeline used the silver tongs to select a biscuit,

altering her selection to a plumper one when Aunt Rachel cleared her throat. "Did Mama tell you she's entering the garden competition again?"

"Why wouldn't she? Heloise has won the last three in a row."

"Four. Mama would be hurt if you forgot one of her victories."

"I'm more worried over the hurt she would do *me* if she knew I'd forgotten one. If she asks about my final conversation, please tell her I remembered all four of her ribbons."

Evangeline didn't want to discuss gardening ribbons at all. Curiosity had been pulling at her since her early morning arrival, in fact, but she refused to succumb. Her aunt had summoned her to Tandey House on the outskirts of London and then spent the subsequent hour talking endlessly about nothing in particular. Whatever had prompted the invitation practically at dawn and a full fortnight ahead of her regular visit, Aunt Rachel would come around to discussing it eventually.

Her aunt sent her a sideways glance, shifting on the mounds of fluffed pillows that threatened to engulf her and the entire bedchamber. "You have the patience of Job, don't you?"

"I know how you enjoy your surprises."

"Yes, though I don't think I quite realized the mortal peril I would face when I embarked upon this particular venture."

"Peril?" Gilly repeated. "You're not going off to India again, are you?"

"Heavens, I'd never survive the voyage. No, this is something I've contemplated for quite some time. Though you know I prefer not to play favorites, I had to make a choice between you and your cousins." Evidently remembering that she was on her deathbed, she coughed once more. "You may wonder why I selected you."

"Since I don't know what you've selected me for, I can hardly comment on it."

"Aha," Aunt Rachel chortled. "That is it, precisely."

Evangeline blinked. "Beg pardon?"

"You possess an astounding measure of practicality, and absolutely no imagination. If you have no capacity for believing in fanciful happenings, you may be immune to their occurrence."

As highly as Evangeline prized her sensibility, that didn't sound like a compliment. "I believe what my eyes, experience, and logic tell me," she said, keeping her voice cool.

"Yes, I know. And while ordinarily I would hope you would learn to seek a broader perspective, one that would perhaps utilize your heart, under these circumstances your logic may be your most valuable tool."

Considering her aunt's flights of dramatics, Evangeline supposed she should be pleased to be excluded from the arm-flailing horde. And the word *valuable* always sounded promising. "I admit, you begin to make me curious."

Rachel Tandey slapped her hand on the rumpled bedsheets. "Oh, very well. You've wheedled it out of me." She reached beneath one of the pillows and produced an ornate wooden box the size of a teacup. "This, my dear, is for you." She handed it over.

With a dubious glance from the box to her aunt, Evangeline took it. "This isn't rhinoceros toenails like you gave me before, is it?"

"*That* was for Christmas. *This* is an inheritance. It's

been in the family for a very long time. We're very careful about to whom it should be passed along. Go on, open it."

She would have preferred another moment or two to study the pretty mahogany box, but it wouldn't do to upset her aunt in the midst of gift-giving. Evangeline flipped up the small brass catch and opened the lid.

The bedchamber windows flashed white, and thunder abruptly cracked in a deafening, echoing crescendo around the room. "Good heavens! That was alarming." Rachel Tandey clutched her chest.

"It's been blustery since midnight," Evangeline said absently. "That's why I was late arriving here."

She scarcely noted what Aunt Rachel said. Her attention was on the contents of the box. A fine gold chain closely lined with multifaceted stones coiled loosely around the interior like a slender, hungry snake. In the middle lay a delicate setting also of gold, and holding thirteen small stones and a much larger blue-tinted one in the middle, sparkling like starlight. "It's not paste, is it?" she asked, knowing from the sparkle alone that it must be real. *A diamond*. Dozens of diamonds. But the blue one . . .

"It's very real. But now that you've set eyes on it, I have to tell you that it doesn't come by itself."

Carefully Evangeline freed it from the velvet-lined box. "There are earbobs as well, then?" she asked hopefully. It was heavy, but not absurdly so.

"Not earbobs. A curse."

"Mm-hm." She held up the necklace, scarcely breathing as she let it spin and sparkle in the candlelight. "This is an heirloom? The centerpiece alone must be a hundred carats!"

"One hundred and sixty-nine carats. As it's been

passed down to me, the tale is that the diamond came from—"

"A hundred and sixty-nine carats? Why have I never heard of it before? This should be the entire family's pride and joy!"

"—from deepest Africa, when a ship broke apart at the Cape of Good Hope and only two sailors survived. The one who found the diamond came down with a—"

"Does it have a name?" Evangeline interrupted. "A diamond with a name is always more valuable."

"I'm getting to that. He came down with a raging fever. On *his* deathbed he gave it to his companion so that at least one of them could profit by it. That very evening his fever broke, and he began to recover. Once on his feet again, he asked for the diamond to be returned to him, but his companion refused. The two men argued and fought over it for days, their friendship ripping into tatters, until the companion was swept away by a raging river. Finally remembering their friendship, the first man ran along beside him, trying to find a way to get him to shore."

"To the bank, you mean. Oceans and lakes have shores. Rivers have banks."

"You're missing the point, Gilly. Sensing his imminent death, the companion tossed the diamond to his friend. Immediately a branch broke from a tree just downriver. The companion reached it and was saved. From then on, unwilling to part with the gem but little by little realizing its deadly power, they traded it off until they found civilization and the sailor who'd discovered it put it safely away. That sailor was your great-great-grandfather's uncle. Over the years your ancestors have had it cut and put into this setting. And now it comes to you."

Evangeline looked at her sideways. "If you actually believe that nonsense, why are you gifting me with a curse?"

"I am passing on an heirloom and a responsibility. Now that you've set eyes on it, I strongly suggest that you immediately put it away somewhere safe, so that you'll enjoy its good luck and protect yourself from the bad. Oh, and it's called the Nightshade Diamond, because of its poisonous nature, I suppose."

It made a very good children's bedtime story. Being nearly nineteen and not the least bit gullible, Evangeline tucked the necklace back into its box and stood to kiss her aunt on the cheek. "The Nightshade Diamond. Don't you think the name could be because it's tinted blue like twilight?"

"No. And you should take what I tell you seriously, Gilly. A lack of passion and imagination might save you, and it might not."

"I do take you seriously," Evangeline returned absently. "Thank you for the very lovely gift. I will treat it well."

"Gilly—"

"And don't fret, Aunt Rachel. You'll be back to your usual self in no time at all."

Rachel Tandey watched as her niece left the bedchamber. "I daresay I will be now," she muttered, shifting as a sudden attack of the vapors caught her. *Ah. Better already*, she thought, then wrinkled her nose in distaste. "Good heavens. Bess! Come in here and throw open a window at once!"

Evangeline opened the wooden box again as her coach rolled into London proper. She lifted the necklace, admiring its sparkle again as muted, blustery daylight danced along hundreds of beveled edges from the fourteen main stones and the dozens along the chain. Such a pretty thing, it was. The most breathtaking necklace she'd ever seen.

"Goodness gracious," her maid exclaimed from the facing seat. "That is the most beautiful bauble I've ever set my eyes on!"

"It's hardly a bauble, Doretta. It's a very valuable family heirloom. Aunt Rachel thought me the most worthy to receive it." Well, not precisely worthy, but she hardly meant to repeat that her aunt found her unimaginative and that the item was purportedly cursed.

With an admiring sigh she returned the necklace to its box and closed the lid.

The next second she crashed to the floor. Her maid, the box, and her book and reticule flew about her. The coach lurched sickeningly sideways in the opposite direction, then with another hard jolt landed back on all four wheels again.

"We've hit something!" Doretta shrieked unhelpfully.

"It seems we have." Evangeline narrowed her eyes as she looked at her maid sprawled along the seat. "Are you injured?"

"No, Miss Munroe. I don't think so."

"Then help me to my feet, if you please."

Outside the coach two male voices spoke angrily over each other's commentary, while above that horses whinnied and snorted. It sounded like absolute bedlam. As soon as Doretta pulled her upright, Evangeline pushed at the door. With a reluctant groan it swung open.

Bedlam indeed. A coach of tremendous size had locked wheels with hers, tilting both of them crazily and tangling the horses into a morass of neighing bay and black bodies. "Good heavens," she muttered tightly.

The step remained tucked under the coach body, so Evangeline grasped the doorframe and jumped the two feet to the street. "Maywing!" she called to her driver, using her most annoyed voice. "Cease arguing with that idiot and untangle the horses!"

Either Maywing couldn't hear her or he chose not to do so. At any rate, he and the other coachman continued bellowing at one another. Evangeline squeezed around to view the opposite door of the other coach. It hadn't budged.

"You there!" she tried again, jabbing a finger at the second driver. "See to your passenger!"

No answer. Some of the insults were becoming rather colorful, and now Maywing's parentage was being called into question. With an irritated sniff Evangeline awkwardly flipped down the large coach's step and climbed up. The curtains were closed, but she grasped the door handle and pulled.

In a flash of blue eyes and dark hair a large figure collapsed forward as the door gave way. Unable to do anything but gasp, Evangeline fell backward, landing hard enough on the street to bruise her backside. Her bottom, though, immediately became the least of her concerns; in fact, she scarcely noticed it as the blue-eyed lump—*man*—thunked face down on top of her.

"Get off of me!" she shrieked, shoving at his broad shoulder and trying to scramble free.

"Ah, Daisy," his low voice murmured, the tone shockingly intimate. The man shifted, but only to bring his face even with hers. Then he kissed her, soft, deep, and tasting of brandy.

She froze, deeply surprised at the sensation of his mouth expertly plying at hers. For a fleeting heartbeat she acknowledged that though she was no expert, this man kissed like sin itself. Then she brought her hand around and awkwardly slapped him across the cheek.

Blue eyes opened only inches from hers. Their mouths separated, and the eyes narrowed. "You are not Daisy."

"I am not," she agreed. "Get off of me this instant."

To her growing annoyance, he lifted his head to look about. "This is not a bedchamber."

By now a crowd surrounded them. The lout was going to absolutely ruin her. "It is the middle of the street. If you don't remove yourself from my person this instant, I will kick you so hard that Daisy, whoever she is, will never wish to set eyes on you again."

"Hm." Setting his hands on the street at either side of her shoulders, he pushed himself up. Their gazes again caught for the briefest of seconds before he twisted off of her to sit up. "You are definitely not Daisy."

Evangeline climbed to her feet as gracefully as she could, leaving him sitting in the road. "It is after nine o'clock in the morning, sir," she said, looking down at his upturned face with his black hair falling across one eye. "How can you possibly be this dissipated already?"

"I am returning home, I think." He frowned, the expression lowering his brows and making her notice his sensuous mouth again. "So for me it's still the previous evening. And it's lord; not sir. I am no knight."

"Clearly not. Knights are supposed to be chivalrous. They do not fall upon women in the streets."

"I wouldn't be so certain of that." With a groan he clasped the coach step and pulled himself to his feet. "Oh, good God."

She put her hands on her hips, having to look up to meet his gaze now, since he stood at least a foot taller than she did. "I will assume you are incapable of rendering any assistance," she assessed. The statement on its face sounded odd, because physically he looked supremely capable—except for the drunken swaying, of course. "Kindly stay clear of the coaches." With that she turned her back on him and stalked up to Maywing and the other driver. "Gentlemen!" she said loudly. "You, set your brake. Maywing, untangle the harnesses and back our coach up so we clear our wheels."

"Epping," the low, masculine voice came from right behind her, "I don't recall asking you to stop off anywhere. Clear the cattle and take me home."

The other driver immediately stopped his exuberant arguing. "But m'lord, it wasn't my fault, and we've near lost a wheel. I—"

"I don't recall asking you for details, either," he cut in. "Home. Now. Exchange information with this fellow, and go."

"Yes, m'lord."

Evangeline stifled a scowl. Very well, the fellow wasn't completely useless. And considering that the object was to get away from the growing crowd without delay, she was glad for that. Many men, she supposed, returned home very late and very inebriated, and his falling on her had been an accident.

A hand touched her shoulder, and she turned around. He did have very nice eyes, though she would have liked them better if they hadn't been bloodshot and barely in focus. "Yes?"

"I assume you are uninjured?"

"I am." No thanks to him. But she wasn't about to admit to a bruised bottom.

"You kiss very well."

Evangeline blinked. She'd been so certain he was going

to apologize for his crass behavior that for a second what he *had* said made no sense. "That was your imagination," she finally fumbled, her cheeks warming. "Pray do not insult me by relying on your faulty recollections of a . . . sodden and mistaken memory."

His mouth curved. "I know a pleasant kiss when I taste one. Tell me your name."

He was so inebriated he probably wouldn't remember it. Now that she'd had a moment to gather her thoughts, she could see that he was indeed dressed in formal evening wear—though his cravat looked as though it had been retied, and poorly, and his waistcoat was buttoned wrong. And his hair was wild, pushed up on one side and tangled across his eyes like a thick black spider's nest. He badly needed a shave, though she had to admit that the overall appearance of masculine dishevelment was rather . . . appealing. Evangeline took a breath. "I'll tell you that my name is not Daisy."

"Yes, I realized that almost immediately. What is your name?"

"I am Miss Munroe," she finally said. "Now please climb back into your coach before you fall down again."

He assessed her for a moment, then gave a charming, lopsided smile. "That's likely very good advice, Miss Munroe."

Before he could continue, Evangeline turned her back and with Doretta's help hauled herself up into her own vehicle again. He wasn't actually attempting to flirt with her, was he? Heavens. Yes, he was handsome, but he'd practically crushed her, and then mauled her. She would remember that, even if he didn't. "Drive on, Maywing," she said, closing the door on the fellow's inebriated smile.

As she sat, she eyed the box holding her new necklace. If she believed in any of that superstitious nonsense, she would say that Aunt Rachel had it backward. She'd been perfectly fine until she'd set it aside. Bad luck, ha. She would wear it tonight, just to prove her aunt wrong. If the diamond held any luck at all, which she doubted, it was *good* luck.

Chapter 2

Connoll Spencer Addison, the very intoxicated Marquis of Rawley, watched Miss Munroe's coach as it rolled over someone's cigar—probably his—and a thick book—probably not his. Leaning a hand against his carriage's wheel to steady himself, Connoll squatted down and retrieved the tome.

"*The Rights of Women*," he read, flipping it over. "Not a bit surprised by that."

"M'lord?"

"Nothing, Epping," he said to his coachman. "Take me home, and for God's sake don't hit anything else. It's been the devil of a night, and I do not wish my sleep interrupted again."

"Yes, m'lord." The driver climbed back up to his perch. Connoll returned to the coach's dim interior, tossed the book onto the seat opposite, and sank back to resume his sleep and try to forget about a certain mistress who'd decided to marry—though thankfully not him. Blasted Daisy Applegate.

Abruptly he sat forward again. He'd kissed the chit,

Miss Mun . . . Mun something. Yes, he'd kissed Miss Someone, and that could be bad. Not unpleasant, but bad. Kissing a Miss in public was always bad. He was generally much more careful about the setting for that sort of activity.

Finally he realized that the coach had stopped rocking, and that the usual noise of London seemed rather subdued. And his head ached like the devil. "Damnation," he muttered, and thumped on the ceiling with his fist. "Epping, if we're lost, I will toss you out of my employment on your bloody backside."

Nothing.

"Epping!"

Frowning, Connoll stood and shoved open the coach's door. They were indeed stopped. They were stopped to such a degree that the horses were gone from their harnesses, and a pair of geese waddled between the near coach wheels in his stable yard.

He grabbed up the chit's book. Avoiding the geese, he stepped to the ground and stalked around the side of the house to his front door. It swung open as he topped the steps.

"Good afternoon, Lord Rawley."

Afternoon. "Winters, how long was I asleep in the damned coach in the damned stable yard?"

"Nearly three hours, my lord. Epping said you'd expressly requested that you not be disturbed."

"By his wrecking the coach again, yes, that half-wit. I didn't mean for him to leave me boxed up and ready for delivery."

"I shall inform him of his error, my lord."

Connoll headed for the stairs, shedding his coat as he went. "And send me Hodges. I want a bath."

"Very good, my lord."

He *needed* a bath, and a shave, and a change of clothes. With a glance at the book he carried, Connoll shook his head. However much he would have liked to busy himself in his office study until nightfall, he'd done some damage—and he needed to determine its extent. The chit was a Miss with a good-quality carriage, and she read progressive literature. And that was all he knew about her. That and the fuzzy memory of frighteningly intelligent hazel eyes, a soft, subtle mouth, and curling honey-blonde hair.

"Winters!"

"Yes, my lord?" echoed up from the foyer.

"I want to have a word with Epping." He could hear the unspoken query in the ensuing silence. "No, I don't mean to sack him, but I make no promise about murdering him."

"I'll send him to you at once, my lord."

He wanted an address—to return a book, and to inquire after any damages to a coach. And to discover whether that female's dismissive practicality had been a ruse to set him off balance while she chose a wedding gown. Women had attempted to trap him into marriage over the Seasons, but he'd never made it so bloody easy for any of them before. Damnation. And still he continued to contemplate that kiss.

"If you knew Aunt Rachel had a diamond necklace sitting in a box in her attic, why did you never say anything?" Evangeline looked beyond her own mirrored reflection to her mother's.

Heloise, Lady Munroe, stood at her daughter's shoulder. "It wasn't actually in the attic, was it?"

"Oh, I don't know. I only said that for effect. It's a hundred and sixty-nine carats, Mama."

"As far as I knew, the Nightshade Diamond was nothing but a silly rumor. My Uncle Benjamin used to talk about a cursed diamond, but no one ever listened to a word he said. The old fool lost a leg in a billiards accident, of all things."

"Did he like to wear diamonds?" Evangeline joked, shifting to see the glint of the one around her throat.

"Oh, please. He was a clumsy fool. He did clumsy, foolish things like trying to ride an old billiards table down a flight of stairs." She leaned down, caressing the stone with her forefinger. "But look at you. A fourteen-diamond pendant. You shone before. Now no man will be able to resist you."

She'd heard that before, and she usually rolled her eyes as she and her mother laughed. This time, though, a tremor ran through Evangeline. Someone this morning had been unable to resist her. And what a kiss that had been. "I would hope the men are more worried about me resisting them," she offered. "Thus far only Lord Dapney and Lord Redmond have survived on our list."

Straightening, the viscountess tapped her chin. "Dapney or Redmond, hm? Good choices, both. You'll find wealth, titles, and prestige with either of them, but Dapney's the younger by far. He's what, one and twenty?"

Evangeline nodded. "Only two years my elder."

"That appeals to me. Young men are often more malleable than older ones. Does he dote on you?"

"He seems to. My thinking, though, is that Redmond will take less effort."

"Either way, we'll have to make certain. Men have a notorious tendency to not show their true dispositions until they've already tricked a lady into a disadvantageous union."

Evangeline smiled. "Except that we know better than to be tricked."

"Precisely. And as you know, deciphering all of the disadvantages and how to counter them gives *us* the advantage."

A rap came at her bedchamber door. Doretta went to open it, and Evangeline's father walked into the room. "I hear your aunt gave you a diamond necklace, Gilly," John, Viscount Munroe, said with a smile. "I came to see it."

Evangeline started to her feet to show it to him, but the viscountess pushed down on her shoulder to keep her in the chair. "Not now, John," her mother said with a dismissive wave of her hand, frowning as she faced him. "And you can't wear that coat this evening; you know I don't show well with beige around me. Put on the hunter green. It will complement my yellow silk."

He nodded. "Of course, my dear. Apologies."

The viscount left the room again. "Normally I wouldn't mind his silliness so much, but you know if I tolerate him wearing beige even once, he'll think he can wear it whenever he pleases."

"He does try, once you point him in the correct direction," Evangeline countered, focusing her attention on the sparkling diamond again.

"I suppose so." The viscountess summoned Doretta to the large wardrobe. "Gilly must wear blue or green, to set off the necklace." She faced her daughter. "You know, it's a pity you can't wear that diamond every night, for it does look well on you. But we can't have people thinking you have nothing else to show."

Evangeline reached up to unfasten the jewel's delicate clasp. Her mother had dismissed the idea of a cursed heirloom even more readily than she had. The carriage accident had been the result of an overly tired driver and a drunken passenger. As for the kiss—well, she hadn't mentioned that. It had only been a stupid embrace from an inebriated man, and didn't signify. Carefully she set the necklace back in its box.

Her bedchamber door rattled again. "For goodness' sake," the viscountess muttered. "Your father is useless." She walked to the entry. "Tell Wallis what I wish you to wear, John. Surely your valet knows something of fashion."

When she pulled the door open, though, it wasn't the viscount who stood there, but the butler. "Pardon me, my lady," he said, "but Miss Munroe has a caller."

"Very well, Clifford," Evangeline said, shutting the diamond away. "I'll be down directly. Who is it?"

"The Marquis of Rawley." He produced an ornate card on a silver salver. Gold filagree in the shape of English ivy bordered the card, the letters bold and black and stylish across the center.

Her mother frowned. "The Marquis of Rawley?" She picked up the card. "We crossed him off your list of potential spouses weeks ago. Why is he calling on you?"

"I have no idea." Evangeline stood. "We've never even met. Perhaps he's admired me from afar and doesn't know he's already been rejected."

The viscountess chuckled. "Very likely, poor fellow. Clifford, you heard Miss Munroe. She'll be down in a moment."

"Very good, my lady."

As Doretta repinned Evangeline's hair, her mother went to the window and pulled aside the curtain. "There's a lovely black Arabian on the drive." She faced her daughter. "Lord Rawley," she mused. "Wasn't he the one buying up all of those French paintings?"

"I heard something to that effect."

"We can't have our friends thinking we have a Bonaparte supporter about."

"Don't worry, Mother. We shan't. And rest assured, if he speaks to me in French I'll send him away immediately."

She actually remembered very little of the research they'd done on Rawley. There'd been so many names on that first list, before they'd begun the elimination process. French paintings and being a reputed liberal in the House of Lords made him unacceptable.

With Doretta trailing behind her, Evangeline descended the stairs. Clifford waited outside the morning room door and pulled it open as she approached. "Lord Rawley, Miss Munroe," he announced, stepping back to allow her entry.

She walked into the room, smiling as the tall, broad-shouldered figure by the window faced her. "Lord Raw . . ." Evangeline trailed off, an odd thump echoing in her chest. *Him.* "Oh, it's you."

Connoll Addison inclined his head. Evidently he'd made quite the impression earlier. Oddly enough, though, even without the pleasant haze a bottle of brandy lent his vision, Miss Munroe was . . . lovely. Perhaps his uncertain senses had exaggerated her sharp tongue, but since he'd been correct about her other attributes, he doubted it. "I found your book," he said, taking it from beneath his arm and offering it to her.

Her soft lips tightened as she took it, clearly doing everything she could to avoid touching his fingers. "Thank you."

"My pleasure. Have you read it, by chance?"

She lifted a fine eyebrow. "Why, do you imagine I carry it with me to quote progressive opinions to the unenlightened? Or perhaps you think me illiterate and merely trying to gain attention?"

A smile tugged at his mouth. No, he hadn't been imagining her prickly tongue. "I imagined that you would have it memorized, actually."

"Hm. Thank you for its return, my lord. Good day." She turned on her heel, her maid falling in behind her.

Faced with this female, some of his male friends would have fainted in terror by now. Connoll, though, found himself intrigued. "It occurs to me, Miss Munroe," he said, taking a half step after her, "that you might wish to give me your Christian name."

She paused, looking over her shoulder at him. "And why is that?"

"We have kissed, after all." And he abruptly wanted to kiss her again. The rest of his observations had been accurate; he wanted to know whether his impression of her mouth was, as well. Soft lips and a sharp tongue. Fascinating. He wondered whether she knew how few women ever spoke frankly to him.

With what might have been a curse she reached out to close the morning room door. "We did not kiss, my lord," she returned, her voice clipped as she faced him directly again. "You fell on me, and then you mistakenly mauled me. Do not pretend there was anything mutual about it."

This time he couldn't keep his lips from curving, watching as her gaze dropped to his mouth in response. "So you say. I myself don't entirely recollect."

"*I* recollect quite clearly. Pray do not mention your . . . error in judgment again, for both of our sakes."

"I'm not convinced it was an error, but very well." He rocked back on his heels. "If you tell me your given name."

He couldn't read the expression that crossed her face, but he thought it might be surprise. Men probably threw themselves at her feet and worshipped the hems of her gowns.

"Oh, for heaven's . . ." she sputtered. "Fine. Evangeline."

"Evangeline," he repeated. "Very nice."

"Thank you. I'll tell my mother that you approve her choice."

Connoll lifted an eyebrow. "You're not precisely a shrinking violet, are you?"

"You accosted me," she retorted, putting her hands on her hips. "I feel no desire to play pretty with you."

"But I like to play."

Her cheeks darkened. "No doubt. I suggest that next time you find someone more willing to reciprocate."

Connoll reached out to fluff the sleeve of her cream-colored muslin with his fingers. "You know, I find myself rather relieved," he said, wondering how close he was treading to the edge of disaster and still willing to career along at full speed. "There are women of my acquaintance who would use my . . . misstep of earlier to gain a husband and a title. You only seem to wish to be rid of me."

Evangeline Munroe pursed her lips, an expression he found both amusing and attractive. "You were blind drunk at nearly ten o'clock in the morning. In all honesty, my lord, I do not find that behavior admirable, nor do I wish to associate myself with it on a permanent basis."

"Well, that stung," he admitted, not overly offended. "Suffice it to say that I am not generally tight at mid-morning. Say you'll dance with me tonight at the Gaviston soiree, Evangeline. I assume you'll be attending."

"Are you mad?" She took a step closer, lifting up on her toes to bring herself closer to his height. "I have been attempting to convince you to leave since the moment you arrived. Why in God's name would that make you think me willing to dance with you? And I gave you no leave to call me by my given name. I only told you what it was under duress."

"I'll leave, but not until you say you'll dance with me tonight. Or kiss me again, immediately. I leave the choice up to you."

She sputtered. "If I were a man, I would call you out, sir."

"If I were a woman, I would kiss me again."

Unfortunately, the morning room door opened before she could reply to that. "Good afternoon, my dear," a smooth, feminine voice cooed. "Oh, I see you have a caller. Pray introduce me, Evangeline."

The chit drew herself in again, while Connoll belatedly took a half step away from her. "Of course. Mama, this is the Marquis of Rawley. My lord, my mother, Viscountess Munroe."

The lady stood several inches taller than her daughter, but their hair was dipped in the same honey, and their eyes were the same hazel. Any other man might have commented that they looked like sisters, but from her too-young hair style and low-cut gown, Lady Munroe seemed to be asking for just such a compliment. Connoll bowed. "My lady. Your daughter and I had a carriage accident this morning, and I came to inquire after her health."

"Oh. This is the gentleman you spoke of, Gilly?"

Gilly. He liked that, but it seemed so . . . friendly for such a spiny chit. Another piece to a puzzle he'd only just discovered, and couldn't let go of.

"It was nothing, Mama," Gilly was saying, "as I told you. And now Lord Rawley has offered to pay for any damages."

"That's quite gallant of you, my lord." The lady swept forward, offering her hand. "Even considering that you were at fault."

Connoll squeezed her fingers, then released her. After eight-and-twenty years he wouldn't be worth a pinch of snuff if he couldn't detect a matchmaking mama from across the street, much less across the room. And this mama didn't like him. "I was, indeed. Hence my offer."

"Very kind. Would you care for some tea?"

Unfriendly female or not, he still wanted a better acquaintance with the daughter. "I—"

"I'm afraid Lord Rawley has already informed me that he has an appointment elsewhere," Evangeline cut in.

He shook himself, not feeling ready to take on both of them without some preparation. "Yes, I do. Would you do me the honor of walking me to the door, Miss Munroe?"

Her expression tightened. "With pleasure, my lord."

As he offered his arm, she wrapped her fingers around his sleeve and practically towed him toward the foyer. Once they were out of the morning room, he drew her to a halt. "So that we may be perfectly clear," he said in a low voice, gazing down at eyes turned green by the lamplight, "you don't like me."

"I do not like you," she agreed.

"I am quite wealthy, you know," he offered with a half smile. "Obscenely so. And I've been told all of my features form an orderly portrait."

"Yes, they do," she admitted, ignoring his renowned

powers of seduction and pulling him toward the door again. "I daresay you are quite handsome."

Ah, now they were getting somewhere. "I'm glad we can agree about something. Say you'll dance with me."

"I do not dally with drunkards," she whispered, releasing him as the butler pulled open the front door. "I find them to be dull and forward and not at all amenable to sound reasoning."

Connoll stepped onto the front portico and opened his mouth to inform her what he thought of chits who stood too high in the instep and considered themselves above any reproach, but she took the door in her hand and closed it on him.

He looked at the door for a moment, then descended to take Faro's reins from a waiting groom. So she wanted him to admit defeat and scuttle away without putting up any kind of fight at all. Obviously she had no idea who he was. For a bright chit, she'd made a miserably simple mistake. He didn't like to lose. A female who kissed like that even when taken by surprise had no right to be so stuffy. Evangeline Munroe could definitely stand to be taken down a peg or two. Or twelve.

With a grim smile he sent Faro in the direction of Grosvenor Street and home. When she arrived at the Gaviston soiree tonight, she would realize that she'd just engaged in a duel with a master.

Chapter 3

"*You've met the Marquis of Rawley?*" Leandra Halloway whispered from behind her fan. "I didn't know he was even back in London."

"Where was he, then?" Evangline asked, curious in spite of herself.

"That depends on who you ask," her friend returned, still keeping her voice low and conspiratorial. "Some say he and his latest mistress were at one of his estates in Scotland."

Undoubtedly this latest mistress went by the name of Daisy. She nodded. "*One* of his estates?"

"Oh, yes. He has several. But my cousin says that Rawley wasn't in Scotland at all, that he was actually in France up to something or other." Leandra fanned herself. "I have to say, I don't care where he's been. All I know is that if it had been me he fell on, I would be the Marchioness of Rawley by now."

"Oh, please. You would be welcome to him." Evangline waved as another of her friends entered the ballroom. Thankfully Rawley hadn't yet appeared; perhaps he'd gotten drunk again and forgotten that he wanted to dance with her.

"But you do know that his mother was a Spencer. He owns half of Devonshire, and at least four estates in Scotland."

"Wealth is well and good, but I can't speak for his manners, because he doesn't have any." Evangeline took another sip of lemonade; it was tepid, but in the stifling, crowded ballroom she felt grateful for any refreshment at all.

Yes, Rawley had a charming smile, and very handsome features, and a devastating kiss, but none of that made him the sort of man she would wish to have pursuing her. He clearly thought himself irresistible, and that self-importance could make him nearly impossible to guide or to control, in addition to his other myriad faults. Still . . . "He's a Spencer, then?"

"You don't even know his given name, do you? I thought you must be mortal enemies already, the way you've been talking about him, Gilly."

"Please, Leandra." He'd been crossed from the list too quickly for her to have learned anything but the very broadest strokes.

Her friend dimpled again. "Very well." She cleared her throat dramatically. "He's Connoll Spencer Addison, Viscount Halford, Earl of Weldon, Marquis of Rawley. And I'm glad you don't like him, because I *do*. Of course, he's never asked me to dance with him."

"How do you know him, when you haven't been in London any longer than I have?"

Leandra shrugged. "Mama and I made a list at the beginning of the Season," she admitted, lowering her voice still further. "You know, of men whose attentions

I might encourage. His name was right at the top. It was very disappointing that he wasn't even here."

Hm. Obviously her and her mother's requirements had been very different from the Halloways'. It made sense, though; Leandra's family needed money, while her own necessities ran toward—how did her mother phrase it?—power and respectability tempered with malleability. Rawley seemed the antithesis of that. And she wouldn't have a habitual drunk about, anyway.

"Enough about Rawley," she exclaimed, flipping her hand. "Did you see my new treasure?" She gestured at her throat.

"I've been attempting not to stare at it since you walked in," her friend returned with a grin. "It's exquisite!"

"It's called the Nightshade Diamond. It's an heirloom, handed down to me from my Aunt Rachel." And whatever her aunt might claim, Evangeline could already dispute its supernatural powers. Nothing untoward had occurred all evening. Even better, Rawley had yet to make an appearance.

"I see someone else who's staring," Leandra murmured, angling her fan past Evangeline's shoulder.

She turned around, putting on a warm smile as she saw who approached. "Lord Redmond. I'd nearly given up hope of seeing you this evening."

At one and fifty, Lord Redmond was two years older than her own father, but he fell into the category of what she termed "distinguished," if a bit portly. He favored her with a deep, reverent bow. "If I'd known for certain you would be here, Miss Munroe, I would have arrived sooner."

"You are too kind, my lord," she returned, offering her hand for his kiss.

"Not a bit. You know how I worship you."

Yes, she did. He said it often enough. "In that case, I think you should ask me to dance."

He smiled, drawing in his gut as he offered his arm. "My pleasure."

"Gilly, you aren't going to save a dance for . . . your cousin?" Leandra broke in, her lips twisting.

"Certainly not. He's not even here."

As she accepted Redmond's escort to her place in line for the country dance, Evangeline made another swift survey of the crowded room. The Gavistons' soirees were always notoriously well attended; the baron and baroness seemed determined to invite everyone with an address in the west of London. And yet she still saw no sign of the Marquis of Rawley.

He'd been rather bold, demanding a dance from her and then not bothering to make an appearance. If he thought she would spend the evening doing nothing but anticipating his arrival, he was sadly mistaken. Her only emotion where he was concerned happened to be relief that he'd taken himself elsewhere.

Across the room her mother gave an encouraging nod as the viscountess sent her husband off to fetch her a refreshment. When she'd been younger, Evangeline had spent countless hours in observation and instruction, learning precisely how to go about being the mistress of the house—asking without asking, expecting without demanding, directing without ordering, and seeing very clearly who truly ruled the family.

Using those same methods herself, she'd narrowed down the selection from her multitude of suitors—weeded out the roses from amid the nettles, as her mother said—and found the two men with the right combination of wealth, power, and potential, and of course a hearty need for her guidance. Redmond or Dapney. Either would do, though contrary to her mother's opinion she thought that with Redmond she would find a usable . . . desperation to be seen as charming by someone less than half his age, a need to be wanted that Dapney at one-and-twenty simply didn't yet feel.

As she wound up and down the line of dancers, everyone seemed to be sending admiring looks at her neck. Bad luck, indeed. She'd never felt more admired. Redmond could barely keep his gaze off her long enough to notice where he was going. If everything continued this well, she could expect a proposal from him within the fortnight. And then Lord Rawley wouldn't dare presume that she'd enjoyed kissing him and might wish to do so again.

"Explain to me again why you need me to be here?" Connoll asked, flipping open his pocket watch for the third time. "I told you I had a previous engagement."

"I need you to be here," his companion said, "because what I know about art wouldn't fill a snuffbox. My grandmama is coming to visit, and she expects to see some refinement burgeoning in my soul if I ever hope to inherit. That's what she said in her last letter, anyway. Just to frighten me into finding some culture, I think. You said you would help me, Conn. You promised."

"For God's sake, Francis, don't you think it's a bit late now to try to develop refinement? You had none the entire time we were at Oxford." And besides, he'd threatened dancing tonight. He needed to follow through with it, or a certain forthright chit would gain even more ground on him.

Francis Henning frowned, the expression further

rounding his generous cheeks. "I *did* have refinement back then. I shared quarters with you."

Connoll snorted. "Then we're both sore out of luck, my friend, because I was just today informed that I have no refinement left to my person. Apparently I drowned it in a very large snifter of brandy."

"Nonsense, Rawley. I saw that stack of paintings in your hallway. You know what you're about, even if you're mad enough to travel to Paris for your precious art."

"Keep that between us, will you?" Connoll cautioned in a low voice. "A confirmation of my travels, whatever the reason for them, could make me very unpopular."

"I'll be quiet as a mouse about it if you'll help me tonight."

Damnation. "Very well." He signaled for a glass of claret. The red liquid was not his preferred drink, but on the off chance that the auction ended quickly and he had time to escape to the Gaviston soiree, he would not give Gilly Munroe another opportunity to call him a drunk.

"What about this one, then?" Henning whispered, elbowing him in the ribs.

He shook himself. "Hogarth," he observed, eyeing the painting as the salon's employees set it on an easel in preparation for bidding. It was tempting just to concur and be done with it, but he'd given his word. "It's fine quality," he said, "but it'll cost you a pretty penny, Francis." He looked down the list of items up for auction. "You might hold off until this one." He pointed at a name.

"William Etty. Is he famous?"

"Not yet. He's still quite young, but I think you'll find his work affordable, and a good investment. He has a remarkable eye for color."

"Splendid, Rawley. You'll have to make me some notes so I'll know what to say about it."

"Yes, well, I can do that tomorrow. May I leave now?" He still had half a chance of arriving in time to take a spot on the chit's dance card.

"No, you can't go," Henning squawked, his soft features paling. "I won't know how much to bid, or when to drop out—if I should drop out. Or whether—"

"Breathe, Francis," he interrupted, stifling another frown as he put his watch away.

"For God's sake, don't abandon me now, Conn. I'll have an apoplexy and drop dead, and then I'll never inherit Grandmama's money."

Connoll sank back into his uncomfortable chair. "Very well. But you will owe me a very large favor."

His friend smiled happily. "I already owe you so many I've lost count."

"I haven't."

"Oh."

The butler had the bad manners to look annoyed when Connoll arrived at Munroe House shortly after nine o'clock the next morning. "I shall have to inquire whether Miss Munroe has risen yet, my lord," he intoned.

Connoll nodded. "I'll wait. A cup of tea would be welcome, though."

"Very good, my lord."

The butler showed him to the same room where he'd waited for her yesterday. Yes, it was early, but considering Evangeline's view of him, he wanted to make it perfectly clear that he did not as a rule stay out all night drinking.

Evangeline Munroe. Good God, she had a mouth on

her, which made her the type of woman he generally avoided like the plague. His life had enough twists and turns without making every conversation into a battle. On the other hand, if she'd wept and fainted after their carriage accident yesterday, he doubted he would have bothered to make an appearance this morning—or at all, for that matter.

It was a conundrum, and clearly Miss Munroe had the answers he required. He didn't know the questions, and yet here he was again, for the second time in twenty-four hours. Perhaps he'd been traveling too much lately and the overabundance of bad roads had rattled his brains.

"I don't know whether to say good morning or good evening to you, Lord Rawley," an enticing female voice said from behind him.

He turned around, smiling as he noted that not only was she attired to perfection in a trim green walking dress, but she even wore a bonnet. "Today it's good morning," he returned, sketching a shallow bow. "I came to apologize."

"We've already established that you were drunk, my lord. Please don't trouble yourself."

That again. "I'm apologizing for not dancing with you last evening. I made plans to attend, but a friend unexpectedly called on me to request my help with a pressing matter." Of course, for Francis Henning nearly everything was pressing, but he recognized true desperation when he saw it.

Something briefly passed through her hazel eyes. Surprise? "Oh," she muttered, taking a half step backward. "There's no need to apologize for that, either. I hadn't expected you to remember, much less to attend."

He followed her retreat, ignoring the cluck of her

lurking maid. "I did remember, and I did mean to attend. So I apologize."

"I . . . then I accept." She cleared her throat. "Now, if you'll excuse me, I'm late for my morning walk."

"I'll join you."

She took another step toward the morning room door. "That isn't necessary, my lord. You owe me nothing."

"I'm not offering anything but my presence and my wit, both of which are reputed to be quite pleasant. After you." He gestured her toward the foyer.

Evangeline frowned, then covered the expression again. "Very well. I do walk quite briskly, though."

"Duly noted."

Not troubling to hide his amusement, mostly because that seemed to baffle her, Connoll collected his great-coat, gloves, and hat before he followed her out the front door. Moving up between the chit and her maid, he offered his arm.

"I prefer to keep my hands free," she said, and struck off in the direction of Hyde Park.

He fell in behind her. "I like mine full," he commented.

"And your brain addled."

Connoll sighed. "You likely won't believe me, but while I do drink socially, the state you found me in yesterday was quite unusual for me."

"You're correct. I don't believe you. You seemed perfectly at ease sprawled in the street and kissing me as though we were both naked. Or you and this Daisy were, rather."

He flinched. "I would consider it a favor if you would not mention her name in conjunction with mine again." If he needed another reminder about what an unhelpful thing it was to be as intoxicated as he'd been, that provided it.

Gilly shot him a sideways glance. "Why, are you worried about your so-called reputation?"

"No, I'm worried about hers." He drew a breath. "She had the bad taste to fall in love with some gentleman who will be far too adoring toward her. I did not receive the homecoming I expected, and instead spent the night at a very ungentlemanly club known as Jezebel's. We—you and I, that is—ran into one another shortly after my driver dragged me out."

"I see." They walked in silence for several moments. "Were you in love with her?"

A surprising question from a seemingly practical chit. "No. But I was fond of her. I still am. And so I shall stay away from her."

"Then I wish you were fond of me, so you would do me the same courtesy."

Connell laughed. God, she was witty. "Unfortunately, I must remain in your company."

Her pace increased as they reached the park. "And why is that?"

"Because we kissed. You've infatuated me."

This time Miss Munroe snorted. "If I infatuated you, you would do as I ask and leave me be."

"Is that how you generally dispose of infatuated males?" he asked, tipping his hat as the Duke of Monmouth trotted by on his morning ride. "An odd method of courtship, Gilly."

Evangeline didn't seem to notice what he'd said. Rather, her gaze followed the path of the retreating duke. "You showed him respect," she noted. "Who is he?"

Mild annoyance touched Connell, and he brushed

it away. Women found him charming; he knew that, because he'd seen ample proof. In spite of what had happened with Daisy, he was the one who generally broke off relations with a chit rather than the other way around. "That is the Duke of Monmouth," he said, "an altogether unpleasant and overly opinionated fellow."

"I see. He's quite distinguished-looking. Is he married?"

"Extremely so." Connoll put a hand on her shoulder, stopping her forward progress and in the same motion turning her to face him. "You're walking with *me*, Miss Munroe."

"Not by choice. You invited yourself along." She returned her gaze, and apparently most of her attention, to the passersby around them. The well-dressed ones, at least—and the men, specifically.

He eyed her. "Are you hunting?" he asked after a moment, beginning to wish that he didn't find her so interesting.

"Hunting?"

"You look predatory." Actually, she looked enchanting, all hazel eyes and honey-blonde hair beneath her prim blue bonnet, but considering the forthright way she had of expressing herself, he would not mistake her for an angel. "I would think you'd find more fertile hunting grounds in a *ton* ballroom."

Her fair skin flushed. "I am being observant. Anything else is your brandy-soaked imagination."

"For the last damned time, I am not a drunk."

She pulled away from him and resumed her race along the southern boundary of Hyde Park. "I don't care."

"And you're not being observant. You're being . . . calculating."

"I am not! I go walking every morning. I did not appear on someone else's doorstep and insinuate myself into their daily exercise regimen."

Perhaps she had reacted a bit too stridently to Monmouth's appearance, but for heaven's sake, he didn't need to stir such a tempest over it. She should have realized the duke was married, because he'd never made even a brief appearance on her list. Evangeline set her attention on the bridge that crossed the Serpentine. If Lord Rawley would leave her alone or at least stop being so . . . distracting, she *would* have realized that.

She was only following her mother's advice, anyway. No one had proposed to her yet, and until someone did, she had an obligation to herself to assess every eligible man. She did not, for instance, wish to end up married to a man as demanding of her wits and her attention as Connoll Spencer Addison was proving to be.

"You know," his cool, masculine drawl came from beside her, distracting her from her thoughts yet again, "if you favor 'distinguished' men, the show you're putting on now by sprinting along the walking path probably isn't helping you."

"I beg your pardon?" she snapped.

"A 'distinguished' gentleman seeing such athletic ability and youthful exuberance in a chit might think twice about forming an attachment to her. You could very likely kill him on your first night of wedded bliss. And though you might consider that a fortunate happenstance, he most likely would not. Any imaginings along that path might even cause him to seek out a meeker, less fit chit than yourself, if only to preserve his own health."

"That's awful!" she blurted, slowing a little to give him a hard glare. "I am not some black widow or other spouse-eating insect. I am only looking for a gentleman who fulfills certain requirements. Age is not necessarily one of them."

"Which requirements are they, then?"

"Why?"

"I'm curious. And quite possibly intrigued."

"Well, become unintrigued this instant, because all I will tell you is that you fulfill absolutely none of those requirements."

He lifted an eyebrow, handsome and collected and less out of breath than she was. "Not one?"

"Not one."

That wasn't entirely true, of course, because he was wealthy and did have a title. In fact, he actually fell quite well into certain categories she hadn't heretofore considered. Lord Rawley spoke to her as though he expected her to be able to keep up with the conversation, for instance, which was actually nice, even refreshing, compared to the gentlemen who called her "my dear" or "my Aphrodite" and then allowed her to lead them about by the nose while they settled into the visions of their own superiority. Ha.

"I think you need a different list of requirements," he said easily, "because I have it on good authority that I am quite the catch."

Daisy hadn't wanted him, but Evangeline refrained from saying that aloud. "If this is your method of courting," she said instead, "I would have to dispute that. I am not impressed."

"You will be."

He said it with such conviction that it startled her. Goodness, did he mean to court her, then? Why? She'd been as rude to him as possible, because earning his affection was utterly pointless, and because having him about was very flustering. She didn't like being flustered.

Any female entered a marriage at a disadvantage—the money was the husband's, as were all of the rights and rules and properties. Her choice would allow her to even those odds, and perhaps even come out in the lead. Anything else, any*one* else, was unacceptable. Period.

Chapter 4

"*Who was that I saw you walking with, my* darling?" Lady Munroe trilled as she swept into the library. Halfway to the chairs arranged in a semicircle before the fireplace, she stopped. "Oh, he's still here." She smiled, dipping into a curtsy. "You're still here, my lord. How wonderful."

"Yes, he won't leave," Evangeline commented, leaning against the back of one of the chairs and folding her arms. "I have asked him to go. Several times."

"I'm perusing your library, my lady," Lord Rawley contributed, running his fingers along the titles stacked in the grand bookcase. "No Wollstonecraft?" he queried, pausing in his viewing only long enough to nod at the viscountess. "What about Swift? He's progressive, for an Irishman and a male."

"We are not a household of anarchists, my lord." The viscountess put a hand over her heart. "What in the world makes you think us so?"

Drat. Evangeline frowned, pasting an affronted look on her face when the marquis glanced at her. Advertising to males how much she knew of female rights rather defeated the goal of having unexpected information to use to her advantage. "I have begun to realize," she said carefully, "that Lord Rawley is very difficult to decipher."

"Yes, I am." He set a book back on the shelf as he faced her. "Abominably so. But Miss Munroe is too kind. I've been called much worse than difficult." He inclined his head in the viscountess's direction. "I did not mean to offend."

"No offense taken, my lord. Shall I send for tea?"

"No, though I thank you for the offer." His sensuous lips curved into a smile that reminded Evangeline abruptly of kissing. "And despite Miss Munroe's reluctance to let me leave," he continued, "I do have an appointment."

"I did not—"

"Do you attend Almack's tonight?" he cut in, as though Gilly hadn't spoken.

"We do, Lord Rawley," her mother supplied when Evangeline clamped her own lips shut.

"Then I shall, as well." Rawley crossed the room to Evangeline and reached down for her hand. Slowly he lifted her fingers, brushing her knuckles with his lips. "Until tonight."

"I will not dance with you," she grated, before she remembered she should probably be grateful that he hadn't mentioned kissing her.

"I haven't asked you to. Yet." With a last, fleeting smile he strolled out of the room.

Belatedly realizing that she still had her hand held up in the empty air, Evangeline clenched her fist and lowered it again. Impossible, distracting, arrogant man. Thank goodness he'd finally left.

"Well, this is unexpected," her mother said, looking at the closed door. "We crossed him off the list."

"He doesn't signify," Evangeline returned feelingly. "I think he enjoys aggravating and provoking people, and I'm merely his latest target—all thanks to an unfortunate carriage mishap. He certainly doesn't do anything I ask of him."

The viscountess pursed her lips. "It's actually a shame, because he is very pleasing to look at." She brushed at the front of her skirt. "On the other hand, that's just another mark of his unsuitability. As you know, a handsome man isn't the best choice. Once a gentleman becomes accustomed to compliments from the fairer sex, he will seek them out in any bedchamber he can find them. You don't want a man who preens."

She had a difficult time imagining Rawley as a preener; he had a multitude of other faults, but not that one. "I want a man who will give over his household and his income to my care, and then do what I tell him regarding everything else." And if she'd already discovered one thing about Connoll Addison, it was that he would never do as anyone else directed him.

"Precisely. Now come along, my dear. Leandra Halloway and Lady Mary have invited us to go shopping, and I would like to see you in something a touch more daring." Her mother smiled. "After all, we don't have to admire men, but they should admire us."

Lewis Blanchard, Lord Ivey, stood as Connoll strode into the Addison House morning room. "There you are, you rogue," he said in a deep, booming voice. "I'd begun to think you'd abandoned London again."

Inwardly flinching, Connoll stripped off his right riding glove and shook hands with the earl. "My apologies,

Ivey," he drawled. "I thought we were meeting for luncheon."

"We were. I wanted to see those paintings you told me about. And I've a bit of news that can't wait."

Connoll could guess what the news was, but he feigned a curious expression anyway. "What news, then?"

"First the paintings. I feel like building some anticipation."

More like dread. "Very well. They're in the upstairs hallway and the library."

With Ivey on his heels, he climbed the stairs. At the top he stood aside, letting his friend proceed on his own. Tall, solid in build and manner, and possessing a surprisingly refined taste, Lewis Blanchard's only flaw seemed to be that he took people at face value and never changed his opinion of them.

"I say, Connoll, these are exquisite. They must have cost you a few fair pounds."

Connoll shook himself. "More than a few. The biggest expense, though, was getting them out of France before Bonaparte could seize them and barter the lot away for cannon shot."

"And before Wellington could burn them and Paris to the ground. A bold move, Conn. And a brave one. You've saved some very significant pieces."

"The bother of it all is that now I'll have to open my own gallery or something. I've room for some of them at Rawley Park, but this is ridiculous. They can't stay in the hallway. Winters nearly broke his neck on a Rembrandt this morning."

"You could loan them to the British Museum. Anonymously, of course, since traipsing about France isn't very popular at the moment—even for a just cause."

A museum loan. He'd actually considered it, but hearing Ivey second the notion gave the idea more credence. "You know, I think I may do that." Connoll cleared his throat, not particularly eager to hear Lewis's surprise, but knowing he was expected to be curious. "Have we built enough anticipation? Because I'm getting a bit hungry, and if you're not going to divulge anything, my frustration will sit better on a full stomach."

"Very well." Ivey drew a breath. "After you left London I met someone. A lady. We've seen quite a bit of one another over the past few weeks, though because her husband died just over a year ago I've been keeping her identity a secret—you know what damage courting too soon can do to a lady's reputation."

"Yes, I know. And?" Connoll prompted.

"Well, a few days ago I asked her to marry me. She said yes."

Connoll made himself smile. "Well done, Ivey. Congratulations." He lifted an eyebrow. "You are going to tell me her identity eventually, aren't you? Sooner or later I'm bound to figure it out."

The earl laughed. "I suppose it's safe now. Daisy Applegate. Lady Applegate."

"Soon to be Lady Ivey." Connoll offered his hand. "I've met her. She's lovely. And you two are well suited, I think. You've made a good match, Lewis."

"Thank you. She makes me very happy."

"I can see that."

"Yes, well, now we must find a chit for you."

With a snort Connoll headed back down the stairs. "They say a happily married man is the worst sort of matchmaker. You leave me be."

"For the moment, then."

Despite his protest, the image of a chit did cross his

thoughts, and it wasn't Daisy Applegate, thank God, but a young lady with hazel eyes and a very high opinion of herself. A lady with whom he meant to dance tonight at Almack's, whether she admitted to wanting to see him there or not.

A blast of warm air hit Connoll as he strolled into Almack's main assembly room. Generally he would rather eat ants than spend an evening at Mayfair's tamest venue, but he'd promised—or threatened, actually—to be there.

As he rounded a flock of debutantes, he spied Evangeline standing with her mother and a tall man who looked to be her father. His pulse stirred. Whatever the devil had happened to him during that carriage accident, Gilly Munroe had seized his attention and refused to let go.

"For heaven's sake, John," Lady Munroe was saying, her tone impatient, "with you skulking about, no gentlemen will approach Gilly. Please just go stand elsewhere and try to look interesting."

"I'm on my way, Heloise. May I fetch you a lemonade?" the viscount returned mildly.

"No. Be sensible, will you? If you fetch us anything, you give gentlemen one less excuse to approach."

Hm. The mother's tirade explained several things about the daughter. Increasing his pace, Connoll reached the Munroes before the viscount could make himself scarce. "Good evening," he drawled, keeping his gaze on the family's patriarch despite the keen desire to look into sharp hazel eyes.

"My lord," the viscountess returned when Gilly kept silent. "You are as good as your word, I see."

"I do try." He paused for a moment, but when no

introductions seemed to be forthcoming, he stuck out his hand. "Connoll Addison," he said. "You must be Lord Munroe."

The viscount shook his hand. "I am indeed," he said warmly. "I was just on my way to . . . elsewhere."

"It is stifling in here, isn't it?" Connoll agreed. "I don't blame you for wanting to escape. In fact, after I secure a place on your daughter's dance card, I may just join you."

When he finally turned his attention to Gilly, her expression had become an intriguing meld of annoyance and surprise. "I already told you that I won't dance with you, my lord."

He smiled, wishing for a moment that her parents weren't present. "Change your mind, Evangeline."

"I don't wish to change my mind."

"Very well. Then I shall keep you company for the entire evening." He eyed her coolly. "That won't prevent any other eligible men from approaching you, I hope."

"You know it will. Why won't you simply go away?"

"Gilly! You shouldn't speak to a gentleman in that tone."

"But he's impossible, Mama. What am I to do? I can't challenge him to a duel."

"All you have to do is give me a dance, and I'll leave you be for the remainder of the evening."

She glared at him for a moment. "Very well." Her jaw tight, she pulled her dance card from her reticule and handed it to him.

Several spaces were already taken. Lord Redmond had reserved the only waltz of the evening, damn the old fool. Waltzes should be left for those who could enjoy them. Keeping his expression mildly amused, Connoll selected a country dance toward the end of the evening and handed the card back to her.

Gilly gazed at his selection, then lifted her eyes to his. "Now you'll have to wait about for two hours, and not in my vicinity."

"Mm-hm. Excuse me. Lord Munroe, would you care to step outside for a cigar?"

The viscount lifted both eyebrows. "I would love to. My thanks, my lord."

Evangeline had some interesting—and unflattering— ideas about men, and about him in particular. Lord Munroe could very likely be the key to why she held those ideas, and Connoll felt in the mood for some answers. With a nod at Gilly and her mother, he gestured for her father to lead the way outside. Bloody Almacks's bloody patronesses didn't allow a gentleman to smoke inside the bloody building. With no liquor served, either, he couldn't imagine how it had become so popular.

"You and my Gilly seem to be having something of a disagreement," the viscount commented as they stopped at the foot of the front steps.

Connoll handed him a cigar. "We've been in conflict since the moment we met," he agreed.

With a deep sigh, Munroe breathed in the scent of the cigar. "Very nice," he said. "Heloise doesn't allow me to smoke—says it's a smelly vice—so you have no idea how much I appreciate this."

"If I couldn't have a cigar on occasion, I think I would consider putting a pistol to my head." With a swift grin Connoll lifted the glass lamp on the side of one of the waiting coaches and lit his cigar. Munroe followed suit.

"It's not as tragic as that, lad, though . . . ah . . . very few things satisfy as well."

Connoll could disagree with that, but since he'd just scheduled a dance with the man's daughter, he kept his silence. "Why is it that I've never seen you in London before?" he asked instead.

"My wife doesn't like me to be gone from Shropshire without her. Now that Gilly's come of age and we can all journey to London together, well, we did."

"You're an indulgent husband, my lord. I doubt anything could keep me from London during the Season. For Parliament, if nothing else."

"Ah, Parliament. If everything goes as I hope, I'll file my intention to sit for next year's session. I would like to do my duty by my country." He sighed, taking another puff on his cigar. "Family does come first, however."

"Of course. If I may say, you've raised a lovely daughter."

A shadow crossed the viscount's face. "Yes, thank you. Just like her mother, she is." He cleared his throat. "You find her amenable, then?"

Connoll snorted. He couldn't help himself. "Amenable? No. But forthright and witty. It's refreshing, despite the blows to my pride. I'm . . . fawned over quite a bit, generally."

"Hm. Interesting."

"Why is that?"

"Oh, nothing. Just an old father musing to himself." The viscount pulled out his pocket watch and clicked it open. "I should go see how they're faring."

From what Connoll had overheard, the viscountess didn't want her husband anywhere near them. Obviously Munroe had some opinions about things, and just as clearly he had no intention of expressing them to a man he'd only just met. If an extended acquaintance was what it took to enable him to decipher Evangeline, so be it. Whatever she'd done to him that morning didn't seem to be waning.

"I'll go with you," he decided, crushing out his cigar on the carriage's wheel rim. "I suppose I need to assess my competition."

"You're sincerely in pursuit of Gilly, then, are you?" her father asked. "With honorable intentions, I presume?"

"I wouldn't be talking with you if they were otherwise, my lord." A few days ago forming that sentence would have sent him screaming into the night. Perhaps Gilly was a witch. If he was under a spell, though, it was an odd one, since a love spell generally meant that the conjurer was attracted to the conjuree. Miss Munroe had several times looked at him as though she would like to throw him through the nearest window. He grinned, then quickly hid the expression. A better explanation was that he'd simply gone mad. "And to clarify, yes, my intentions are honorable."

"Perhaps you should call me John, then."

"Only if you call me Connoll."

"Agreed, Connoll. I have to say, it's pleasant to have another gentleman about for me to converse with. A household of females, you know, requires a certain restraint."

Where the Munroe household was concerned, the level of restraint seemed extraordinary. He declined to comment on that, at least for the moment.

The sight of Gilly standing before Lord Redmond, though, set him back on his heels again. As he watched, she giggled behind her fan, then playfully cuffed the old man with the ivory-ribbed confection. *Good God.* Who was this chit? If that had been him standing there, she would have attempted to remove his head with that fan.

"We've returned to see whether you require anything, my dears," the viscount intoned, smiling at his wife.

"We're quite well," Lady Munroe said, her jaw clenching. "Lord Redmond, are you acquainted with Lord Rawley?"

The earl shuffled his feet around to face Connoll. "Indeed I am. Welcome back to London, Rawley. I'd heard you had embarked on some expedition or other."

Damnation. "Oh, you know me," he said nonchalantly. "I like to wander. It keeps me out of trouble—for the most part."

Redmond chuckled, then began wheezing. "For the . . . most part . . . Very good, Rawley."

Sending a glare at Connoll, Gilly offered her arm to the earl. "Goodness, my lord. Shall I have someone fetch you a drink?"

"John will go," the viscountess broke in. "Go get the earl a lemonade, John."

With a shallow bow, Munroe vanished. Redmond's coughing fit continued.

"Perhaps you might take a seat, Redmond," Connoll suggested, beginning to wonder whether he'd killed the old fool. His quip had been only mildly amusing at most. Certainly not apoplexy-worthy.

"Yes, I think . . . I shall." With another wheeze, the earl released Gilly and grabbed for Connoll's outstretched arm. "Too much exertion tonight, I think. I did dance with Miss Allenthorpe at the beginning of the evening."

"Yes, she's very energetic," Connoll agreed, half carrying Redmond to the nearest chair and dumping him into it. "I suggest you sit there for a few moments and recover yourself."

"But I have a waltz with Miss Munroe," the old man exclaimed. "I wouldn't miss that for anything."

"I'm certain Miss Munroe understands that you are a mere mortal, Redmond." He glanced up to meet furious hazel eyes. If Gilly carried a pistol rather than a fan, he would probably have found himself on the floor, dead. "If it pains you to miss a dance, I have one with her later in the evening. We could trade, and then nothing is lost."

Her glower deepened. "But—"

"You are too kind, Rawley. I accept," Redmond returned, nodding his thanks as Munroe reappeared with a glass of lemonade. "Just need a few minutes to catch my breath, is all."

The music for the waltz began, and Connoll straightened. "Shall we, then, Miss Munroe?" he intoned, keeping his expression innocent and polite.

Her jaw tight, she draped her fingers over his. "Dastard," she hissed as he led her to the dance floor and slid an arm around her waist.

"I made it possible for him to dance with you later," Connoll commented, drawing her closer and then stepping into the waltz. "If I hadn't appeared, you would still be standing with the old fool, commiserating over his advanced stage of portliness. This way you get to waltz, and still dance with him at the end of the evening, if he's recovered."

"You poisoned him or something, didn't you?"

He lifted an eyebrow. "My dear, I find you attractive, but I don't yet know you well enough to commit murder. Perhaps by Tuesday next, if you continue to be this charming."

"I should never have accepted that diamond," she muttered.

"Redmond gave you a diamond?" The surprising stab of jealousy made his muscles shake. Connoll took a breath. He was behaving like a madman; this chit had only crashed into his life yesterday, and obviously Redmond was in the midst of courting her. Why she accepted the codger's suit, he had no idea, but he had no intention of giving in to the abrupt desire to thrash the old earl.

"No, not Redmond," she countered, her hazel gaze meeting his. "My aunt gave it to me as an inheritance."

"My condolences on your aunt's passing, then." That was better. Very civilized of him.

"Oh, she's not dead." A flicker of amusement touched her face. "I suppose I should explain, since I brought up the subject."

"Yes, that would be pleasant of you."

"Aunt Rachel's apparently had the thing for years— the diamond necklace, I mean—and believed the family mythology that it's cursed. She thought herself on her deathbed and so gave it to me with one of her silly, dire warnings. At any rate she wrote me yesterday saying that she's feeling much better and hopes I'm using the 'cursed gem'—that's what she's calling it now—wisely."

"But you said that you wished you hadn't accepted it. Does that mean you believe its curse, too?"

"No! Of course not. It's superstitious nonsense." She scowled. "On the other hand, the moment I accepted it, your carriage crashed into mine and nearly killed me. And now you've begun hounding me and won't go away."

"I see. So if this diamond *is* cursed, then I am the personification of its evil."

"Precisely," she agreed easily.

"But I've never set eyes on it. If it and I are doing the devil's work, shouldn't it call to me or something?" He caught the glitter of amusement in her eyes again. "Wait, I think I hear it now." He gazed about the room. "No, that's Redmond with the vapors."

"Oh, stop it," she said, a chuckle in her voice.

"My point is, if the diamond and I are both evil, why am I only about when it's not?"

"That is my thinking precisely. I'm beginning to believe that my aunt had it sideways: The diamond is *good* luck. And that's why you only appear when I'm *not* wearing it."

"Hm. You begin to wound my feelings, Gilly." He drew her a breath closer and lowered his voice. "Tell me in all honesty that you never wish to set eyes on me again, then, and I'll go away. But be honest, because I will acquiesce to your wishes."

"I never wish to set eyes on you again."

"Balderdash. I don't believe you."

She sighed, not sounding as irritated as he expected. A little bit of her *did* like him, then; just not the part she could admit to. "Why don't you believe me, Lord Rawley?"

"Call me Connoll."

"No."

"Yes, if you wish me to answer your question."

"You insist on bullying me, don't you?"

"You began it. I give as I receive. Call me Connoll."

"Connoll, then. Why don't you believe me, Connoll?"

He liked the way she said his name, with a kind of exasperated affection. It very much reflected the way he'd begun to feel about her. Exasperated, at wit's end, but not willing to give her up yet. Not even close. "I don't believe you because you kissed me."

"That was not—"

"Not your idea. I know that. But in addition, I've noted your . . . strong will. If you didn't want me about, you wouldn't have walked with me, and you wouldn't be dancing with me now. So you protest, but I think only for show. To please your mother, perhaps—I'm not certain, yet. But you enjoy my company, and I enjoy yours. I see no reason for us to go our separate ways. In fact, I intend to take you on a picnic luncheon tomorrow at noon."

"No."

"Yes. If you wish to test the necklace, wear it. Put it in your pocket. Burn rare spices to invoke its power. Sacrifice a chicken to it. But I will be on your doorstep at noon, and we will have a pleasant, amusing, interesting time together. I swear it."

"Do you, now?"

"Yes, I do."

"Then I accept your challenge, Connoll Addison."

Chapter 5

Evangeline lifted the diamond necklace out of its velvet-lined box and then out of the velvet bag she'd found for it, and held it up to the window. Good luck or bad luck? Oh, the idea of it being either was ridiculous. All wearing it to a picnic would mean was that she was terribly overdressed.

Still, Lord Rawley had challenged her to wear it, or at least to keep it with her. And she supposed that she didn't need to convince herself of its power; she only needed to convince *him.* Therefore, if she kept it in her pocket and remained resolved to dislike him and made certain they both had a miserable time, then producing it for his viewing pleasure would ensure that he would leave her alone. Or it would at least improve the chances that he would do so.

Yes, he was handsome, and witty, and very intelligent and wealthy, but he'd already demonstrated that everything had to be done his way, at his pleasure, and for his own satisfaction. She couldn't think of a life more miserable than one spent in the company of that aggravating man.

"Are you going to wear that today, Miss Munroe?" Doretta asked as she entered the room, Evangeline's newly cleaned slippers in her hands.

"No. I'm going to put it in my pocket." With a deep breath she placed it back in its bag and then did so, patting the outside of her pelisse to make certain it was secure. It would never do to lose it somewhere, with or without the curse.

"In your pocket," the maid repeated. "May I ask why?"

"It's a test," Evangeline returned.

"For pickpockets?"

"No. It's complicated, Doretta. Just help me with my shoes, will you?"

"Right away, Miss Munroe. But it's only half eleven. Isn't your gentleman calling at noon?"

"He's not my gentleman. He's an annoyance."

"A very handsome one. Those blue eyes . . ."

Evangeline snorted. "Doretta!"

Her maid blushed. "My apologies, miss."

"No harm done. He is quite well favored."

The sound of a carriage rattling up the drive drifted in through her open bedchamber window. Her heart skipped a beat. Was he early? And why did the mere thought of him make her muscles shiver? She didn't even like him, for heaven's sake.

Leaning a hand on her chair for balance, she stepped into her pearl-colored shoes, a match for her pearl and green muslin gown. As she straightened, the butler scratched at the door.

"You have a caller, Miss Munroe."

She wanted to smile, and sternly stopped herself. Rawley was dangerous, with his easy wit and charming grin. She would not be dominated, and he clearly didn't care about anything but his own amusements. "Please tell the marquis I'll be down in a minute."

"The earl, miss. I'll inform him." He backed out the door.

Evangeline put out a hand to stop the butler's retreat. "Wait a moment, Clifford. Who is downstairs?"

"Lord Redmond. Shall I still have him wait?"

"Oh. Yes. Thank you."

Another flutter ran through her. This time it didn't feel as much like anticipation as it did . . . annoyance. Evangeline shook herself. No, of course she wasn't annoyed to have Redmond calling on her. It was only that she hadn't been expecting him, and her mind had been preparing for a different kind of encounter altogether.

"Come along, Doretta. Let's see what the earl wants."

Her maid giggled. "He wants to marry you, miss. That's no secret at all."

"I mean this morning." He'd barely survived Almack's last night. She'd hoped that he knew enough to stay in bed and rest. If he expired now, he wouldn't be doing anyone any favors.

She swept into the morning room. The earl rose from his seat and gave a reverent bow. "Miss Munroe. I apologize for calling without making prior arrangements, but I'd hoped you would be available to have luncheon with me today."

"Goodness," she said, letting the annoyance she felt color her voice just a little. "I'm so sorry, but I've already made plans. I wish you had asked me last evening. You know how I dislike having to tell you no, my lord."

"Oh, my humble apologies again, Miss Munroe." He hurried forward and clasped both of her hands in his. "I didn't mean to upset you."

"It's of no consequence. If you like, we can sit for a few minutes and you can say complimentary things about me. You did come all this way, after all."

The earl chuckled, releasing one of her hands to guide her to the couch. "You've given me a very easy task. How can I not accept?"

For the next ten minutes he did exactly as she asked, complimenting her features, her hair, her gown, her overall keen sense of fashion, her voice—every insignificant quality she possessed. Evangeline smiled and contemplated the silliness of men that they could be so easily convinced to apologize for having the audacity to appear with a luncheon invitation. Her mother was correct; they needed to be guided, if only for their own sakes.

She glanced at the clock above the fireplace. Rawley was already ten minutes late. Perhaps he'd had another friend in need of assistance and had decided not to come calling at all. Again.

"You know," Redmond was saying, "I feel the need to mention especially your fingers."

"My fingers? There are ten, an altogether unremarkable fact."

"Oh, no, my dear. It's not that. It's how well one of them would look with my signet ring on it."

Good God, he was proposing, and better than a week ahead of her estimate. Of course, marriage to Redmond was precisely what she wanted, and it didn't matter that he smelled of moths and horse liniment. But she had to admit she was somewhat disappointed that Rawley hadn't even bothered to appear for their luncheon.

The diamond. More than half convinced that absolutely nothing would happen, she slipped it out of her pocket and tucked it under the closest couch pillow. Then she smiled. Now for the experiment. "You say the most flattering things, Lord Redmond. I—"

The morning room door opened. "My apologies," Rawley's deep drawl came, and he strolled into the room as confident as if he actually owned the place. "I seem to be tardy."

"Yes, you are," she returned as coolly as she could manage, considering that his appearance the moment the diamond left her possession had nearly stopped her heart. So if the jewel did alter luck, had her fortunes just changed for the better, or for the worse? "Another friend in need, I presume?"

"A damned milk cart overturned right in front of me. My tiger and I spent twenty minutes chasing urchins and cats and one rather frightening elderly woman out of the street before further carnage could ensue." For the first time he glanced at her other guest. "Hello, Redmond. Didn't see you there."

"Rawley. If you'd give me a moment, I was speaking with Miss Munroe."

For a second Connoll Addison's gaze met Evangeline's, his expression unreadable. "Of course. I'll be in the foyer, Gilly."

He'd used her familiar name deliberately. Not that she found it in the least significant that the man who'd been courting her for better than a month still called her Miss Munroe, while the marquis who'd known her for less than a week had already absconded with her pet name. He was simply rude and arrogant.

Once he'd left the room, Redmond seized her hand. "Say you'll wear my ring, Miss Munroe."

"My goodness," she returned. "This is rather sudden, my lord. Might I . . ." She paused, looking at his brown, adoring eyes. "Might I ask you a favor?"

"Ask me anything. I would purchase you the moon, if you but asked for it."

"Heavens, I don't want the moon. But . . . well, will you kiss me?"

It was a stupid request, since as her mother had many times informed her, personal attraction had nothing to do with a marriage. On the other hand, however weakminded a husband, he would still expect to share a bed on occasion with his wife—at least until she could convince him otherwise.

"I would be honored," he breathed, then clenched her shoulders, drew her up to him, and pressed his tightly closed lips against hers.

It was like being kissed by a pig's snout, or how she imagined that would be, anyway—damp, slightly bristled, and eliciting nothing but a faint disgust. She sat back, blinking. "Thank you, my lord," she said faintly, resisting the urge to wipe the back of her hand across her lips.

"I would kiss you whenever you wish it, if you would only answer my question," he said fervently.

Doretta shrieked and leaped to her feet. Dancing about like a madwoman, she flapped her skirts, brushing at them frantically. "Doretta! What's—"

The door burst open again, Rawley striding into the room. "What's amiss?" he asked, turning his gaze from Evangeline to her maid.

"A very big . . . a spider! On my dress!"

"Then hold still a moment," he instructed, grabbing her arm. He gazed at the maid critically, then reached down to the level of her ankle, flicked a finger at something, and stomped as a dark spot landed on the hardwood floor. "There you are. No harm done—except to the spider, of course."

"Oh, thank you, my lord. I'm terrified of those crawly things."

"Yes, I know what you mean. I refuse to feel kindly toward anything that can move in more directions than I can." With a last reassuring pat on her arm, he faced Evangeline again. "Not to be rude, but I've been chasing about the street all morning, and I'm famished. Are you ready for our picnic?"

"Yes, I am." She spared Redmond a glance. "I beg your pardon, my lord, but I do have a previous engagement. Perhaps we can continue our discussion at a more opportune time."

"Of course. I am all patience for you, Miss Munroe." His brown eyes slid over to the marquis. "Perhaps I'll have a chat with your papa."

"Please do," she returned. As if it would be her father who granted her permission to marry. Everyone in the household knew that Lady Munroe would have the final say in that particular matter.

With a last glance in the direction of the couch and the hidden necklace, she touched Doretta's shoulder. "Get the diamond and put it back in its box," she whispered, and the maid nodded.

While Doretta hurried upstairs, Evangeline joined Connoll Addison in the foyer. Good luck or bad luck, he seemed to appear only when the diamond was not on her person. Today she would find out for certain which kind of luck he was for her, and she had more than a suspicion that she couldn't do that with the Nightshade Diamond in hand.

* * *

Connoll kept an eye on Lord Redmond as he, Gilly, and her spider-fearing maid left the house. The earl, though, seemed content to remain inside. Better there than making a fool of himself over a girl less than half his age.

But it wasn't just Redmond being foolish. Obviously Gilly felt the need to encourage the fellow, though he still wasn't quite certain why. Money? Title? He had more of both than the earl did. And if he did say so himself, at least he hadn't begun to sag in embarrassing places yet.

He shook himself as they reached his curricle. "Any luck yet, Quilling?" he asked his tiger.

The lad looked up from the bundle he held in one arm, the other hand being engaged with holding the horses. "No, m'lord. He still won't let go."

"What won't let go?" Evangeline asked.

"No matter. He can have my coat until he changes his mind," Connoll returned, offering a hand to help Evangeline onto the high seat. "While we were chasing children and felines out of harm's way, one of them latched on to my greatcoat. One of the cats, not the children. Otherwise that could have been awkward."

She chuckled. "May I see it?"

"Certainly, miss." The tiger released the horses as Connoll took the reins, then walked back and held up the bundle to Evangeline before he and the maid climbed onto the back of the vehicle.

"Oh, it's adorable," Gilly said, peeling back a layer of coat to reveal a small gray ball of fur. "It's just a kitten, poor thing."

"Yes, I'm afraid the cart driver was a little too vigorous in defending his spilled milk, and he kicked the lad. I don't think he hurt it, but the animal hasn't set foot on the ground since. I carried him on the back of my leg for five minutes before I realized he was there."

"Why do you think it's a he?" she asked, stroking its back and making attractive cooing sounds. "I think it's a girl."

"Until we know for certain, she can be whatever you wish. I'm in no hurry to get my eyes scratched out for trying to discover its gender."

"What are you going to do with her?"

"Wear her, apparently, if she won't relinquish my coat."

"You won't throw her out in the street?"

He turned his head, gazing at her. "Providing a bowl of cream isn't a very great sacrifice," he said slowly. "I think we'll manage."

"Good," she said, smiling.

"Unless you wish her."

"Oh, no. Mama would never have an animal in the house. She doesn't like to trip over things."

There seemed to be a great many things her mother didn't tolerate. "Then she'll stay with me. I would appreciate if you would name her, though. The only thing I could come up with is Claws, or perhaps Scratchy, but that's when she was a boy cat."

With another chuckle, Evangeline freed the kitten's claws from his coat and lifted her up to look her in the eye. "Elektra," she said after a moment.

"Ah, the father-killing heroine of Greek myth." Somehow, her choice wasn't a bit surprising. She seemed something of a man-killer, herself.

"If you don't like it, then choose something else."

"Elektra is fine."

"Hmph."

"Truly. I like it. Elektra. Very nice. A strong name for a brave young kitten. All of the others ran away, you know. She stayed to get her share of milk."

Finally Evangeline's mouth softened again. Good. At least she wasn't mad at him. Now, though, at the sight of her upcurved, slightly parted lips, he wanted to kiss her. He'd been dreaming of kissing her again for the past three nights, uncertain whether it had been as pleasant and stimulating as he remembered, or whether he'd been too drunk to realize that nothing spectacular had happened at all.

"You are an unusual man," she commented quietly, cuddling Elektra against her chest, "taking in stray kittens and inviting women who've slapped you out to luncheon."

So she remembered the kiss, too—or at least the end of it. "I kissed you without invitation. I deserved to be slapped."

"And so now you're a completely proper gentleman?"

"No. But the next time we kiss, I will ask you first."

Her cheeks darkened. "What makes you think there will be a next time?"

"Because I can't imagine there not being one."

That stopped her for a moment. She sat beside him, absently scratching Elektra and gazing at the crowded London streets around them. Apparently he'd given the correct response, since she hadn't slapped him or thrown the cat at his head. And oddly enough, he'd also given a completely honest response. He did want to kiss her again, and however efficiently she seemed to evade him, he knew—*knew*—he would kiss her again.

"Where are we going?" she asked finally, still not facing him.

"St. James's Park. I thought we might picnic beside the pond."

"That sounds nice."

He nodded, fighting against the urge to smile. "Did you bring your evil gemstone?" he queried, mostly to give her a moment to recover her usual, more acerbic self.

"No, I didn't. I told you it was nonsense. There's no such thing as a diamond giving someone bad luck or good luck."

"There are those who would dispute that. As we're here together and it's elsewhere, I, for instance, would say that its absence is good luck."

"For you, perhaps."

"But if my theory is correct, to prove it you would only need to wear it, and I would fall off the carriage and break my neck."

Finally she faced him again, her expression serious, but her hazel eyes dancing. "If only I could be certain, I might risk it."

"Very amusing, Gilly. I consider that your leaving it behind means you like me and don't wish me to lose any appendages."

"Suit yourself, but *I* merely considered a diamond necklace too much decoration for a picnic."

Connoll grinned. "Very well. I'll be grateful and keep my peace." They turned onto the park's main path, and he slowed the team of chestnut mares to a walk. "Did I interrupt Redmond's visit earlier?" he asked in a hopefully offhand tone. Whatever her intentions regarding the earl or vice versa, he refused to be jealous of the old windbag. He did, however, want to know what was going on. And he'd already given himself permission to do anything necessary to disrupt it.

"He came by to see whether I might be available for luncheon," she returned, waving as they passed another carriage.

"He actually is a suitor, then? Not just some very, very, very old friend of the family?"

"He's one-and-fifty. That's not so very old."

"Not for dirt or some select bottles of wine," he retorted. "As a suitor for a young lady not yet twenty, it is *very* old. And that doesn't even take into account the fact that he has barely half a wit."

"You're jealous?" she asked, obvious surprise lifting her voice and her fine eyebrows.

"I am curious," he countered. "Is he your idea of a good catch, or your mother's?"

"I am not going to spend my luncheon debating the merits of the Earl of Redmond with you. At least he's never knocked me off my feet."

"I knocked you down, but I never knocked you off your feet, Gilly. I don't think any man ever has. And that is what you need."

She continued to scratch the kitten. "I assume you're speaking metaphorically. And you're wrong."

"You have been knocked off your feet, then? I doubt—"

"I meant that that is not what I need. I am not some trembling, fainting miss. I know what I wish to have in my life, and I know who can provide it."

"And that person is Redmond?" he asked skeptically.

"Yes."

"Then you're wishing for the wrong things."

Turning away, she muttered something under her breath. The only word he could make out was "diamond."

"What was that?" he prompted.

"I said, I should have worn the diamond. Let's eat our luncheon and conclude this appointment, shall we?"

Connoll stopped the curricle beneath a likely tree. As

soon as his tiger hopped to the ground and went to hold the horses, he tied off the ribbons and jumped down himself. Evangeline puzzled him—a young lady with wits, beauty, and money enough that she needn't marry to provide for herself, didn't pursue matrimony with the likes of the Earl of Redmond. And yet she was pursuing it, as much as the old earl was. Why?

"Are you going to leave me up here?" she asked, handing Elektra to her maid and twisting on her perch to look down at him.

Shaking himself, Connoll strode around to her side of the carriage. Putting his hands around her waist, he lifted her to the ground. The curricle momentarily sheltered them from the view of anyone in the park who might be passing by. With a slow breath he tilted her chin up and leaned beneath the brim of her bonnet to kiss her.

The soft *oh* of surprise her lips formed molded against his mouth. Even braced for a blow as he was, her feathery breath, the smooth, warm line of her jaw, lifted him inside until he couldn't even feel the ground beneath his boots.

She shoved at his shoulders. Breathing hard, Connoll took a reluctant step backward. "You can't want that old m—"

Gilly grabbed him again, the bonnet slipping back off her honey-colored hair as she pressed against him. Her arms wrapped fiercely around his shoulders, fingers digging into his back. He felt all of it, everywhere they touched, the tremble of her lips as she parted them for his questing tongue.

He pressed her back against the wheel of the carriage, tilting her face up as he deepened the kiss. God, she tasted of . . . of warm sunshine, of ripe strawberries, of something he couldn't put a name to but that abruptly became vital to his continued survival.

"Miss Munroe!" her maid squeaked in a hushed, horrified voice. "Lord Rawley! You must stop that at once!"

No, he thought, sliding his arms down from her waist to her hips, drawing her harder against him. *Never.*

"Someone is coming! Please!"

That caught his attention. "Damnation," he swore against Gilly's mouth. Blinking, half surprised they were still clothed, much less upright, he tore his mouth from hers. Pulling the bonnet back over her hair, he wiped a hand across his lips and turned just in time to see the barouche stop beside his curricle.

"I thought I recognized your carriage, Conn," came the booming voice of Lewis Blanchard, Lord Ivey. "You know my betrothed."

Clenching his jaw, Connoll faced the slender, raven-haired chit seated beside Ivey, her arm wrapped around his. "Of course I do. Good afternoon, Daisy."

Chapter 6

Daisy. Evangeline looked from the lovely young lady to Connoll, standing there looking calm as anything, except for his hands, clenched so tightly into fists that his knuckles were white.

She cleared her throat. "Aren't you going to introduce me, Connoll?" she asked, forcing a smile and choosing not to question why she felt the need to step in.

Black eyes gazed at her, assessing, curious . . . and jealous? She wasn't certain. But little as she liked the idea of being a bit player in someone else's theatrical production, at the moment her foremost thought was that she wanted Connoll Addison to kiss her again.

He stirred. "My apologies, Gilly," he said easily, taking her hand in his and gently squeezing before he placed her fingers on his sleeve. "Gilly, Lewis Blanchard, Lord Ivey, and his fiancée, Daisy, Lady Applegate. Lewis, Daisy, Miss Munroe."

"Hello," she said, with a nod and a smile.

"Miss Munroe." The large Lord Ivey grinned. "No

wonder you didn't want my services as a matchmaker, Connoll. You might have said something."

"I don't gossip, even about myself," the marquis returned. "Lady Applegate, best wishes to you on your betrothal."

"Thank you, Lord Rawley. I hope you and Miss Munroe will come to our engagement ball."

"I can't speak for Evangeline, but I would be honored."

"As would I," Evangeline echoed, rather surprised to hear herself volunteering. It had been a very exceptional kiss, however, even better than the first one. And to herself she could admit that though it wasn't supposed to matter, the kiss from Lord Redmond had repulsed her.

"Splendid." Ivey chuckled again. "Very well. We'll leave you to your picnic, then." He doffed his hat. "Good day, Miss Munroe, Conn."

"Ivey, Lady Applegate."

She watched them down the path. "So that was the famous Daisy, eh?" she asked, facing Connoll again.

He grabbed her shoulders and kissed her hard on the mouth. "Thank you," he murmured, running a finger along her lips as he straightened.

Good heavens. "Don't trouble yourself. It was a small matter." She blinked, trying to pull her mind back to the events at hand, and to what exactly she was doing there. "Did you kiss her the same way you kissed me?"

"What kind of question is that?" With a quizzical look at her, he returned to the back of the carriage and lowered Doretta and the picnic basket to the ground.

"It's a very pertinent question," she returned, taking the blanket out of his hands and spreading it on the grass. "The first time you kissed me, you thought I was her. Daisy, Lady Applegate. Now you seem to be courting me or something, but I have to wonder whether you might merely want to have some other female on your arm so your lady won't think you miss her."

She sank onto the blanket, congratulating herself on figuring out his motives, and pretending that she didn't want to be absolutely incorrect.

"You are very wrong about me, you know," he commented, setting the basket beside her and dropping onto the blanket opposite.

"How so?"

"I wish Daisy well, and I suppose I do miss some things about her." He scowled, shredding a piece of grass in his fingers. "She was amiable, and convenient. And honestly, I didn't think her capable of forming a deep attachment to anyone. I realize now that she could—just not to me. Which may have been my fault, because I wasn't interested in a deep attachment with anyone."

Hearing that, her heart thudded harder. Evidently his interests had changed. Did he want to form a deep attachment to her, when Daisy hadn't tempted him to do so? Evangeline shook herself. Whatever attachment he might want to form, he'd been crossed off her list for a reason—he was not the sort of man she wanted in her life. "And then you turned around and saw me, and decided I must be the one."

"Yes, I did."

"Forgive my skepticism. And please don't call on me again."

"Now who's being absurd?" Connoll pulled out a bottle of Madeira and two glasses, which he handed over to her. "I didn't lose my virginity to Daisy. She wasn't my first mistress. And I didn't love her. She . . . wounded my pride, a little. I recover quickly."

"But you do love me, now."

However flippantly she made the statement, more than a little of her own pride rested on his answer. *What was wrong with her today?* To cover the sudden flutter of nerves, she held out the glasses for him to fill.

"That's an odd question coming from a chit encouraging an old fool's suit."

Hm. He was correct, and she was stupid to have asked. "My question was about you," she improvised. "It has nothing to do with me."

"Ah. Explain."

"Certainly. Before I waste any further time in your company, I would like to know whether or not you're simply a magpie, pursuing whatever sparkles the most in your sight at any given moment."

To her surprise, he sent her a slight grin as he accepted one of the glasses back from her and took a sip. "You don't converse like this with Redmond, do you?"

"I have no need to be cross with him. His adoration has been unwavering since we met."

"So has mine."

She smirked. "Oh, please, Connoll. You thought I was someone else. You don't adore me."

"I admire you," he countered.

"Why?" she blurted, before she could stop herself. *Ninny.*

He gazed straight at her, his deep blue eyes serious and considering. "Because whatever web you're spinning for Redmond, with me you've been honest and forthright to the point of painfulness. You are, I'm beginning to realize, exceptionally brilliant, with a wit most others would weep to possess." He clinked his glass against hers. "And that is why I admire you, Gilly."

Evangeline took a drink of Madeira. Not a conventional compliment in the mix, and yet she'd never felt more genuinely flattered. This was one of the traps her mother had warned her about, obviously. Any man could be pleasant and compliant for a short time. She didn't want her opinion listened to, her requests granted, for merely a moment; she required a lifetime of being integral to her spouse.

"Tell me, Connoll, if we attended the Howlett ball on Friday next, and I wore a dark blue gown, would you wear a light blue coat to complement my apparel?"

"No."

She frowned. "Well, why not?" He might at least have considered it for a blasted minute before he refused her.

"Firstly, I don't own a light blue anything, and secondly, I'm not a doll you dress to match your fancy. Now, if you said you were going to wear nothing, *then* I would dress in nothing as well. That is the only exception."

Hm. "Lord Redmond would wear light blue for me."

"So would a pet monkey."

She thought she heard a snort. When she looked toward the tree beneath which the maid rested, though, Doretta appeared absorbed in her needlework, the kitten in her lap. The tiger was too far away to overhear their conversation, thank goodness.

"Insulting me is an odd way to show your admiration," she said stiffly, digging into the picnic basket when he showed no inclination to do anything but sip Madeira and gaze at her all afternoon.

"I'm insulting your suitor, not you," he returned smoothly. "And monkeys, I suppose."

"Well, for your information, Lord Redmond is not my only suitor."

"I know of two," Connoll said, taking a peach and

pulling a very sharp-looking knife from his boot to slice it, "including myself."

Her cheeks warmed. "Not that it's any of your business, but Lord Dapney has already proposed to me twice."

"Dapney," he repeated, frowning a little. "Dapney. Do you mean Viscount Dapney?"

"Yes, that's him."

"But he's older than Redmond. Good God, Gilly, you may as well hold your wedding at a cemetery."

"His grandson, for heaven's sake," she exclaimed. "The old Lord Dapney died over a year ago."

Connoll handed her a slice of peach. "That makes a bit more sense, at least. I hope he's not the grandson who bought that yacht in Dover and then immediately sank it when he decided to steer it up the Thames himself."

"William has never mentioned any such thing. It must have been one of his cousins."

"Any other gentlemen pursuing you? I wish to know my competition."

"They are in earnest, my lord. You can't be considered to be in competition unless you are, as well."

"I'm not going to commit to an enterprise after three days, Evangeline, however tempting that may be. Dapney's proposed twice, you said, and obviously you've turned him down. I won't accept him as a serious rival. Redmond troubles me more, mostly because I can't for the life of me figure out why you tolerate him, much less encourage him."

Redmond *troubled* him. Evangeline wondered how she would feel if the old earl began to court another woman, or if someone else showed an interest in him. The answer was easy—without a second's hesitation she would turn around and look for another man who fulfilled her requirements. She absolutely didn't wish to become embroiled in a conflict with anyone else over either Redmond or Dapney. How distasteful that would be.

"What are you thinking?" Connoll asked, leaning back against the oak tree trunk and looking like the image of . . . well, of precisely what he was—a handsome, virile, powerful member of the peerage. And those eyes . . .

"I'm thinking that your presence presents something of a puzzle for me," she answered truthfully.

"Did you expect that I wouldn't be interested in you?" He handed her another slice of peach.

It was a very good peach. "It's not that."

"So you *did* expect that I would be interested in you."

Evangeline shrugged. "I'm pretty." As he grinned at that, she threw an acorn at him. "I have no more control over my features than keeping them clean," she said defensively. "Their arrangement is God's decision. I daresay you know you're devilish handsome, Connoll. Refusing to admit something so obvious and so insignificant is mere silliness."

"An interesting point. Very well, we are two well-favored individuals, stamped with our features by the Almighty. Why do I puzzle you, then?"

She hesitated. A few days ago she wouldn't have been able to imagine herself having such a straightforward conversation with anyone, much less a gentleman. Even more surprising, she enjoyed talking with him, even when they were battling. Especially when they were battling. She didn't think she'd ever witnessed her mother and father arguing—the viscountess made a statement, and the viscount agreed with it. No matter what it was, and no matter who might be correct.

"I've been rude to you from the moment you fell on

me. Why are *you* here?" she countered. "Aside from your admiration of my character, which you didn't know until later."

The marquis laughed. She liked the sound, merry and open—rather like she'd begun to think he must be. "Because when I kissed you, you slapped me."

"That's—"

"But before you slapped me, you kissed me back. You didn't faint, you didn't panic, and you didn't scream bloody murder and compromise both of us." His smile softened. "You kissed me back. And it was a very nice kiss. I wanted to experience another one. Several, in fact."

Evangeline sat back. What was wrong with her? This man would question absolutely everything she ever said or did, he would never give in and let her win an argument, and still what she wanted most at that moment was to throw herself on him and just let him kiss her. It had been a *very* nice kiss. And the successive ones had each been better than the first.

"Don't tell me that now I've stumped you," he murmured, setting aside the remains of the peach in favor of some delectable-looking sandwiches.

"I don't want to discuss kissing any longer," she said flippantly, hoping her cheeks didn't look as heated as they felt. For goodness' sake, if Redmond only kissed a little better, and Rawley a little worse, she wouldn't have to be considering anything at all.

"Actions speak louder than words, eh?" He set aside the plate and leaned toward her.

"No!" she blurted, blocking his mouth with her glass of Madeira. "Go back onto your side of the blanket."

"Very well," he returned with a jaunty grin, complying, "but I'd rather be over there."

Talk about something else, she ordered herself. *Think about something else.* "Are the rumors true?" she asked, shifting about for anything to set him as much off balance as he'd put her. "The ones that said you just returned from Paris?"

"I will only answer that question while waltzing. With you, in case you were going to attempt something nefarious and substitute someone else."

"But—"

"We've already established that I'm escorting you to the Howlett ball on Friday, and that you're wearing blue and I'm not. We'll dance there."

"That was a hypothetical situation."

"Not if you want me to answer your question."

She sputtered. "Oh, very well."

"Excellent." He grinned again. "Have some cheese."

"There you are," Lewis Blanchard said, pausing beside a potted palm tree. "What the devil are you doing skulking in the shrubbery?"

Connoll grabbed his friend's shoulder and yanked him behind the fronds. "I'm observing unseen. If you stand out there and talk to me, people will either think you're mad or they'll see me. While I don't mind the former, the latter could be slightly embarrassing."

"What are you observing, then?" the earl boomed in his version of a whisper.

"Lower your damned head. You look like a lighthouse."

Somehow Lord Ivey managed to fold most of himself behind the palm tree. "Good God. I think I've broken my spine. What are you looking at?"

"Not what. Whom. Miss Munroe."

"Your Miss Munroe?"

He liked the way that sounded, though Gilly would be the first one to correct that misapprehension if she ever heard it. "Yes, my Miss Munroe. Hush."

"But—"

"I'm also listening." He'd spent evenings in an odder fashion than this, he supposed, but not recently. After going to the bother of securing an invitation to a very loud and long-winded lecture on Shakespearean metaphor, he should at least be flinging similes about the room. That, however, would have defeated his purpose in being there, which was nothing more and nothing less than deciphering young Miss Munroe.

It seemed she'd coerced the equally youthful Lord Dapney into accompanying her this evening. Even without being able to overhear every word of their conversation, Connoll had no doubt that Dapney fell into the same category as Redmond—the half-wit adored Gilly. At that moment the viscount trudged back to her circle of friends, his arms laden with drinks.

"Oh, thank you, my lord," Evangeline said with a brief smile. "They hadn't any Madeira, then? I do prefer that, you know."

"My apologies, Miss Munroe," Dapney stammered. "I hadn't thought to inquire. I'll return directly." He scurried off again.

"*Your* Miss Munroe has another suitor," Lewis noted.

"She has several," Connoll said absently.

As she half faced him again, he got his best look yet at the jewel glittering against the base of her throat. The diamond. Everyone she'd encountered had taken turns admiring it, but no one had dropped dead or gone blind. She certainly didn't look cursed, herself; actually, seeing her in the soft green silk that lightened the hazel of her eyes, he could only describe her as stunning. His gut clenched.

Perhaps the curse was meant for him, to tangle her into his thoughts and dreams until he went mad from seeing her and knowing she wanted someone else. And the someone she wanted—he didn't consider himself particularly vain, but why in God's name would she prefer either Redmond or Dapney over him? At least he had a full share of wits.

"Isn't that Dapney?" the earl whispered, as the lad returned with her requested drink. "The one who slammed his yacht into a bridge piling an hour after he took possession of it?"

"That's him."

He felt Lewis's gaze on him. "Oh."

"Shut up."

Gilly accepted the drink, taking a dainty sip. "I've heard that the rose garden here is lovely," she commented.

"Allow me to escort you on a tour," Dapney said, reminding Connoll of a puppy trying to please its master. Or mistress, rather. "It would be my greatest honor."

"A breath of fresh air would be welcome. Excuse us for a few moments, everyone."

The two of them wandered off toward the back of the house. With a curse Connoll pushed past the earl. He knew why couples went to admire gardens in the middle of the night, and it wasn't for the view.

"Conn, are you—"

"Apologies, Ivey. I need to go skulk elsewhere."

Brushing past the behemoth, Connoll slipped around the fringes of the room toward the row of floor-length windows that lined the ground-floor entrance to the gardens. If Daisy had been in Lewis's company, he never would have confessed to spying on Gilly. He wasn't certain what he would have said in the face of Gilly's obvious flirtation with Lord Dapney, but he knew how he felt. He didn't like it. Not one damned bit.

He'd nearly reached the windows when a hand grabbed his arm. Scowling, he turned. "Francis. Didn't expect to see you here tonight."

"I was told the desserts were top-drawer," Mr. Henning returned. "I think someone was bamming me. I ain't even seen any desserts."

The tail of Evangeline's emerald gown disappeared through the windows. Bloody hell. "I thought I saw cake over by the hearth," Connoll lied, sidestepping as Henning stampeded by him.

Before anyone else could detain him to ask for a report on the weather, he dodged outside, taking cover in the deep shadows of a hedge while he listened for Evangeline and the idiot with her. Unless she could see by the light of the half-moon and had a very large affection for roses, she was up to something. If it was an amorous tryst, he wanted to know, though in his mind he was already making excuses as to why in God's name she would wish to be with Dapney and not him.

Slipping unnoticed past Lord Gunden and his latest mistress, Connoll made his way around the small pond to the back of the garden. As he heard Evangeline's voice and a lower-toned answer, he moved in closer. Just behind a stand of red roses, he caught his sleeve on a clump of sharp thorns and stopped short.

"Damnation," he muttered, yanking. The thorns, long and curved like the teeth of some carnivorous beast, dug in deeper, finding flesh.

"You know I live only to please you," Dapney's admiring voice came from the far side of a hedge.

By twisting sideways, Connoll could just make out the leafy outline of Gilly's profile and the thicker bulk of the young oaf with her. Whatever they were up to, it seemed to involve sitting very close to one another on a stone bench.

"I know you do," her rich voice came. "And *you* know that I must have someone in my life who will always look after me."

What? Look after her? She'd several times demonstrated that she could take care of herself quite capably. Connoll pulled away again, and the tail of his coat flipped over another branch, tangling him further.

"I would die for you, Miss Munroe."

Yes, but I'm the one who's bleeding, Connoll supplied silently. Hodges was going to weep over the damage to his coat. Hearing Gilly spewing such nonsense and Dapney lapping it up, however, troubled him more.

It was the next sound, though, that froze him. Lips smacked against lips. He could just see Dapney pressed up against her. That bloody poacher. And that blasted minx. With a barely stifled growl he yanked himself backward, taking half the substantial rosebush with him.

"What was that?" Dapney's voice came. "Is someone coming?"

"Oh, dear," Gilly said. "You go back inside. I'll follow a minute later. Hurry, my lord."

Booted feet thudded down the path. With a last twist and a bad scratch across the back of his hand, Connoll managed to hurl the last stubborn branch away from him. "Your hero seems to have left you all alone in the dark," he said, rounding the hedge to gaze at Evangeline.

She had her diamond necklace in her hand, her reticule open as she dropped it inside. For a bare second she froze, her mouth forming a surprised *oh*, before she pulled the strings of her bag closed. "You," she breathed.

"Yes, me. Though with what I just overheard I have no idea why I bothered to make an appear—"

Evangeline lunged at him, grabbing his shoulders and yanking him down to cover his mouth with hers. To keep his balance Connoll flung an arm out to grab a branch of the nearest elm tree, pressing her back against the solid trunk as he deepened the kiss.

She moaned, clinging against him. *Christ.* "What the devil are you up to?" he managed around a dozen deep, rough kisses.

"I like the way you kiss," she whispered against his mouth.

"What else?"

Lifting her face, breathing hard, she frowned at him. "What do you mean, 'what else'? I'm not the one sneaking about in the shrubbery."

"Yes, you are."

Her cheeks darkened. "Oh, yes. I forgot. Still, at least I was on the path."

Connoll gazed down into her pretty hazel eyes. "Have I mistaken something about you, Gilly?" he murmured.

"What do you mean? You surprised me at a . . . a weak moment."

"More likely a rare moment of clarity."

"What the devil are you talk—"

"Why Dabney, and why Redmond?" he interrupted. "And what makes you think I will happily dawdle about while you kiss one or the other of them?"

She let go of his shoulders and took a step backward. "I don't need to explain myself to you."

"Mm-hm. I notice that Lord Dapney wore green. That was at your request, I assume, to complement your own gown?"

"What if it was? Simply because you're unwilling to grant me the tiniest request doesn't mean that every other man is as arrogant and stubborn as you."

Some things were beginning to make sense. Resisting the urge to rub at the scratches on his hand, Connoll continued to eye her. "That's it, isn't it? You're trying to become your mother."

"Don't be absur—"

"You don't want a lover, or even a husband. You want a servant. Someone to wear matching colors and fetch you things and be otherwise unobtrusive and unnoticed."

She put her hands on her hips. "Go away."

He laughed grimly, shaking his head. "If I'm wrong, then please correct me."

"If you won't leave, then I will." With a stomp of her foot, she turned around and stalked back to the house.

Connoll watched her retreat to the safety of the yellow chandelier lights, then sat on the stone bench she and Dapney had vacated. Damnation. How could a woman as . . . obstinate and aggravating and intelligent as Evangeline Munroe want—not even just want, but actively seek—a mate who offered her nothing but a mindless shell? An income and a title, and . . . and what? An arm to hang on?

Whatever she looked for, it obviously wasn't him. Which meant that he could either step back and let Redmond or Dapney have her, or he could step forward and prove to her that she didn't know what she was doing.

He rubbed his hand across his mouth. Walking away without a fight—it wasn't in his nature. And he wasn't ready to let Evangeline Munroe get away, whatever she might think she wanted.

Chapter 7

"I don't want to wear it," Evangeline said, scowling at the wooden box resting on her dressing table.

"But everyone will be attending tonight," her mother countered. "You'll never have a better opportunity to show it off. Aside from that, you'll look so elegant in a sapphire gown with a blue diamond necklace."

"I've already decided to wear the pearls." Rubbing the tips of her fingers nervously, she nudged the box farther away from her.

It could still all be coincidence, she supposed; in fact, it probably was. But with the Nightshade Diamond on she'd experienced two very unpleasant kisses and a proposal that pleased her much less than it should have. The moment she put the thing away, each time she did so, Connoll Addison appeared. And whether she happened to be angry with him or not, she didn't like the idea of a jewel controlling when they were able to meet.

"But the Howlett soiree is legendary."

She faced the viscountess. *"You* should wear it."

"What? I couldn't. Rachel gave it to *you*."

"And I'm saying it would look very nice on you to-night if you will accept its loan."

Her mother gazed at the box. "It is a lovely piece."

Burying her uneasiness, Evangeline lifted the box and handed it to her mother. "I'm still not certain about the whole curse nonsense, but I leave the choice up to you."

"I think I will wear it, then." With a rare grin, the viscountess took the box and opened it, removing the velvet bag. "Because the curse nonsense is just that, you know. Nonsense. I hope that's not the reason you don't wish to wear it."

"Of course not."

"And if it is bad luck," her mother continued, "per-haps Lord Rawley's coach will lose a wheel, and we'll have to attend the ball without his escort."

A shiver ran beneath Evangeline's skin. The man had actually laughed at her the evening before last. She cer-tainly hadn't expected him to send over a note remind-ing her that he would be by at eight o'clock to escort her and her parents to the Howlett ball. The viscountess had suggested that she decline the invitation, but the more Evangeline considered it, the more she welcomed the opportunity to inform Connoll just how little she cared about his opinion.

Of course she didn't want to marry a servant; a butler couldn't make her a viscountess or a countess. If it made her mercenary to wish for a husband's title but not his dictates or stupid opinions, then so be it. Probably the most efficient way to prove just that point would be for her to accept the next proposal either Redmond or Dap-ney handed her. But that would mean no more of those wondrous Connoll Addison kisses.

She scowled. After the other night, neither of them was likely to be kissing the other again, anyway. Doretta fastened the pearls around her neck, and she stood. "I don't doubt that he'll arrive late, regardless of luck," she said to no one in particular.

"I don't know why you accepted his offer of escort, anyway," the viscountess responded, motioning for Doretta to assist her with the diamond. "Lord Redmond has a fine carriage."

Admitting that she still wasn't quite certain how it had happened would only earn her a lecture. "I couldn't have declined his invitation without appearing rude," she improvised.

"Perhaps he and your father will begin a conversation about horses or cigars or something, and they'll leave us be. You know Lord Redmond will be attending, and so will Lord Dapney."

"Lord Dapney had mentioned it," Evangeline returned.

"Have you decided which of them you prefer? They both have their merits, I have to say." The viscountess walked to the bedchamber door, pausing with her fingers on the handle. "Dapney will provide you with a longtime escort, and you'll be able to guide the course of any investments, and social or political alliances. Redmond will most likely tire easily and will leave you to go to whichever soirees you choose and with whomever you choose, and of course you will have a very comfortable life as a wealthy widow."

Now, *that* seemed a bit mercenary, making the older man's death a part of her plan for a comfortable life. "I'm not in a hurry to decide," she said slowly. "I don't want to make the wrong choice, after all."

"Very wise of you, my dear. I'll see you downstairs."

"Miss Munroe?" Doretta asked as the viscountess left the room. "If I'm not overstepping, do you think your diamond is cursed?"

"No. Of course not. People only spread those rumors so thieves won't try to steal their valuables."

"Then why did you take it off the other night?"

Why had she? She'd kissed Dapney once previously, and the sensation had been completely acceptable, if unexciting. The night of the Shakespearean discussion, though, she might as well have kissed a fish. Wet, amateurish, and awful. Yes, she'd pursued a match with him, but the idea that the diamond might . . . encourage him, encourage another proposal, had made her queasy. And as soon as she took the thing off, there had been Connoll.

"I took it off," she finally said, when she realized Doretta was still looking at her, "because I wanted to see what would happen. Nothing did, naturally, and then I forgot that I'd removed it."

"Well, if you were to ask me, I think it *is* cursed. Before you had it, you were set on getting Lord Redmond to propose to you. Now, though, it's not him you're thinking about. And that will *not* please your mama."

"Now you're overstepping, Doretta," Evangeline said sharply, pulling on her white, elbow-length gloves. "Nothing has changed. I very likely will marry Lord Redmond. If before that I choose to indulge in a kiss or two with a very accomplished gentleman, that's no one's concern but my own."

"I beg your pardon, then, Miss Munroe." The maid dipped a curtsy.

Evangeline stood. "No matter. And I suppose if the diamond is either bad luck or good luck for the wearer, we'll find out tonight. I know quite well what Mama wants for me."

Surreptitiously Doretta crossed her fingers and turned a circle. Evangeline pretended not to notice—protection against even an imagined curse couldn't hurt.

The grandfather clock on the landing showed five minutes of eight as they descended the stairs. She wondered again why, precisely, Lord Rawley still wanted to provide her an escort tonight. As she recalled, the last thing she'd said to him had been "go away," or something very close to that.

If he meant to take the opportunity to tease her again for having a plan to secure her future, she would box his ears. Or she would bring up again the fact that they'd met because he'd been drunk and had fallen on her. If anyone deserved to be laughed at, it was him.

As she reached the foyer, someone rapped at the front door. Her heart skittered—which annoyed her. Yes, his kiss had been the devil's inspiration for thinking up sin, but he had nothing else in his favor at all.

Clifford pulled open the door. "Good evening, my lord," he said, bowing as he backed out of the doorway.

"Good evening," Connoll's low drawl returned, and then the man himself stepped into the foyer.

"Good—" Evangeline's jaw dropped as she looked at him.

"I assume you're speechless in admiration," he said, brushing at the powder-blue sleeve of his coat. "It is what you requested."

"But . . . but you said no," she stammered. With light gray pants tucked into polished Hessian boots and a blue-thread paisley pattern on his cream-colored waistcoat, he looked like a dandy—a muscular, slightly dangerous one, but in those colors he couldn't be anything else. The colors did have the effect of making his eyes look the deep blue of the top of the sky at noon; in fact, she could barely tear her gaze from his long enough to take in the rest of him.

"I've decided that doing as you request is more pleasant than arguing," he said easily.

Her mother stepped out of the sitting room. "My," she said after a moment. "The two of you look very well together."

"It was Evangeline's idea," Connoll replied. "She asked me to wear a coat that complemented her gown." He smiled. "May I say, my lady," he continued, "that necklace is exquisite."

The viscountess lowered her lashes, one hand fluttering up to touch the diamond. "Thank you, Lord Rawley. It's a family piece." After a glance about the small foyer, she gestured at the butler. "Go fetch Lord Munroe," she instructed, "and tell him that if he isn't prompt, we will leave without him."

Evangeline wiped the surprised, suspicious scowl off her face to look at Connoll. Rather than making a cynical comment about how much mother and daughter now resembled one another, however, he was looking at his reflection in the hall mirror. As she watched, he fluffed up one side of his cravat. As blue eyes caught hers in the mirror's reflection, his smile deepened.

"What?" she whispered, strolling up behind him.

"You look lovely," he returned. "I'm glad to be a planet orbiting in the light of your sun."

"Mm-hm."

Before she could comment further on that nonsense, her father appeared, hurrying down the stairs with Clifford on his heels. "My apologies, my love," he said. "I was reading, and lost track of the time."

The viscountess gave him a dismissive look and turned for the entry. With the butler still halfway up the stairs, Connoll moved in to open the front door for her. As much as he'd meant to surprise Gilly tonight with his wardrobe and his cooperation, she'd surprised him, as well. He'd only gotten a glimpse of the diamond necklace the other night, but he recognized it—and he recognized that it was the viscountess wearing it, and not Evangeline.

He wanted to ask her why, but that wouldn't fit with his plan for the evening. And so he bit his tongue and smiled as he helped both ladies into his coach and then followed Lord Munroe inside. Wearing what he was to a very popular soiree was probably going to be the stupidest thing he'd ever done—except for getting drunk and falling on Gilly—but if his assessment was correct, giving her precisely what she claimed to want could be the very best way to prove that she was in error.

She was gazing at him again, her expression still wary and suspicious. If she thought he meant to try something tonight, she was too late. They were already well into the game.

"What were you reading that so engrossed you, Papa?" she asked after several moments of silence.

The viscount stirred, sending a swift glance in his wife's direction. "Ah, just the newspaper. A fascinating article on the reinstatement of the French monarchy once we've dealt with Bonaparte again."

Connoll lowered his brow, wishing everyone would stop talking about France, then smoothed the expression as the viscountess looked up at him and smiled. "That was kind of you to dress in coordination with Evangeline," she said.

"Oh, I worship your daughter," he said, repeating

what he'd heard Dapney say the other night. "I would do anything for her."

"Would you, now?"

"Anything. Ask it of me."

"I'm sure that's not necessary," Gilly broke in to the conversation.

"We might at least know what Lord Rawley's intentions are toward you," her mother countered.

"Surely I'm not Miss Munroe's only suitor. Though I am the most sincere, I assure you." He clenched his jaw at the silliness spilling from his own lips. Whatever he was getting into, however, he'd already vowed to see it through. "My annual income is in the vicinity of twenty-five thousand pounds," he said with every ounce of unctuousness he possessed—a means to an end. "I could provide her with anything she wanted. I would be happy to do so."

"Twenty-five thousand," the viscountess repeated, her eyes growing larger. "And a marquis."

"My main estate in Devonshire is rumored to be the finest in three counties," he continued. "My great-great-great-grandfather had it built in 1612."

"Your main estate? How many do you own?"

"Well, four in Scotland," he returned, ticking them off on his fingers, "one in Devonshire, one in York, and a seventh in Cornwall. And the two houses here in London, though I've given one over to my cousin and his family. They also have use of the estate in Cornwall. One can only live in so many places."

"Indeed."

Evangeline gazed at him, her lips pursed. "There are some rumors," she said slowly, flicking her skirt, "that you recently spent some time in France, and that you have sympathies with Bonaparte and the French."

The little minx. "I have sympathy *for* the French," he answered, keeping his tone easy. "They will have a great deal of work ahead of them once Bonaparte's been stopped."

From the flash of her hazel eyes, Gilly realized that he hadn't answered the question of whether he'd been in France or not. To her credit, though, she didn't pursue it further. He'd already told her that he would explain his whereabouts during their waltz tonight—and not a bloody second before that.

"I don't envy Wellington that task," the viscount put in. "Bonaparte's a popular fellow."

"There is nothing more tedious than politics," Lady Munroe said airily. "I've heard that Lady Howlett actually has a tent erected in the stable yard to accommodate all of the additional servants and supplies needed for tonight."

"Indeed she does," Connoll answered. "As a result, there is nowhere for the horses and coaches. The entire three streets surrounding Howlett House are jammed solid." *And I will look like a bloody sugar-glazed croissant in front of everyone.*

"That sounds very exciting."

"It is. Just watch where you step."

Gilly snorted, then coughed to cover it. "Thank you for your advice, my lord."

"I mean to please."

"So you say."

They had to stop the coach six houses away and walk. Connoll offered his arm, and after a barely noticeable hesitation, Gilly wrapped her fingers about his sleeve. He would have had them take the lead, but she pulled against him until her parents moved on ahead of them.

"All right, what the devil are you up to, Connoll?" she whispered.

"Nothing at all. I wish to be with you, and I've realized what you seek in a gentleman. I have become that."

"Just like that."

"Yes, just like that."

"I need to fix my gloves. Carry my reticule for a moment, will you?"

Wordlessly, his eyebrow barely lifting, he took the strings from her fingers and held her small blue bag. At least it matched his coat. After fiddling with her white gloves for several moments too long, she sent him an annoyed sideways glance and held her hand out again.

"I do hope no gentlemen attempt to crowd in for attention while I'm attempting to greet my friends. I rather dislike being interrupted."

So this was what he was in for tonight. "Am I permitted a space on your dance card?"

"What if I say no?"

Connoll stifled the urge to grab Gilly and kiss her until her senses either appeared or left her—the opposite of whatever condition she was in now. *Patience.* He could be patient. That was how he'd acquired some of his most precious paintings and antiques, and it was how he would win Evangeline Munroe.

He shrugged. "If you say no, then we shan't dance."

"Aha! That's what you want, isn't it, so you won't be obligated to tell me about your sojourn to France?"

"*If* I was in France," he pointed out. "But I'm not opposing you at all, Evangeline. If you wish to dance, we shall. If you don't, we won't."

"And you'll abandon my parents and me here."

"I will escort you home regardless. That is a matter

of honor. And with that, there is no playing about."

From the look she gave him, he might have spoken too forcefully. But considering how they'd met, the point he most wanted her to understand was that he *was* a man of honor. One who did *not* make a habit of going about drunk in the middle of the morning.

"Very well," she said slowly. "I apologize for suggesting that you would do other than the proper thing."

Any other night he would have jumped on her apology as a way to prove that she wasn't infallible. Tonight he smiled and stopped beside her parents to greet Lord and Lady Howlett. As he shook hands with Howlett, he drew a breath. The looks from Gilly were nothing compared to the ones he was beginning to receive now. Lights blazed from every window, and even at this early hour there were easily two hundred guests in attendance. *Wonderful.*

It was for a good cause—or so he hoped. If Evangeline truly wanted a Lord Dapney or a Redmond, then he wanted no part of that misery. What he saw beneath her very stubborn exterior, though—the flashes of humor, the wit, the passion—caused him to believe that one night of dressing like a fop would be worthwhile if it helped him find a way to encourage her to keep those particular charms permanently on display.

"My goodness, it's warm in here," Gilly said, fanning at her face with her free hand.

"Shall I fetch you a lemonade?" he asked, wondering whether he should hunch his shoulders and look submissive.

"That would leave me standing here by myself," she returned.

"Ah. Apologies. You were only priming the pump, so to speak, so you could be rid of me more efficiently later." With a nod, beginning to find her little barbs and tests amusing, he gestured her to guide their forward progress. "I still have some things to learn, obviously."

"I was not priming anything. Stating the temperature does not equate with trying to be rid of you."

"Then I apologize again," he said, offering her a slow smile as he realized that she was trying very hard to pick a fight with him. "I would never wish to upset you."

"Why not? That's never troubled you before."

"Because I've learned that you don't want a man who will—who might—upend your sensibilities."

Her eyes narrowed, but she didn't seem to know what to say to him. *Good.* Before she could conjure something, a flock of her colorfully feathered friends surrounded her. That, then, would be his signal to go away and fetch some lemonade.

Before he did that, though, he wanted a swallow of something stronger for himself. He signaled a passing footman, then sank back against the nearest wall to watch the proceedings.

"I say," a familiar voice drawled to his left, "I almost didn't recognize you, Conn."

Connoll straightened, offering his hand. "Francis. I almost didn't recognize myself."

"You'll have to give me your tailor's name," the shorter man said in an obviously admiring tone. "I've never seen a more stunning ensemble."

This from the man who'd tried to start a fashion of pink cravats. "I'll send you his card," he said. In truth, this coat and waistcoat were two of the most expensive garments he owned—the consequence of giving his tailor less than forty-eight hours to put them together.

"Did I see you arrive with Miss Munroe?" Henning continued.

"You did." He glanced at the abruptly uncomfortable look on his friend's face. "Why?"

"Oh. Nothing. Nothing, of course."

"Francis, save us both the time and bother and speak up."

Henning scowled. "Very well. I had luncheon today with Dapney and his cronies. He, ah, mentioned that he would be offering for Miss Munroe by the end of the month. He seemed to have some confidence that she would accept his proposal."

She probably would, if Connoll couldn't convince her of what a miserable life she would be letting herself in for. "No worries, Francis. My eyes are open."

Henning rolled his shoulders. "Good, then. Because I—"

"Thank you for telling me."

The plump fellow smiled. "Thank you for not killing the messenger."

At that moment Gilly looked in their direction and lifted an eyebrow. "If you'll excuse me," Connoll said, handing Francis his glass of port, "I'm being summoned."

"You—oh. Of course."

Francis wasn't the only one surprised that he'd so readily put himself at someone's beck and call. More bothersome, though, was that Connoll could see her mother's mannerisms emerging as he became one of the empty-headed enthralled. If Gilly didn't learn or at least comprehend the lesson tonight, he would have to consider her cause a lost one. And that would be a damned bloody shame.

"Here you go, Miss Munroe," he said with his brightest smile, delivering her a glass of lemonade.

"There you are," she returned, taking the glass. "I'd begun to wonder where you'd run off to."

Strictly speaking he'd been away from her side for less than five minutes. Since he refused to argue, though, he only dipped his head. "It does seem an eternity since I last stood beside you. My deepest apologies. I didn't intend to leave you stranded."

Evangeline actually batted him on the arm. "You are too amusing, Lord Rawley. It was only lemonade, after all." She gestured at a tall, spindly girl standing beside her. "Have you met Leandra Halloway? No? Leandra, Lord Rawley. Connoll, Miss Halloway."

He took the girl's hand, finding it trembling. "Miss Halloway. Your uncle is the famed mathematician, is he not? Robert Halloway?"

She smiled shyly. "Yes. He's working on a new project at Oxford."

"His economic theories are fascinating. It's a pleasure to make your acquaintance."

"Thank you, my lord."

Gilly cleared her throat. "I thought," she said, sending a glance from Connoll to her friend, "that as I will be dancing the first waltz of the evening with Lord Dapney, you might partner with Leandra."

That bloody interloper. "I would be honored, if Miss Halloway is available."

"Oh," the chit squeaked. "I am. Available, I mean."

"Splendid." As the herd began giggling again, he took a step closer to Gilly. "May I see your dance card?"

"Afraid you'll lose the second waltz?" she murmured, handing it over.

"I'm just hoping the curious part of you outweighs the nonsensical one that wants to dance with Dapney," he returned in the same tone. The space next to the second waltz remained empty, and he wrote his name there in pencil. "Shall I make myself scarce until then?"

"Oh, no," she returned, taking the card back and then wrapping her fingers around his sleeve. "You may hand me off to Lord Dapney."

He would rather flatten the pup. "Certainly. Whatever pleases you, Evangeline."

"I know you're behaving counter to your own character," she said with a sniff, "so don't bother thinking that you've fooled me into believing you to be the least bit amenable."

"Why don't you ask yourself why, if you prefer an amenable gentleman, you keep attempting to goad me into an argument?" He looked up as Dapney approached, the sallow-faced fool's expression hesitant. "Ah, Lord Dapney. I believe you've won the first waltz of the evening with our Miss Munroe," he said in his most jolly voice.

"I, ah, yes, I have," the viscount said, offering a forced smile.

Connoll handed her off to Dapney, wondering if she would ever realize just how close she was treading to the edge of disaster. Whether she knew it yet or not, Gilly was his. And he didn't like to share. "Enjoy yourselves," he said smoothly, and without a backward glance walked over to find Miss Halloway.

The second waltz would be his. And between now and then he needed to conjure a way to convince a very stubborn young lady that her views of married life in general and men in particular left a great deal to be desired. And that over the past week he had come to desire one thing above all others—her.

Chapter 8

"*May I ask you a question, Lord Dapney?*" Evangeline queried as they circled the dance floor.

"Of course, Miss Munroe." He smiled at her. "And then I have a bit of news you might enjoy."

"Tell me your news first, then."

"Oh. Very well." He cleared his throat, giving a surreptitious glance about the crowded room before he faced her again. "What would you say if I told you that I am in the midst of acquiring a very fine thirty-foot yacht?"

"A yacht?" she repeated, hiding her abrupt frown. Though she hadn't heard the rumor herself, according to Connell the viscount had recently sunk just such a vessel after less than a day of ownership.

"Yes. I thought that it might be a pleasant way to travel to Italy for a . . . honeymoon, say."

Wonderful. He meant to sail them through the combined battling forces of Bonaparte and England and Spain in order to crash them on some pier in Venice. "Italy," she said slowly. "That's interesting. Who would you be honeymooning with? My dream for my own honeymoon has always been to visit Scotland. We shall have to compare our adventures."

"Scot . . ." The viscount swallowed audibly. "As I said, the purchase hasn't been completed yet. But what was your question, my precious?"

"I wanted to know if you would describe for me how you see yourself in five years. Family, politics, that sort of thing."

It was a silly, useless question; if things went as she planned, in five years he would be exactly where she told him to be. But still, she wanted to know what he would conjure on his own.

"Five years?" His brow furrowed. "Well, I'll be six-and-twenty."

Good—he could do basic arithmetic. Evangeline reined in her abrupt annoyance at Dapney's lack of imagination. That was one of the reasons she'd chosen him, after all. And her aunt had accused her of suffering from the same malady. "Yes, you will be," she prompted after a moment. "And?"

"And I presume I'll be married to a particular young lady," he continued, smiling at her. "And we'll hold grand house parties at my estate, and everyone will beg to be invited. Even Wellington and Prinny."

No mention of political ambitions, business or income advances, and no children. All of those decisions, then, would be hers. She drew a breath, smiling back at him and wishing impatience and the stirring desire to be elsewhere hadn't begun crawling beneath her skin. His life could be a successful, admired one—with her assistance, of course.

Beyond them, Leandra twirled about the dance floor in Connoll's arms. She was smiling, laughing at some undoubtedly witty comment from the marquis. Leandra had already admitted that she would jump at the chance to become the Marchioness of Rawley; Evangeline supposed she should wish her friend well.

Except that she didn't. Despite his arrogance and self-importance, she enjoyed having Connoll Addison pursuing her. Who wouldn't be flattered? He was titled, wealthy, and exceptionally handsome. He was also both very intelligent and very witty—which some women might consider of even more importance than the other assets, though she didn't know who those women might be. And even the way he'd been pursuing her demonstrated quite clearly that he would accept no outcome but the one he wanted.

She had other plans—which left her with either Dapney or Redmond. "Do you like to read?" she asked abruptly, returning her attention to the viscount.

"Not particularly," he responded easily. "It takes far too much energy and concentration with no reward. I'd rather play cards."

"Cards?"

He must have heard the consternation in her voice, because he cleared his throat. "I'm a fair hand at faro, if I do say so myself. Just last night I won forty pounds at the table."

Another flaw of which she would have to rid him if they married. *If.* She wanted to rub her hands across her face, to clear her head of the jumble of thoughts filling it. She still had an alternative choice in Lord Redmond. The earl probably didn't wager—at least not heavily—because he preferred to be at home and in bed by eleven. The worst of the gamblers had barely begun their evenings by then.

The waltz ended, and she joined in the applause. As

Dapney returned her to her mother's side, Leandra grabbed her arm. Laughing and out of breath, her friend's face was flushed and excited. "You never told me he was so amusing," she gasped, still chuckling.

"Yes, Lord Rawley is full of wit," Evangeline said succinctly, turning to find that cool blue gaze of his on her.

"You wish another lemonade, I suppose?" he asked, his expression contorting into what was undoubtedly his interpretation of blandness.

"Actually, Lord Rawley," she said, the noise of the room around her rising into an alarming, suffocating shriek as the orchestra wandered off to scavenge a meal from the kitchen, "I could use a breath of fresh air."

"Ah. Does one usually deliver that to you in a bottle? A corked one, I would assume."

Beside her, Leandra giggled again.

Evangeline wanted to knock her friend sideways. "Perhaps you could deliver me to it," she said in her calmest voice, "as I think you understood."

He offered his arm. "Just trying to be accommodating." Connoll nodded at her mother. "May I bring you anything, my lady?"

"Nothing but the return of my daughter in time for the quadrille with Lord Redmond," she said.

"Of course."

Together they crossed the room to one of the four doorways that opened onto the Howlett veranda and garden. "I know what you're trying to do," she said, releasing his arm as soon as they left the house for the cool, torch-lit darkness. The breeze brushed across her face, but did nothing for the tangle in her mind.

"I'm trying to be exactly what you want," he returned, crossing to the top of the veranda's shallow stone steps. "That's not a secret."

She faced him. "No. You're trying to convince me that what I want isn't what I want. I'm perfectly aware of your underhandedness, and you're wrong."

Connoll leaned a haunch against the brick of the raised flower bed. "Am I doing all that? It sounds like a great deal of bother."

It *was* a great deal of bother. "I want a husband," she said. "I want a particular kind of man, just as some people want a particular kind of . . . dog."

"I think I'm insulted."

She shook her head, refusing to be sent off her track. "We both know that you don't fit into my list of preferences. Why are you bothering to pretend that you do?"

For a moment he gazed at her in silence. Finally he straightened. "I suppose I'm hoping you'll realize you've fallen into a Greek play with the moral of 'Be careful what you wish for.'" Connoll took a step closer to her. "Tonight, I am what you wish for. I have no opinions which aren't yours, no thoughts which aren't about pleasing you." Another step. "The question then becomes, do you like me better tonight than yesterday?"

"And what if I like you better tonight?"

He looked down for a heartbeat, the expression that fleetingly crossed his lean, handsome features almost regretful. "If you like me better tonight, Gilly, then you'd be equally satisfied with Dapney or Redmond, and I will respectfully bow out of the pursuit."

For a second she gazed at him, dumbfounded. It didn't make any sense. He didn't make any sense. "But you—" She stopped, tilting her head to look at him from a different angle. "You wore blue—light blue—just as I asked. Why did you do that, if it was merely to make some statement about me being wrong?"

Connoll shrugged. "It's only clothes, Gilly." He reached

out, running a finger gently along her left cheek. "I'm hoping you're worth the expense of the—"

"Of the lesson?" she finished, batting his hand away. "You're a very stupid man."

His brow furrowed. "Beg pardon?"

"Why am I wrong? Why is it that you're in the right? Because you think that a man should do nothing to accommodate a woman? That she should dress to reflect well on him, but he needn't bend to any of her wishes or requests? That—"

"That's enough, Evangeline," he broke in.

"Why, because you say so?" She put her hands on her hips as she warmed to the argument. "It seems to me that you like me, while I don't like you. *You* are the one who needs to become someone else. Not me."

"Are you finished?"

"Yes, I am." With a last glare at him, she turned on her heel. "I'm going to get my diamond. Good or bad luck, it seems to keep you away from me."

Two steps later, a hand grabbed her arm. Before she could do more than open her mouth to protest, Connoll pulled her around to face him. "No."

"No, what? That's hardly—"

He kissed her. She forgot to breathe as his mouth moved against hers, the scent of port and shaving soap filling her nostrils and making her feel giddy. Evangeline put her hands on his shoulders and shoved. This was about how wrong he was for her, not about goose bumps and breathlessness.

"That does not—"

He moved in again, slower, teasing, nibbling, until the tangle fled her mind to be replaced by one word only—Connoll. Good Lord, he knew how to kiss. Feeling helpless as a moth to firelight, she leaned into his chest, sliding her arms around his shoulders, tangling her fingers into his black, wavy hair. If all they ever had to do was kiss, they would have no problems at all getting along.

His body dipped, and abruptly she was in the air, cradled in his arms. "Put me—"

"Do not say another word," he murmured, steel beneath the velvet of his deep voice.

Evangeline frowned. "I will not—"

"No. I am not going to listen to you logic yourself into a marriage with one of those idiots. Not until you understand what a union between two people involves."

She would have protested his high-handedness again, but the glint in his eyes made her reconsider. Why he was now the expert concerning what she required in a marriage, she had no idea, though he probably thought he knew everything. For the moment, scooped up in his arms and holding tightly to his shoulders, feeling the hard beat of his heart against her arm, she would observe and bide her time.

Three-quarters of the way along the terrace he shouldered open a door which led into a dark room cluttered with outdoor furniture—sheet-covered chaises, umbrellas, stacks of padded cushions, and wooden chairs. Everything necessary for a large al fresco luncheon party. After he kicked the door closed behind them, Connoll plopped her down on the nearest chaise. The white covering sheet billowed up around her in a wave and then sank down again.

"I have a quadrille in less than half an hour," she said as he latched the outside door and then strode across the room to secure the inner door. "So if you're kidnapping me, I will be missed very soon."

He faced her, blue eyes black in the gloom. "This would be a fairly pitiful attempt at a kidnapping, don't you think?"

The marquis actually sounded amused. And apparently she was permitted to speak again. "Then what is this?"

"My last chance, I think." He sat beside her, the chaise shifting a little with his weight.

She supposed she should be angry. After all, he'd kissed her without permission—again—and told her to be quiet, and then he'd carried her off and dumped her on a dustcover in an abandoned room. With him right beside her, though, close enough to touch, the emotion that stirred her pulse was excitement. And arousal. And a fair measure of confusion.

"Your last chance at me, I suppose?" she asked, her voice sounding unsteady even to her own ears. Blast. "You should know that nothing you say can convince me that you will—"

"I told you, Gilly, no more words. I'll just have to show you why we belong together." He smiled at her expression. "You see," he continued, running a finger along the knuckles of the hand she clenched on her thigh, "I happen to believe that your Nightshade Diamond *is* cursed. And I think that its idea of bad luck where you're concerned is a life with Redmond or Dapney. Your gem doesn't seem to care which mushroom you pick. I also think that the diamond's view of ill luck for your mother is the two of us sitting right where we are now. Or worse, kissing."

Connoll leaned in, taking her mouth in a slow, heartstopping kiss. She moaned, curling her hands into his lapels. Desire, lust, sank through her. Oh, why couldn't Dapney make her feel this way?

"Are you trying to seduce me?" she managed, shivering.

His lips crept along the line of her jaw. "No. I *am* seducing you. I want you, and I mean to have you."

"But I really don't like you." She closed her eyes, clutching his shoulders as his lips traveled to her throat.

"Yes, you do. Just not in the way you think is important."

She could argue with that, but then he might stop the kissing, and the way he drew her ever closer against him. "Why do you like *me*, then, Connoll?"

His mouth lowered to her collarbone. "Well," he murmured, his voice muffled against her skin, "you speak your mind. It's ironic, I suppose, that most females speak to me the way you'd prefer that men speak to you. 'Yes, my lord. No, my lord. Isn't the weather fine today, my lord?' They're so intent on being what they think I want that they've forgotten about passion." He lifted his head to look her in the eye. "You, Gilly, are full of passion."

"No. No, I'm not. My aunt said so."

He knelt at her feet, taking her ankles and removing her slippers one by one. "Yes, you are. Your aunt is wrong." He kissed her calves, sliding her skirts up as he trailed his mouth toward the backs of her knees.

Good heavens. "You're going to ruin me, aren't you?" she whispered, sliding sideways on the chaise as he lifted her legs onto the furniture.

"With your permission. And in my favor, Gilly, I would like to point out that even if I'm wrong and you actually don't like me, neither of your lapdogs will care about the state of your virginity."

Obviously he'd thought this through, and she couldn't disagree with his conclusions. Dapney might raise an eyebrow, but Redmond probably wouldn't even notice. As for the alternative, abruptly she didn't even want to consider it. With Connoll at least she would have one evening—one moment, really—where her foremost thought wasn't how quickly she could escape her spouse's embrace.

"It won't work," she said belatedly, noting that he'd paused his trail of kisses.

"It's working quite well for me, Evangeline."

Truth be told, it was also working quite well for her. And obviously she wasn't fooling him, much less herself. For a moment she watched him in the gloom, watched as he tugged up her skirts, his mouth following the trail of his hands. Everywhere he touched her felt heated, sensitive, and alive. And aching for more of his attentions.

"Very well," she conceded, gasping as his warm hands brushed the insides of her thighs, "I will accept you as a lover. Nothing m—"

"That's enough for tonight, then. We can begin the debate again tomorrow."

His smile, full of lust and everything wicked she could think of, sent heat spearing down to her depths. As his hands moved higher, brushing the apex of her thighs, she gasped again. The bodice of her gown abruptly felt very tight and confining.

Logically she should be kicking him in the head and screaming for assistance, but then she wouldn't feel the ache of pure sensation as he moved in to . . . oh, to lick . . .

"Connoll," she rasped, curling her fingers into his hair.

His chuckle reverberated through her into muscle and bone. "If I only did as you requested," he murmured, straightening to pull her frothy sleeves down her shoulders, "would you have thought to ask for this?" He released her gown to slide a finger inside her.

"Oh, goodness," she squeaked, writhing beneath his hand. "I had no idea."

He shed his coat, leaning in as he did so for another deep, long, tongue-teasing kiss. This time he sank slowly along her, pausing at the low neckline of her gown. Dipping his fingers beneath the silk, he pulled the material down to her waist.

As that capable mouth of his kissed the swell of her bare breasts and then closed over one nipple, she bucked. The sensation left her feeling weightless and stretched tighter than a violin string all at the same time.

For the briefest of seconds she tried to imagine whether she would feel the same physical pleasure with one of her other suitors looming over her—but since neither of them had the passion or imagination of a turnip, she didn't see how they could ever make her feel so wanton. So wanted. So free.

A country dance began dimly, and Connoll glanced toward the doorway. "Damnation," he muttered. "Your quadrille is next."

She was surprised he'd been able to keep track. "Don't you dare leave me like this, Connoll," she panted, squirming as his nimble fingers brushed her breasts again. "Please."

His smile appeared again, dark and possessive. "I won't. I wouldn't be able to appear in public, either. I . . . I want more time with you. To convince you."

She felt half convinced as it was. Settling back on his knees again, Connoll unfastened his breeches and shoved them down to his thighs. The bulge that tented the material of his trousers sprang free, hard and erect.

He wanted her. She knew that, but seeing the proof

made it real. And if she said no, he would leave. The moment, and what happened next, was up to her.

This was real power. And oddly enough, she had no wish to use it against him. Not here. Not now. Taking a shallow breath, her hands shaking as much as the rest of her, Evangeline reached out and grasped his manhood. His muscles jumped in response. "Are you . . . exceptional?" she asked, running her fingers down his girth.

"Exceptional?" Connoll crouched forward, kneeling between her thighs to kiss her again. "I've never been made fun of, if that's what you mean."

No, she didn't imagine he would have been. "This feels nice, doesn't it?" she continued shakily, stroking the length of him once more.

"If you want me to continue, you'd best stop," he whispered into her ear, his own breathing unsteady. "That is how good it feels."

Immediately she released him. "I hope there are a great many people dancing," she managed. The more there were, the longer it would take for all of them to go through their paces, and the longer the dance would continue.

"So do I." He settled his weight along her, his hard manhood pressed between her thighs. "I've never bedded a virgin, Gilly," he said, splaying his large right hand across her breast as if he still couldn't stop touching her, "but I have it on good authority that it will hurt. Briefly, and not again."

She lifted her chin. "I have it on good authority that if you don't hurry up, someone will come looking for us."

"Mm." Lifting up on his elbows, he kissed her again, at the same time shifting and pushing his hips forward.

Evangeline gasped with surprise and then pain at the

sensation of him entering her. "Oh, God," she gasped, clinging to shoulders still covered by the fine lawn of his shirt.

He froze, shaking a little as he held himself still inside her. The pain began to fade, and her muscles relaxed a fraction. The sensation that remained was . . . exquisite. "Apologies," he murmured, nibbling at her ear. He began to move his hips again, back and forward.

The chaise longue squeaked beneath them in time with his thrusts. Evangeline grabbed on to him, digging the pads of her fingers into his shoulders, wishing they could somehow be closer together than they already were. The bowstring tension ran through her, tighter and tighter, as he moved inside her. Suddenly she shattered, crying out as everything went white. Time, sound, everything stopped but sensation. *Glorious.*

A half dozen heartbeats later, Connoll gave a fierce grunt, holding to her, and kissed her again. Still inside her, he twisted them so that she lay sprawled and spent across his chest.

"The next time, you have to take the rest of your clothes off," she panted. *The next time.* She wanted a next time, and a time after that. Obviously her mother had failed to describe all of the aspects of marriage.

"I hope I've adequately demonstrated the benefits of compromise," he said, his heart beating hard beneath her cheek.

Oh, he'd done that. At the moment, all she wanted to do was lie there in his arms and have him hold her as he was now. And then, like the crack of doom, the music of the quadrille began.

Chapter 9

Connoll did a last quick check of Gilly's and his clothes. Shoes, ribbons, jacket, gown—everything looked perfectly in place. With a quick lift and kiss of her fingers, he led the way from the terrace back into the ballroom.

Lord Redmond stood close by the terrace windows, his generally bland expression bordering on annoyed. More troubling, though, was Lady Munroe, standing beside the earl.

"There you are," she said, her voice clipped, as Gilly moved in front of Connoll and stopped beside her dance partner.

"Apologies," Evangeline said easily. "We were talking with one of the gardeners about the Howletts' glorious roses."

"My fault," Connoll put in, very aware that the conversation was eating into the time remaining for Redmond's dance and quite willing to nibble every bit of it away. "I neglected to check my watch."

"It's no matter," Redmond said, offering his arm. "I believe we have a quadrille, Miss Munroe."

"Indeed we do." With a glance at Connoll, she took the earl's arm and joined him on the dance floor.

Previously Redmond had been an easily outmaneuvered piece of a puzzle. Now, though, as he and Gilly touched hands and swished about the floor, Connoll wanted to flatten him. It wasn't just that the fool was touching *his* Gilly—though that certainly played a part in it. Rather, it was the knowledge that he'd done his best to sway her, to convince her that a union between two participants was so much more interesting than one between a ruler and a servant, and yet he still didn't know who she would choose.

"Are you genuinely in pursuit of my daughter's hand?" Lady Munroe asked abruptly, shaking him from his thoughts.

He'd forgotten she stood there. "Yes, I am," he answered.

"You won't succeed; you're not the sort of man she wants in her life."

"Not the sort of man *she* wants, or not the sort of man *you* want?" Connoll returned, gazing directly at her. "Because if she would but open her eyes, I think she would find that there is more variety to her taste than she might previously have believed."

"You think you know everything; you think you know Gilly. But you do not." With that, the viscountess glided away, her nose in the air.

Connoll very much hoped that Lady Munroe was wrong. Because though he'd never been one to believe in deep and lasting love, the past week had served to change his perspective. He wanted Evangeline Munroe in his life. But that could only happen if she changed her own perspective.

More time would have been nice, so that he might at least have had the opportunity to remove his shirt and boots. Not just for his sake, though; he'd never met a woman with so much passion in her bones and yet so dedicated to following a path leading to an emotionless future.

He gazed across the dance floor at her. Had tonight been the beginning for her? Or would she see it as a once-only excursion to a place she never intended to visit again? His fingers curled into fists. If this had been a matter for someone to smash down walls and throttle villains, he would have been more than willing. It was harder to wait and see what she would do. But however much he wanted to go about swinging his sword, the decision was up to her.

"You wouldn't happen to have another one of those cigars, would you?"

Taking a breath, Connoll turned away from the crowded dance floor. "I would," he said, pulling one from his jacket pocket and handing it to Lord Munroe.

"My thanks."

"May I ask you a question?" Connoll continued, as the viscount tucked the cigar into his own jacket.

"Certainly."

"Lady Munroe seems to have a certain negative opinion of our sex."

"Oh, I'm aware of that. Believe you me."

"I do. But my question is, why?"

"Ah. Walk with me, will you?"

Reluctant as he was to let Gilly out of his sight, Connoll nodded and headed for a second time out to the terrace. *Steady*, he reminded himself. *Patience*. It wasn't as if she would accept a proposal from Redmond in the middle of a quadrille, whatever decision she ultimately made.

"Heloise's father," Lord Munroe began, pulling out the cigar and lighting it on a torch, "was a baron. He was also a drunk and a gambler and a brute who very nearly lost the family fortune on several occasions. She rarely speaks of him, but when she does . . . well, her contempt is obvious."

"Her contempt doesn't seem to be limited to her parent," Connoll noted, walking to the doorway to glance at the well-lighted room inside.

"When we met, I made it my primary task to prove to her that not every man was like her father." The viscount grimaced. "It's taken a bit longer than I anticipated, I'm afraid."

Hm. It seemed more as though the viscount had only reinforced her beliefs. By doing only as she asked, by being little more than her manservant, he'd proven that a life with her in control was better than one where she shared or relinquished power. And she'd passed that mind-set on to her daughter.

Munroe was looking at him as though he expected a response, so Connoll nodded. "You're a very patient man," he commented.

"Too patient, I sometimes think, but I'm a bit outnumbered now."

"I've been trying to convince your daughter that a balanced partnership might be more rewarding." He couldn't be any more explicit without risking making an enemy. And he could use an ally, ineffective or not.

"Considering that we're both dressed to complement the ladies of my household, Rawley, I'm not convinced of your success."

"You're not convinced of *my*—"

"And your particular lady is dancing with Earl Redmond, who means to propose to her tomorrow."

Connoll looked back at the doorway. *Tomorrow.* "That doesn't give me a hell of a lot of time," he said aloud.

"You've arrived late to the race."

"I had business elsewhere." He couldn't regret acquiring the paintings in Paris, especially when his absence had given Daisy the opportunity to make Ivey's acquaintance. Hm. So now he was grateful that his mistress had found someone else. What a difference a week and a carriage accident, not to mention a cursed diamond, could make.

"Do you have a plan?" the viscount pursued.

"You could deny Redmond your blessing," Connoll returned. "That might give me some time to convince her to see things my way."

"Heloise has already given her blessing. Mine doesn't count."

"Maybe it should," Connoll snapped, drawing a sharp breath.

"Excuse me, lad, but that's a race *I've* been running. And I'll thank you to refrain from commenting about it."

Swearing under his breath, Connoll paced to the terrace steps and back. "Apologies. It's just that . . . it's one thing to lose when the battle's been fought fairly and the ground is level. This, I don't understand. What in God's name would make Gilly want to spend the remainder of her life—well, his life—with the Earl of Redmond? Or Dapney, for that matter?"

"I think I've explained—"

"No, I understand Lady Munroe's prejudice. What I don't comprehend is why Evangeline is so content to look through her mother's eyes." Even as he said it, though, of course he understood—her mother's had been the only voice influencing her. For her entire life all she'd heard was the worthlessness of men and the only conditions under which they should be tolerated. And whatever changes her father had been trying to bring about were so subtle as to be nonexistent.

With Redmond planning a proposal for tomorrow, he was running out of time. If their interlude in the storage room had done nothing to sway her, he'd probably already lost. All he had remaining tonight was one waltz. It had best be one hell of a dance.

Evangeline looked toward the terrace door through which her father and Connoll had vanished. If he meant to confess their sins in order to force a marriage, he was speaking with the wrong parent. And if he attempted any such thing, she would never forgive him.

". . . spending a great deal of time with you lately," the earl was saying as he took her hand. They turned and separated and then joined again. "The fellow spends far too much time in France, for my taste."

He was also approximately twenty-three years younger than the earl. "I enjoy traveling," she said, mostly to see how Redmond would respond to that.

"A married lady may travel as much as she likes," he returned with the predictability of a clock. "And there are other benefits, as well."

"Such as?"

"More of those delicious kisses," the earl breathed as they passed one another. "You fill me with desire, Miss Munroe."

Previous to Connoll she'd heard enough talk among the servants to have a fair idea of what intimacy entailed.

Experiencing it, and even more, feeling it, was another matter entirely. And now the thought of doing either with Lord Redmond made her shudder. The idea of him on top of her, inside her . . .

Once they'd consummated the marriage, though, she could make fairly certain he would never touch her again. And then she could travel, she could attend dances, she could entertain friends, or read, or anything else a married woman wished to do, and Redmond would be nothing more than the man who shared the house with her and held her shawl.

No need or desire for conversations or kisses or long, warm nights in bed—they wouldn't even share a bed-chamber. Evangeline shook herself. If she had it all settled in her mind, then why was she imagining all of those things, and with Connoll? Yes, he'd taken her virginity less than half an hour ago, and yes, the way she'd felt, the way he'd made her feel, surprised and pleased her down to her bones. But had it really changed anything?

His goal, most likely, had been to let her know that he was a proficient lover. She'd already experienced his skills at kissing. But it was more than that, and while half of her was angry with him for presuming that he could change the way she viewed her entire life because of twenty naked minutes, the other half wanted an additional twenty minutes, and twenty more after that.

She supposed if she married Redmond she could take lovers, but that seemed rather contrary to her stated purpose to have as little to do with men as possible. Choosing the least demanding, most easily swayed of men meant freedom. But now because of stupid Connoll she had to ask herself, freedom to do what?

Across the room her mother watched them dance the quadrille. The viscountess didn't have affairs, and, from what Evangeline had been able to decipher as she'd grown older, gave her husband what she termed his "birthday present" no more than once or twice a year.

"And now that blackguard's with your father," Lord Redmond huffed abruptly, his gaze on the terrace door. "I have the primary claim. I hope he realizes that."

Evangeline turned her head. Connoll and her father strolled back in from the terrace, her father wearing the guilty expression that said he'd been smoking cigars again. Connoll, though, didn't appear to be feeling guilt about anything. Rather, his deep blue eyes searched the dancers until he found her. And then he smiled.

Warmth spread from her insides out to her fingers, lust tugging at her like a summer breeze. Heavens. This wanton was not who she was.

But it could be. Easily. And every time Connoll Addison looked at her, she wanted it more. The dance ended, and she headed them in her father's direction rather than her mother's.

"Lord Redmond," she said, "I will marry whom I wish. My parents will not make that decision for me."

"Of course, my sweet. Of course. I know that. It's just that I don't like the idea of a pretty-faced pup poaching my territory."

He'd done more than poach; he'd caught the prize game. Evangeline stifled an unexpected grin. "A pretty face to gaze at is well and good," she said loudly enough for Connoll to hear, "but I prefer adoration."

Redmond seized her hand, smothering her fingers with damp kisses. "I do adore you, Miss Munroe. You know that."

Of course she did; he'd made it extremely clear on every possible occasion. "I know your feelings, my lord," she said, freeing her hand. "You've never hidden them from me." She sent the marquis a sideways glance. "Goodness, I hadn't realized how warm it is in here."

"I'll fetch you a drink," the earl said, nearly growling at Connoll, and trundled off into the crowd.

"I can see I still need some practice, if Redmond can outsycophant me," the marquis noted easily.

"If you two will excuse me," her father put in, "I'll go see if Lady Munroe requires anything."

Once they were alone, Connoll spent a moment gazing down at her, his eyes promising things she knew he didn't dare say aloud in a crowded ballroom. Warmth began again between her legs. *Good Lord*.

"How was your quadrille?" he asked, lifting his head to glance in the direction Redmond had vanished.

"Brief."

"Ah. Do you wish an extended dance, then?"

"Not with Lord Redmond," she muttered, reaching out to wrap her fingers around his warm sleeve. "I can't remember where the sweets table is," she improvised, to cover this new desire to touch him. "Do you?"

"Not a clue. Shall we have a look?"

He hadn't offered to guide her or show her the way, which she considered promising. Evidently he realized that she wouldn't be led about like a dog on a leash. Of course, neither would he be—which she considered to be a fault on his part. Probably.

"What did you and my father discuss?" she asked.

"Is that really what you want to talk about?" he murmured back, drawing her closer against him.

"Do you expect I should become moon-eyed and hang on your every syllable as though gold dripped from your lips?"

The marquis snorted. "That would be rather messy, wouldn't it? Very well. We discussed you."

"Me. A price, perhaps?" So he'd made the same mistake as Redmond and gone to the wrong parent for permission for . . . for whatever it was he wanted from her. "Not a confession, I hope."

"I've no wish to cross swords with your papa, Gilly. The conversation was private, but we did touch on your likes and dislikes."

As if her father knew anything about her. "And?" she asked anyway. "Did you come to any interesting conclusions?"

"Everything about you is interesting." He leaned closer. "I look forward to further exploration."

"What—" She had to clear her throat. "What makes you think I'll allow further exploration, as you call it?"

"Because you got rid of Redmond the first second you could do so," he whispered. "I want you to know, Evangeline, that bit in the storage room was my best effort under the circumstances. Given more time and more privacy, however, I don't think I'll disappoint."

Disappoint? He'd had her making sounds she'd never dreamed of.

He must have read the expression on her face, because he laughed. "What I mean to say, my dear," he continued in the same low, intimate tone, "is that it gets even better." His lips brushed her ear. "And I intend to have you again so that I may properly show you. And again after that, to demonstrate that the previous time wasn't a fluke."

She shivered. His words were just that—words—and yet the tense fire began low in her gut again. "Stop that," she ordered unsteadily.

"No. In fact, now I'm going to describe how we will remove one another's clothes. We'll begin with my cravat, because I want to feel your lips kissing my throat. The—"

The musicians on the balcony above the ballroom be-gan playing a waltz. Their waltz. "If you continue speak-ing like that while we're dancing," she said, allowing him to lead her onto the dance floor, "I will faint."

"I doubt that," he returned with a jaunty grin, "but as you wish." Sliding an arm around her waist, he swung them into the waltz.

She'd noted before that he was a proficient dancer, but now that she had something to compare it to, she could say that he danced as well as he made love. And that was quite a compliment to both skills, if she said so herself.

"A penny for your thoughts," he murmured, pulling her closer than was strictly proper.

"I was just thinking about the level of your skill," she admitted, her cheeks warming along with the rest of her.

"And what is the level of my skill, if I may ask?"

"If you were a student, I would put you at the head of your class."

He laughed again. She liked the way the merry sound lacked the sarcasm that colored much of his speech. "I will merely say thank you, and return the compliment in kind."

"You promised you would tell me about France," Gilly said, pretending that his comments hadn't pleased her greatly.

"So I did. Very well. Do you want to ask questions, or shall I just tell the entire tale?"

"The entire tale, if you please."

"Let me preface this by saying I would prefer that you keep this to yourself," he returned, holding her gaze.

She nodded. "I will."

Connoll smiled. "Thank you. I collect artworks.

Paintings, mostly, but also sculptures on occasion. Usually I'm fairly discriminating, acquiring one or two works each year. Earlier this year, however, one of my . . . contacts, I suppose you would call him, informed me that his studio in Paris had been raided by Bonaparte's men, with the paintings that weren't destroyed being sold for well below their value in exchange for cash."

"Cash. Isn't that the usual—"

"Cash for Bonaparte, which he used for the purchase of weapons. I also began to hear that Wellington had started sending in spies to destroy items of value before Bonaparte could use them to solidify his own standing in France. So I went to Paris and purchased approximately sixty paintings from various artists and even museums. I didn't wish to see them destroyed or lost to history."

"Sixty paintings?" she repeated.

"I would have acquired more, but Bonaparte's people were trailing me. I didn't want to be held up as a traitor or as an idiot nobleman who needed to be ransomed back to England, so I bundled up ten crates and slipped home across the Channel."

Something told her he was leaving out a good portion of the danger and intrigue that must have been involved, but she agreed that the Howlett ballroom was not the place to discuss such things. "Where are they now? The paintings, I mean."

"Mostly leaning in my hallways at Addison House. Lord Ivey suggested I loan them to the British Museum, and I may do that with some of the better-known ones. They deserve to be seen, especially considering that I was attempting to save them from obscurity and destruction."

"I would like to see those paintings," she said.

"Because you don't believe me?" He lifted an eyebrow.

Evangeline grinned. "Because I like art."

"Then it would be my pleasure to show them to you."

She liked the way he looked at her, the humor and the interest in his gaze. Redmond and Dapney spent so much time bowing and scraping to her, she wasn't even certain what color their eyes might be. "Lord Ivey is your friend," she said quietly, "but you and Lady Applegate were—"

"Ivey didn't—doesn't—know. And that was before the two of them met," he interrupted. "And truth be told, I'm more concerned with keeping my friendship than with continuing or renewing any assignation with Daisy." He smiled. "In fact, over the past few days I've been feeling rather grateful that Daisy found someone else."

"Have you, now?"

His smile softened. "Yes, I have."

The waltz ended before she was ready, and Connoll placed her hand back over his arm again. "I think we need another breath of fresh air," he whispered, brushing her ear with his lips again.

Her breath shivered. "I don't—"

A hand grabbed his free arm, pulling him to an abrupt halt and nearly overbalancing both of them.

"Maintain a proper distance from my daughter, sir," her mother's low voice hissed. "I will not see her mauled in public."

Connoll straightened. "Evangeline and I were discussing what time I should bring my phaeton around tomorrow for our ride in the park. Ten o'clock, Gilly?"

His expression remained amused, but his blue eyes were colder than ice. Evangeline swallowed, looking from him to her mother. She'd never seen this version of Connoll before, and despite the fact that his arrogant self-confidence went against everything she was supposed to want in a man, she was struck by the fact that she liked it. His abrupt possessiveness thrilled her and aroused her. "Ten would be fine," she heard herself say.

"You already have an engagement tomorrow morning, Evangeline."

An actual engagement, no doubt, from the hints her mother and Lord Redmond had been dropping all evening. "I didn't make one," she said, putting a puzzled expression on her face and wondering how much yelling her mother would favor her with later for being defiant. "Perhaps whoever it is might come by tomorrow afternoon, instead."

"Afternoon." Her mother looked at the number of people standing within earshot, and nodded tightly. "Certainly. I'll speak with . . . I'll make the arrangements."

"Thank you, Mama."

The diamond glittered against her mother's neck. Connoll said he thought its curse was a real one, but she still had her doubts. Still, tonight had certainly gone his way rather than the viscountess's. And considering how he made her feel, and the way she'd abruptly begun looking forward to an outing that hadn't even existed five minutes ago, Evangeline at that moment decided she would not be wearing the diamond again in the foreseeable future. Or rather, in the unforeseeable future.

Chapter 10

"*Are you certain you don't wish her to accompany* you, my lord?" Winters asked.

Connoll straightened from scratching Elektra behind her gray ears. "Not today," he returned, eyeing the butler. "You're not afraid of her, are you?"

"She's sneaky, my lord. Nearly frightened the wits out of me this morning when she popped out of the silver closet."

"Perhaps I'll bring someone by to have a talk with her." Shrugging into his greatcoat, he rubbed Elektra beneath the chin with the toe of his Hessian boot. "You've made arrangements to give everyone the day off today, as I requested?"

The butler nodded. "Only myself, Hodges, Quilling, and Mrs. Dooley will remain, my lord."

He wasn't entirely certain how necessary his valet was, but by his actions he'd already made it fairly clear that he was up to something clandestine, as it was. "Just make yourselves scarce until I call for you. And be certain Mrs. Dooley has the sandwiches ready by eleven."

"I will see to it."

Winters pulled open the front door, and Connoll trotted down the shallow steps to the waiting phaeton. As Connoll settled into the high seat, Quilling released the team and stepped back, and he set off down the street. If he didn't make it back with his "visitor" for Elektra, his servants would think him eccentric, but then again, he already had paintings strewn across half the house and no one had batted an eye.

The plan he contemplated could ruin Gilly, but if she'd become pregnant last night, then he'd already done his worst. And considering that he meant to marry her regardless, he had a difficult time seeing the downside to his plot. Gilly might have a different opinion, but he looked forward to hearing that, too.

The team of bays hitched to the phaeton wanted to run, and he couldn't blame them for their impatience. Apparently he'd managed to sweep in ahead of Redmond for the day, but he wouldn't put it past Lady Munroe to have the earl arrive at dawn with a pastor in tow. The viscountess could definitely be a problem, especially since he didn't want to make a direct enemy of her. Not when he intended that they should be in-laws.

In-laws. A fortnight ago the idea that he would have met someone—crashed into her coach, actually—and then a week later decided they should marry would have sent him into spasms of laughter. He still couldn't quite believe he'd known Gilly Munroe for only eight days. In fairy tales, or in *Romeo and Juliet*, perhaps, eyes met across crowded rooms and people fell for one another at first sight. He'd heard of such things in the actual world, but he'd never believed the accounts.

Now he seemed to be one of those few who could make such claims. The idea of marrying Evangeline didn't even frighten him—it excited him, but he'd never been in any situation where he felt as sure of himself as he did now with her.

Unfortunately, a few questions did remain, mainly about her feelings regarding him. And nearly as importantly, whether she would follow her own path, or the one her mother had set for her apparently from birth.

He turned up the semicircular drive of Munroe House and whistled for a groom. A moment later a liveried servant came running around from the stable yard to take the team while Connoll hopped to the ground and walked up to the front door.

"Good morning, my lord," the butler said, pulling the door open as he reached it.

"Good morning. Is Miss Munroe available?" he asked, doffing his beaver hat and gloves but declining to remove his greatcoat. He didn't intend to be there for that long.

"If you'll wait in the morning room, I shall inquire."

With a nod Connoll walked into the nearest room, then paused. "My lady," he said, offering a shallow bow and inwardly cringing at the sight of the female seated on the couch before the fireplace.

"Lord Rawley. Come sit with me." Lady Munroe indicated the space beside her on the couch.

Bloody hell. "With pleasure, my lady," he said aloud, sitting.

"I have some questions for you, my lord," she continued, twisting a little to face him.

Questions that in a more traditional household, the patriarch of the family would more than likely be asking—had asked, actually. But Connoll doubted that Lord and Lady Munroe shared information. "I am at your service."

"Your parents," she began without preamble. "What kind of marriage did they have?"

With the ease of long practice, Connoll hid his scowl. "My parents are both deceased. Ask me about me."

"I find that the parents influence the child. I would like to know about them."

He couldn't argue with her statement, little as he liked the discussion. "My parents had a very close marriage. So much so that when my father died of influenza, my mother followed him for no apparent physical reason a month later."

"Hm. The morning Evangeline met you, she described you as a drunkard. I will not have my daughter courted by a drunkard."

"I beg your pardon, my lady, but Gilly and I have had this discussion, and she is satisfied with my answers. I won't be interrogated for your amusement."

The viscountess gave a stiff nod. "Very well. I will only make a statement, then. I don't believe you and my daughter will suit, and I ask that you cease calling on her."

So much for being polite. "I will cease calling on Gilly if and when *she* asks me to do so."

"How dare you d—"

"Good morning," Evangeline said, as she swished into the room. From her fixed smile she'd heard at least part of the discussion, and he wondered how far she would go in defying her mother, or if she'd travel in that direction at all.

Connoll stood, taking her hand and bringing it to his lips. Just looking at her sent the blood rushing beneath his skin. "Good morning," he returned, holding himself back when he wanted to pull her into his arms and kiss her senseless. "Shall we go?"

"Yes." She glanced at her mother. "I'll be home in a few hours, Mama."

"Where is your chaperone?" the viscountess demanded. "Doretta!"

"I have my phaeton, my lady," Connoll interjected. "Room only for two."

"Scandalous."

"Nonsense, Mama," Gilly cut in, smiling harder. "We wouldn't be able to get out of the carriage without the team running off. You know I may ride in a phaeton without a companion."

Lady Munroe sniffed. "Do as you will, then. But remember, you are to meet someone here at two o'clock. Do not be late."

"Yes, Mama."

Outside, Connoll handed Evangeline up onto the phaeton's high seat while the Munroe groom continued to hold the fidgeting team. Taking the reins as soon as he climbed up the far side of the carriage, without a backward glance, Connoll headed them off down the street.

"I still haven't decided anything yet, you know," she said abruptly, her gaze on the houses they passed.

She'd decided something, if she hadn't dismissed him out of hand, but he refrained from commenting on that. "I know you haven't. And I also know that the someone you're meeting today at two o'clock is the Earl of Redmond, and that he means to propose to you."

"And how do you know all of that?"

"Your father told me, last night."

She sent him a glance. "My father told you? You mean you wheedled it out of him."

Trying to put the annoyance of the chit's mother out of his mind, Connoll gave a short smile. "He was actually quite forthcoming with the information. I imagine he doesn't look forward to welcoming into the household a son-in-law who's two years his senior."

"Humph." She looked back at the street and frowned. "Shouldn't you have turned there?"

"Hyde Park's in that direction."

"I know. That's what—"

"We're not going to Hyde Park."

"We're not? Then where are we going? This isn't another of your kidnapping attempts, is it? Because it doesn't seem any more put together than the last one."

She didn't sound the least bit upset. The grin pulled at Connoll's mouth again. "I'm not kidnapping you now, and I didn't kidnap you last night. I arranged for us to have an intimate interlude. One which I don't recall you objecting to."

Her cheeks flushed in a way that made him want to run his fingers across them. "I daresay our . . . intimate interlude was quite pleasant."

"Then you wouldn't mind repeating the experi—"

With a resounding crack the phaeton pitched sideways and forward. Connoll reflexively grabbed Gilly, bracing his feet and hauling on the reins with his free hand. The left front of the carriage dug into the ground, nearly dumping them forward over the horses. With another lurch they came to a grinding, sliding stop.

"Are you injured?" he barked, twisting to look her in the face.

"No," Gilly said breathlessly, one hand clutching his arm and the other, the back of the seat. "Goodness."

A crowd immediately began forming, loud with advice but completely unhelpful. The team, already frightened, pulled harder on him and skidded the phaeton another foot sideways. "Climb across me and step down," he instructed, levering her across his lap. "Can you do that?"

"Of course." Using his thigh and lapel as handholds, she scrambled over him and hopped shakily to the ground.

Once she was clear of the carriage, he wrapped the lurching reins harder around his hand. Keeping a steady pull on them, he angled sideways and jumped down. "Woah, lads," he said soothingly, talking in his most calming voice as he worked his way up to the head of the nearest of the pair. "Good boy, Paris. That's a lad, Benvolio. Steady there."

Hauling on the leads, he had them drag the phaeton out of the middle of the road. The front axle lay cracked in two beneath it. *Bloody hell.* "You there," he snapped at a stout-looking man standing to one side. "Hold the team while I unhitch them."

The fellow tugged on his hat brim and came forward. "Aye, m'lord."

Relinquishing the team, Connoll strode back and began undoing buckles. Someone else had joined him on the far side of Paris, and he looked up. With a quick smile Gilly met his gaze, then went back to work freeing the restless bay.

His heart thudded. In itself, stepping in to aid him might have been both logical and incidental, but for a woman who claimed to view the men in her life as little better than servants, he considered it extremely significant. Of course, he had already been working toward bedding her again, so he might have some tendency to overread her actions—but he didn't think he was doing that. She was changing, and so was he.

Before he'd met Gilly he'd never considered that the relationships between men and women could be or should be other than what they were. All he'd known was that he'd never met a woman who could cause him more than a night of drunken self-pity, and he'd never wanted anything more. Until Evangeline.

The horses freed, he took back the leads and faced Gilly again. "We're two streets from my house," he said, digging in his pocket for a shilling to pay the man for his assistance. "Care to walk with . . ." His searching fingers curled around something large, hard, and rimmed with smaller protrusions.

Lifting his hand halfway out of his pocket, he looked down. The diamond. *The damned diamond.*

"Connoll?" Gilly queried, looking at him curiously.

He shook himself, releasing the jewel and finding a coin. Once he handed it over, he returned his attention to Gilly. "Shall we?"

She fell into step beside him, while he led the team south toward Grosvenor Street. "What's wrong? Other than your ill luck with vehicles, of course."

"Check my left pocket," he said. "Go ahead. Take a look."

Frowning and eyeing him as though she expected a mouse to leap out of his coat, she delicately dipped her fingers into his pocket. A heartbeat later her eyes widened. She snatched her fingers back as if they'd been burned. "What—"

"You didn't put it there, I presume."

"No! But—"

"I didn't put it there, either. I wondered why your mother wanted to speak with me earlier."

"She wouldn't have put a family heirloom—a very valuable one—in someone else's pocket."

"Then the alternative is that I stole it from you." He took a breath, trying to level his temper. "From wherever you were keeping it."

From her expression, she was weighing all the evidence,

his statement against her mother's knowledge. Finally she blew out her breath. "Why would she do that? It's worth a thousand pounds."

"Perhaps she counted on accusing me of its theft later," he suggested, shrugging. "I don't know. What I do know is that I believe it's cursed, and I think you do, as well. And so does your mother. If her purpose was to accuse me of foul deeds, she might have put a piece of silverware in my pocket. She wanted me to have ill luck. And as a result, you might have been killed. Or *I* might have been, which upsets me nearly as much."

For a few moments Evangeline walked beside him in silence. He didn't know what might be going on in that agile mind of hers, but she obviously had a great deal to consider. And so did he. With a cursed diamond in his pocket every carriage, every unsettled horse became a potential threat—and not just to him. Because the worst thing he could imagine was not injury or death to himself, but separation from Gilly.

"Connoll," she said, her hands clutched together in front of her, "it's actually cursed, isn't it?"

"This could be a string of coincidences, but it would be a very odd one. So, logical-minded though I try to be, and silly as I feel saying it, yes, I think the diamond is cursed."

"Aunt Rachel said that once the Nightshade Diamond's been in one's possession, setting it aside can bring as much good luck as holding it can bring bad luck."

"I'm tempted to throw it into the Thames and risk losing both." He hit a rough patch of ground and stubbed his toe. "Ouch."

She touched his arm, her fingers lingering there for longer than she needed to make certain he wasn't going to fall on his head. "Maybe I should carry it for a bit."

"That depends. What's your idea of ill luck?"

"I don't think it matters what my idea of luck is. Or yours. It's what *is* good or bad luck for the bearer, whether that person realizes it or not."

Her pretty hazel eyes were thoughtful and serious. "Explain, pray tell," he urged.

"The first time I set it aside, I crashed into you. At the time I certainly didn't consider the addition of you in my life to be good luck."

" 'At the time'?" he repeated. "Does that mean you've changed your mind about me?"

"I know I would never expect my own mother to try to cause me ill luck," she returned. "I know why she supports Redmond's cause, but *she* knows that he can't—won't—make me happy. And I've recently begun to realize that I *can* be happy in a man's company. A different sort of man than she's been recommending. And that she left out some things in her lessons on married life." She sent him a glance. "I still haven't decided. I have more to contemplate now."

As they walked up the front drive of Addison House, Paris and Benvolio in tow, Connoll hoped to give her even more to contemplate. Being in her presence seemed to give him a fever, a low heat running just beneath his skin, a longing for the deeper warmth of her body around him. One thing was for certain, though: However she made him feel, before he tried a second seduction he needed to get the damned diamond off his person and somewhere safe.

Winters pulled open the front door. "My lord, is something amiss?"

"No, Winters. I always lead my phaeton team about behind me."

"I beg your pardon, my lord."

"Send Quilling to Brook Street. My phaeton's there, with a broken axle."

"I'll see to it."

Connoll looped the ribbons around the hitching post and took Gilly's hand. "I'm not in, should anyone call."

The butler backed away from the door to allow them entry. "Understood, my lord. The sandwiches are in the morning room."

"Good. Make yourself absent."

With a nod the butler left the house in the direction of the stable yard. Connoll closed the door behind him.

"So this was your plan all along?" Gilly asked, hands on her hips as she assumed her usual stubborn pose.

He held up one hand. "Follow me." Without another word he led the way into his office, unlocked the top drawer of his desk and put the necklace inside, then closed and locked it again. Then he handed her the key.

"I trust you," she said, looking from him to the key.

"I don't know what the lingering effects of the Nightshade Diamond might be. In case I drop dead, you'll be able to show people why. I'll find you a box to take it home."

He went back into the hallway, but she remained. "Are you going to answer my question?" she asked.

"Yes, this was my plan all along. Not the phaeton coming apart or getting my toe stubbed, but yes to the rest of it. I intended to bring you here and show you the paintings, and I intend to remove all of your clothes and have you again."

She looked at him, several expressions warring with one another on her sensitive face. Then she gave an unladylike snort. "You are unexpected, Lord Rawley."

"I will take that as a compliment." A gray shape darted by him as Gilly left his office. "Your friend remembers you."

"Elektra!" Evangeline bent down and scooped up the kitten. "You kept her."

"I said I would. She likes to try to knock Winters's feet out from under him, which is an added bonus to her presence."

She smiled at him. It seemed impossible that a few weeks ago she would have been willing to marry Lord Redmond, and would never have looked back. Everything orderly, everything predictable and according to plan. The things she would have missed in her life were only beginning to dawn on her—and these were things she'd realized just in the past eight days. Now, if she made the right decision, she could spend a lifetime being surprised.

But her mother obviously opposed Connoll's suit, to the point that she'd been willing to risk the loss of a very valuable heirloom. A tremor of uneasiness ran down her spine. Was eight days enough to know the character of a man? Could she be certain he wouldn't become a controlling, demanding monster if eight additional days passed?

Redmond or Dapney would be safer, definitely. She could predict every moment of her future in a life with either of them. But *safe* had lately become a less attractive word. And she'd begun to learn a new vocabulary—one that included words like *surprise*, *amusing*, and *romance*.

"Would you like to see the paintings?" Connoll asked, moving closer to rub Elektra behind the ears. The cat began purring; with him that close to her, Evangeline felt like doing the same thing. What a difference eight days could make.

Chapter 11

"*Good heavens,*" *Evangeline said, kneeling to* look more closely at the painting leaning in front of her. "This is a Rembrandt, isn't it?"

"You have a good eye."

Many of the others she didn't recognize, though they had at least one thing in common: They were magnificent. "Connoll, how much did all of this cost you?"

He squatted beside her. "A little over forty thousand pounds," he said matter-of-factly. "If I'd been able to go through completely legitimate channels without the threat of Bonaparte on my heels, I probably could have managed a bit better, but I had already witnessed a handful of them lost or destroyed. I didn't wish to take the chance."

"You know, some men might attempt to lure naive young ladies into their homes by claiming to have a painting or two."

Connoll chuckled. "Yes, but *I* would be telling the truth." He reached over to tuck a strand of her hair behind her ear.

She shivered again. "Where are your servants?"

"Gone for the day."

"You were that certain I would accompany you here?"

Connoll leaned in to kiss her softly. Evangeline released Elektra to slide her arms around Connoll's neck. The question of whether he would be the one to provide her with what she wanted became moot as he sighed against her mouth; at this moment, *he* was precisely what she wanted.

Around them a naked Venus lounged in the company of a Dutch Puritan and a French shepherdess and her flock, all of them watching silently. She smiled. Her mother would absolutely faint if she ever discovered either her daughter's present location or her actions.

"Shall we adjourn to somewhere I'm less likely to put a foot through a Le Moyne?" Connoll murmured, kissing her again.

"That sounds reasonable."

Standing, he held out his hands and drew her to her feet. She knew why he'd brought her to his home, and she knew just as clearly why she hadn't raised one objection once she'd realized where they were going or that he'd sent most of his servants away. Whatever it was about Connoll Spencer Addison that had inspired her to kiss him back that first morning they'd met, pulled her to him even more strongly now. It was as though they were connected before she ever knew of his existence.

He twined his fingers through hers and led her down the far hallway to what was obviously his master bedchamber. The deep blues and golds and browns of the curtains and walls and bed hangings spoke of his taste as strongly as did the paintings he'd chosen to hang inside the large room. Pastorals of exquisite skill, some of them probably centuries old.

"What?" he asked, releasing her to close and latch the door.

"I don't know," she answered truthfully. "I like this room."

Connoll smiled, his gaze on her rather than their surroundings. "Thank you. I like having you in this room." He stepped closer, tugging on the front of her pelisse to undo the buttons there one by one. "Everything's more interesting when you're about, Evangeline."

That was quite possibly the finest compliment she'd ever received. Together with his fingers toying with the front of her gown, his words lifted her so that she could scarcely feel the floor beneath her feet. It was an odd sensation, because in every other aspect she felt so . . . aware—of her body, of the warmth emanating from the man standing before her, of the cool breeze from the half-open window whispering along her bare arms.

She leaned up along his chest to kiss him again. They'd been in such a hurry last night that she hadn't been able to touch him, to experience him. Today she would do as she wanted. And what she wanted. Slipping her fingers from his jawline down to his throat, she pulled out the intricate knots of his cravat and slid it free.

Dropping it to the floor, she kissed his bared throat as he'd said he liked. Connoll's hard muscles shuddered in response, and he drew a shaking breath. Warm damp began between her thighs. Encouraged by his reaction, she pushed his coat down his shoulders, and he shrugged out of it. Then she went to work on his cream-colored waistcoat.

"We're in no hurry, you know," Connoll commented, sliding one sleeve of her gown and shift down her shoulder.

"I'm not hurrying," she retorted, pulling off his waistcoat and dropping it from her fingers. "I'm curious. And interested." And aroused, but he could probably tell that by the way her fingers were shaking.

"Proceed, then. Just try not to destroy anything; I don't want to have to explain that to Hodges."

Evangeline pulled his shirt from his trousers to run her palms up his chest. Warm, velvet skin with the steel of muscles beneath. Glorious. Then she realized what he'd said. "Why do you care about explanations?" she asked.

His blue-eyed gaze held hers. "I apologize. I was attempting to be amusing," he said quietly, twining a strand of her hair around his fingers. "We both know that yours is the reputation at risk. But you should know that I have no intention of going anywhere."

"Ah. You mean if this happens to ruin me, you'll stay by my side and dance with me even when everyone else turns their back and whispers?"

He pulled down her other sleeve none too gently, exposing both her breasts. "I mean, Gilly," he said, running his fingertips feather-light across her nipples, "that I intend to ask for your hand in marriage whether today remains our private secret or whether the diamond somehow inspires a columnist with the *London Times* to put our tale on the front page of the newspaper tomorrow. Is that clear enough?"

She gasped at the sensation of his touch. "But you still haven't asked me, and I still haven't decided."

Connoll lifted her around the waist and set her down on the edge of his very large bed. "Sex," he said, yanking his shirt off over his head, "is not about talking. It's about feeling."

"Are you telling me to shut up again?"

"I'm telling you to try to imagine Redmond doing this." He knelt at her feet, leaning in to slowly run his tongue across her right breast, circling closer and closer until he took her nipple into his mouth.

She gasped again, digging her fingers into his hair and arching against him. *Good Lord.* Could she imagine Redmond touching her like this? At the moment she couldn't even conjure the earl's visage. The only thing in her mind was Connoll, Connoll's hands, his mouth, his skin against hers. Yes, he was cheating, using unfair tactics to make his point, but for heaven's sake he was good at it. She moaned, shuddering, as he shifted his attentions to her left breast.

"Or that pup, Dapney," he continued in a muffled growl, pressing her back onto the bed and lifting her hips to slide her gown down her legs and off. Her shoes followed, vanishing somewhere over his shoulder.

Evangeline lifted her head to watch as he trailed his mouth from her breasts down her stomach, and then dipped between her legs. She jumped, her muscles clenching.

With a low laugh that resonated all the way through her, Connoll briefly met her gaze. "Don't crush my head, love; you'll knock loose any sense remaining in my skull."

She nodded, unable to form a response as he went back to licking and nibbling. Dapney? He probably had . . . oh . . . no idea what to do. Curling her fingers into the coverlet, she lifted her hips to him. Abruptly she began to spasm, shuddering. Between her knees, Connoll murmured something very naughty-sounding and redoubled his efforts.

When she could breathe again she struggled onto her elbows. "Con . . . Connoll, you still have clothes on," she managed.

He straightened to sit on the edge of the bed beside her. "I was just about to comment on that myself," he said, and yanked off his boots. When he began unfastening his trousers, she sat up.

"Let me," she offered, twisting her legs beneath her as she faced him.

"Very well. If you insist."

She'd hoped the action would give her a moment to recover her breath and her senses, but as she leaned across him, Connoll reached up and began pulling pins from her hair.

"I'll never get it to look right again," she protested, but he batted her interfering hand away and placed it back on his trousers.

"If I can tie a cravat, I'm certain I can pin up your hair," he replied, kissing her again while her hair began its disheveled cascade down around her bare shoulders.

With him running his fingers through it, she felt wanton and wicked. When she opened his trousers and he sprang free, hard and ready, the sensation running through her doubled and trebled. "Lie down," she said.

Somewhat to her surprise, he kicked out of his trousers, then scooted farther up on the bed and did as she asked. She sank down on one elbow next to him and ran her fingers over his chest much as he'd done with her.

"Do you like this?" she asked, skimming the light dusting of dark hair that ran across his chest and trailed in a line down to the darker curls below.

"Yes."

When she ran her lips over the small buds of his nipples, he jumped. Before she could inquire about what that reaction meant, he reached up to cup her breasts.

"Is this because of the diamond, do you think?" Evangeline curved herself along his chest for another of his deep, slow, delicious kisses. "Us being here?"

"No. I like your idea that it knows what's good or ill, whether we realize it yet or not. If it's magical, which I'm nearly ready to wager it is, then perhaps it caused our carriages to collide. It didn't make me kiss you. I did that on my own. And I have to say, it's one of the most ingenious things I've ever done."

With that he pulled her arm to turn her flat onto her back again, then moved over her. Slowly he pushed his hips forward, burying himself inside her. This time there was no pain. Instead, the incredible, indescribable sensation of being filled, of having him be a part of her, ran like fire through her.

"Connoll," she breathed, moaning as he thrust into her.

"Gilly," he returned softly. "My Gilly. No one else ever gets to be here with you like this. Promise me."

Demands. The first thing she watched for. But in this moment, she didn't care. She didn't want anyone else, ever. "I promise."

Connoll gazed critically at the soft tangle of honey-blonde locks, then readjusted one of the pins. "Well, I'm rather astonished at my skill as a hairdresser," he said, holding up a mirror so Gilly could see the back of her head. "What do you think?"

She tilted her head, then nodded. "If you fail as a nobleman, I see a definite future for you as a lady's maid."

"My thanks, I think."

As Connoll shrugged back into his coat, he kept his gaze on the young lady seated at his dressing table. He liked seeing her there, liked seeing her in his home. It felt comfortable and exciting all at the same time, and for him that combination was a rare and surprisingly pleasing one.

"You're staring at me," she said, bending down to pull on her shoes.

"Marry me."

Gilly blinked. "You—that—that wasn't very romantic."

Grinning, he knelt in front of her, helping her on with her second shoe. For a chit who'd been contemplating marriage with either a near corpse or a monkey, she certainly had odd requirements now. "I'll send you a hundred roses if you wish it." He placed his hands on her knees to look up at her. "Marry me."

"I . . . haven't been acquainted with you long enough to know of your poorer qualities," she said slowly, frowning.

Connoll ignored the prick to his pride. Time enough to lick his wounds later. "And my poorer qualities worry you?"

She bit her lips. "Yes. I—you may think me silly, but I know all of Lord Redmond's. That's how I decided to allow him to pursue me—all of them were either controllable, alterable, or dismissible."

"Ah. And so were Dapney's, I presume?"

"Yes."

He stood, drawing her to her feet with him. "We have known one another for a relatively short time," he agreed. "I won't bring up the fact that Romeo and

Juliet married within three days of meeting, because I hardly consider them to be beacons of long-lasting love."

Her lips twitched. "I would agree with that."

"I am happy to court you, Evangeline," he said, leaning down to kiss her soft, sweet mouth again. He should have been sated after three hours in bed with her, but he still couldn't help wanting to touch her. "But I happen to know that someone else is going to propose to you in just under an hour. And I know which match your mother would prefer. I don't want to lose you because of her sentiments."

She cupped both sides of his face in her hands, gazing up into his eyes with her bright hazel ones. His heart simply stopped. God, he could stand this way forever, just looking at her. As he'd told her, he wasn't a virgin and hadn't been one for some time, but he'd never met a woman who affected him as she did. And he knew deep down that he never would again.

"Give me a week," she finally said, releasing him to collect her reticule, "to convince my mother that we will suit. She'll see reason."

He had his doubts about that. And if after a week Lady Munroe still refused to give her blessing, he wasn't certain what Gilly would do. But asking for a week more wasn't so much, when a week ago she probably wouldn't have been able to imagine even having this conversation. "A week," he agreed.

She turned and grabbed his hair, pulling his face down for a deep, hard kiss. "Thank you," she whispered, her voice shaking a little.

Yes, he could wait a week if it would give her some peace of mind. If he pressed for a definite answer, threatened her with ruination or the specter of pregnancy, she would probably acquiesce—and she would hate him and consider that everything her mother had ever told her about men was true.

Of course, the deeply male part of him didn't want to play any games or waste time placating any suspicious mothers. Gilly belonged to him already, and that was why he hadn't taken any precautions to avoid a pregnancy even though he could have and should have. Possession. Her image, her voice, her spirit, had begun burrowing their way into his heart, and he liked her there. He meant for her to stay. Now all he needed to do was convince her to do so, and to find his way into *her* heart. He had more than a suspicion that he was already halfway there.

"How are you going to take me home with the phaeton wrecked?" she asked as they reached the foyer at the bottom of the stairs.

"We'll say the wheel was loose, so we stopped on the way back to Munroe House for my curricle and my tiger," he decided. "A bit unconventional, but considering that I was being mindful of your safety, I think your parents will accept the story."

He sent Winters off to fetch a box, and took the moment to twine his fingers with hers. "Will you be wearing the diamond again?"

"Absolutely not. I prefer to make my own luck." She grinned. "Though I may stick it in Mama's pocket for the recital tomorrow night."

"Which recital?"

"Lord and Lady Baxley's four daughters. You didn't receive an invitation? I thought they would invite every single gentleman in London to attend."

"They did. I declined. I shall have to send over a note of apology and reacceptance."

"I don't believe they play very proficiently. That is the rumor, at any rate."

"I have no doubts on that count. But I intend to be self-serving and make an appearance for my own selfish reasons." He kissed her again, closing his eyes as her lips molded to his. She could almost tempt a fellow to try his hand at poetry.

Winters in the doorway cleared his throat, and Connoll reluctantly took a step back from Gilly. "Will this do, my lord?" the butler asked, holding up what looked like one of his good cigar boxes. One that had been nearly full.

"Perfect," he said, taking it. "You have the key," he reminded Gilly, gesturing her toward his office.

Beside the desk she handed the small brass key back to him. "Don't touch it, Connoll," she blurted as he unlocked the drawer and pulled it open.

A responding smile curved his mouth. "Thank you for saying that," he returned. "And I have no intention of risking bad luck now." Sliding a quill pen through the gold, diamond-encrusted chain, he lifted up the glittering beauty and deposited it in his cigar box. "There you go." He closed the lid and handed the box over to her.

She took it with clear reluctance, both hands keeping the lid securely closed. Considering that thus far the bad luck had seemed to involve separating the two of them, he took her care not to touch the Nightshade Diamond as a very good sign.

"Are you going to tell your mother that I found it and returned it to you?" he asked.

"I haven't decided yet."

Connoll hid another smile as he helped her outside to his waiting curricle. They still had a ways to go, but he would take any sign of Gilly defying her mother as a step taken in his direction. And he considered that to be very, very good luck.

Chapter 12

"*There's that blasted man again,*" *Lady Mun*-roe hissed under her breath. "No, don't look at him, Gilly, you'll only encourage him to . . . Oh, wonderful, here he comes."

Gilly smiled as Connoll crossed the floor of the Baxley music room to greet her. She couldn't help herself; when he appeared she felt instantly warmer, on the inside where it didn't show.

"Good evening, Lord Munroe, Lady Munroe, Evangeline," he said, sketching an elegant bow. "I had no idea you were so fond of musicales."

"Lady Baxley is a dear friend of mine," her mother said, not even the hint of a smile in her voice or her eyes. Evidently the conversation Gilly had begun about happiness hadn't made even a slight dent in Lady Munroe's prejudice against Connoll.

Showing more life than he generally did, her father smiled and shook Connoll's hand. "Good evening, lad. How fairs your phaeton?"

"I had the axle replaced this morning. Damnable bit

of luck, that. The thing was as sound as stone until yesterday."

This time her mother's eyes did flash. "I should hope so, Lord Rawley. It was very poorly done of you to drive my daughter about in such a dangerous vehicle."

"Mama," Evangeline broke in, "I'm certain Connoll would never have driven the phaeton if he'd known something was amiss."

"Let's find some seats, shall we?" her father suggested. "Connoll, sit with us."

"Glad to."

Apparently Connoll Addison—or his cigars—had won over the viscount. If only the viscountess could be convinced, Evangeline would sleep much easier. As it was, what she wanted to do and what all of her mother's advice said she should do couldn't possibly be any farther apart. And she'd only given herself seven days to convince her mother that a lifetime of lessons delivered and learned were wrong.

"Did you forget, John," her mother grated, "that I've already invited Lord Redmond to sit with us?"

The viscount frowned. "I didn't—"

"Please fetch me some Madeira," his wife interrupted. "Lord Rawley, perhaps you might assist Lord Munroe in finding a footman."

Connoll glanced at Evangeline, the question clear in his eyes. Did she want him to stay? The answer was yes, but obviously her mother wished to talk to her about something in private. She angled her head in her father's direction. "I would appreciate a glass as well, if you don't mind," she said.

"Not a bit." Nodding, the marquis gestured her father to precede him.

"You see what Rawley's doing?" her mother whispered

sharply. "He already has your father making all sorts of mad decisions. Can you imagine what he would do if you married him?"

"Perhaps you should make an effort to know him, Mama," Evangeline replied. "He's very nice."

"He's a drunken lout who has French sympathies and probably keeps a dozen mistresses. Open your eyes, Gilly. Don't be blinded by a handsome face. Faces change. It's a man's character you must consider. And his is lacking."

"If you would converse with him, I think you would find that Connoll has a great deal of character." An almost overwhelming quantity, in fact, but she wasn't about to say that aloud.

"Bah. And you should not refer to him by his Christian name. It will make him too familiar."

"Mama, I do not wish to have this discussion here. And since Con—Lord Rawley—is here and has been invited to sit with us, we—"

"Yes, by your idiot father."

"—we should make the best of it."

"Oh, very well. But I don't like it. Not one bit."

Evangeline knew she was going to win the argument, whether her mother realized it or not—because her mother carried the Nightshade Diamond in her reticule. It colored how Evangeline argued, and the way she was able to keep a reasonable tone even in the face of her mother's obvious venom. And it might make the viscountess understand that they would all be better off if she would at least listen to what Connoll had to say.

Aunt Rachel had been right when she'd indicated that the owner of the jewel could benefit from *not* wearing it. And Gilly was beginning to understand that she owed her aunt a debt of thanks. Halfway across the room,

Connoll turned to look at her and grinned. A very large debt of thanks.

"Ah, there's Redmond." Brushing past her, the viscountess went to greet the earl.

Surprised, Evangeline quickly searched the area immediately around where they'd been standing, fully expecting to see that the diamond had fallen onto the floor. Instead she caught sight of her mother's reticule lying across the chair she'd claimed for herself. "Damnation," she muttered.

"What is it?" a low, familiar voice asked from just beyond her elbow. Connoll handed her a glass of Madeira.

Before she answered, she took a generous swallow. "Redmond's here, and I'm going to have to sit between him and Mama because she's left her reticule on her seat."

Connoll eyed her. "Oh, heavens. Then I suggest an immediate elopement to Gretna Green," he returned easily. "Or an attack on Calais."

"This isn't amusing."

"Tell me why not, so I may be alarmed, as well."

"It's not amusing because the diamond's in her bag."

He gazed from her to the reticule and back again. "You actually hid it on her person?"

"I was angry with her. And she still won't listen to me."

"Well done, Gilly."

She couldn't help smiling at his obvious admiration. This man wanted her, wanted to marry her. *Goodness.* "I only have a week. I thought the Nightshade might assist me. But she put the diamond down, and now she'll have my—our—good luck."

"Hm. Allow me." He went to the chair, then turned back around and handed her his glass. "Just in case," he drawled, and picked the bag up by the strings.

"What are you going to—"

"Lady Munroe," he said in a conversational tone, strolling to the viscountess's side, "the room's becoming rather crowded. I didn't want your reticule to be misplaced."

She snatched it from his fingers as though she expected him to make off with it. As if Connoll on his worst day could be mistaken for a common cutpurse. "Let's take our seats, shall we?" Evangeline suggested, wrapping her arm around Connoll's until they were firmly seated beside one another.

With a humph the viscountess sat on Evangeline's other side and drew her husband down beside her, probably so she wouldn't have to sit beside her elderly prospective son-in-law. Redmond looked lost for a moment, then sat down beside her father.

Once the recital began, Connoll dug into his breast pocket and handed her the folded piece of paper he liberated. "For you," he murmured.

"What is it?" Surely he hadn't written her a poem. She'd never thought of him as that . . . flowery.

"It's a list. Of all my faults, in case that was your next question." He frowned briefly. "All the ones I could think of, anyway. You said you were worried that you didn't know me better. I asked Winters and Hodges for suggestions as well, but Winters declined to answer, and Hodges fled the room."

She laughed, covering her mouth as her mother elbowed her sharply in the ribs. Once the viscountess returned her attention to the musicians, Evangeline unfolded the note. Whatever it said, she had the feeling she wouldn't consider anything written there insurmountable. Or even a fault, probably.

" 'I enjoy arguing,' " she read in a whisper. "Yes, I'm aware of that."

"Keep going. I began with the obvious ones."

" 'I am impulsive.' " She looked over at him. From her admittedly limited experience, he seemed to be quite the strategist—not something she thought very compatible with impulsiveness. "How so?" she asked.

He shrugged. "I went off to France to save paintings in the middle of a war. Not the wisest thing I've ever done."

"But you did save them."

"Presumably. Some or most of them might have been perfectly fine without my interference. In return for my excursion, though—well, you've heard the rumors."

She could hardly avoid them, with the way her mother flung them about. "One impulsive act doesn't necessarily make you an impulsive man."

His mouth curved into that pulse-speeding smile of his. "I also kissed a lady once and then almost immediately decided that I wanted to—needed to—marry her."

"Ah. And what was this lady's name?"

"Evangeline Munroe."

The answer certainly didn't surprise her, but he was right that she would consider impulsiveness a fault. "What will happen when you next kiss a lady, then?" she asked slowly.

"I kissed several ladies previously, and never felt the least desire to marry any of them. And now that I've met you, I don't feel the desire to kiss anyone else. Only you, Gilly."

"You might add glibness to your list of faults."

"That's not a fault. It's simply the ability to speak the truth in a hopefully pleasing manner."

She sighed unsteadily, wishing they were alone so she

could kiss him. He'd said that he found her intelligent, witty, and forthright, and she didn't have any reason to think him merely attempting to flatter her. She certainly hadn't given him cause to pursue her unless he did admire those qualities.

Connoll's hand brushed hers. "Have I set your mind at ease? Or do you wish to continue torturing me?"

"That's one of *my* faults," she returned with a smile. "And besides, I haven't finished reading yet."

"Torture it is, then." He settled in closer to her. "I suggest you read more quickly, though, if I'm working to convince you, and you still wish to convince your mother."

She swallowed. A week seemed such an arbitrary figure for convincing anyone of anything. What had she been thinking? That at a given hour her mother would suddenly begin seeing things through different eyes? She was just being a coward. If she wanted a marriage with Connoll, she would have to stand against the viscountess. Or she could turn him away, avoid an argument, and avoid finding a life that would be filled with anything resembling happiness and romance.

"Very well. 'I have been known, on very rare occasions, to drink to excess,'" she continued reading. That was fairly self-explanatory, and with a swift glance into his beautiful eyes, she went on to the next item. "'I like to eat tomatoes.'" Evangeline snorted.

"Caught you by surprise, did I?"

"That is enough," her mother hissed, jabbing her again. "Trade seats with me if you can't comport yourself properly in his presence."

"I like him, Mama. And I like sitting beside him."

The viscountess's eyes narrowed. "We are leaving. I'm not feeling well." She started to her feet.

Connoll abruptly leaned across Evangeline. "Leave if you're feeling poorly," he said quietly, gazing at the viscountess. "I will see that Gilly returns home safely." His easy, amused expression was gone, replaced by a cold, hard look that said he generally got what he wanted. And he wanted *her*. Evangeline's heart thudded.

"I'm not leaving without my daughter," her mother retorted.

"Then stay with us." He leaned closer, lowering his voice further. "I have been polite to this point, Lady Munroe, out of respect for your daughter. But do not make the mistake of thinking that because I am good-natured, I am also one of your mindless sheep. I will not acquiesce beyond all reason."

For a long second they glared at one another, while Evangeline, stuck in between them, wanted to sink through the bottom of her chair and disappear. "Let's be reasonable, shall we?" she finally uttered, deliberately sitting forward to break their line of sight.

"I need a breath of air," the viscountess said, practically hurling her reticule onto Evangeline's lap as she stood and made her way to the nearest door.

As Evangeline grabbed for the bag, the diamond spilled out like a shimmering, deadly snake. Moving with surprising speed, Connoll caught it before it could hit the floor. "Damn," he muttered, curling his fingers around the thing. "Open the bag, Gilly."

While Evangeline hurried to comply, a skinny form took the vacated seat beside her. "Miss Munroe," Lord Dapney breathed, pulling her hand from the reticule to clasp it in both of his, "I must speak with you."

Blast it all. "I'm listening to the music," she offered, trying to free her hand from his clammy grip.

"But this is urgent," he protested, ignoring the annoyed

looks they'd begun getting from the other guests seated around them.

On her other side, Connoll stirred. And he still held the diamond necklace, which troubled her immensely. That worry spoke very clearly to her—she didn't want anything to harm what she'd begun to think she'd found with him. Seven days to reason with anyone else be damned. "What is it, then?" she asked, keeping her voice brisk and cool. The fewer people unsettled here tonight, the better.

"You've been avoiding me, Evangeline."

"Of course I haven't," she lied. "I've been very busy, is all."

"Busy being pursued by him, you mean," Dapney retorted, his voice rising further. "I could accept Lord Redmond as a fellow suitor—the old fool is hardly competition. But Rawley—"

"I beg your pardon?" Lord Redmond grumbled from the far side of her father. "I have been assured by Lady Munroe that she favors my suit over yours, you young pup."

"I am speaking to Miss Munroe," Dapney shot back. "Say you'll marry me, Evangeline. You know how I adore you. You're—"

"You can't propose," the earl protested. "I've already done so."

"Don't listen to that old goat," the viscount snapped. "And you certainly can't believe anything that . . . that womanizing traitor says to you," he continued, gesturing at Connoll.

On her other side, Connoll climbed to his feet. "A word outside with you, Dapney," he said very quietly, his voice level and ice-cold.

"Gentlemen, please allow me to enjoy the recital,"

Evangeline muttered, yanking down on Connoll's sleeve to pull him back into his chair. "I know what the wishes of all three of you are. I will make my own decision."

Dapney leaned across her. "You should withdraw, Rawley. You're late to the game, and you can have any woman you want. You've *had* half the women in Lon—"

Connoll hit him square in the jaw.

As the viscount reeled backward, falling across her father's lap, Connoll pulled Evangeline to her feet. "You'd best get clear of this," he muttered, his gaze on his opponent as Dapney climbed back to his feet.

"Give me the necklace," she said instead of moving.

"Gilly, get out of the way."

"Give me the blasted necklace before you ruin everything." She held out her hand.

Dapney lunged at him, slamming his shoulder into hers as he attacked. Evangeline stumbled into Connoll's chest. He grabbed her, keeping her from falling to the floor, just as the viscount's fist impacted with his cheek.

They all went over in a pile of chairs and legs and flailing arms. A female seated somewhere behind them shrieked, and the Baxley girls scattered, leaving their instruments behind. Evangeline saw it all in a blur as she tried to squirm out from the sandwich of the marquis and the viscount.

Abruptly someone took hold of her arm and hauled her free and upright. She grabbed his arm to steady herself, turning to look up at her father. "You have to stop them," she said breathlessly, horrified.

"That seems a bit risky, Gilly. Let's get you out of here and leave the scandal to them."

"But Connoll has my necklace, and now I'll end up with Redmond, and I don't want him," she blurted.

"What?"

"The diamond. He has my bad-luck diamond. I put it in Mama's purse and it fell out, and now Connoll has it, and Dapney's going to ruin everything, and I'll have to marry the only one left."

"I see." He looked from her to the struggling men for a heartbeat. "Move out of the way," he instructed, and strode back into the melee.

"Miss Munroe," Lord Redmond said, grasping her elbow, "allow me to escort you away from this inexcusable fracas."

"No, thank you," she returned, pulling free of his grip. "I believe Lord Dapney is having a seizure of some sort. I should be nearby to assist Lord Rawley and my father, if necessary."

Whatever tale she attempted to spread, though, she realized that that was how it would happen—two suitors were disgraced, and Redmond would sweep into victory by default. Oh, that necklace. That stupid, stupid—

Connoll stumbled free as her father grabbed Dapney by the shoulders. "Take my daughter home at once, Rawley," her father bellowed. "I'll deal with this."

With a nod, Connoll swept in between her and Redmond, taking her hand and placing it over his somewhat battered sleeve. "Do you wish to lose what teeth you have remaining?" he asked the earl.

Redmond stepped back. "You young blackguard," he muttered, still backing.

"I thought not." The marquis faced her. "Quickly," he murmured, heading them toward the door.

"But the diamond," she whispered, hitching up one side of her skirt with her free hand as they made their way outside through the boisterous crowd. They'd probably never attended such an exciting recital. "We'll never make it to Munroe House in one piece." Or at least not together.

"I think we may," he returned, signaling his driver. "Your father has the Nightshade."

"What?" She stopped, pulling against him. "You put it—"

"He took it. Right out of my hand." He pulled open the coach door and helped her inside. "Then he pushed me out of the way."

"But . . . Goodness." Did her father favor Connoll's suit, then? This was the first time she could recall him doing . . . well, anything. "Goodness."

"Exactly my thought." He climbed inside after her, leaning out to close the door. "Munroe House, Epping. And no crashes."

"Aye, my lord."

"The question then becomes," he continued, "what is your father's idea of bad luck?"

What *would* her father consider ill luck? They needed to know, but the moment the carriage rocked into motion all of her attention, all of her being, centered on the man seated across from her, and the realization that the two of them were together, alone, again.

Connoll gamely tried to straighten his cravat, but half of it seemed to be missing. A thin line of blood ran from the left side of his lower lip down his chin, and his black hair stuck out crazily on one side where Dapney had apparently pulled it.

"Why did you hit him?" she asked.

He half stood, shifting to sit beside her. "I'm impulsive, if you'll recall." Leaning closer, he kissed her softly. "Ouch. You see? Impulsive. And I refuse to sit by and allow some fool to insult me."

"I knew it wasn't true," she commented.

His eyes smiled at her even as he touched his lip again and winced. "Thank you." He gazed at her for another moment, then cleared his throat. "So should I worry about a tree falling on us, or a sudden flood sweeping me out the door and down to the Thames?"

She shook herself. They still had a very large problem to deal with. Several of them, really. "I don't know. I've been trying to figure out how the diamond might affect my father's luck, but it's beginning to occur to me that I don't know all that much about him." She drew a breath. "When he jumped into the fight, I . . . I've never been so shocked in my life."

"Dapney's venom surprised me a bit, as well." Connoll took her hand, stroking her fingers almost absently. "I want you, Gilly. I want to marry you. But I've presented my case. So have Dapney and Redmond. I'm not like them. I can't prance about you like a poodle while you look for the perfect ingredients to avoid making any kind of mistake. I may not be a better man than either of them, but I'm better for you."

God, what had she been thinking, encouraging Redmond and Dapney? That fight had been her fault, for stringing along men she'd already manipulated into becoming dependent on her supposed admiration. Connoll was right; she'd been ticking off items on a list of someone else's making, and had never really looked beyond those items. This one had no imagination, while that one never lost his temper. And the one sitting beside her didn't fit any list at all. He aroused her, intoxicated her, and certainly more than kept her on her toes. But because of that, she could see herself sinking into his life, spending her days wanting to please him. Would that leave anything for her?

"I don't want you to order me about, or to completely control my life," she said slowly.

"And I don't want you doing that to me, Evangeline." He frowned briefly. "I'm not some bloody damned tyrant. My parents loved one another deeply, you know. Recently I've begun wondering if that isn't why I've never been tempted to marry. Just like you shaped your expectations because of your mama's, I had an expectation of what I wanted to feel, of what sort of woman I wanted in my life, because of them."

"And I'm that woman?" she asked, trying to sound skeptical rather than contrite and hopeful.

"I've kissed several women, as we've discussed. But you're the only one I've asked to marry me." Connoll blew out his breath. "Your father told me about your mother's experience with her own father, and I can assure you that I'm not that man. In a marriage most rights, laws, advantages—whatever you wish to call them—belong to the husband. I can also assure you that I won't use any of them to hurt or smother you. But—"

" 'Assurances,' as you call them, are one thing. I prefer a guarantee."

He shook his head, and a lock of his disheveled hair fell across one eye. Without thinking, she brushed it away.

"We've been acquainted for only a handful of days," he said quietly, "but you know me. Probably better than anyone. I can't give you a guarantee without proof. And until we're married, I can't prove anything but what you've already seen. Have some faith in me. If you don't or won't, then tell me goodbye."

"I—"

"I'm not finished," he pressed. "To be perfectly candid, I have faith in you. Faith that you're smarter than your mother, and that you *know* what you've been looking for won't make you happy."

"This from a man with a bloody lip." She ran a finger gently across that same lip. "As you know, I've been reading Mary Wollstonecraft. She was a very bright woman, very sure of herself and what she wanted. But I wouldn't call her happy. I can describe my mother the same way. I'm not so certain what I want any longer. But I do know that I thought I would prefer comfort over happiness."

He shifted. "Gilly, you—"

She flattened her hand over his mouth. "You got to be profound and eloquent. Now it's my turn to talk."

The fact that he didn't protest said more than any of his words ever could. Still, she continued. Thinking aloud had never been one of her favorite things to do; she preferred to come to her conclusions in silence before she spoke them. But she needed to hear it, probably as much as he did.

Evangeline closed her eyes for a moment, trying to slow the hard, fast, hopeful beating of her heart. *Faith.* He was certainly right about that. She just hadn't realized how difficult it would be when the moment came to demonstrate hers, newly forming as it was.

"When I'm in your company," she continued, "I'm happy. It's not just that you make me happy, which you do, but that I feel happier, lighter, since I've met you." An unexpected tear ran down her cheek.

Connoll brushed it away with his thumb. "Are you finished being eloquent?"

"Yes."

"Then I have two questions."

Two? That surprised her; he always surprised her. "Very well," she returned, wishing she had better control of her voice, and knowing that he probably wouldn't be fooled, regardless.

"You asked for a week to convince your mother not to object to me, and there are six days of that week left. Is she going to be the one to decide your—our—future?"

"I—" She cleared her throat. "I think I should wait to hear the second question before I answer the first."

Nodding, Connoll reached for her other hand, clasping them both in his. His own fingers shook. *Goodness.* "Will you marry me, Gilly?"

She gazed into his dark blue eyes, seeing his humor and intelligence and quite a bit of worry there—worry that she would evade him or refuse him again. *Faith.* "The answer to your first question is no. And to the second one, I say yes," she whispered unsteadily. "Yes, and yes, and yes again."

Connoll laughed, drawing her hands up to kiss her fingers. "That's handy, because my third question was going to be whether you would prefer a short engagement to a lengthy one, and now you've already answered it."

"Very clever of y—"

She couldn't finish her sentence, because he kissed her.

Chapter 13

"No! I refuse to allow this!"

Connoll sat beside Gilly on her parents' couch and did his best to keep both his temper and his silence while Lady Munroe stalked about the room like a madwoman. She hadn't sat down from the moment she and the viscount had walked into the Munroe House drawing room.

"Mama, I am nearly nineteen years of age. I've come into my inheritance, and nothing you say will convince me to change my m—"

"You are ungrateful! Ungrateful and obstinate."

"She should look in a mirror," Connoll muttered, and Gilly squeezed his fingers.

"Hush. No more brawls tonight, and especially not with Mama."

"He makes her happy, Heloise," her father said abruptly, from his seat across the room.

"What?" The viscountess whirled on him. "You have no idea what you're saying." She whipped back to glare at Connoll. "You put that diamond in my pocket, didn't you?" She began clawing at her gown. "I don't have a pocket. Where is it? I demand you tell me at once!"

"It's here, darling," Munroe stated, lifting his arm. The diamond dangled from its chain, sparking in the firelight. "I have it."

"You? But I put it—" Lady Munroe stopped, pinching her lips together.

"You put it in Connoll's pocket yesterday," Gilly finished, her voice admirably calm. "He found it and put it in a box to return to me. I put it in your reticule this evening, to teach you a lesson. It fell out and Connoll caught it, which is when the fight began. Papa took it from him to save us."

"To save you?" she repeated, stalking up to the viscount. "How dare you interfere when you—"

Munroe stood. "It's true that this is bad luck, isn't it?" he asked, looking past his wife at his daughter.

"I think it is. There've been far too many coincidences for me to dismiss them as . . . well, as coincidences."

"I agree," Munroe said slowly, placing it on the end table. "I've been thinking about what bad luck would be to me."

Your wife, Connoll thought silently, but continued to hold his tongue. Considering that he had proposed and Gilly had finally accepted, he was extremely curious about how the viscount's poor luck might have affected them.

"Did it bring you bad luck, Papa?" Evangeline asked.

"It cost me my daughter." He smiled. "That is the worst thing I could imagine, Gilly, losing you. My only consolation is that you've found the one good apple in the bunch of wormy fruit your mama's been throwing at you."

"Thank you, sir," Connoll said feelingly. At least one member of the Munroe family had apparently been on his side all along.

"John! How dare you!"

"You haven't given me any choice, Heloise." He walked forward to kiss Gilly on the cheek, and to shake Connoll's hand. "The two of you have *my* blessing, if that counts for anything."

"It does, Papa," Evangeline answered, taking his hand and squeezing his fingers. "Thank you."

"You don't have mine!" Lady Munroe broke in. From her high color and wringing hands, she looked on the verge of an apoplexy.

"Mama," Gilly said, rising, "you wore the necklace for an entire evening and nothing untoward happened to you. You had it in your reticule for over an hour tonight, and again, nothing happened."

"What are you trying to say, Evangeline?"

"The Nightshade Diamond finds what you want least, and that is what it provides. For you, it didn't change anything. It affected Connoll and me and Papa, but not you. To me that says that you're already living what you want least."

"That is not—"

"I want you to have it," Gilly pressed, squaring her shoulders before she stepped over to pick it up and bring it to where her mother stood glowering. "I'm happy, and I'm fearful that this thing will ruin that. It doesn't seem to hurt you, so I'm giving it to you. Do what you want with it. But I am going to marry Connoll. He is a good man."

She took her mother's hand and dropped the diamond into her palm, then returned to her seat. As she sat, Connoll could feel her muscles shaking, and he took her fingers in his again. To stand up against the parent to whom she'd looked to for her entire life—it took courage. And faith. Faith in him.

"I love you, Evangeline," he murmured, gazing at her.

Without warning she flung her arms around his shoulders, hugging him tightly. "I love you, Connoll," she whispered into his ear. "Thank you for saving me from myself."

He held her close. Thank God that Daisy had tired of his playing about, thank God she'd met Ivey. And thank God for that damned diamond, which he hoped never to set eyes on again.

"I suppose I shall have to accept this," the viscountess bit out, closing her fingers over the diamond. "But I am not happy about it, Evangeline. And you will live to regret it. Mark my words, you stupid girl."

That was enough of that. Connoll climbed to his feet. "If your worry, my lady, is that Gilly will find herself belittled and broken by her spouse, you have nothing to fear. I will, however, ask that you stop doing to her the very thing from which you claim to wish to save her."

Lady Munroe clamped her jaw closed again. "I'm sorry if I've been such a burden to you, Gilly," she ground out, and left the room.

Lord Munroe blew out his breath. "I'd best go fetch her something. That should improve her mood."

"Papa," Gilly said, before he could leave, "why have you let her rule you? Obviously you do have . . ."

"A mind of my own?" her father finished. "I love your mother. I met her father; I knew what sort of man he was. I've done my best to not be anything like him. Apparently I've stepped too far in the other direction, and you've paid the price." He glanced at Connoll. "Or very nearly."

"I wish I'd come to know you better."

He grinned. "Heavens, girl, I'm not dead yet. And she'll come around. It's mostly that she's terrified you'll make the wrong choice. Once she sees that you've done well for yourself, I think some of the chill will leave the air."

"I hope so, Papa. Thank you."

He gave a slow smile. "And thank you. Both of you. The wind seems to have changed; perhaps I'll keep the breeze blowing."

As the viscount left the room, Connoll swept Gilly into his arms and kissed her again. He meant to spend a great part of each and every day from now on doing that. "So, my dear, I believe we have a wedding to plan," he said. "I think a special license and a marriage next week might be appropriate. And you?"

She slipped her arms over his shoulders to look up at him. "I think that is a good idea," she murmured, leaning up to kiss him once more. "A very good idea."

Six weeks later

Evangeline took a turn about the upstairs drawing room of Rawley Park in Devonshire. Connoll had several times told her the size of the house, and mentioned the splendid fishing in the lake at the rear of the estate. Setting eyes on it, though, had been startling.

"Are you dancing again?" his low, amused drawl came as he leaned into the doorway.

"I can't help it. I knew you had excellent taste in paintings, but this is the most beautiful house I've ever seen."

"And it's yours."

"Ours," she corrected.

He straightened, joining her by the window. "We could wrestle for it. I can almost guarantee that you'll win." He slid his arms around her waist, and she leaned back against him.

"'Almost'?" she repeated, chuckling.

"Very well. I can absolutely guarantee it. You know me; it's the wrestling part I enjoy."

"Mm-hm."

A hand rapped at the open door. "Lady Rawley, another box just arrived for you," Doretta said, hefting a wooden container about the size of a hatbox in her hands.

"It's smaller than the other ones, anyway," Connoll said, releasing her. "Perhaps you're finally running out of clothes to be delivered."

"Nonsense," she shot back over her shoulder as she left the window to take the box. "This is probably the earbobs."

"Good God," he muttered. "In that case, I'll go have the stable expanded." Kissing the back of her ear, he headed out again.

Evangeline laughed as she scooted Elektra off the bed and sat to pull open the lid. A small mahogany box rested in a pile of straw, a note wrapped around it. "Connoll," she said, instinctively pulling her hands away from the box.

Immediately he turned around and strode back into the room. "What's wrong?" he asked sharply.

"It's—"

"Damnation," he said, spying the box. "I thought she'd decided we had a slight chance of having a tolerable marriage."

"I did, as well." Wiping her palms on her skirt, she reached in and untied the string holding the note to the box.

"Gilly, don't. I'll throw the whole thing in the lake."

"That would probably kill all of your very tasty fish. And I'm touching the letter; not the box."

"I doubt the Nightshade Diamond cares about semantics," he noted darkly.

She understood his uneasiness. With the news she'd given him yesterday, they both had reason to want nothing but good luck for the next eight months or so. Still, her mother wanted grandchildren, and she couldn't imagine that the viscountess would risk that out of vindictiveness.

With a shallow breath she opened the note. Swiftly she read through it, and then handed it to Connoll as tears welled in her eyes. "Here," she said, wiping her cheeks.

"Good God, Gilly," he grunted, wrapping his free arm across her shoulders.

"Read it."

" 'Dearest Evangeline,' " he obediently began aloud, " 'I have recently discovered that a woman can learn important lessons from her own child—children, for I must include Connoll in this.' " He glanced at Gilly's face. "That's the first time she's referred to me as other than 'that man.' "

"Keep reading, Conn."

"I am, I am. 'Your father took the Nightshade and hid it from me. Since then he and I have had several interesting—and enlightening—conversations. As a result of them and your marriage, we have decided to journey to Scotland for the autumn. And I cannot—no, I WON'T—take the diamond with us. I seem to have developed some good luck, and I don't wish to jeopardize it. So the Nightshade is yours again, since your Aunt Rachel continues to deem you the most worthy. Do with it what you think best. My most loving regards, Your Mother.'"

They sat silently for a long moment, looking at the box. "That's unexpected," Connoll finally said.

"What are we going to do with it?"

"I have an idea." Stepping forward, he lifted the larger box, the diamond container still inside. "Come with me."

"You can't just throw it away. Someone will find it, and then whatever happens to them will be our fault." She followed him down the stairs to his office, where he sat behind the desk and pulled out a piece of paper. "What are you doing?"

"Writing a warning," he said, continuing to scrawl out something. "I'm not going to throw it away." He blew on the paper, then folded it. Taking a breath, he opened the box and glanced inside, nudging something inside with one finger. "It's there, in the velvet bag. And I told you that I have a plan."

"And you're still not telling me what it is."

"I'm showing you." He shoved his note inside the mahogany box and slammed the lid again, then lifted the larger box. "This way, my heart."

This time they left the house, heading out to the large stone stable. He shooed the half dozen grooms out, and walked to the far back corner of one of the stalls. Finally he set the box down.

"You're going to bury it in the stable."

"No." He pulled over another large box and stood on it. Then he reached out just above his head and pulled at one of the stones. After a bit of wiggling, it shifted and came loose in his hand. He set it down beside the box. "I used to hide my treasures in here when I was little," he said, glancing at her over his shoulder. Reaching in, he pulled out a lead soldier and a shilling. "Very little," he continued, handing them down to her.

"Do you remember," Evangeline said as he stepped back down and gingerly picked up the mahogany box, "what I told you about my aunt's explanation of the curse?"

"About good luck following bad once you set the damned thing aside?"

"Yes, that."

"I remember."

Carefully he pushed the box with its note deep inside the wall, then retrieved the stone and set it back in place. Once he was finished, the corner looked as though it hadn't been touched in decades.

"You're a very brilliant man," she concluded, taking his hand as he jumped to the ground again.

"I know. I married you."

"Do you really think it'll be safe there?"

"Not only do I think it'll be safe, I think that the Addisons for generations to come will benefit from having it lodged in the Rawley Park wall."

"As long as no one tears down your stable."

"As long as no one actually finds it." He grinned, tilting her chin up to kiss her. "And if they do, I can only hope they know how to read and put it back immediately."

She kissed him back, reveling in the feel of his strong, warm arms around her. "Or that they're so unlucky the Nightshade will have no effect on them whatsoever."

"You're talking about our descendants, Gilly. They can't possibly be unlucky."

Evangeline laughed, wrapping her arms around his neck as he scooped her up off the floor. "But sometimes bad luck can become good luck. You're a prime example of that."

"And don't you forget it."

Diamonds Are <u>Not</u> a Girl's Best Friend

Chapter 1

June 2007
Wednesday, 8:51 a.m.

"Forget it, Rick!" Samantha Jellicoe called over her shoulder. "You volunteered me for this job, so keep out of it!"

"It's my building!" the low, British-accented drawl came in return.

"It's your building being loaned to the V & A. Butt the hell out."

To prevent further argument, and to keep him from hearing her laugh, she shut the garden gate and strode out through the Devonshire sunshine toward the old Rawley Park stable. It actually wasn't a stable any longer; years ago an ancestor had turned it into storage in favor of a new, larger stable. And then Rick Addison had further converted it into a huge temperature-controlled safe room for paintings and works of art he didn't have room to display.

And it wasn't even that, at the moment. "Hey, Armand," she greeted as she reached the locked door and the very properly dressed bald man standing in front of it. "Sorry I'm late."

"No worries, Miss Jellicoe," Armand Montgomery returned, looking as though he were fighting the instinct to salute. "I only just arrived, myself."

He was lying, because she'd seen his blue Mercedes pull up the long estate drive twenty minutes earlier. But he was also British, and even the assistant curator of the Victoria and Albert Museum would never complain about being made to stand around. "Here's the new alarm code," she said, pulling a card out of her jeans pocket and handing it to him.

He stared hard at the set of numbers, obviously trying to memorize them, then tucked the card into his inner jacket pocket. "I'll shred it once we get inside," he said, obviously reading her expression.

He'd better; she was getting tired of reminding him. It continued to amaze her the way most people—even those who had things worth stealing—looked at security. As someone who had once benefited from those same it-won't-happen-to-me attitudes, it seemed both wrong and extremely vital that she warn them to keep their damn guards up.

With a quick, uncertain smile at her, he entered the five-digit code, waited for the alarm light to switch from red to green, and then pulled open the heavy fireproof door. "Will Lord Rawl—I mean Mr. Addison—be joining us?"

She shrugged. She was used to living in the shadows, being someone that no one would notice, but she had a legitimate job now, dammit. And it irked her that however good she happened to be at it, everyone's first question was still about Richard Addison. Okay, yes, he was one of the richest guys in the world, and yes, he was gorgeous, and yes, they'd been living together for eight months, but this gig was hers. Not his. "He's pretty busy. I don't know if he'll show today or not." Especially since she'd warned him not to.

"Oh, very well. Of course. It was very kind of him to loan the hall to us for the gem exhibit. I think it's the finest location we've had."

They walked into the building. The walls were still old stone, though much of it had been replaced or remortared to accommodate electrical and security wiring. The dirt floor was now a gray slate covering insulated concrete, and the timber roof above the bare oak beams had been sealed with a protective lacquer and reinforced with concealed steel brackets.

All along the walls and down a trio of rows running the length of the long building, she and Mr. Montgomery had overseen the installation of displays designed to match the appearance of the old stable, but so wired and sensored that they practically hummed.

Samantha punched in another code and swung open a panel set into the near wall. All of the control switches were inside, and she flipped on the display lights.

"So this is what it will look like when we go live?" Montgomery asked, strolling between two of the rows of glass-topped displays.

"That's what I wanted to check with you about," she returned. "The display lighting's great when it's just us, but add a couple hundred people all leaning over to look inside, and the room's going to be dark enough for pickpockets." It would actually be dark enough for axe-wielding giants, but from his tight-lipped expression, she'd made her point.

"The gems are arriving tomorrow, and the exhibit opens on—"

"On Saturday. I know. Which is why I brought in an electrician while you were touring with the jewels in Edinburgh. What do you think of this?" She reached into the panel again.

"But we said that overhead lighting would . . ." He looked up as she flipped the switch. "Oh."

The glass covering the displays was of a very expensive non-reflective material, but the gems themselves would be highly reflective, which had meant a very different kind of problem altogether. Her solution had been to install indirect lighting along the upper walls of the stable-cum-museum hall, so that the top half of the room was bathed in soft white light that faded to a barely noticeable glow just above the level of the displays.

"I like it," Montgomery said, turning a circle. "Very innovative. You have quite a knack for this, don't you?"

She shrugged. "I try."

In her time as a cat burglar she'd probably seen every type of artifact lighting known to mankind, and she had a good idea of what worked and what didn't. That, though, would have to stay a trade secret. As long as she was living with a very high-profile businessman, the fewer people who knew about her nefarious past, the better. And that didn't even take into account the fact that she'd only been retired for eight months or so, while the statute of limitations for stealing Picassos and Remingtons was, on average, seven years.

"The, uh, fire exit area bothers me a bit," the curator was saying.

Samantha shook herself. She knew better than to get lost in self-reflection in the middle of a gig. Even a legitimate one. The corner he indicated was twice as dark as the rest of the room. "Crap," she muttered. "The reflector came loose again. I'll fix it."

"I can—"

"No, it was the first one we put up, and we were still kind of experimenting."

Dragging over one of the stepladders that still littered the floor, she climbed up and reached high along the wall to reattach the reflector to its base and push the clip back into the holder. Abruptly the stone she'd been leaning on to steady herself shifted beneath her hand.

"Shit," she muttered, flinging her other hand out to keep her balance.

Mr. Montgomery grabbed her around the ankles, nearly making her shriek. She absolutely hated being grabbed, no matter the circumstances. Rather than kick him in the face, though, she took a breath.

"I'm fine, Mr. Montgomery. Just a loose stone."

He released her. "We'd best get it remortared before the show—don't want it falling into a case of diamonds."

"That we don't." She tugged on the stone, and it slid out from the wall. With the diffused light pouring down the wall she could clearly see the open space behind it. Or what would have been an open space, if not for the box resting securely inside the hollow. Her heart began beating faster. Anybody would love the idea of hidden treasure, she supposed, reaching carefully in to pull out the box. For her, it was practically orgasmic.

"What do you have there?"

"I don't know," she said absently, brushing dust off the top of the box and stepping to the ground. Mahogany, polished and inlaid—and old. Not some child's treasure box.

"Goodness," Montgomery said, looking over her shoulder. "Why don't you open it?"

She wanted to. Badly. She was in charge of security for this building, after all, so technically she needed to know about everything inside it. Even old, hidden things. Especially when they were inside the stable walls of Rick's ancestral property.

And a closed box, of all things—she'd spent the last eight months pretty much resisting temptation, but nobody could expect her to ignore a box that had literally fallen into her hands. Rick wouldn't.

Taking a deep breath, she opened the lid. A small velvet bag lay inside. Still hesitating, she reached in to tilt the bag into her fingers. A diamond-encrusted chain spilled out, attached to a blue diamond the size of a walnut. It winked at her.

At the same instant the light over her head popped and exploded, showering her with sparks. Gasping, she snapped the box closed again. *Christ.*

Montgomery gaped at the ceiling. "That—"

"E-excuse me for a minute, will you?" she stammered, and headed for the door.

The box gripped hard in her hands, she crossed the corner of the temporary parking lot they'd put in for the exhibition, opened the low garden gate with her hip, and strode up to the massive house.

A diamond. A *fucking* diamond. That sneak. They'd been dating—hell, living together—since three days after they'd met, and Rick had made it clear that he wanted her in his life for the rest of his life. But he also knew that she had an abysmal track record for staying in one place for very long, and that she didn't work with partners.

If this was his way of giving her a gift without sending her running for the hills . . . well, it was pretty clever, really. He knew she liked puzzles—and a hidden box in a secret hole in a wall was definitely a puzzle. But a diamond wasn't just a gift. Diamonds meant something. And ones this size—

"Rick!" she yelled as she reached the main foyer.

"What?" A moment later he leaned over the balcony railing above and behind her. "You didn't kill Montgomery, did you?"

For a heartbeat she just looked at him. Black hair, deep blue eyes, a professional soccer player's body—and all hers. The smart-ass remark she'd been ready to make about the diamond stuck in her throat.

"What is it?" he repeated in his deep voice with its slightly faded British accent, and descended the stairs. He wore a loose gray T-shirt and jeans, and his feet were bare. Yep, her billionaire liked going barefoot.

Still clutching the box in one hand, she walked to the base of the stairs, grabbed his shoulder, and kissed him.

Rick slid his hands around her hips and pulled her closer. She sighed, pressed along his lean, muscular body. Out of the corner of her eye she saw Sykes the butler start through the foyer, see them, and turn around to head back out the way he'd come in.

Pulling away from her an inch or two, Rick tucked a strand of her reddish hair back behind her ear. "What exactly were you and Mr. Montgomery discussing?" he asked. "Not that I'm going to complain about it."

She took another breath, her heart pounding all over again. "I found it, Brit. It's . . . thank you, but . . . it's too much."

His brow furrowed. "What are you talking about, Yank?"

Samantha moved the box around between them. "This. When did you put it—"

Rick took it from her hands, glanced at her face, then opened it. "Good God," he breathed, lifting the sparkling orb out of the box by its diamond and gold chain. "Where did this come fr—"

"You didn't put it there."

Of course he hadn't. She was an idiot. Did that mean she'd been hoping for a diamond? So much for independent Samantha Elizabeth Jellicoe. *Schmuck.*

"Put it where?"

"It was in a hole in the wall in the exhibit hall. Come on. I'll show you."

"Hold a minute." Setting the box down on a side table, he pulled out a folded piece of paper stuck to the lid. "Did you see this?"

She shook her head. So not only was she an idiot, she was an unobservant one. What the hell was wrong with her? Leaping to conclusions and missing clues only led to nice ceremonies over pine boxes—or whatever it was they made coffins out of these days.

Gingerly he opened it. The edges were crumbled, the paper yellowed and badly creased. " 'To whom it may concern,' " he read, angling the paper to catch the morning light through the generous front windows, " 'The item you have discovered is known as the Nightshade Diamond. It was previously owned by the Munroe family out of Lancastershire, and through my marriage to Evangeline Munroe and with her permission has passed to mine.' "

"Who's Evangeline Munroe?"

"Hush. I'm reading. 'The diamond was discovered by a Munroe in southernmost Africa in approximately 1640, and has been an object of misfortune since that date. Because you have discovered it, the decision must be yours, but I must warn you that touching the diamond, carrying it on your person, inspires the worst luck imaginable. Conversely, once having touched it and then set it aside, an equal share of good luck results.

"'I advise you, nay, beg you, to replace this letter, and this box, from whence you found it, or if that is impossible, to place it in an alternate safe, secure location. That is the only way to benefit from the Nightshade Diamond. I have witnessed both aspects of the curse, and can vouch for the truth of the legend. May the best of luck be with you. Yours in Respect, Connoll Spencer Addison, Marquis of Rawley.'" Rick glanced up at her, then looked down again. "It's dated nineteen July, 1814."

She watched his expression. For a guy with so long and rich a heritage, he rarely talked about it. In fact, he winced whenever anyone referred to him as the Marquis of Rawley, preferring, especially in the States, to go by plain old Mr. Richard Addison. "Do you know these people?" she finally asked.

"Yes. Connoll and Evangeline are my great-great-and-then-some-grandparents. There are portraits of them in the gallery hall."

"So this Nightshade Diamond has actually been sitting in a hole in the stable for nearly two hundred years."

"It would seem so."

She looked at it, draped across the box where he'd set it to read the letter. "We should put it back."

"Are you mad? If this is genuine, and it looks like it is, this thing's at least a hundred and fifty carats, not counting the smaller ones around it or the chain. And it's blue. Do you know how rare that is?"

"It's bad luck. Your great-great says so."

"You're too superstitious. Show me where you found it."

He picked it up and started to hand it to her, but she backed away, putting her hands behind her back. "No way."

"The note said carrying it on your person has the same effect as wearing it. You saw it, and you carried it to the house. Did lightning strike you? Did you fall in a hole?"

"Rick, that—"

"Two hundred years ago my great-great, as you call him, was superstitious enough to put a diamond worth several million pounds in a hole. I think we're a bit more enlightened than that, don't you?"

When he put it that way, it did sound a little silly. Still reluctant, she put her hand out and he draped it across her fingers. It was lovely. Stunning. For a second she couldn't help waiting, breath held, for the sky to crack open or something, but nothing happened. No lightbulb even dimmed. "I can't help being superstitious, you know," she said, seeing Rick grinning at her. "Black cats, ladders, all that shit, it's—"

"Yes, I've heard that criminal types look for warnings everywhere." He kissed her again. "But you're not a criminal type any longer. Show me the hole."

She clenched the diamond in her fist, sighing and pretending that she wasn't still jumpy as a long-tailed cat in a room full of rocking chairs. "Okay, but if the ground caves in, I'm pulling you down with me."

"I wouldn't expect anything less."

Chapter 2

Wednesday, 9:44 a.m.

Richard Addison went up the stepladder and peered into the small, irregularly shaped hole in the wall of his old stable. After several renovations in over two hundred years, and especially with the massive one he'd commissioned seven years earlier, the fact that this hiding place had remained intact was something of a miracle.

Deep in the far left corner his fingers touched something, and he pulled it free. An old lead soldier, its paint flaked and faded away to nothing, emerged into Sam's expertly lit exhibit room.

"What is it?" she asked, standing on her tiptoes to look.

"A fusilier," he returned, handing it to her and stepping down. "George the Third, I would think."

She gave him a quicksilver grin. "I knew you were an expert in Georgian painters, but I had no idea about the toy soldiers."

"I was an English lad, you know." He glanced around the cluttered room. "Where's Armand?"

"Mr. Montgomery took your diamond outside to examine it in the sunlight." Samantha handed him back the soldier. "I've never seen an English guy look so excited."

Richard lifted an eyebrow. "I beg your pardon?"

She snorted. "Well, not outside a bedroom, anyway."

"I just hope he doesn't try to run off with it."

"I could totally run him down if he tried," she commented, heading with him to the door. "Besides, jewels are his life. And that one's a stunner. Even if it is bad luck."

"There's no such thing as an object causing luck," he said, taking her hand as they left the stable and walked over to where Armand Montgomery stood with the diamond in one hand and his cell phone in the other. "Peoples' reaction to an object, yes," he continued. "The object itself, no."

"How logical of you, Mr. Spock." She pulled free of his hand as Armand ended his call. "So, what do you think?" she asked him.

"It's a blue diamond," he returned, a muscle beneath his left eye jumping. "Expertly cut."

In his career as a buyer and seller of properties and businesses, Richard had become very proficient at reading people. Their Mr. Montgomery was upset about something. "Armand? What's troubling you?" he asked.

"I, um, was just called back to London. A question about the authenticity of a very prominent item in the museum collection."

"But the exhibit opens here in three days."

"Yes, I know. I'll send my assistant up here with the

delivery tomorrow." He cleared his throat. "Abysmal timing, I'm afraid. And it's been a pleasure working with you, Miss Jellicoe. And you again, Mr. Addison." He opened the door of his Mercedes and slid onto the seat.

"Eventually, I will convince you to call me Rick. And Armand?"

The assistant curator looked up. "Yes?"

"The diamond?"

Montgomery blanched. "Oh, good God." He handed the necklace over. "My apologies. I'm just, well, a bit distracted."

Richard took a step back from the car. "No worries. Have a safe trip."

As soon as the Mercedes left the gravel parking lot, Samantha clapped her hands together. "Great. I get the assistant's assistant to help me put together a showing of a shitload of jewels."

"You don't need anyone else, my dear," he commented, beginning to regret leaving the house barefoot if they were going to keep treading about on the gravel. "You know Montgomery was just window dressing."

"Except that the exhibit belongs to his museum and goes where he says. And this is my first big gig like this, and I only got it because you own half the countryside, and the—"

Richard grabbed her around the waist, pulling her in for a long, soft kiss. Green eyes, auburn hair, slim and athletic—she'd attracted him the moment he set eyes on her, and that had been while she'd been in his Palm Beach house trying to rob him. But it was the rest of her—the way she could disarm an alarm system in five seconds flat but refused to rob museums, the way she would full-on tackle an armed bad guy but hated killing spiders—that mesmerized him.

Obsession, heart, whatever term he chose to describe her, he loved her. So much that it frightened him sometimes. And she'd thought he had planted the diamond for her to find. And she hadn't screamed and run away into the night. She'd thanked him, and kissed him—which made a certain item he'd picked up a few weeks ago even more interesting.

"What say we go out somewhere for dinner tonight?" he suggested, gingerly leading the way off the gravel and back to the grassy garden path.

"As long as we don't go anywhere that has the word *pudding* on the menu. You people do not know what pudding is."

"I was actually thinking of dining at Petrus."

"I am not driving to London; the gems and the assistant's assistant will be here first thing in the morning."

"That's not a problem," he returned. "I'll call for the helicopter."

She laughed, tucking herself into his shoulder. "You are so cool."

"Yes, I know."

She glanced up from his hand to his face. "So that's pretty weird, huh, finding that necklace like that? A two-hundred-year-old family heirloom. The last person to set eyes on it was probably your great-great himself."

"I have a multitude of family heirlooms. Connoll Addison, though, was the one who began the collection of European Masters. Family legend has it that he rescued a handful of paintings from Paris so Bonaparte couldn't seize and sell them for ammunition."

"He sounds like your kind of guy. You . . . don't talk about your family very much."

"Neither do you," he pointed out.

"That's because I don't know who my mom is, and until three months ago I thought my dad had died in prison."

"And now he's wandering about Europe and points east scamming Interpol. I remember. He nearly got you killed."

"Mm-hm. You're changing the subject, Rick."

He took a breath. "I'll have the copter pick us up at half five." Richard checked his watch. "I've got a proposal to finish reading before then."

"And what about the Nightshade Diamond?"

He looked down at the necklace in his hand. It was "weird," as Sam had said. It felt strange, to be holding something so directly connected to his own ancestor, reportedly the one he most resembled in both appearance and temperament. Yes, he owned other items passed down from that generation and even earlier, but hundreds of hands had touched them, hundreds of eyes had gazed at them between then and now. The Nightshade Diamond felt like a direct link between him and his great-great-grandfather, and it had come with a bloody warning.

"Hey," Samantha said, nudging his rib cage with her elbow, "you don't have to have everything about the diamond sorted out in ten minutes. I get the being-thrown-for-a-loop thing. And I can be cool and understanding."

He chuckled. "And here I thought you were the peppery, temperamental one."

"Peppery. I like that." She released him as they reached the house. "I'm going to do another video and sensor check. Can't be too careful. There might be a me out there somewhere looking to make a score."

"There is no other you. I can guarantee that."

She leaned up and kissed him again. "Thanks. See ya."

"See you later," he returned, nodding.

Inside the house he headed upstairs for the library and some of the old property and inventory ledgers. Surely somebody would have noted the ownership of a 150-plus-carat diamond, whether they knew of its location or not. And before he let anyone else know that he now owned a very rare blue diamond, he wanted to authenticate a few things—including the value and quality of the gem itself.

No, he didn't believe in bad luck, but Samantha did. And she'd discovered a diamond lost for nearly two hundred years, three days before Rawley Park was to host a traveling precious gem exhibit. Fate. Now, that was an odd bird, and apparently one with a sense of humor. Or so he hoped.

When Samantha blew out her breath in the early morning air, it fogged. Chilly and damp, even in the middle of June—she'd never really called any one place home, but it was mornings like this when she missed the warmth of Palm Beach, Florida, the city where she'd lived for most of the last three years.

Rick had a house there, as well, if anyone could call a mansion boasting thirty rooms, a pool, two tennis courts, and three acres of garden a house. Even Solano Dorado, though, was dwarfed by the Rawley Park estate here in Devonshire.

She looked toward the main road again, visible far down the hill beyond the estate's stone walls. Additional security personnel already manned the gates, watched the security monitors, and walked the perimeter of the stable outbuilding. Everything was as ready as she could make it, but she couldn't help pacing.

The tips of her fingers tingled, and adrenaline pumped through her muscles. It felt like the preamble to a robbery, without the underlying layering of hard tension that came when she put her freedom, and sometimes her life, on the line for a crime. She rotated her arms, stretching her muscles and speeding her bloodflow. Yep, she was ready for anything. Now all she needed was for the trucks and the white hats to arrive so she could get started.

Footsteps crunched on the gravel behind her. "This is early for you, isn't it, love?" Rick said in his low, cultured drawl, pushing her hair forward over her shoulders to kiss the nape of her neck.

For a minute she let herself sink into him. What had Dr. Phil called a good partner? A soft place to fall, or words to that effect. Rick had made it possible for her to start a new life. Whether she'd meant to retire in the near future anyway or not, without him the temptation to go back into the heart-pounding nights of cat burglary would have been almost too much to resist.

"Just waiting for a delivery," she returned, facing him. "Ooh, very James Bond."

"I'm not James Bond," he said, giving his standard reply.

"This morning you are. Wow."

He'd dressed for business, in a dark blue Armani suit and a blue and gray tie that made his eyes look as blue as sapphires. When he grinned, her heart skipped a beat.

"Then kiss me, Moneypenny," he said in a very good Connery accent. He wrapped his hands around her waist and dipped her.

With a yelp she grabbed his shoulders, arching her back as he kissed her, mouth, teeth, and tongue. *Good glory.* "Oh, James," she breathed, when he gave her a second to talk. "What brought that on?"

"You were asleep last night when I came to bed," he returned, slowly swinging her upright again. "And I was such a gentleman that I didn't wake you up for the sex."

Samantha snorted. " 'The sex'?"

He nodded. "Yes, you're familiar with the sex, I believe. If not, read up. I'll be home this evening, and if you're asleep this time, I *will* wake you up."

Rick kissed her again. It continued to amaze her that even after eight months he could just look at her and make her knees go weak. As for his kisses and the sex, hoo mama. "I'll be awake."

"Very wise of you. Call me if you need me." He gripped her fingers, then slowly released her to head toward his stadium-sized garage. "I love you."

"I love you." She watched him walk away. "Why are you driving?"

He glanced over his shoulder. "It helps me think. By the by, I'm taking the Nightshade with me to have it appraised."

A low shiver of uneasiness ran through her. "Be careful, Rick."

"I will be."

He could be to London and back by helicopter in the time it took him to drive there, but if he was carrying a cursed diamond, she was happy that he was on the ground rather than a thousand feet above it. Still, she'd seen him drive. He didn't take as many risks as she did, but he did like to go fast.

The red '61 E-type Jaguar growled down the drive and out the gate, then headed down the narrow road to the main highway intersection. He would still be on his land for another ten minutes, but he'd only walled off the house from the prying eyes of the press and the star-struck public.

Samantha only had five minutes to consider whether he should be more worried about carrying the diamond, or she should be less worried about it. She was still undecided when she caught sight of a trio of white-paneled delivery trucks winding up the hill toward Rawley Park. As they drew closer, the four accompanying police cars came into view.

That was the biggest downside of working with the white hats—constantly rubbing shoulders with cops and lawyers and other people she previously would have avoided with a vengeance. "Showtime," she muttered, as the caravan stopped momentarily at the main gates and then continued up toward her again.

A couple of months ago and despite the many times Rick had said he trusted her, she couldn't quite picture him driving away while the V & A delivered the glittery equivalent of several million British pounds into her care. And yet there he went, out of sight now down the road.

The trucks and police cars stopped in the gravel parking lot. Wow, they'd sent bobbies with M-16s just to show how seriously everybody took the safety of this little traveling display. She blew out her breath and picked up the paperwork attached to her official exhibit clipboard.

"Miss Jellicoe," a tall guy in a cheap, tan-colored suit said, as he emerged from the lead truck and approached her. "I'm Henry Larson, Mr. Montgomery's second-in-command."

That sounded better than the assistant's assistant. "Mr. Larson," she said, shaking his hand and examining his photo badge. With the blonde crew cut and brown eyes that spent more time looking at the picturesque land around them than at her face, he didn't quite fit her idea of a museum curator. But then she couldn't quite imagine herself as the mistress of the house behind them—if that's what she was. "Do you want to take a look at the room before you start off-loading?"

"Indeed I do." He signaled, and half the cops together with a dozen ID-badge-wearing museum employees joined them.

"You've all seen the layout schematics, I presume," Samantha said, leading the way to the stable and feeling like she needed a little tour-guide flag to wave. "The displays are set up nearly identically to the layout in Edinburgh."

"How many people will have access to the door code?" Larson asked, nodding at the pair of estate guards standing at either side of the door.

She turned her back on the crowd and punched in the set of numbers. "Just you and me," she returned, facing him again. "It changes daily, and you'll have to get it either from me or from the computer in the estate cellar, which is where I have all the monitoring equipment set up."

"Excellent," he returned, giving the control pad and heavy door the once-over before they walked inside.

She'd turned on the bright overheads already, figuring that the group setting up the displays would favor good illumination over atmospheric lighting. "The exit door to the gift shop's set up the same way, and I'll have guards at each door when we open."

"How many cameras?" Mr. Larson asked, turning a slow circle.

Evidently he and his boss didn't communicate very

well. "Twelve, including the four outside covering the outer walls and doorways."

"Overlapping views in here, I see," he commented, then bent down to look into the nearest display. "Pressure sensors on the glass?"

"And weight and motion sensors inside the cases, all currently deactivated."

"I'd like to do a live test before we bring the gems in."

"Okay." Samantha pulled her walkie-talkie from her pocket. "Craigson, make 'em hot," she instructed. "This is a test, everybody." All she needed was for the estate guards to come in and tackle Larson.

"Everything's green, Sam," Craigson's voice came a moment later.

She faced Mr. Larson again. "Break in to your heart's content," she said, stepping out of the way and covering her ears.

Ignoring the many "Do Not Touch the Displays" signs affixed to the walls, Larson gripped either side of one of the smaller cases and yanked up. The lid stayed put, the secondary scary red overhead floodlights came on, the doors locked, and a high-pitched wail screamed from the hidden wall speakers.

Releasing one of her ears, Samantha faced the nearest camera and drew her fingers across her neck. The siren shut off and the lights and doors returned to their standby positions.

Larson was nodding. "Is there a fire override?"

"Yes. If a fire sensor goes off, the doors unlock and the sprinklers go off, or we can do it from the control room. We had the sensors turned all the way up; when guests arrive I'll turn them down so a little jostling and glass-tapping won't set off the fireworks."

"Well done, Miss Jellicoe. What about metal detectors?"

"They pull out from the doorframes, with a second one inset into the gift shop exit doorway for the merchandise tags. They were off," she commented, indicating the cops with their M-16s.

The assistant's assistant clapped his hands together. "Very well. Let's get started, then, shall we? McCauley, get your people organized."

Samantha hid a frown as a spindly young woman with bright red cropped hair nodded, gathering the museum employees together for some quick instruction and then sending them out the door. It made sense, she supposed; the V & A people had been touring with the gems for four months and could probably do the setup with their eyes closed. Henry Larson was the second-string quarterback.

"While they're bringing in the safe boxes, would you show me the command center?" he asked on the tail of her thought.

"Sure. This way."

Much as she wanted to see the jewels being settled into their temporary homes, walking away was probably a better test of her character. And even though she and Montgomery had spent most of the last month reviewing security and viewing concerns and trying to balance the two, she couldn't blame Larson for wanting to cover his ass and see the setup for himself.

"I hear you'll be opening your own exhibit here soon," he said conversationally as they walked through the garden.

"Mm-hm. The entire south wing of the house is being remodeled to display the art and antiques Rick's collected. We're hoping for a December opening. The

V & A exhibit is turning out to be great for helping me answer some of the security concerns I've had for the main house."

"Speaking of Mr. Addison, is he in residence?"

Ah, another fan of the rich and famous. "Not at the moment," she said noncommittally. As her old dad had used to say before they'd parted company and he'd been arrested, only give out information when it's to your own benefit. Talking about the house gave her some additional credentials, and it was public knowledge, anyway. Talking about Rick—that was Rick's business.

"You know," Larson continued, following her in through what had used to be the servants' entrance and down the narrow hall at the back of the house, "I've been doing some studying. You have a rather interesting résumé."

She glanced sideways at him, but his attention was apparently on the cellar door they approached. "Do I? Just run-of-the-mill artwork security stuff and some art restoration, I thought."

"Hardly. Two months ago you helped foil a robbery at the Metropolitan Museum of Art in New York."

"I made a phone call," she countered. That was the public story, anyway. "My father foiled the robbery."

"Yes, the famous Martin Jellicoe. I was quite surprised to read that he wasn't dead, as had been widely reported."

She shrugged, keeping a relaxed stance even though her Spider-sense was beginning to tingle. If this guy was a low-level museum curator, she was Wonder Woman. "Martin used to be a cat burglar; sneakiness was kind of his MO."

"Indeed. There was also a mystery you solved involving Mr. Addison's stolen paintings, and something about a robbery and murder in Florida which you also solved."

"What can I say? I'm good at my job."

"To a rather miraculous degree."

Samantha stopped, blocking him from descending the last few steps to the cellar floor. "You know, now that I think about it, I do have an interesting résumé. My project with Rick has put me in contact with the curators of most of the better-known museums in Europe. And you know something else?"

"I—"

"I have a nearly photographic memory. If I see a face or hear a name, I pretty much remember it. But oddly enough, I don't remember ever hearing your name before you gave it to me this morning."

He frowned. "That's—"

"So in my mind that means you're either running a scam on me and the V & A—which makes me kind of unhappy—or you're a cop. Which is it, Henry Larson?"

"Cop," he answered stiffly, his scowl deepening.

"Badge?" she returned, holding out her hand.

Reaching into an inside jacket pocket, he pulled it out and handed it to her. "Scotland Yard," she said easily, as if she'd expected exactly that. *Great.* "So, Inspector Larson, what are you doing pretending to be a museum curator?"

"We should sit down," he said, still looking glum that she'd figured him out. "And put on some tea. This might take a bit of time."

Chapter 3

Thursday, 8:12 a.m.

Richard slowed his classic '61 Jaguar as he passed three delivery trucks and four police cars heading up the long slope to Rawley Park. He downshifted, aiming for the section of road past the next curve where he could turn around.

The idea of leaving Samantha alone with truckloads of precious gems amused him. A half dozen or more police officers, though, didn't seem nearly as funny. He didn't know about all of the robberies she'd pulled, but he knew enough to be deeply worried whenever she and law enforcement officials were in the same vicinity.

As he reached the spot where the road widened, he pulled over and stopped. Why the devil he hadn't realized that the jewels would have a police escort, he had no idea, but if he went back now, Samantha would know that he'd done so to keep an eye either on her or over her. She hated hovering as much as he did.

"Bloody hell," he muttered, and pulled out his cell

phone. Swiftly he dialed the estate security office number.

"Craigson," came his security chief's professional voice.

"It's Addison."

"Yes, sir. What may I do for you?" the soft Scottish brogue returned.

"Just a small favor," Richard said, frowning into his rearview mirror. "If, ah, Miss Jellicoe at any time today appears to be in some . . . difficulty, please call me at once at this number."

"Is there anything in particular I should be looking out for, sir?"

Richard hesitated. He liked Craigson, and obviously Samantha did as well, or she never would have hired him, much less put him in charge of overall estate security. They seemed to have a shorthand for discussing things, but Rick had no idea how much the Scot knew of her past. And the fewer people who knew of her Achilles' heel, the better. "No, nothing in particular," he said slowly. "I can almost guarantee that you'll know it if you see it."

"Very well, sir. I'll take care of it."

"Thank you, Craigson. Ta."

He hung up and stuffed the phone back into his pocket. Samantha had several times told him that he had knight-in-shining-armor instincts, and every one of them told him to turn around and go back. It wasn't that he didn't trust her; he didn't trust the people around her. But then he would be implying that she couldn't take care of herself, and he wanted to have sex tonight. Spending the evening fighting would be counterproductive.

With a last glance behind him he put the Jag back in gear and pulled again onto the road heading toward

London. If he'd learned anything by now it was that Samantha Elizabeth Jellicoe could take care of just about any odd thing thrown at her. And he had a meeting he needed to attend if he didn't want to lose out on the Blackpool waterfront redevelopment project.

An hour later, just short of the A-1, something popped. Loudly. The Jaguar lurched to the right, nearly sideswiping a lorry. "Shit," Richard muttered, hauling the wheel back purely by brute force. Pumping the brakes, he managed to slide to a stop at the side of the road.

Behind him, most of a tire bounced and skidded along the highway while traffic obliterated it. He blew out his breath, shoved the Jag into park, and opened his door. The right front hubcap and tire were gone, the wheel dug four inches into the soft mud. Bloody wonderful.

Leaning against the hood, he pulled out his cell phone to call Sarah in his London office. As he hit the speed dial, a flock of pigeons swooped in from somewhere behind him. One of them apparently mistook him for a telephone pole and tried to land on his head. Cursing, he batted at it—and the cell phone flew out of his hand.

It landed on the highway and was promptly flattened by a sedan. For a second he just looked at it. As Sam would say, unbefuckinlievable. She in fact would probably find it hilarious that he, one of the wealthiest, most powerful men in the world, was stuck by the side of the road in a classic car without automated roadside assistance and being attacked by pigeons. He, however, had a meeting to get to.

Blowing out his breath, he pulled off his jacket and tossed it onto the passenger seat. As he did so, the velvet bag he'd placed in one pocket spilled onto the floor. The bag containing a very large and supposedly cursed blue diamond that had once belonged to his great-great-grandmother.

"There is no such thing as a bloody cursed diamond," he muttered, leaning over to pick it up and shove it back into an inside pocket. Then he popped the boot and pulled out the jack and spare tire.

Squatting on the muddy ground, he found a flat rock to place under the jack and went to work. A few minutes later a breakdown lorry came up behind him, and he straightened, stifling the urge to whip out his wallet and offer the driver every pound in it just for stopping. "Good morning," he said.

"Morning. Got a flat, eh?"

"A blowout. Did someone call you?"

The beefy fellow nodded. "Dispatcher radioed and said some git called to say that Rick Addison himself was stuck on the side of the road in his Jag. You'd be Rick Addison, then?"

"That's me."

"You're a wealthy bugger, ain't you?"

Surreptitiously Richard tightened his grip on the box spanner. "I am." Hopefully most people had learned by now that rich or not, he wasn't an easy mark. Far from it. If it came to it, the illegal Glock in his glove box could back him up on that.

"I was gonna say something about your choice in cars, but since it was the tire and since the car's a 1961 E-type, I guess that won't work."

"At this point, you can insult any part of the car you feel like."

The fellow snorted and offered his hand. "I'm Jardin. Angus Jardin."

Richard shook hands with him. "Good to meet you, Mr. Jardin."

"Ha. Angus suits me just fine. You want a tire change or a tow?"

"The wheel rim's bent, so I'm not sure we can change the tire."

"A tow it is. I'll pull around in front of you."

By the time Angus had the Jaguar hooked up to his lorry, Richard was already twenty minutes late for the Blackpool meeting, with another twenty minutes or so of road between it and him. He checked his watch again as he sat beside his rescuer in the breakdown lorry. "You wouldn't happen to have a cell phone, would you?"

"Here you go," Angus returned, pulling his phone out from under a scattering of papers on the seat between them and handing it over.

"My thanks." Rick dialed his secretary. "Sarah, it's Rick. I had a flat, and I'm just pulling onto the A-1."

"Sir, I've been trying to call you. The—"

"My cell phone met with an accident. Has Allenbeck contacted you?"

"Yes, sir. He . . . wasn't happy."

Fuck. "What did he say?"

"That if you can't manage to arrive for a meeting on time, he doesn't want you trying to meet construction deadlines for an entire city. There was profanity, but I won't—"

"Not necessary. I'm fairly familiar with Allenbeck's colorful expletives. Give me the address and phone number again, will you? I had it on my phone, but that's gone."

She read off the information, and he jotted it down on the back of an envelope. That done, he closed the phone and handed it back to Angus. If this meeting had been with practically anyone else in the world, they probably would have either delayed beginning it or sent out a search party to join him wherever he happened to be. But not Joseph Allenbeck, the pompous little rooster.

"Trouble, m'lord?"

Richard rolled his shoulders. "As usual." He eyed the driver. "You know, if you'll agree to drive me to this address in Westminster, I'll *give* you that Jaguar."

Angus laughed, a loud, unpleasant sound reminiscent of bears fighting. "You give me thirty quid and let me take your Jag to my brother's garage, and I'll drive you to Westminster and call us even."

"That is a deal."

Samantha leaned against one of the few sections of bare wall inside the exhibit room and watched the flow and sparkle of precious jewels all around her. Yesterday, even this morning, she'd been excited and a little nervous about helping to look after a very mobile fortune. Now, though, her enthusiasm had pretty much been squashed flat as a pancake.

She thought about calling her former fence and current business partner to complain about the general suckiness of life, but Walter "Stoney" Barstone was holding down the fort at their security office in Palm Beach. If she started bitching to him without at least giving Rick a chance to get his ear chewed first, he would only point out that in the four months since they'd opened the office, she'd spent more time out of town than in it.

As for Rick, not only was he in a meeting, but he wasn't answering his damn cell phone, which she knew because she'd called it four times. Four calls in two hours was pushing it—five would make her a resident of pityville or stalkytown. *Just deal, Sam*, she told herself.

She knew enough to watch and wait until the players around her showed more of their cards.

Her cell phone rang, not in one of the familiar tunes she'd assigned her various friends and family. Giving an apologetic wince to the museum people around her, she flipped open the phone and headed past one of the armed bobbies guarding the door.

"*Hola*," she said.

"Hello, sweetheart," Rick's voice returned.

Even through the phone she could tell that he was unhappy about something. *Join the club, bub.* "Where are you calling from?"

"The lobby of the Mandarin Oriental," he said. "I'm having lunch and waiting to have a new cellular and a rental car delivered."

"Ah. What happened to your old stuff?"

"A Volvo ran over my phone."

"And the Jag?"

"It blew a tire."

She took a breath, the sudden sharp worry that squirreled down her spine surprising and scaring her. "Are you okay, Rick?"

"Safe as houses. I met a very nice breakdown driver named Angus, and now I'm trying to charm bloody Joseph Allenbeck into accepting vehicle failure as a legitimate reason for being tardy to a meeting."

"So you've had a good day, too."

This time he paused. "You haven't jumped into any mystery or mayhem without me, have you?"

"No more than I usually do."

"Care to explain that, Samantha?"

"Not over the phone while you're standing in the lobby of the Mandarin Oriental."

"Right." For a moment he was so quiet that she

could hear the concierge calling for a limousine in the background.

"Rick?"

"Will you be all right for the next forty minutes or so?"

She frowned at her phone. Since he was two hours away, it seemed like kind of an odd question. Then it dawned on her. "Finish your meeting," she said. "Don't you dare start helicoptering around the countryside just to hold my hand."

"You're certain."

"I'm certain. We'll exchange war stories tonight. And Rick?"

"Yes, love?"

"Are you starting to believe that diamond curse thing yet? Because I totally have the wiggins."

She heard his sigh. "Don't blame it on an old rock. I think true bad luck for us, Yank, can be and has been so much worse than this."

"That's what you think," she muttered.

"Beg pardon?"

"Nothing. I'll see you tonight. Be careful, Rick."

"I will."

Slowly she flipped the phone closed again. The conversation with Rick made her feel a little better in that at least she knew he was okay. It also made a couple of other things clear. He would always come riding to her rescue, ready to pluck her out of danger—or more likely, to jump in with her. In this instance, though, plucking and jumping wasn't exactly what she needed. No, today she had to admit that old friends would be more helpful than new ones.

With a sigh she opened the phone again and hit speed dial number two.

Four rings later the line clicked open. "Your damn clothes had better be on fire, Sam, because it's . . . it's five twenty-one in the morning here."

"Just be glad I didn't call you four hours ago when I wanted to," she returned, automatically relaxing a fraction at the sound of Stoney's voice. He sounded exactly like who he was—a big black man with a deep streak of poetry running through him, and an even deeper streak of larceny combined with Mother Hubbard alongside that.

"If you'd called me then, I still would have been awake."

"Oh. Are you still seeing Kim, the real estate lady?"

"If that's why you're calling me I'm going to hang up and yank you out of my damn Rolodex."

"Okay, okay. Can you talk business?"

She could almost hear him coming to attention. "Hold on."

Sam grinned. "Oh, my God! She's totally over there with you, isn't she?"

"For your information, nosey, I'm at her place. Now what's up?"

"You still have some contacts over here, right?"

"A few. People tend not to answer my calls when they find out I'm a partner in Jellicoe Security."

That reminded her that she still needed a better name for her business. One thing at a time. "See if you can run down anybody who might be trying to bag a big profit with a traveling precious gems exhibit, will you?"

"Would that be *your* exhibit, honey?"

"It would. Scotland Yard got a tip that we might get hit. I'm supposed to step back and let the experts handle it."

He snorted. "If they only knew. What does Lord Big Wallet say about this?"

"He doesn't know yet. And I thought you two were allies now."

"Only when it comes to backing up your fanny. I'm going back to bed now. Thanks to you she's probably awake and now I'll have to be studly again."

"Oh, gross. Don't be telling me shit like that."

"Like I want to hear about you and the English muffin. 'Bye, sweetie."

" 'Bye, Stoney."

She hung up. Okay, she had help on the case now, so probably the smartest thing to do would be to go back in and make sure everything was getting set up according to plan and that none of the white hats had fiddled with any of the sensors or cameras. It was a sad day when you couldn't even trust the good guys anymore.

As she walked back inside the main exhibit room, one of the bobbies was arguing with one of her guys, Hervey, about who had the authority to let whom into the building. "Hey," she snapped, "today you both agree that they get in, or they don't. Clear?"

"As glass, ma'am," Hervey returned, practically saluting.

The bobby nodded; apparently he thought that looked cooler. Swearing under her breath, Samantha made her way through the displays and safe boxes until she found Larson on a ladder beside one of her cameras.

"That's for authorized personnel only, Mr. Assistant to the Assistant Curator," she commented, just barely resisting the urge to yank him down to the floor.

He stepped down. "Please, Miss Jellicoe," he said in a low voice, taking her arm and leading her to a less crowded corner, "I've taken you into my confidence for convenience's sake. As far as all but the senior museum personnel know, I am a new appointee to this position. The officers know they're to cooperate with me, and that's all."

"Convenience, my ass. I found you out," Samantha said, pulling her arm free. Nobody grabbed her, except maybe for Rick. But no cops. Ever. "So stop fooling with the security equipment like it's part of your job. The V & A asked for this location, and they asked for me to oversee the venue's safety. If you want to blow your own damned cover, then keep it up."

He frowned, the expression joining his eyebrows together in one long, shaggy line. "Listen, Miss Jellicoe, I tried to be diplomatic, but let's not fool ourselves. The museum asked to use Lord Rawley's land, and he agreed on the condition that his girlfriend, a cat burglar's daughter, be included. I know that with Lord Rawley's help you've had a few lucky breaks, but I am a professional. The V & A and Scotland Yard want me here. You go on and make certain your lights are plugged in, and let me do what I'm best at."

Which was being an idiot, apparently. She bit that comment back. Okay, so what if, with the possible exception of her dad, she'd probably bagged more loot than any cat alive or dead. She wasn't about to tell Inspector Henry Larson that. And if somebody did mean to hit the place, it would definitely take some of the heat off her if he took the credit for shutting them down, *or* for letting them get away with it—except that she wasn't going to let that happen. Not for anything.

Everything looked fairly normal when Richard drove up past his guarded gates in the Jag, repaired courtesy of Jardin's Auto Repair. Appearances, however, as he'd learned upon meeting Samantha, could be extremely deceiving.

He stopped the car at the front of the house and topped the shallow granite steps as his white-haired butler pulled open the front door. "Sykes. Have Ernest put up the car, will you? And check the tires and whatever else he can think of."

"Yes, sir. Dinner will be ready in twenty minutes. And Miss Sam is in the cellar."

"Thank you."

He descended the stairs at the back of the house. Once he reached the large cellar he first headed through the door on the right and into the temperature-controlled room beyond. A bottle of wine tonight seemed like a very good idea. The door to the left was closed, as well. It had been since Samantha had agreed to manage the security for the gems exhibit. He punched in the code and pulled the door open.

She sat beside Craigson, her eyes on the monitors lining the back wall and her back to him. "Greetings, Lord Rawley," she said, waving over her shoulder. "I thought you were bringing a rental car home."

"Jardin's Auto Repair apparently keeps Jaguar parts in stock," he returned, not surprised that she'd watched his approach on camera. They had agreed that with the exception of the south gallery wing the interior of the house be void of security cameras. They each had their own reasons for wanting it, but they both valued their privacy.

She stood, stretching her back, and joined him by the door. "How was the rest of your day, my English muffin?"

He distinctly heard Craigson stifle a chuckle. Wordlessly Richard took her hand and pulled her into the main part of the cellar, closing the security door behind them. Then he drew her up against him, leaned down, and kissed her softly on the mouth. "Hi," he said, pulling away a few inches to gaze into her sharp green eyes.

"Hi," she breathed back, sliding an arm around his waist and the other over his shoulder.

" 'English muffin,' " he repeated, shifting his kisses to the top of her head. "That's one of Walter's. You've been talking to him, then? About whatever happened today that *we* couldn't discuss over the phone, I presume?"

She fisted her hand and cuffed him on the shoulder. "I said we couldn't discuss it with you standing in the middle of the Mandarin Oriental lobby. We can definitely talk about it now, unless you're too busy being tall, dark, and jealous."

"I'm not jealous," he lied. "It's just that generally your conversations with Walter in lieu of me signify trouble in the offing." And he *was* jealous, if only because Walter Barstone kept her connected to a past that still held plenty of temptations for her—and a great many more dangers.

"Well, I can't argue with you and your multisyllabic British logic this time."

Eight months of practice kept his muscles from tensing, though nothing could prevent the heady combination of worry and arousal that curled down his spine. "I'm listening."

"First let's crack open that bottle of"—she twisted his wrist to look—"Merlot and adjourn to the sitting room, my dear."

She didn't seem overly concerned about anything,

though adept as he'd become at reading her moods she could still on occasion surprise him. Shifting to tuck her against his side, he headed them back up the stairs to the main part of the house.

The sitting room sat on the ground floor directly adjacent to the south wing, and the wide floor-length windows opened onto a terrace that overlooked the lake at the rear of the house. She walked straight through to the terrace, while he paused to sweep up two glasses and a corkscrew.

Samantha had taken a seat at one of the small bistro-style tables on the stone terrace, and she pulled out the chair beside her for him as he set down the bottle and glasses. "Have I mentioned that I like this place?" she asked absently, her gaze on a pair of swans meandering across the water.

"Once or twice." He studied her profile in the waning daylight. Nine years younger than he was or not, she matched him in every way possible. After eight months together, he couldn't imagine being without her. "My ancestors had good taste, building here."

She stirred, half facing him. "Speaking of your ancestors, did you have time to get the diamond appraised?"

"I did. The Nightshade Diamond is one hundred sixty-nine carats, surrounded by thirteen diamonds of thirteen carats each. On the open market, it's presently worth approximately sixteen million dollars, American."

"Wow." She gave a low whistle. "Do you still have it with you?"

He pulled the velvet bag from his pocket and held it out to her. Samantha took it with her fingertips and immediately set it on the table between them, then wiped her hands off on her jeans.

"Sam, it's not bad luck," he commented, beginning to feel a little exasperated at her relentless insistence on superstition.

"Mm-hm. Thirteen diamonds of thirteen carats, and big blue's one hundred sixty-nine carats. That's thirteen times thirteen, by the way."

"Fine. I was going to give it to you for real, but have it your way."

"Fine. I don't want your stupid cursed diamond. Just touching it this morning already caused me enough trouble, thank you very much."

And again she hadn't panicked at the hypothetical gift of a diamond. Richard set that thought aside for later consideration. "All right, unbelt," he said, reaching for the bottle and corkscrew.

"That means talk, right? Not get naked? Because it's getting a little chilly out here."

"You know what it means. Stop stalling." He twisted the corkscrew in and pulled.

"Armand Montgomery's replacement showed up with the gems today. Henry Larson."

"The assistant's assistant, as I believe you referred to him."

"Yep. AKA Inspector Henry Larson of Scotland Yard, Crime Prevention Unit. AKA, the guy currently staying in the Aquitaine Room upstairs."

"Bloody—"

The cork came free, taking the top of the bottle with it. Red wine splashed out over his leg, across the table, and liberally on Samantha's pale yellow blouse.

"Shit," he muttered, setting the bottle down as Sam shot to her feet.

"See?" she said with an amused snort, wiping at her front. "Bad luck."

"Bad bottle-making." The wine had missed the velvet bag, but he nudged it farther away, just in case. "Come on, let's get cleaned up. And tell me more about Henry Larson. Specifically why the devil he's staying in my house."

Chapter 4

Thursday, 9:45 p.m.

"If Scotland Yard wants to run an investiga-tion, then let them run it. I've been wanting to do some fishing up at Maldoney in Scotland, anyway."

"I knew you were going to say that," Samantha returned, grabbing the bowl of popcorn from him and plunking herself down on the couch. "And what am I supposed to do while you're catching bass at your moldy old castle?"

"It's not moldy, and it's trout."

"I don't care what kind of fish it is." She flipped on the DVD player and dimmed the lights. "I'm not going anywhere."

Scowling, he sat beside her. "You're still in the process of starting up a business, which will see increased revenue based on your success. If the Yard stomps all over your 'gig,' as you call it, and the exhibit gets robbed anyway, that hurts *your* credibility. And therefore your future in your new-chosen line of work."

"If it goes south I could always snatch up what's left of the jewels and go on the lam. A couple million would replenish the retirement fund I've been dipping into to go straight."

"When I go to hospital with chronic high blood pressure, I'm going to tell the doctor it's your fault." He reached over, sliding an arm around her shoulder and digging into the popcorn bowl with his free hand.

She smiled, sinking back against his side. He liked to be in physical contact with her, and skittish as she'd been at first, at the moment she couldn't see a thing in the world wrong with it. Rick Addison had always felt so . . . safe, and so exciting at the same time. She could probably spend a lifetime figuring him out, if one of them didn't kill the other before then.

But at least this time he was worried about her reputation in the security and stolen items retrieval business and not about whether she'd get blamed if something went missing. And he hadn't freaked out when she joked about going crooked again. Wow. Either he was getting soft or she was losing her touch.

On the plasma screen, Godzilla roared. "This is the black and white one?" Rick asked. "With Raymond Burr? We've watched this seventy-two times."

"We have not. And this is the original original. Before the U.S. distributor edited in Burr. Back when it was called *Gojira*. And sorry, it's subtitled."

"Have you seen it before?"

"I watched it a couple of weeks ago while you were in Paris."

"So this is for my benefit."

"You betcha. By the time I'm finished with you, you'll know all the Godzilla monsters from Gigan to Destroyah."

"Good thing I've been taking notes, then."

In all fairness, while he seemed to think her fascination with Godzilla was pretty funny, he watched most of them alongside her. Probably because she hadn't lodged any complaints against his Dirk Bogarde WWII movie collection. Guys and their heavy artillery. Building-stomping aside, she actually preferred a little more finesse, herself. The basic Grants—Cary and Hugh—now, they could get the old ticker going.

"Do you have any idea who might go after the gems?" Rick asked abruptly.

So much for *Gojira* tonight. "You have a very larcenous mind."

The muscles of the arm he had draped over her shoulders tensed a little. She'd been waiting for that. He'd been amazingly easygoing throughout her explanation of Larson's presence, and dinner had come and gone without a single thing being punched, kicked, or thrown. Now, however, he apparently wanted the details. She sighed.

"Okay, okay. Stoney's trying to get some info, but his contacts aren't as forthcoming as they used to be. There are probably three dozen guys and gals who think they could pull this kind of thing off, and maybe a quarter of them actually could. That was before I took over the security here, though."

"So nobody can get past your setup?"

She shrugged. "I could, but I know all the wiring schematics. As for anybody else, I'm not so sure."

"Then we have nothing to worry about. I suppose Scotland Yard can sniff around all they want, as long as they're not sniffing after you. Fishing can wait until autumn."

"Except that just because *I* know they'd never pull it off doesn't mean nobody else will give it a try."

"Okay. Fishing is on again."

She elbowed him in the gut. "I'm not bailing on the exhibit, and you know it. Like you said, I'm at the beginning of a new business. And whether I'm handling security for valuables or recovering stolen ones, I have a reputation to maintain."

"That's what I'm talking a—"

"Not just with potential clients. With the guys who might think it would be fun to show up Sam Jellicoe. The ones I used to be in competition with, the ones who couldn't handle the jobs that I could. If those guys make me look bad, I may as well become a professional trout fisherwoman, because anybody would be stupid to hire me to protect anything."

"I'd still hire you."

She glared up at him. "Oh, gee whiz, thanks."

"Mm-hm. You're welcome."

Rick took the bowl of popcorn from her and set it on the table. Then he pulled her legs across his and leaned over to kiss her. One hand slid up the thighs of her jeans, dipping between them and pressing.

Arousal spun down her spine. Mm, this was more like it. Tomorrow was the local press preview and the last rehearsal, and then the exhibit opened on Saturday. Rick had a way of focusing her tension and releasing it that no one else had ever been able to manage. There was good sex, there was great sex, and then there was Rick Addison sex.

He pushed her back flat along the couch, following her down and sliding his hands up beneath her T-shirt. This time when he kissed her, their tongues danced. Samantha yanked the loose open shirt he wore down his arms, and he released her long enough to shrug out of it.

"You could go to Scotland without me, if you want to stay clear of this," she said in a rush, arching her back as he pushed her bra up and flicked his tongue across one nipple, then the other.

"Stuff that," he said, his voice muffled against her tits.

His voice reverberated and tickled into her chest. "Christ," she muttered, digging her fingers into his black hair. "But the exhibit's going to be here for four weeks, stud muffin. I'm going to be pretty busy anyway, so—"

"Forget it." He unzipped her jeans and slipped his hand down beneath her panties. "I know how it's going to be. You, watching over all those shiny rocks all day and not being allowed to touch any of them. And I'll be here to sympathize with your frustration."

She reached one hand down to cup the considerable bulge at the crotch of his trousers. "Speaking of rocks," she murmured, gently squeezing.

He moaned. "And they're both for you."

Samantha chuckled breathlessly. "Hey, that reminds me, where's the cursed one?"

"In the safe upstairs." He began tugging her pants down.

She lifted her hips, wriggling to hurry the naked part of the evening. "Good. I don't want anything important falling off of you."

With a snort, Rick finished removing her pants and underwear, then straightened to pull off his own gray T-shirt and unzip the jeans he'd donned after the wine incident. "No, we wouldn't want that."

Eight months together, and she still went wet when he looked at her sideways. In moments of sanity it occurred to her that an art-collecting billionaire and a semi-retired cat burglar with over forty robberies for which she could still be arrested probably weren't the wisest combination. But he'd made his way into her heart so thoroughly that she couldn't imagine—didn't want to imagine—the scenario that would send them on their separate ways. Whatever it was, she was certain it would be her fault; she knew she needed to stay on the right side of the law, but she knew way too many people who thought otherwise.

She wrestled her shirt and bra onto the floor, and wrapped her hands around his shoulders as he settled over her and slowly, steadily, entered her. This was where everything worked, where whatever arguments or differences they had could just melt away. This was where they fit. Perfectly.

Rick kissed her, the motions of his tongue matching the thrust of his hips. In the background, somebody screamed something in Japanese about a giant monster, and Godzilla roared. Mm, even with a probable burglary attempt on her watch and a cursed diamond upstairs, life was good.

Samantha tightened and came, fast and hard. "There you go," Rick murmured in her ear. "I've been waiting for that all day."

She locked her ankles around his hips. "Your turn now, bucko," she gasped, clenching around him.

"Jesus." His pace increased, he roared, Godzilla roared, and he sank down over her, shaking.

Their hearts pounded against one another. He was heavy, six-foot-two and all lean muscle, but she liked the weight. Her white knight, ready to slay dragons and black hats whenever the situation called for it.

Rick lifted his head. "So much for the appetizer," he

said, grinning as he kissed the tip of her nose. "Let's take the main course upstairs, shall we?"

"Hot damn."

Richard held the diamond up by its delicate gold clasp. He'd always considered Connoll Addison to be an intelligent man—after all, he was the one who'd begun the expansion of the Addison collection, now considered one of the finest, if not *the* finest, privately owned art and antiques collections in the world.

Stuffing a very rare diamond in a wall, then, didn't quite seem Connoll's style. Maybe he'd done it to appease his overly superstitious new bride, Evangeline. But she'd had fine taste herself, and from everything he'd heard and read had been a fair and equal partner in the marriage. Their three children, two sons and a daughter, had been of sound mind and body, and Rick couldn't think of a reason why neither of the parents would tell any of the children about the heirloom in the wall.

His new cell phone rang, and he dropped the diamond back into its bag. "Addison."

"Good morning, sir," Sarah's voice came.

"You don't sound particularly pleased," he noted, wiggling his fingers at Samantha as she emerged, naked but for a damp towel, from the bathroom.

"I just heard from Mr. Allenbeck. They've decided to go with Pellmore Construction, sir."

Fuck. "Thank you for telling me. Anything else on the agenda this morning?"

"John Stillwell called from Canada. He says the Montreal city council is being surprisingly cooperative, and he'll e-mail you the details today."

Well, that figured. The Quebec project looked to be time-consuming and not nearly as profitable as the Blackpool one. The perils of sending a new and enthusiastic assistant, though, were that he would be doing his best to impress the boss. "I'll look for it. And Sarah?"

"Yes, sir?"

"I'm expecting that package from Tom Donner today. If it arrives, let me know, and have it forwarded to me here. I'll take a look at it over the weekend."

"I'll see to it."

"Cheers."

He closed the phone and turned in time to see Samantha's terry-clothed backside disappearing back into the bathroom. Hm. Swiftly he grabbed up the velvet bag and stuffed it into the pocket of the jacket she would be wearing for the press preview today. Maybe that would convince her how silly she was being—especially since he wanted her to have the diamond. *His* diamond.

"Are you certain you don't mind me hanging about for the preview today?" he asked, leaning into the doorway.

She finished fastening her bra. "I would have told you to get lost if I didn't want you here. And I heard the Donner word a minute ago. What's he doing now, trying to get me permanently deported?"

Richard chuckled. If he didn't know that Sam and Tom admired one another far more than either would ever admit, he would have been less amused. But his closest friend and attorney had proved several times that he would take steps out of his comfort zone to see that Samantha remained safe, and so he would tolerate the public antagonism. "It's some property tax reports. I'd have John handle them, but he's doing my bidding in Canada."

"You and your minions." She turned around and kissed him. "And yes, come to the press preview. That way if anything goes wrong, I can throw you to the paparazzi while I make my escape." She faced the mirror again, reaching for her eyeliner. "You didn't get the Blackpool gig, did you?"

"No. Though after yesterday, I can't say I'm that disappointed to miss out on working with Allenbeck. The man's a twit."

"I love when you get all British."

He lifted an eyebrow. "I'm always all British."

God, she looked so lovely, her hair still hanging damply around her face as she critically eyed her application of what she called her war paint. Before he'd married and after he'd discovered his former wife, Patricia, in bed with his former college roommate, he'd done his share of dating—actresses and models, mostly, because they were used to the cameras and press that seemed to follow him everywhere. And then he'd met Samantha. She'd been in his Palm Beach house, halfway to stealing a priceless stone tablet that had come from Troy. And she'd ended up saving his life when his security guard accidently set off a bomb planted by another thief.

Insanity, all of it, and at the end they'd emerged together. He wanted them to stay that way. And so he'd learned to be patient, to treat their relationship with far more care than he did any business partnership. So far it was working, but he still had no idea what she would do if and when he decided to take the next step with her.

"What?" she asked, eyeing him in the mirror.

He shook himself. "What what?"

"You're smiling. That scares me."

Richard laughed. "Nothing scares you. I'm just proud of you. You've earned the responsibility the V & A's giving you today."

"Save a few priceless paintings from being stolen from the Metropolitan Museum of Art, and suddenly all the museums want you to be their lunch buddy."

"So you know not to listen to the tripe being shoveled by our houseguest. I had nothing to do with your being asked to install and supervise security for the exhibit."

"I intend to listen to very little coming from Inspector Henry Larson, but thanks."

"You're welcome. I suppose I should go introduce myself to him."

"Go ahead. I'll be down in a few minutes. Just don't punch him, Rick; I want to do that."

He grinned as he left the bathroom and the master suite. "No promises, my love."

Henry Larson was already downstairs in the traditional breakfast room when Richard made his way inside. His chef, Jean-Pierre Montagne, was the third of his cooks to be charmed by Samantha, as evidenced by the three separate piles of sugared strawberries on the sideboard and the champagne bucket filled with ice and chilled Diet Cokes. Larson had made liberal use of both selections, not a good sign for the inspector's continued well-being.

"Good morning," Richard said, selecting scrambled eggs and a pair of sausages to go with his tea. He'd take out one of the horses and go riding this afternoon to compensate. Maybe this time he could finally convince Sam to join him.

The inspector pushed back his chair and stood. "Good morning, my lord."

With a slant of his head, Richard indicated that Stilson, one of the downstairs housekeepers, should leave the room. "Addison, if you please," he said aloud. Generally he preferred Rick, but this fellow was making some problems for him. "And you must be Mr. Larson from the Yard."

"Oh, Miss Jellicoe told you, then?"

"We don't keep secrets. I would appreciate a few more details, however."

"Of course. I'm with the Crime Prevention Unit of the Yard, Mr. Addison. Three days ago we received a tip that someone might attempt to hit the exhibit while it's here at Rawley Park. So my superiors assigned me to replace Mr. Montgomery in order to keep an eye on things."

"But this exhibit's been traveling through England and Scotland for the past two months. Why here and now?"

"We think it's because of your . . . of Miss Jellicoe."

Richard snapped into a frown, any amusement gone. "If you're implying that Miss Jellicoe is doing anything nefarious, I suggest you leave and return with a proper warrant and personnel to begin an investigation. You are no longer welcome here under my—"

"No, no, no, sir," the inspector stammered. "I misspoke. What I meant was that Miss Jellicoe's father, Martin Jellicoe, was a fairly infamous cat burglar. Somebody might get the idea that Miss Jellicoe's soft on that sort of thing."

"And that would be based on her helping to uncover an international art theft ring eight months ago? Or perhaps the investigation she did into Charles Kunz's death, resulting in the arrest of both of his children for murder, theft, and attempting to defraud?" He could mention the Met job, too, but only a select few knew she'd had any part in that.

"Or," Larson continued hurriedly, "or, it might be that somebody thinks they'll make a name for themselves if they can get past a Jellicoe. Her father being so famous in those circles."

"Ah. I see. Very well. But I suggest you not misspeak regarding Miss Jellicoe in my presence again."

"No, sir. I will not."

"Good."

Samantha took that moment to stroll into the room. Her timing was so perfect that he had no doubt she'd been standing outside the door listening. When she winked at him from behind the inspector's back, he knew it for certain.

"Hello, Mr. Larson. All ready for our big day today?" she asked, making a beeline to the sodas.

"I believe so, Miss Jellicoe."

"Good. Because the press will be asking you all sorts of questions about the different gemstones. Especially the cursed ones, or the ones somebody was wearing when they got beheaded."

"I'll defer those questions to the museum staff," he said stiffly.

"That makes sense. And don't forget I want to see your authorization from Scotland Yard in writing before I give you today's access codes."

"It'll be here before the press arrives."

"I hope so, for your sake." Selecting strawberries and toast, she took the seat beside Richard.

For a second Rick felt guilty that he'd put the diamond in her pocket without telling her, because he would have hell to pay if she found it before or during the outing with the press. She was giving hell to Larson right now with no other ill effects, though, and if they made it until afterward, it would be worth the risk to prove to her that this superstitious nonsense was just that—nonsense. And that owning a diamond didn't spell doom.

Chapter 5

Friday, 9:58 a.m.

Press cars and television vans were already lined up outside the main estate gates by the time Samantha and Larson walked through the garden to the old stable. The V & A crew had assembled from the hotel down the road where they'd been staying, and her security team had been doing patrols since the gems arrived yesterday.

Larson hit the day's new security code and pulled open the door. Samantha helped her guys roll the metal detectors out from the doorframes and set up the purse-check tables. Privately, as both a former thief and a citizen of the world, she hated the idea of opening her private possessions for some stranger's perusal, but neither did she have any intention of letting anybody in with so much as a pocket knife. She'd done jobs with just that much equipment.

The museum gang took up their information stations throughout the large room, while the remaining three manned the small gift shop at the far end. So far, so good. She lifted her walkie-talkie. "How do we look, Craigson?" she asked.

"We're good, Sam," he replied in his Scottish brogue. "One hundred percent on cameras and sensors."

"Okay. Have Hervey open the gates."

"I'd like one of those walkies," Larson said, coming up beside her.

"It's my name on the contract, Larson," she returned. "I'll work the security with my team. If you want a radio, get your own guys to order around. Or hold drills for the museum personnel. You're supposed to be their boss."

"I don't want to have to report your lack of cooperation to my superiors, Miss Jellicoe."

"I gave you the security codes on your superiors' say-so, Larson. That's it. If anything goes hinky, then we'll talk. Until then, you don't get a walkie-talkie."

His lips tightened. "I could order you to hand one over."

"Go ahead." She folded her arms across her chest. For once she hadn't done anything shady to precipitate the law showing up, and she wasn't about to let this guy walk all over her. She'd let him in the door, and that was already going to give her nightmares. Her, working with cops. Again.

"Give me a walkie-talkie."

"No."

"You have to."

Samantha narrowed her eyes. "You might have gotten a tip from some rat about a possible robbery here. You might have bullied or conned Armand Montgomery and the V & A into letting you step in here. But I know my job, and I know you're here because you told your boss you'd use your own time to do it. That sounds to me like you want really bad to impress somebody, and that your career is in the crapper."

He actually took a step backward. "I—"

"Now," she cut in before he could get started, "if you're actually here to keep an eye out for bad guys instead of to impress the gang at the Yard, that's fine. Hang out, eat my strawberries, drink my sodas. But this is *my* responsibility and it's my show. You're just the guy with the handcuffs and the shiny badge. Got it?"

A warm hand slipped around her upper arm. "Inspector, Samantha," Rick drawled. "Put on your happy faces, because you're about to make the evening news."

Without giving her or Larson a chance to comment, he steered her toward the door. As soon as they were out of close earshot of anybody else, Samantha yanked her arm free. "Stay the fuck out of my business, will you? For the—"

"Two things," he interrupted, putting on his placid professional face as he gazed toward the entrance. "First, things that affect you, affect me. So stop telling me to ignore that fact. Second, you live to a certain extent by virtue of your bravado. So do people like Inspector Larson. Tearing him down like you just did could be hazardous to his health. And by extension to ours, for as long as he's here. Try to keep in mind that you two want the same thing."

Samantha blew out her breath. "Yeah, fine, whatever. Smart-ass. I'm not apologizing."

"I didn't expect that you would." Before she could head out through the door, Rick took her free hand. "Good luck."

"Thanks." She shrugged, tugging him forward before pulling free again. "But luck's for schmucks."

Holding his hand would have been nice, but Larson obviously thought she'd gotten this job because of Rick rather than because she deserved it. She damn well wasn't going to give the press a jump-start to reaching the same conclusion.

Larson waited with Diane McCauley from the V & A just inside the entrance. He'd probably realized that if he went forward alone he would be faced with a lot of questions he couldn't answer. Samantha led the way around to the front of the building where the press waited. Holy crap, she hated this part—the publicity, her face in print and on TV. In her past life, that would have been a death sentence.

"Good morning," she said with a smile as they reached the herd of reporters. "I'm Sam Jellicoe, and I'm supplying the security for this exhibit. Sorry, but I'm not going to tell you about any of that. Instead, I'm happy to introduce Dr. Diane McCauley with the Victoria and Albert Museum, who's been traveling with the *All That Glitters* exhibit since its inception. Diane?"

Dr. McCauley stepped forward to explain the reasoning behind the exhibit and how it was determined which pieces should be included. Samantha moved out of the way as the museum thanked Rick for allowing them to use the beautiful Rawley Park location.

As soon as Samantha stopped beside Rick, cameras began clicking in earnest; apparently even after eight months the Addison-Jellicoe cohabitation was still big news. Bigger even than a ton of money in the form of precious gems.

"Hey, I have an idea," she muttered, nudging Rick's arm with her shoulder.

"Fishing in Scotland?"

"Donating the Nightshade Diamond to the exhibit. Nobody would be holding it or owning it, so nobody would have bad luck. Especially us."

"*I* would have bad luck, because you would have forced me to give away a priceless family heirloom because of a bloody superstition."

"Just wait until that safe of yours falls through the floor and kills Sykes or something."

"Technically, according to Connoll's note, since we've both seen it and have set it aside, we should have *good* luck now."

"Tell that to Sykes after he gets flattened. That thing was in a wall for two hundred years. It's probably going a little wacky with the evil mojo."

Diane finished her introduction and led the way to the entrance. The press filed through the metal detectors one by one, handing over cameras and bags for a quick inspection by her guys. Probably perfunctory, but if it got them to write a line about the exhibit's tight security, it would be worth it.

One of the photographers turned around to snap a picture of her, grinned, and handed his camera over for inspection. Samantha shifted from annoyed to alert in the space of one hard beat of her heart. *Shit. Shit, shit, shit.*

"Are you all right?" Rick asked, touching her arm. "You look—"

"You know how much I love having my picture taken," she improvised, shaking herself. "I'll get over it."

Okay, Rick was wrong about having good luck once they set the diamond aside, and she was right about the bad juju. And Henry Larson's stupid tip had been correct; someone was making plans to hit the exhibit. She just hadn't expected that it would be Bryce Shepherd.

How the hell had he gotten press credentials? Of course she could have done it, and easily. In fact, she would probably have approached this gig in exactly the same way—go in legitimately, at a time when photos would be allowed, and use the pictures to create a layout and pinpoint any weaknesses in security. Samantha took a breath, working to keep her expression the alert and calm one she'd been practicing all morning. That had been for the benefit of their guests, though now she had to convince Rick, too—at least until she figured out what was going on.

Bryce Shepherd. Dammit.

"I think I'll go mingle," she told Rick, "just to make sure nobody touches anything they shouldn't."

He nodded. "This is your moment, Sam. I'll join Larson and try to puff up his punctured ego a bit."

"Don't go overboard with that," she returned, because he would expect her to.

She left his side and strolled up to the entrance. The last of the press passed through, and with a quick word of thanks to her team, she skirted the detector to follow them in.

A quarter of the way through the exhibit she spotted him, leaning over a case of sapphires that showed their progression from raw form to exquisite piece of jewelry. She cleared her throat.

"Surprise," he murmured in his charming Irish brogue, his gaze still on the gems. "You've got some real beauties here."

"What the hell are you doing here?" she hissed.

He lifted his head, lanky blonde hair falling across his deep brown eyes. "Is that any way to say hello to an old friend, sweetheart?"

"Don't call me that."

"As pleases you, Sammi—though I know about doing that as well, don't I, now?"

It took everything she had to keep from looking over her shoulder for Rick. "Do you even have film in that thing?" she asked, indicating his professional-looking camera. "Or are you just here to bother me?"

"Ah, Sam, it's not always about you. Sometimes it's about some very fine jewelry. And I've gone digital—it's easier to crop out the parts you don't need. Like that rich fella, for instance."

"Just leave, Bryce. Otherwise things are going to get ugly."

Shepherd clucked his tongue. "If you tattle on me, darlin', I've a few tales I could tell about you."

"Not without taking yourself down."

"I don't mean any of our illegal feats, Sammi. I could have a nice little chat with your new fella about some of the windows we steamed up, though."

Fuck. "He'd squash you like a bug." She took a reluctant step closer. Bryce Shepherd hadn't lost an ounce of his looks or his charm in the last two years. His job description evidently hadn't changed, either, and he was on the short list of guys who might actually have a shot at making it through her gauntlet of security. "We parted on good terms, Bryce. Don't make me regret liking you."

"So you really have switched sides. Pity, that. But don't expect me to quit a score because you're guarding it. In fact, it might be fun to dance with you again— though I imagine we'll keep our clothes on this time."

She wasn't going to follow along just because he kept trying to make this personal. Well, it *was* personal, but not in the way he kept suggesting. "I'm better than you are," she said bluntly. "If you come back here again, I'll nail you. In the bad way, in case you were going to ask."

"Now, Sam, don't—"

"If you want these gems, hit 'em at their next stop. Otherwise, take a pass. I'm not warning you again."

He smiled that charming smile she remembered. Two years ago, he'd given her a great couple of weeks—the best she'd had as a thief. "I'm warned, then. Now you'd best move along, or people will think you're flirting with me. Unless you are, of course. In which case, I came here in a big white van with plenty of floor space."

Aggressive and sure of himself as he was, that was what had attracted her to him in the first place. It still did, partly. "Goodbye, Bryce," she said, turning her back and walking away.

"Cheers, Sam."

He hadn't added an "until we meet again" or a "see you soon," but she heard them anyway. Bryce Shepherd had come by today knowing she would see him. Intending that she would see him. He'd issued his challenge loud and clear, and she'd answered the same way.

So now it was just a question of when—and of whether she would tell Rick that her former lover was the black hat who was going to try to rob the exhibit.

Richard stood beside Inspector Larson at the fake diamond display. Larson was muttering something about instincts and being underappreciated, but Rick wasn't paying much attention to that.

Instead, he was watching Samantha talking with some bloke a dozen yards away. He couldn't hear what they were saying, but he was fairly adept at reading faces and body language. The fellow was good-looking, four or five years younger than himself. And he was poised forward, smiling, head tilting—interested.

As usual, Samantha was more difficult to read. The most he could tell was that she wasn't relaxed, and that she was standing very close to the man. From the press pass clipped to his pocket and the camera around his neck, he had authorization to be there. And he was the one who'd snapped the photo of Samantha outside.

The two of them finally parted company, Samantha walking over to a fairly uncrowded spot and lifting her walkie-talkie, while the fellow moved on to the next display. Richard glanced around. Half the press present seemed to be focused on him rather than the gems. *Bloody marvelous.* Press tended to know press, but the second he asked anyone for the name of the bloke who'd been talking with Samantha, the headline would be— *Jellicoe Takes Secret Lover; Addison Flips Out.*

That left him only one choice, because he was not going to leave without knowing why he suddenly felt so uneasy. Jealous, obsessed, whatever label he put on it, he'd learned the perils of letting Samantha get so much as a single step out in front of him.

"If you'll excuse me," he said to Inspector Larson, stepping away, "I need to mingle."

"Oh, of course, my l—Mr. Addison."

The second he emerged from the shadows, cameras and microphones surrounded him. This was getting ridiculous. Taking a breath, he gave his professional smile.

"Good morning. If you don't mind, I would very much prefer that the gems be the stars today. I'm merely a visitor, just as you are."

"But Mr. Addison, are you taking any extra security

precautions, knowing that the public will have access to Rawley Park for the next four weeks?"

"Miss Jellicoe has arranged the security; that is her expertise. I defer any questions to her."

"Haven't you discussed it?"

"Are you not speaking?"

"We are speaking, and we have discussed it," he countered, continuing to move along the line of displays, "and I defer any questions regarding security to her. Now, if you'll excuse me, I would like to see the rest of the exhibit."

"But Rick, the—"

"Excuse me," he repeated, gazing steadily at the reporter who'd begun the question.

She backed down. "Of course."

Continuing on his way, he rounded the rubies and caught up to the blonde man at the emeralds. "Gorgeous, aren't they?" he offered.

The fellow didn't look surprised. "Aye, they are," he said in a light brogue.

Richard stuck out his hand. "Rick Addison."

"Oh, I'm aware of that."

He wasn't offering any information in return. That seemed distinctly familiar. For a time he hadn't thought Samantha would ever tell him her last name. "Newspaper or magazine?" he pressed, indicating the camera.

"*Glasgow Daily.* Generally a political rag, but whether they print my photos or not, it was worth the drive just to see all of these beauties."

Richard narrowed his eyes a fraction. He knew bloody well when he was being stonewalled, and he didn't like it. Of course, there was a small chance that he was wrong, that this bloke was exactly what he claimed to be. "How do you know Samantha?" he asked. His instincts rarely let him down, and they were practically shouting at the moment.

"Ah, Miss Jellicoe. She is lovely, isn't she?"

Silently Richard counted to ten. This was so damned familiar that he might have been talking to Samantha during their first day of acquaintance. The question became, did he play along? Or did he let this bastard know that he'd been found out? "Yes, she is," he slowly agreed. "Why don't we step outside, and I'll give you a chance to take some photos the rest of the press won't get?"

"Are you propositioning me, Mr. Addison? Because I don't—"

"Rick," Samantha's sharp voice came, and she wrapped a hand hard around his arm. "May I speak to you for a minute?"

"Certainly." With a last, hard look at the other fellow, he allowed Samantha to lead him through the small gift shop and back out to the gravel parking lot.

"What the hell was that about?" she demanded.

"Why don't you tell me?"

"So I can't speak to anybody who has a dick anymore without you attacking? That is not going to work."

"Who is he?"

"Aren't you listening to me? I am not—"

He grabbed her arm, yanking her closer to him. "He's a thief. I got that much. I also got that you know him. So who is he? And don't play any fucking games with me, Sam."

"You need to calm down," she snapped back, trying to pull her arm free. He let her go, only because he knew that being trapped pushed her panic button. "Yes, he's a thief. Did you expect me to announce it in front of everyone? You might have given me five damn minutes. But no, you have to charge in like a fucking bull. I guess I should be grateful that you didn't knock anyone down."

"Don't—"

"Don't what?" she interrupted, staying right in his face. "Are you taking over, or is this still my gig? Because I seem to remember you saying that I'd earned it, and I deserved it. If you only meant that I could do this job until something actually happened, then you and I have a problem."

He blew out his breath. She had a point. A good one. He hadn't given her any time to do anything, and he had tried to take over. She'd been on the walkie-talkie. In all honesty, she might very well have told Craigson to keep an eye on their Irish visitor.

"Apologies," he said, gazing at the gravel.

For a long second she stayed silent. "Okay. I'm keeping an eye on him, and I warned him not to come back. He knows I'm on to him, so I doubt he'll be trying anything." She jabbed a finger into his chest. "And you so owe me a good old American hamburger. Deal?"

His life had changed a great deal over the past eight months. Before then, before Samantha, he never apologized for anything, never backed down, and certainly never admitted defeat. They matched, all right—so much so that if they both stayed on the offensive, they would probably kill one another. And so he backed down. "Deal."

She gave him her heart-stealing, quicksilver smile and kissed him on the cheek. "I'm going back in. Be calm; I've got this handled."

Still breathing hard, he watched her slip back in through the gift shop. It was only then that two things occurred to him: one, she had the diamond in her pocket, so perhaps he'd been too hasty about the no-such-thing-as-curses business. And two, she hadn't given him the Irish bloke's name.

Chapter 6

Friday, 4:32 p.m.

Samantha perched on the back of a chair in the security office. Munching on an apple, she flipped through her checklist. "Two more guys on horseback? I like it. At least for the first weekend."

Craigson made a note on his assignment sheet. "Well, after we had to run that television crew off the lakeshore, it occurred to me. We need more mobility in patrolling the grounds, or you'll have tourists in your bedroom."

She chuckled, not sure whether she was amused or annoyed. "That would put a crimp in things."

"Can I ask you a question, Sam?" he asked, tossing his clipboard onto the desk behind him.

"Sure."

"I have a bit of an . . . odd résumé. Why am I your second-in-command here?"

"Stoney vouched for you. He said after you got nicked and did your two years in the slam, you told him flat out that you were retiring. And you took a job as a wedding videographer, which pretty much tells me that you were serious about not getting back into the game."

"Aye. The life's addictive, but I like my blue skies without bars across them. And thank you for knowing the difference between retiring and *retiring*."

"Well, Jamie, I'm kind of going through the same thing, myself."

Movement on one of the monitors for an exterior camera caught her attention. Rick galloped up on his gray horse, Twist, and headed for the newer building that now housed the actual stable.

He'd been avoiding her all afternoon, and while her instinct for self-preservation told her to avoid him right back, she couldn't do it. This whole relationship thing continued to baffle her—not so much the rules and rituals, but the way her happiness had become tied so closely to the way *he* felt.

"Do you want me to call Hurst and see if he's got a couple of bonded guards who can ride?" Craigson asked, following her gaze to the monitor.

"Yeah, thanks," she returned, standing. "And as soon as your night relief gets here, go home. Get some sleep. We've checked everything checkable."

"All right. Cheers, Sam. I'll see you in the morning."

Tossing the remains of her apple in the trash can, she headed upstairs and around the back of the house. She reached the stable just as Rick was leaving it, slapping his riding gloves in his hand. He stopped when he saw her, his jaw working before he assumed his infamous don't-fuck-with-me expression.

"Hi," she said anyway.

"Hello."

"How was your ride?"

"Fine. You should try it sometime," he commented, resuming his long-legged walk toward the house.

"I will."

He stopped again. "When?"

She stopped her advance, as well. "Oh, this is going to be one of those fights."

Rick eyed her. "Which kind of fight is that?"

"The kind where you push me to do something I'm not comfortable with because you don't like the way something else went."

"Whatever you're blathering about, it's ridiculous."

So he wanted to get nasty, then. That figured, since they'd barely had a disagreement over the past month, and she had the biggest day of her new career coming up tomorrow. He expected her to bite back, so instead she brushed past him and strode toward the stable.

"What are you doing?" he asked tightly.

"I'm going to ride a stupid horse. Then the next time we argue you'll only be able to get on me about deep-sea fishing."

"Sam—"

She left him behind, shoving open the door and walking in. "Hi, Briggs," she said to the groom currently brushing Twist.

"Hello, Miss Sam. The boss just left. You—"

"I'm right here," Rick interrupted, striding in behind her.

"Would you saddle a horse for me, Briggs?" she asked, shoving down her bout of nerves. A horse was just a big dog, really. If she could drive a car, she could steer a horse.

"You don't have to, Samantha," Rick commented, his tone lowering a little.

"Yes, I do. I'm tired of you cutting at me sideways."

"Fine. Briggs, would you please saddle Molly? And Livingston, too."

She kept her back to him. "I'm not riding with you."

Rick didn't like when they argued in front of anyone else, but right now the anyones seemed to be everywhere. And she damned well wasn't going to fight him in the house in front of Inspector Clouseau Larson.

He moved up right behind her. "You *are* riding with me," he murmured into her ear, "because if you fall someone will have to take you to hospital."

"That is not what I want to hear right n—"

Rick yanked at the pocket of her light jacket. She turned on him, slapping his hand away.

"Hands off, bucko," she snapped, reflexively digging her hand in to protect her pocket. Her fingers curled around a velvet-soft pouch covering something harder and heavier inside. "You son of a bitch," she snarled, pulling the small bundle free.

"That's—"

Pushing past him to the door, she hurled it at the lake. It landed in the water a few feet from shore with a soft plop, then sank. "There's your sixteen-million-dollar priceless fucking family heirloom." *Dammit*. No wonder they were fighting. No wonder Bryce had appeared literally on her doorstep after two years. No wonder—

He dangled a bag in front of her eyes. "This is my sixteen-million-dollar priceless fucking family heirloom," he murmured. "That was a little something from me to you."

Samantha looked over her shoulder at him. "That evil mojo thing was in my pocket, though, wasn't it?" she demanded. If it hadn't been, she was just plain-and-simple cursed.

Blue eyes regarded her. "Yes. I just switched them. I didn't want to risk you breaking your neck riding."

For a long moment she looked back at him. "Put the diamond somewhere else," she finally muttered. She headed for the lake, shrugging out of her jacket as she went.

"Sam?"

Hopping, she pulled off one ankle boot. "If you'll excuse me, I'm going for a swim before my ride."

It was one thing to get rid of a cursed diamond when he'd planted it on her. It was quite another to have him remove it and for her to get pissed after it was too late to do anything about it. And he'd replaced it with a gift. Okay, she couldn't call herself stupid, but just really, really slow. She dumped her phone into one boot.

He pulled off the loose shirt he wore over his black T-shirt and kicked out of his riding boots. "No. I put evil in your pocket. I'll get it."

Samantha straightened. "Maybe it'll help you cool off, too." She watched as he cautiously stepped off the bank into the chilly water.

"Christ, it's cold," he muttered, casting around with his bare feet.

"I'm going to get the Nightshade out of here before you break *your* neck," she said, "or swans eat you."

"Or catfish."

Samantha looked from Rick's shivering, half-submerged figure to the velvet bag beside his riding boots. Then she pulled out her cell phone and flipped it open. "Sykes? Come out to the lake for a moment, will you? And bring a blanket."

"Right away, Miss Sam."

No way was she going to miss Rick wading in his

lake. She only hoped a catfish hadn't swallowed her gift. She drew a breath, still torn between anger and amusement as he dug with his toes through the muck at the bottom of the lake. He'd planted that damned diamond on her, and she hadn't even realized it. So good, he deserved to go wading through his swan-infested lake.

"Anything yet?" she called.

Rick gave her a two-fingered salute, took a breath, and sank down under the water. Whatever the value of the item in that bag—and she had no idea about that—he certainly seemed determined to find it.

"Miss Sam?"

She faced Sykes, taking the blanket from the butler. "Please take that," she said, pointing at the velvet diamond bag as Rick surfaced again, "and lock it in with the silverware. Rick will collect it from you later." She frowned as Sykes bent down to retrieve it from the grass. "And don't look at it," she added, hearing the splash as Rick dove again.

When Sykes left, Samantha faced the lake once more. Okay, it was Rick's fault she'd tossed the present, but *she* had tossed it. She sat down to pull off her other boot. Besides, item retrieval was kind of her specialty.

His head broke the surface again and then he stood, lifting his right hand. He had the bag clutched in his fingers. "Bang on target, I was," he said, wading back out of the lake.

With a half grin, Sam pulled her boots back on. "I should never have doubted."

"Bloody right."

He didn't seem to notice her sarcasm. Still, at the moment, with his black hair scraggling wetly and his wet shirt plastered to his skin, the urge to argue didn't feel quite as strong. *Wow.* Closing the distance between them, she reached up to wrap the blanket around his shoulders. "You seem to be all wet."

"I shouldn't have tried to fool you." He took her hands, tugging her closer.

Samantha pulled back. "Mm-hm. Why don't you go upstairs and get out of these things?"

"That is a very good idea. Care to join me?"

She looked at him. "Nope. I'm going riding."

"Samantha, I'm soaking wet."

"And you just want to have sex so you can wheedle your way back into my good graces."

With his fingertips Richard took her chin and tilted her face up. Then he kissed her softly. "That's what the present was for," he murmured, "though I'm thinking that it's my good graces you need to wheedle back into."

"Me? What did I do? Besides toss your present into the lake, and that was because *you* made *me* mad."

"Who was that fellow this morning? I did notice that you didn't give me his name."

"Sucks to be you," she retorted, stalking toward the stable. "Who was the guy you were trying to get the Blackpool job from? I'd like to call him and yell at him for not cooperating with you."

Richard followed her up the slope, picking up his discarded things as he went. "That's not the same thing, and you know it."

"Why not?" she retorted. "A guy from your line of work versus a guy from my line of work. Only you get to practically grab mine and toss him out on his ass."

"I did no such thing. I only wanted to know who he was."

"Why? Because you thought he was a thief? Or because I was talking to him?"

"Both," he answered, clenching his jaw.

"And did you ever consider that he wouldn't have shown up at all if you hadn't put the Nightshade in my pocket? You know, the cursed diamond that brings bad luck to whoever's carrying it?" She rounded on him. "That was really low, by the way. Whether you believe it or not, I told you it made me nervous. But no, you had to try to prove that you were right and I was wrong. Well, you were wrong. It *is* cursed. So there."

Just inside the stable door he grabbed her, pushing her back against the wall and kissing her again, hard and deep. She was as likely to win any argument as he was, and he'd found that the best way to shut her up was to seduce her. Thankfully she liked being seduced.

The blanket fell to the floor as Samantha slipped her arms around his shoulders, holding him tightly against her. He was wet, but she didn't seem to care. She was so strong, and so independent, that when she finally leaned on him, clung to him, it felt intoxicating. More than that, but he still didn't quite know how to describe the deep sense of satisfaction and pure joy that filled him when they were together, when he knew he'd made her happy.

Still kissing her, and fairly certain the stable was wired into Samantha's bloody video security system, he trailed his fingers down her arm until he set the wet velvet bag into her fingers. The original plan had been for her to discover the gift at her leisure and when he wasn't present to add any pressure to the process.

Since she'd let him go diving in his lake to recover it, though, he assumed that she was fairly interested in receiving it. Backing off a little, he undid the soggy, delicate ties and pulled the mouth of the bag open.

Samantha watched his hands as he took the bag back and turned it upside down over her palm. A small gold triangular setting, a sparkling diamond at each of the three points, and a gold chain pooling beside it, winked at them.

"Oh, Rick," she breathed. "It's beautiful."

Carefully he opened the clasp and looped it around her throat, fastening it behind her neck. "I bought it when I was in Paris. My timing—"

She put a finger across his lips. "Your timing sucks. Thank you." Removing her fingers, she replaced them with her lips.

"You're welcome. Have your fellow turn off the security cameras in here, why don't you?" he suggested.

She chuckled against his mouth. "I am not having sex in here with the horses watching us."

"Sex is perfectly natural in the animal kingdom. I'm certain they won't mind."

"*I* will. And so will Briggs. Besides, I'm going for a ride."

"You don't need to prove anything to me."

Her brow furrowed. "It's not really about you—except to stop you from saying I'm scared to ride."

"Ride me," he murmured, unbuttoning the top fastening of her blouse and slipping his hand along her collarbone.

"You are so slick," she returned with a slow smile.

"Here you are Miss Sam, boss." Briggs emerged from a stall, Molly in tow while Livingston already waited.

"Cool," Samantha answered. "You'll have to show me how to . . . get on board."

Richard slid an arm up the back of her shoulder and leaned down to brush her ear with his lips. "Riding at this moment is going to be extremely uncomfortable for me."

She snorted. "That's your own fault."

Bloody splendid. He did his best to conjure images of

ski crashes in the snow and the Queen in a thong, though that felt distinctly unpatriotic. It only helped a little, but hopefully enough that sitting in the saddle wouldn't permanently damage him.

Briggs was demonstrating how to step into the stirrup when Richard walked forward. "I'll take it from here," he said.

With a nod and a grin that said he'd heard or seen at least part of their exchange, the groom retreated to the tack room. Samantha tugged Richard's damp open shirt forward over his hips. "Are you sure you want to participate?"

"Yes. Plant your foot in my hands and swing your other leg over."

"Okay. You know, I thought that a dip in the lake might have helped you out," she commented, running her gaze along the length of him in a way that had him going from the Queen to John Cleese in drag just so he could keep a little dignity. "Maybe you should try it again."

"After dinner," he returned as smoothly as he could, "I want to see you wearing that necklace and nothing else."

She sat in the saddle while he pushed her toes through the stirrups. "Are you trying to distract me, or warm yourself up?"

"Distract you from what?"

"From realizing that I've just put my life in the hooves of a very large animal with only a thin strip of leather to get him to do what I want."

"Her," he corrected. "And Molly's the calmest animal I own." She should be; he'd made the purchase with Samantha and her lack of horse experience in mind. He attached a line to Molly's bridle and, hanging on to the other end, stiffly mounted Livingston. "Besides, you've dealt with people a great deal more frightening than her."

Samantha settled a little, clearly uncomfortable, before she looked across at him. "Are we still arguing?" she asked.

Yes. "I don't know yet. Why do you ask?"

"Because I'm letting you lead me around."

Coming from the background she'd had, even as small a concession as this was a big deal for Samantha. Especially if they were still fighting. "I hope you know by now that arguments or not, you can still trust me."

She nodded, not quite able to hide her grimace. "Okay."

"Okay." With a cluck he sent Livingston forward at a sedate walk through the tall, wide stable door. Molly followed obediently along behind them. Samantha gripped the low saddle horn with both hands and muttered to herself. He couldn't hear it all, but he caught a few words. Apparently she felt stupid and was about to break her neck.

Considering that she'd never attempted anything without excelling at it, Richard wasn't overly concerned about her neck. Not because of Molly, anyway. It was the rest of Samantha's life—the parts she wouldn't discuss with him—that would get her killed. And that was becoming more and more unacceptable to him.

"How are you doing?" he asked, twisting in the saddle to look back at her.

"I haven't fallen off yet," she returned tightly. "Maybe we should have started with a Shetland pony."

Self-deprecations aside, she had a good seat and a firm grip on the saddle. Mentally crossing himself, Richard kneed Livingston into a canter. Most of his attention on Samantha, he angled them along the lake-shore.

"Rick, stop it!" she snapped, grabbing for the reins with one hand and missing.

"What's that man's name?" he asked.

"What?"

"From this morning. Tell me his name."

"Fuck you. Stop!"

"You're not in any danger. You just don't like this because you're not in control. That's how I feel every time you step into trouble and then won't talk to me about it."

She pulled her cell phone out of her pocket and threw it at him. She had exceptional aim, even on horseback, and it bounced painfully off his skull. With a curse he pulled up. "Dammit! That was not—"

Samantha wiggled her feet out of the stirrups and half fell to the ground. Leaning down to swipe up her phone, she strode back toward the house. Rubbing his temple, Rick kicked out of the saddle and charged after her.

He tackled her to the ground. Very aware that she would come up swinging, he grabbed for her wrists, using his greater weight to keep her pinned. Instead of fighting against him, she shoved hard with her feet against the upside of the slope. Before he could brace against it, they were rolling down the slight hill toward the lake.

"Fuck," he muttered, as they splashed into the shallows and he went under. Again.

Releasing her, he shoved to his feet. A few yards away, Samantha scrambled back onto shore.

"You fight dirty," he panted.

"Look who's talking, Mr. Canterbury Death Trot." Shaking out her hair, she squelched free of her shoes and jacket. "Don't ever do that again."

"I was making a point. Your life isn't just about you any longer."

"I know that. And you challenging that guy to his face this morning is not the way to scare him off a job. So try to keep in mind that it's not all about you and your hefty testosterone levels, either."

"Fine." He slogged out of the water. "Include me, or don't. You know I'm willing to help. But if you choose to keep me out of it, I expect to remain out of it. Publicly, legally, politically, socially, and any other adverbs I can think of. So you decide, Samantha. Once again, I'm leaving it up to you."

Grabbing Livingston's reins, he strode with the two horses back toward the stable. Silence followed him. Bloody hell. Why was it that he could negotiate billion-dollar deals without breaking a sweat, but he couldn't manage a discussion with Sam without losing his temper and causing a fistfight?

"Shepherd," she said from behind him. "Bryce Shepherd. That's his name."

Thank God. He slowed. "Is he any good?"

"He's pretty good. I can handle him."

"Thank you for telling me."

It didn't answer his other questions—the ones about whether Bryce Shepherd had been flirting with her for a reason, and how well she knew him. He would trust her for now, because he quite simply had no other choice. Not if he wanted to keep his sanity—and his heart.

Chapter 7

Friday, 11:20 p.m.

Samantha closed her eyes, putting everything to sensation. Rick kissed the nape of her neck, sliding his hands thickly from her hips up her backbone to her shoulders, and out along her arms to twine his fingers with hers. Her breath caught as he parted her thighs with his knees and then pushed inside her from behind.

She rocked with him as he thrust, her eyes still closed. God, she could feel him everywhere. The cool sheets warming beneath her pressing breasts, the pair of pillows beneath her hips, his feet holding hers apart from one another, the heavy way he filled her, pushed and retreated, then pushed again.

Groaning, she came, pulsing and writhing beneath him. She squealed girlishly, the only time she ever made such silly, carefree sounds. Rick chuckled breathlessly against the back of her head, then abruptly withdrew.

Her eyes flew open again. "Hey!"

"Turn over," he panted, pulling on her left shoulder.

Like she'd argue with him now. Samantha turned over to look up at his face. With his fingertips Rick ran his finger along the gold chain of her new necklace, straightening it between her breasts as he leaned down to lick across her nipples.

"That does look good on you," he commented.

"So do you. Get down here." Pushing the pillows onto the floor, she grabbed for him with her hands and her feet, pulling him back down on top of her. He entered her again, and their dance continued.

Now she kept her eyes open; she enjoyed watching him as much as he did watching her. His deep blue gaze, charcoal-colored in the light from the fireplace, took her in, reading her expression probably better than anyone else alive or previously dead had ever been able to do.

"I love you," he whispered, kissing her hard.

Resting his weight on her hips and one elbow, with his other hand he teased at her breasts, revving her up all over again. The necklace jolted rhythmically up over her shoulder and down onto the sheets again.

"I love you," he repeated. "I love you."

That sort of talk wasn't supposed to count during sex, but she'd never heard him say anything he didn't mean under any circumstances. He didn't seem to expect an answer, though. Whether he was talking to her or just saying what was uppermost in his thoughts, she didn't know. But she knew how he felt; he'd said it to her a hundred times, and never once when he didn't mean it, and never once when it didn't give her shivers and warm fuzzy feelings all over.

"Come for me, Samantha," he urged, shifting his weight.

"Christ, again?" she moaned, laughing. "Demanding much?"

His hand teased at her tits again as his pace increased. "Join me," he groaned, kissing her openmouthed once more.

She came all at once in a shivering rush. Samantha gasped, digging her fingers into his shoulders as he heaved against her, shuddering. Mmm. That was it. Knowing that she excited him as much he aroused her. Fighting or frustrated or standing on different sides of the law, they fit.

When they could breathe again, Rick turned over onto his back beside her. Silently he tugged her closer, until she lay on her stomach half across his chest. With a slight smile she listened to his heartbeat. He twiddled his fingers into her hair, obviously as reluctant as she was to start talking about anything outside the bedroom again. That was where all the damn trouble was.

"Did Walter ever call you back?" he asked finally. "From what you've told me in the past, I presume this Shepherd would have been hired by someone. It could be handy to know who that person is."

She sighed. "No, he hasn't called me back yet. Since I helped get two art thieves here arrested, and a fence got killed because I was digging around, it's gotten kind of hard for Stoney to find any Brits who'll talk to him."

"Well, considering that if you hadn't become involved in that mess there would have been one more dead Brit— one with my initials—all I can say is that I'm sorry for his troubles."

She snuggled closer. "I'm not complaining. Just stating facts."

"Mm-hm. Thank you for clarifying."

"You're welcome." Her eyes closed again. That was her—warm, very satisfied, and sleepy.

"I canceled tomorrow's meeting in London," he said offhandedly.

Samantha opened her eyes again. "And why did you do that?" *As if she didn't know.*

"I thought I'd stay home and watch your opening day."

"What, through the upstairs windows? Do you have any idea how many tourists are going to be crawling around here hoping for a look at Rick Addison?"

"Nearly as many as will hope to see Addison's girl-friend, who's actually working this . . . gig, as you call it."

"No way. I'm the fries; you're the Whopper. Besides, like you said, I'll be working—and in the security room. Nobody's going to see me unless there's trouble. And since you're not going to put the diamond back in my pocket, there won't be any trouble."

"I'm staying here," he repeated, less diplomatically.

"For four weeks, then? I thought you had a big dinner thing Monday night."

"I do. I've already called Sarah to have her inform my guests that the dinner will be here rather than at the London flat. Rawley Park is more impressive, anyway. And besides, now you won't have any excuse not to attend with me."

"I knew that damned diamond was bad luck."

Rick chuckled. "Not for me. I get to have dinner with you. Maybe it's only bad luck if you believe in that sort of thing."

"Do you really call dinner with me and twenty of your closest minions *good* luck?"

"I'm thanking them for a very profitable quarter. You could wear this." He flicked a finger at her new necklace.

"Cool. I'm calling it the Fuck Me Diamond Triad."

He laughed outright. "Call it whatever you like. You make it sparkle."

"Me and the unbelievable pressures and heat acting on subterranean coal deposits."

"So pragmatic, you are."

She raised up and kissed his chin. "I love you," she murmured. There. He got one when it counted.

"I love you, Sam."

As for her pragmatism, she hoped that wasn't a lesson she would have to teach Bryce Shepherd. Because whether they'd once been friends and lovers or not, what she had now was so much more than that. And if push came to shove, she would take Bryce down.

Richard sat on one of the stools at the rear of the control room. All four occupants had their eyes on the red-numbered digital clock in the lower right-hand corner of one of the monitors. At eight fifty-nine and thirty seconds, Craigson began counting backward aloud. Just what they needed—more drama.

Richard took a moment to glance at Samantha. Far from the relaxed, sexy, funny woman of last night, this morning she was all business. Today was important for him in that he'd been able to foot the bill and provide the location for a prestigious exhibit just about to open to the public for no charge. For her, she'd been able to come out of the shadows for this one. And she would be able to put it on her résumé when it went well.

"Three . . . two . . . one," Craigson chanted. "Blast-off."

Samantha hit the talk button on her walkie-talkie. "Open the gates, Hervey."

"Roger that," the guard's voice came back. "Blimey,

it looks like the line for the next *Star Wars* movie out here."

"*Attack of the Tourists*," Samantha muttered. "A journey to the Dark Side."

Richard and the two guards chuckled.

"Just remember that the exhibit would be kind of a failure without them here," Craigson noted.

"Oh, I'm not going to forget that, Jamie. Have your riders stay on this side of the lake. I want to catch any strays before they get into the meadows."

"Will do."

Richard stood and kissed Samantha on the temple. "Are you certain you want to sit here in the cellar and watch all this on camera?"

"I don't want to see what'll happen if either of us goes wandering out amid the huddled masses."

Neither did he, particularly. "Let's go up on the roof," he suggested.

She pursed her lips, no doubt gauging all of the angles of a change of venue. She also looked very sexy while doing it.

"Okay." Samantha patted Craigson on the shoulder. "I'll have my walkie on," she said.

As soon as they were back in the main part of the cellar and away from the security guards, Richard took her hand in his. He loved touching her, though it had taken a great deal of patience to demonstrate the difference between an embrace and a restraint. Since she was working today, he let her go again before she could pull away. Balance. He was still learning, just as she was. He'd thrown out his book of rules the day he'd set eyes on her, and the new one had more asterisks and exceptions than it did actual rules.

"I've been less nervous about some of the jobs I've

pulled," she admitted in a low voice as they topped the stairs.

"Well, the Nightshade's in the safe, so you should have splendid luck today."

Samantha sent him a sideways glance. "You're still making fun of me, aren't you?"

He put his hand over his heart. "Me? Be amused because the smartest, most fearless woman I've ever met screams and runs at the sight of a priceless blue diamond?"

"Mm-hm. I thought so."

They went upstairs, then up into the attic. The roof-access ladder stood in the far corner. "Have you ever stolen something that was supposedly cursed or bad luck?"

"Once."

That sounded intriguing. He climbed the ladder first, unlocking the door to the roof and shouldering it open. "And that's all you're going to say about it?"

As she joined him on the narrow catwalk, she squinted. The pale morning sun turned her auburn hair bronze and lightened her green eyes to emerald. He sighed as he looked at her. *Glorious.*

"The gig was only four years ago," she returned, following him to what, if they'd overlooked the sea, would have been the widow's walk. Since they were in the middle of Devonshire, he'd always reckoned it was there so his ancestors could survey their vast domain.

"So you're warning me that I could be an accessory after the fact if you tell me anything about it," he said.

Samantha nodded. "The statute of limitations doesn't run out for another three years. If I go down, the less you know, the better."

"I think if you were ever arrested, I've already done

enough to be considered an outright accomplice."

"Way to bring down the mood, Rick."

"I didn't mean it that way. It was supposed to sound more like, 'In for a penny, in for a pound.' Or, 'You jump, I jump.' One of those we're-in-it-together clichés."

"Ah. Thanks for clarifying." She sent him her quicksilver grin. "It was a crystal Mayan skull. Creeped me out. The alarm short-circuited and went off, and then my getaway car blew its engine in the middle of Pompano Beach, so I had to boost a VW Bug from a Dairy Queen. Not my finest moment."

"I bet you looked good, though."

"Always." Below the edge of the roof, cars streamed in through the gates and onto the gravel parking lot. "Man. It looks like an after-Christmas sale at Wal-Mart."

"Have you ever actually been to an after-Christmas sale anywhere?"

"I watch the news, baby." She leaned farther forward, fearless as always. "When we open the gallery wing here, we're going to have to either expand the parking lot or limit the number of cars that come through at any given time."

"We'll worry about that later, Samantha. For now, enjoy the moment. Because I would call this a success."

This time she smiled more easily. "I suppose I would, too. The V & A's going to be happy about this. Especially if the tourists hit the gift shop like they're hitting the show."

"Speaking of the V & A, where's Henry Larson?"

He stationed himself as a docent beside the rubicon McCauley must know he's a fraud, because she gave him a cheat sheet in case anybody actually asks him any questions."

"At least he seems pretty harmless."

"There's no such thing as a harmless cop," she returned, her gaze still on the growing crowd. "At best I would call him incompetent, which still means he could cause a shitload of trouble."

"Only if your Mr. Shepherd makes another appearance."

"He's not 'my' anything, and there could be any number of black hats strolling through those doors right now. I just hope Larson doesn't kill anybody, or screw things up so badly that somebody actually makes off with the gemstones."

"You have met some competent law enforcement officers, if you'll recall."

She shrugged. "I know they're out there. I also know that I've been breaking the law since I was six. Number of cuffs put around my wrists? One pair. And that wasn't my fault."

"Okay, okay. I see your point. But have you considered that the more obvious Inspector Larson is, the less likely anyone is to attempt anything with him standing there? And the object is, after all, for the exhibit not to be hit."

When Samantha faced him again, she was grinning. "You're a pretty smart fella, Brit. You should consider going into business. You'd probably be fairly decent at it."

He kissed her softly. "Thank you for the advice. I'll consider it."

They headed back downstairs. "Ooh, and then I could be your secretary and sit on your desk in a really short skirt and take dic . . . tation."

For a second Richard stopped to watch her black-slacks-clothed backside sway as she descended the main staircase. When she half turned to look coyly over her shoulder at him, he went after her.

Shoving her against the wall on the landing, he planted his hands on either side of her shoulders. "I believe I've warned you about teasing me," he murmured.

"Who's teasing?" Tangling her fingers into his hair, she pulled his face down for a deep, openmouthed kiss.

For a long moment he concentrated on kissing her back, on the ebb and flow of dominance and control and passion between them. No wonder they butted heads so often—in a great many ways they were very much alike. Added to that, Samantha had some serious boundary issues that eight months had only just begun to wear down.

Slowly she lifted her palms to his chest and pushed him away a few inches. "Okay, that's enough fun. I have work to do."

"It's not even close to being enough fun," he returned, capturing her mouth again, "but very well. I'll be in my office if you need me."

"For this gig? I think I've got it covered." With a last, quick kiss she headed back in the direction of the cellar.

She probably did have it covered. And he still turned on the walkie-talkie he'd nicked from downstairs. It was one thing to have confidence in her; it was quite another to trust that everything else would go swimmingly. Yes, he trusted her—but he was also an exceedingly cautious fellow where Samantha Elizabeth Jellicoe and her safety were concerned.

Chapter 8

Saturday, 5:12 p.m.

Samantha reached the exhibit doors as Henry Larson emerged into the early evening. "We just cleared the building," he said, nodding his chin in the direction of her security people.

"That's great," she returned, "but I think I'll just take a last look, myself. Bennett, care to join me?"

The beefy guard nodded, falling in behind her. Larson looked annoyed, but she didn't much care. He might suspect that someone was after the gems, but he didn't know it was Bryce Shepherd, and he couldn't possibly know as much about Shepherd's methods as she did.

"I'll accompany you," the inspector put in, stepping in front of Bennett. "You can't be too careful, I suppose."

Oh, brother. If he suspected her, she would ordinarily have considered him a smart cookie. But since she'd been the one to wire this place within an inch of its life and very publicly declared herself its protector, he was just being stupid. Of course, even if she had been up to something and he was standing right on her head to keep watch, he still wouldn't have caught her at it.

"So everybody's equally capable of making away with the goods?" she asked just to make conversation, opening the wall panel and turning on the bright overhead lights.

"Everyone has their price," he agreed. "And these jewels represent quite a lot of blunt."

"Did you notice anyone suspicious?" she continued, beginning her walk to each of the displays and checking first to see if all the gems were in place, and second to make certain the tiny green sensor lights were still on.

"There were a few possibilities. I stayed close on them, and they didn't dare make any trouble." He cleared his throat. "Is it always going to be so crowded, do you think?"

"The weekends will be bad, but today and tomorrow will probably be the worst," she said absently, picking a wad of gum out from one of the latches on a display's underside. *Blech.* Gross, but pretty lame if it was an attempt at being evil. She could do much better with just the junk in her pockets.

With that thought, she reached her fingers into both her jacket pockets. Nothing she hadn't placed there. After yesterday she didn't think Rick would attempt to plant the Nightshade Diamond on her again, but she wasn't willing to take any risks where her own luck was concerned. Of course, he kept going around boasting that since he didn't believe in luck, the thing had no effect on him. Even after the blown tire and wrecked cell phone and lost business deal. What he probably needed was some more proof—the kind he couldn't dispute.

Could she do that to him? Samantha frowned as she

made her way down the second row. *Why was she even asking herself the question?* He'd done it to her. And she'd learned the lesson a long time ago about not letting anyone even *think* they had the advantage over her. Weakness meant failure, and failure meant jail—or death.

"Don't all of the sensors show up on your computer?" Larson asked.

"Yep."

"Then why are you bothering to check whether the little lights are on? It seems to me you should be doing more patrolling of the property here."

Samantha glanced at him. "I'm cautious and paranoid," she returned. "Why aren't you?"

"Oh, I am. I just think that you need to have faith in your own system. If you don't, then why did you install it?"

She put her hands on her hips as weariness pulled at her. Just as stubbornly she pushed back. "Is this because I wouldn't give you a walkie-talkie?"

Bennett snorted, covering the sound with a cough.

"It has nothing to do with that," the inspector retorted. "I spent all day in here keeping an eye on things. You got to sit in a comfy chair, *and* you have employees to help you. I did *my* job, Miss Jellicoe. And I did it well."

For a Scotland Yard guy, he didn't seem to know much about bypassing circuits and looping connections to give false positives. She knew, though, and so she kept checking the displays and the other doors one by one. He might have been keeping watch in person, but with a couple hundred visitors inside at any given time, he couldn't possibly see everything. Even with experts like Craigson and herself watching, even with the ability to zoom and replay, she still wasn't going to leave for the evening without giving everything a closer look.

After ten more minutes she had to admit that everything was shipshape and nobody was hiding up in the rafters. And even better, no one had seen any sign of Bryce Shepherd. She lifted the walkie-talkie. "Okay, Craigson, switch the display sensors to night."

"Roger that."

On the wall panel a fourth and fifth light blinked on red, then switched to green. Now if anybody so much as breathed hard on the glass display covers, the alarm would go off. Taking a last glance around, Samantha flipped off the overhead lights and the display lighting. "Gentlemen," she said, gesturing Larson and Bennett to precede her out the door.

"Maybe now you'll trust that I know what I'm doing," the inspector said smugly. "A pair of eyes is still better than all the expensive equipment you can install."

"You're a jerk, Larson." She closed and locked the door. "Reset the door codes, Jamie," she instructed.

"Done and done."

Whew. Day one, finished. "Thanks," she said into the walkie-talkie. "Say good night, Gracie."

"Good night, Gracie."

With a nod at Bennett, she headed back for the house. One down, twenty-seven days to go. Yay, her.

Abruptly Larson grabbed her shoulder. "I do not appreciate being scoffed at or ridiculed, Miss Jellicoe," he snapped. "I am a pro—"

"Get your hand off my arm," she interrupted, instantly going from relieved to extremely pissed off.

Evidently reading her expression, Larson did probably the smartest thing he'd managed all day and let her go. Samantha took a steadying breath. She'd been all set to kick the crap out of him—or at least smack him—and his sudden reasonableness was a little disappointing.

"My apologies, Miss Jellicoe. As I was saying, I am a professional. And I hope that by working together rather than in opposition, we can thwart any—"

"Rick and I will be having dinner in our private rooms tonight," she broke in. "See you in the morning."

She left him in the garden, ignoring whatever it was he was muttering about Americans in general, and her in particular. Pip-pip and Bob's your uncle—Christ, that stiff, polite British upper lip shit drove her crazy sometimes. Especially when it came from incompetent boobs she couldn't even insult the way she wanted to because he was a cop and might go digging and actually turn up something.

Her cell phone rang as she stepped inside Rick's office, so with a quick wave at him she reversed course and went on to her own office next door. "Hey, Stoney," she greeted the caller, recognizing the ring tone.

"Enough small talk," he returned. "How did opening day go?"

She grinned. "Nothing got ripped off. You'd be just as happy if every gem went missing, though."

"Only if you were the one who pulled the job."

"Oh, you're sweet." She sat back against the edge of her Georgian mahogany desk. "Did you find out anything about Bryce?"

"Not a word."

"Damn. Nobody talking, or no info?"

"No info."

The other end of the line went quiet. Considering that Stoney *always* had something to say, that didn't bode well. "Okay, what's up?" she prompted.

"A couple of brokers I talked to practically started drooling when I mentioned the V & A traveling exhibit. Bryce could be going in on spec—there's plenty of interest for anything he might be able to grab."

Great. "He knows better than to go up against me, especially without a guaranteed paycheck."

"I don't know, honey. You're retired and doing security. That doesn't sound like top-of-your-game-type stuff."

She scowled. "I'm not a janitor. Christ."

"Or," he put in hurriedly, "maybe it's just Bryce. One of his games."

"That's not very helpful. Is it one of his games where he's just teasing, or one of his games where he wants to prove he's better than me?"

"My crystal ball's in the shop. You know him better than I do, Sam. What do you think?"

Samantha blew out her breath. "I don't know. I warned him off pretty directly, but then Rick went all King Kong on him. Bryce used to do shit just because I told him not to, but I'm hoping he's got more sense now."

Movement by the door caught her attention, and she looked up in time to see Rick's backside heading away down the hall. *Crap.* She pushed upright.

"Gotta go, Stoney."

"But the—"

Snapping the phone closed, she tossed it onto the desk and sprinted out the door. "Rick!"

When she reached the master bedroom they shared, the door was locked. Oh, like that would stop her.

"Very mature," she called, banging on the old oak.

As she dug into her pocket for a paper clip, she tried to bury the ill feeling in the pit of her stomach. Obviously he'd overheard her conversation with Stoney. His usual response to realizing she'd kept something from him, though, was to fling it back in her face.

Oh, swell. She'd kept enough secrets from him that she'd been able to develop a catalog of his responses. Samantha twisted open the paper clip and slipped it into the door lock. A second later the lock popped, and she turned the handle.

Opening the door, she walked into the room. And stopped.

"Close the door," Rick ordered.

She closed the door. Okay, she could add another entry to the catalog of his responses. "What are you doing?" she asked.

"What does it look like I'm doing?"

"It looks like you're taking off all of your clothes."

He straightened from removing his second sock. "That would be correct."

"Why?"

"Because I'm going to take a shower." He straightened, naked and hot as anything.

Samantha frowned. "You heard me talking with Stoney, right?"

"I did. Walter doesn't have any leads on who might have hired Bryce Shepherd, I presume?"

"That's right. He might be freelancing."

"Then I imagine you'll have to keep a watch out for him until the exhibit leaves."

"Since I don't have his timetable, yep, I imagine I will."

He looked at her for a moment, then nodded. "Very well. If you'll excuse me."

"No."

Halfway to the bathroom, he stopped. "Beg pardon?"

"I know you heard me talking about how well I knew Bryce. So don't give me that excuse-me shit."

"Let's continue this in the bathroom, then, because I'm getting a bit chilly." Without another backward glance he left the room.

Samantha stood there for a minute. This was not the usual Rick Addison response to learning something she'd been trying to keep quiet about. Hell, the second he'd seen her talking with Bryce he'd been ready to start beating heads.

What if he'd given up on her? A chill ran through her chest. She'd worried about that day, when he decided he'd put up with enough of her very colorful past—and present, apparently—and just stopped caring. She'd tried not to lie to him. In fact, she told him the truth more often than she ever had anybody else in her life, with the possible exception of Stoney.

The water turned on in the bathroom. He was really just going to jump in the shower. Clenching her jaw, her chest still tight with unaccustomed worry, she watched steam begin to seep into the bedroom. She could break into a mansion and lift a Rembrandt like nobody's business, but relationships were hard. This one was hard— because it mattered.

Richard glanced at the half-open bathroom door once more, then stepped into the shower. If he hadn't traveled in the realm of high-stakes business for the past twelve years, he wouldn't have been able to shrug off his anger well enough to fool anyone.

He wanted Samantha with him for the rest of their lives. But he couldn't accomplish that by himself. And so now it was her turn to decide how to handle this latest little revealed secret of hers, even if it half killed him to jump in the shower without first confronting her.

The shower door swung open, and Samantha in all her naked glory stepped in with him. *Thank God*.

"Bryce and I were together for about a month," she said, "about two years ago."

Richard wanted to ask how they'd met, why they'd parted company, and whose idea it had been to go their separate ways. Instead he lathered soap across his chest. "None of my business," he said aloud.

Her lips twisted. "I can't tell if you're throwing a tantrum or if you really don't care," she returned. Her eyes lowered. "Though I can see that you're interested right now."

The one part of himself he couldn't control while naked and in the shower with the woman he loved. "What do you want my reaction to be?" he asked. "Not to wanting you. To the other bit."

"That's not really fair," she noted after a moment. "I see pictures of you and Julia Poole in all the old magazines lying around the dentist's office. I don't throw a tizzy while I'm getting my teeth cleaned."

"You don't see me in new pictures with Julia. I saw you with Bryce Shepherd just yesterday."

"We weren't naked and doin' it on the display case, doofus."

"But you were at one time. Not necessarily on a display case." If they had been, he absolutely did not want to know about that.

"Yep, we did the deed. Just like you did with Miss Golden Globes."

He clenched his jaw. "I thought you weren't jealous of Julia and me."

"I'm not. But I don't have to like her, either."

In a perverse way, it pleased him to hear her say that. Richard reached out to stroke her breasts with his soapy hands. "I don't like Shepherd. But you'll notice that I didn't throw a tizzy in your office."

"Okay, points for you. But you lose some for jumping all over him yesterday." She patted his cock gently, like it was a faithful dog. "And I'm not going to have sex with you just to make you feel like you're planting your British flag in my Tranquility Base, sweetheart."

"You're—"

"I told Larson that we're having dinner up here, by the way. I'm mad at him for being stupid." He thought he heard her snicker as she backed out of the shower and shut it again.

So much for his grand plan to teach her a lesson. Richard glanced down at his lowering flagpole. "Sorry, lad," he muttered. "Maybe later."

Quickly finishing his shower, he went back into the bedroom to find Samantha gone. All hope of predinner sex vanished with her. Grumbling, Richard dug into his wardrobe for a jumper—sweatshirt—and jeans. Craigson would be gone for the night now, which meant that Bill Harrington would be on night duty. Sam and Craigson had a rapport that only thieves seemed to share— a bit like old army buddies, he imagined. Harrington, though, was strictly business, which meant he could be reasoned with.

Down in the cellar, he slowed as he reached the security office door. Harrington was definitely in there with somebody, but it didn't sound like Samantha. *Larson*, he decided after a moment of listening to the muffled voices.

He punched in the security code and opened the door.

"Hello, Harrington," he said easily, then lifted an eyebrow as he spied Larson standing over the night security supervisor. "Is something wrong with the exhibit?"

"No, sir. Nothing."

"Then what is the museum's assistant assistant curator doing down here?"

"Debating security measures," the inspector said shortly. "Excuse me." With a stiff nod he left the room.

"Trouble?"

"No, sir." Harrington glanced at the door as it swung closed. "Sir, I think you and Miss Sam should know that Mr. Larson's not actually with the V & A. He's an inspector with Scotland Yard."

"How did you discover that?"

"The git told me. Flashed his badge, wanted one of the extra radios."

"Did you give him one?"

"He said he would dig up something on me if I didn't. When I was younger, well, I did a few—"

"No worries, Harrington." Samantha had found yet another lost, illegal puppy, apparently. "You could answer a question for me, though."

"Certainly."

Richard turned a chair to sit on it backward. "If someone trips an alarm in the exhibit hall, how does Samantha get notified?"

"She'd probably hear it," the guard returned with a snort. "She said a silent alarm is to nab a bloke on the way out. She wants them stopped before they get in, and she wants 'em to know trouble's coming."

And it would probably frighten the bejeezus out of all lower-level thieves who managed to get that far—which most wouldn't. He didn't doubt for a second, though, that Samantha could get in, take everything including the rafters, and leave again, all without causing the sensors even to twitch. "That makes sense," he said belatedly. "Mechanically what happens, though?"

"Oh. Right." Harrington turned his chair to face the computer monitor. "If any sensor trips, the system calls the authorities, turns on all the exterior lights, puts out an automated alert on the portables, and dials Miss Sam's cell phone." He grinned briefly. "She set her ring tone to the theme from *Psycho*."

Of course she had. "Can you add my phone to the list?"

"I, ah, well, Miss Sam didn't—"

"The exhibit hall does belong to me, after all, even if the contents don't."

"You're right about that, sir. Give me the number you want dialed, and I'll add you to the list."

Richard recited the number and waited while Harrington ran through several computer screens, adding information as he went. Craigson probably would have complied as well, but *he* would have told Samantha about it. Then she would have started a new tirade about who'd been entrusted with what. He preferred to avoid both the tirade and the explanation, where he would have to reveal that it wasn't as much about trust as it was about keeping Samantha safe. And if that alarm went off and she charged in to confront an old lover, he intended to be there to provide backup or whatever else she might need. If that help involved beating Bryce Shepherd into paste, then so be it.

"There you go, and . . . Bob's your uncle," Harrington said, hitting the enter key once more.

"Thank you, Harrington. I appreciate your assistance. And your discretion."

"My pleasure, sir. I am going to have to tell Miss Sam that Larson's got one of the walkie-talkies, though."

"By all means."

He watched the silent, still images on the monitors for another minute, then patted the guard on the shoulder and left the security room. Once the door shut, he took out his cell phone and dialed long-distance.

"Hello, Rick," came a deep Texas-born drawl two rings later.

"Tom," he returned. "How's the weather in Palm Beach?"

"Warm and leaning toward sticky. How's Devonshire?"

"Cool and leaning toward damp."

Whether Samantha referred to Tom Donner, chief partner in the corporate law firm of Donner, Rhodes, and Critchenson, as a Boy Scout or not, Richard had long ago come to consider him as both his most-trusted advisor and his closest friend. And these days he chose his friends very carefully.

"I know it's Saturday afternoon there," he continued, "but I'm wondering if you could dig up a bit of information for me."

"Uh-oh. What'd Jellicoe do this time?"

"And why is it that whenever I ask for something, you assume Samantha must be involved?"

He could almost see the exasperated look on Donner's face. "Is she?"

Richard scowled at the phone. "I need to know whatever you can dig up on an Irishman named Bryce Shepherd, between twenty-five and thirty years of age. Don't limit your search to the United Kingdom—he's fairly well traveled." If he ran in the same upper echelons of thievery as Samantha had, he would have to be.

"Okay. Should I start anywhere in particular? Business, medical, bank—"

"Try outstanding warrants, Interpol, FBI, and Scotland Yard watch lists, and prison records for B&Es or theft."

Silence.

"Tom?"

"Aha! I knew it. What kind of trouble is Jellicoe in?"

"None. And I'd like to keep it that way, so get moving."

"Okay, okay. I'll call my buddy in the Bureau. He owes me one since we tipped him to the Met robbery."

"Which we were able to do because of Samantha," Richard pointed out. "And Tom?"

"Yeah?"

"This stays between us."

"I figured that. I'll call you when I find something."

"The sooner, the better."

He slowly closed the phone and clipped it back onto his belt. Samantha could be as circumspect as she pleased about his former lovers, but he was considerably more territorial where she was concerned. And Sam still seemed to like this Bryce Shepherd—which meant that he didn't. At all.

Chapter 9

Sunday, 2:47 a.m.

Samantha sat up, going from dead asleep to wide awake in the space of a heartbeat. The phone on the nightstand buzzed again, loud and annoying in the dark. "Christ," she muttered, climbing over Rick to grab it.

He got to it first, shouldering her arm out of the way as he hit the talk button. "Yes?" Sitting up, his bed hair crazy and sexy, the phone to his ear, he glared at her. "It's for you. Harrington."

"This is why I wanted the phone on my side of the bed," she grumbled, taking a second to look at the clock. "What is it, Harrington?"

"The floodlights on the north side of the exhibit hall have tripped twice in two minutes, now. Since we lifted the sensor range six inches off the ground and set it for over fifty pounds of mass, it's probably not mice or grouse."

"Could still be deer or really big rabbits," she returned. "Who's checking it out?"

"Will Q and Danny. You said you wanted to know if I got . . ." He paused. "It just tripped again, and I'm still not seeing anything deer-sized on the monitors."

"Okay." She kicked off the remaining tangle of covers. "Let Will and Danny know I'll be down in five."

Handing the phone back to Rick, she slid off her side of the huge bed and reached under the nightstand for the shirt, jeans, and shoes she always kept there, just in case. Some old habits just made sense.

"Why didn't he use the radio?" Rick asked, scooting off his side of the bed.

"Because Larson got hold of a walkie, and I wanted a head start on any trouble."

"I'm going with you," he said, digging in the dark for the clothes he'd discarded two hours earlier.

"Rick, I've got it h—"

"I'm going with you," he repeated, in his don't-mess-with-me voice.

"Fine."

A minute later she grabbed her walkie-talkie, turned it on low, and headed for the bedroom door. "Let's move, Brit."

"I'm moving."

With her adrenaline pumping, she was enjoying this. It wasn't as good as pulling a B&E, and it was probably nothing, but since she'd gone straight, any excuse for a little excitement was welcome.

"You're cranky at two in the morning."

"I am not," he retorted in a low voice, joining her at the door. "I jammed my bloody toe. Do you need a torch?"

Ah, British-speak. He always fell back on it more when he was riled. "I've got a flashlight."

Quietly she opened the door and led the way to the

main staircase, then through the kitchen and out into the garden. The north side of the exhibit hall was the farthest from the house, bordering close on a pretty stand of old elm and oak trees that had probably been acquainted with Robin Hood. With a half smile she couldn't get rid of she hurried them through the garden, automatically avoiding the most blatant of the light sensors out there. White hat or not, blundering into something and being spotlighted was amateurish.

Rick stayed close behind her, moving with a lot of stealth for a businessman. She'd never really worked with a partner, but he would have made a good one—if he'd decided on a life of crime instead of high-profile business and philanthropy, that is.

As she reached the edge of the garden she saw the lights snap on at the opposite end of the exhibit building. The light reflected against the closest trees and sent a greenish sheen along the top of the ankle-high grass below. She lifted her radio. "Danny, Will, I'm at the garden exit."

"We're in the trees across from you, Miss Sam. No sign of anything."

"Okay. Harrington, light it up." She glanced behind her. "Rick, look away."

"What—"

All of the floodlights flicked on. Rick muttered a curse as she angled her gaze toward the gravel parking lot. At night like this, the building looked like the mother ship from *Close Encounters*. Nothing moved beneath the glare.

"Harrington?" she asked into the walkie-talkie, her attention still on the outer edge of the lights' reach.

"Nothing here."

"Here, either. Guys, move in."

Slowly, checking shadows and thick patches of grass, they closed in on the north side of the building from three different angles. Not even a rabbit could have gotten past them in that light, but she didn't see anything. Weird.

Danny and Will joined up with them just outside the gift shop door. Now that she was standing full in them, the lights made her feel way too exposed, but she shrugged it off. Putting them out again would leave all four of them blinded.

"I'm getting a sunburn," Rick commented quietly.

"It must have been a tree branch in the wind," Will suggested, taking another glance at the darkness around them.

"I made sure that couldn't happen," she returned, lifting her radio again. "Harrington, which sensor tripped?"

"Northwest corner of the building."

She looked over there. And frowned. "Turn that light off," she instructed.

A second later it blinked out, sinking into a fading orange glow.

"What the devil is that?" Rick asked, passing her to approach the sensor.

Dammit. "It's a cat toy." The small, feather-covered bird hung from fish line just to one side of the sensor, so that a slight breeze would just swing it to the edge of the sensor plate, setting it off. It was way less than the fifty-pound mass limit, but it was also only six inches from the sensor. "Boost me up, Rick."

She grabbed his shoulder, putting her foot into his cupped hands. He lifted, and she yanked the toy free. A red-ink mark in the shape of a heart covered the yellow chest.

"Shepherd?" Rick asked, his face still as granite.

"Yep."

"How did he get this close without setting off the lights?"

"He's good." *Fuck.* "Harrington, do a real-time check on all the monitors inside the building."

"I just did. We're all clear."

Still cursing under her breath, she faced Will and Danny. "Do a door check, and make another sweep of the trees. We'll leave the lights on for the rest of the night."

"You aren't going into the exhibit?" Rick asked quietly, as the two men moved off.

"He's not in there. This was just a little hello gift, to let me know he's still around."

"And that he can get through at least some of your security without you knowing it."

"That, too."

Past Rick's shoulder, the bright silhouette of Henry Larson charged toward them. "Why wasn't I informed?" he yelled, waving his stolen walkie-talkie.

"Because nothing happened," she snapped, brushing past him.

He grabbed her shoulder. "This looks like something to me. I don't need you people stumbling around and compromising my investigation."

She jerked free and threw the bird at his chest. "Investigate this. It was just a prank."

As she walked back to the house, Rick didn't try to hold her hand. He stayed behind her, in fact, though she was pretty sure he was glaring at her backside rather than watching the shadows. While she was very aware of his large, glowering presence back there, most of her attention was farther back, listening for someone to move on the slanted shingle roof of the exhibit hall.

He kept quiet all the way up the stairs and down the length of the north wing to the bedroom suite. That wasn't good. It meant he wanted to yell about something, and he wanted privacy to do it. Hm. Maybe she should try taking off all her clothes. It had definitely thrown her off when he'd done it earlier. The problem this time was an unusual one—she had no idea what he was mad at.

The bedroom door clicked closed behind her. Feigning a yawn, she sat on the edge of the bed to pull off her shoes.

"You're certain the cat toy was a gift from Shepherd?" he said into the silence.

"I'm sure." She pulled off her emergency jeans and T-shirt and folded them, shoving them back under the nightstand before she slid beneath the soft, cool sheets again.

Rick still stood beside the bed. "So Shepherd was here, with one wall between him and all those gemstones."

"One wall and a lot of high-tech security," she returned.

"Then why didn't you give Shepherd's name to Larson? And why did you tell a Scotland Yard inspector that the toy was just a prank?"

"It *was* just a prank." She curled onto her side. "He wanted me to know he was there. That's why I left the lights on—I'd bet a Picasso that he was up on the exhibit hall roof when we got out there. My little gift to him."

"*What?*"

She frowned up at him. "What what? So he made it past the outside motion sensors. He won't get in—not from the roof, unless he makes a lot of noise. He either wasn't planning on it or he'd already given up. Otherwise he wouldn't have started tripping the lights. He just wanted to pull me out of bed at two o—"

"A known cat burglar tripped our alarm system and is still on the premises. Even if you think he either can't or won't be able to pull off a robbery, I'm not certain it's up to you to decide that. And as for you declaring it's a prank and choosing to keep information about Shepherd's probable location from a member of Scotland Yard who's here for this very reason—you're crossing the line, Samantha." His frown deepened. "In my opinion, of course."

Samantha blinked. She'd been raised a thief, but she figured she knew right from wrong. As far as she'd been concerned, Bryce was trying to push her buttons. The fact that he'd broken the law just by being on the property and that she should have reported him for that reason hadn't even occurred to her.

Rick looked at her for a long moment. "No response?" he murmured, then turned around and headed back for the door.

"Where are you going?" she asked.

"To get Larson and pull a damned thief off my roof."

Moving fast, Samantha scrambled across the bed and put herself between Rick and the door. "No, you're not."

"You really think you can stop me?"

With her standing there in nothing but her panties and him tall, angry, and fully clothed, she wasn't so sure. One of her dad's rules, though, had been never to let 'em see you sweat. "He's gone by now," she hedged.

"I'm going to check anyway. And Larson needs to know."

"No." She didn't budge from blocking the door.

His fists clenched, but he didn't move in on her. "You'd bloody well better tell me why I shouldn't roust every police officer in the county."

Shit. "Because Bryce is testing *me.* If the cops grab him before he tries anything more than hanging cat toys, it's going to get out."

"What'll get out, exactly? That you made a preemptive strike?"

"That I had to call in reinforcements because I didn't trust my own security setup."

"Samantha—"

"I can't. It's my fault, Rick. If I was just . . . normal, then I'd say yes, call the cops. But I'm not normal, and I have to prove to both the good guys and the bad guys that I can do this. Do you get that?"

"I get it."

"Right."

"I get it," he repeated more firmly. "But I think there has to be a point where you stop making things harder on yourself because of what you used to be."

Well, he didn't seem to be trying to bulldoze the door down any longer. "Can I get back into bed to continue this?" she asked. "Because it's kind of cold out here."

Richard's gaze lowered to her bare breasts. They were spectacular, and he couldn't help himself. "Yes, fine," he returned stiffly, leading the way since she probably wouldn't have left her guard station otherwise.

She jumped back into bed and pulled the covers up to her neck. "Okay, get in here. But first, that's bullshit."

Of course, she'd waited to say that until his shirt was halfway over his head. He finished yanking it off. "What's bullshit—that you don't have to compensate, or the 'used to be' part?"

"The compensating part. Because what I used to be is never going to go away. We met because of it."

"We're not still together because of it." Kicking off his shoes and shrugging out of his pants, he slid into bed beside her.

"Yes, we are. You get off on me being bad." Her brow furrowed. "Or that I might be bad. And I still have people looking for me. Do you know how many jobs I pulled in the seven years before we met? I'm still wanted for those, Rick."

"I know that. That's why we take steps to—"

"And that's not even what this is about," she interrupted before he could finish saying that no one was going to arrest her for her past because he wouldn't allow it. He had a hell of a lot of weight to throw around, and for her, he would do it.

"What's it about, then? You covering for a former lover because you used to work in the same business?"

"Jerk. I'm with you. Because I'm with you, the people I used to know figure either that I'm stealing on the side and using our public relationship as a shield, or they figure that I'm unfairly living the good life. Either way, they're going to try to hit you, and me. If I can't prove that I'm capable of holding them off without calling for help, they're going to keep hitting us. Now do you get it?"

He leaned on one elbow, facing her. "How many people did you know?"

Her mouth crimped. "Let's just say that among us we've pulled every major job recorded over the last decade."

Carefully he kept his expression relaxed. "And what percentage of those were yours, just so we can eliminate them from the total number?"

"Ones that made the news, probably eight percent. Major jobs, probably ten or fifteen percent. Really difficult jobs, probably sixty percent."

She said it so matter-of-factly. He'd seen her work, and he knew that she was one of the best at what she did. But numbers-wise, the figures startled him. And scared the shit out of him—not because of the other people involved, but because every one of those jobs meant at least one person looking to arrest her. Or worse.

"Is that why you weren't particularly excited about beginning your own security business? Because of the likelihood that anything you set up would be hit?"

"That's one of the reasons."

"What are some others?" he asked skeptically. Samantha the security pariah—no wonder she hadn't wanted to discuss her business with him.

"Excitement. There isn't much in keeping things safe."

"Your adrenaline addiction."

"Yep. See what you signed up for?"

She sounded tough, but he noted that she didn't meet his gaze as she spoke. "I will admit," he said slowly, reaching over to curl a strand of hair behind her ear, "that you and I are similar. We see something, and we go after it. At times, our methods aren't even all that different."

"Ah, you use glass cutters and lock picks when you take over businesses?"

"I use whatever information I can get my hands on. And the way I get my hands on that information isn't always completely aboveboard. You know that."

"My point is, I'm a bad bet, Rick. This is just the clearest example of why."

"My ex-wife had an affair because I was more concerned with business than with whether she was happy or not."

"Yeah, well, Patricia's kind of a loony, so—"

"So we're both bad bets, depending on how you look at things. I love you, Samantha, and you could have told me about Bryce, and about why you didn't like installing alarm systems in Palm Beach."

"I just want you to understand that as long as we're together, you're going to have cat burglars on your roof. If you don't want that, then—"

He pulled her up against him, kissing her hard. "I want you," he growled, turning onto his back and pulling her over him.

God, he always wanted her. It seemed the only time he could be sure that he had control of her, of the situation, was when he could make her moan and come at his command. The way she could slip in and out of shadows—touching her, holding her hand, being inside her, it was then he knew she was there, and she was real, and she was his.

Samantha pushed his hands away to press herself closer against him. They both lived such high-pressure lives; sex had become both a way for them to reassure one another that they were still partners, and a simple, explosive release of tension. As Samantha slipped a hand beneath the sheets to gently massage his balls and his cock, he moaned. Yes, it was definitely a release. And very, very satisfying.

"Mm, somebody's happy," she breathed, biting his left earlobe.

He pulled her hips across his, trying to keep his eyes from rolling back in his head as she shifted to grasp him more firmly. "I can only think of one thing that could make me happier," he returned, running his mouth along her throat.

"And what might that be?"

"Returning the favor." Taking her shoulders, he flopped her over onto her back. His thighs beside her shoulder as she continued to stroke the length of him, Richard pulled her panties off and tossed them aside. He tugged her legs apart, drawing one of them beneath him so he could reach her with his mouth.

"It's a good thing I'm bendy," she rasped, jumping as he parted her folds with his fingers and caressed her with his tongue.

He chuckled against her. "A very good thing."

Her fingers flexed around him. "Oh, God, that feels good," she panted, her voice unsteady.

Richard found her sensitive nub and flicked it with his fingers. "This?"

She spasmed around his fingers, making a pleased, mewling sound. That alone was nearly enough to send him over, as well, especially with her clever hand on his cock. He fought back from the edge, his hard breathing mixing with her moans in the quiet evening.

"Get on your back," Samantha ordered shakily, releasing her grip.

He complied immediately. Then, wrapping his hands around her thighs, he pulled her down over him, impaling her. "Sam," he grunted, while she settled on his cock until he was fully engulfed in her tight, damp heat.

Samantha sat up, planting her palms on his chest, and lifted up and down, deep and fast. *Christ.* Even after eight months together, eight months of learning what the other liked and didn't like, he still felt on the very frayed edge of control with her. It was as if his body completely took over, letting his mind come along for the ride.

"Rick," she said shakily, bouncing faster.

She came right as he did, holding her thighs down hard against him until they were both finished. With a satisfied sigh, Samantha sank down on his chest, stretching her legs out to tangle with his.

"I won't butt out," he said quietly, into her tousled auburn hair, "but this, as you say, is your gig. Unless things change, I'll let Larson figure this out on his own. That is his job, after all."

"Thanks," she said, shifting just enough to kiss his shoulder.

He held her until he felt her relax, her breathing soft and even against his chest. Normally the sensation of her falling asleep in his arms left him humbled and moved, but tonight he was more grateful than anything else.

Ten minutes later he began a slow shift until she lay on the bed and he could slip out from beneath her. He waited again as she stirred and settled in again. Then he silently rose and pulled his clothes back on, swiping her walkie-talkie as he left the room and closing the door quietly behind him.

"Harrington," he said, after he flipped the radio on.

"Mr. Addison?"

"I'm going back out. Pay special attention to the roof of the exhibit hall while I'm there."

"Will do, sir."

However Samantha wanted to handle it, if he had a chance to catch Bryce Shepherd for so much as trespassing, he wasn't going to pass it up. The stakes were too high to do anything else.

Chapter 10

Monday, 8:12 a.m.

Samantha crept through the north wing and down the stairs, avoiding detection by the three people who passed her as she went, people who might have wished her good morning and ruined the stalking. At the breakfast room she leaned against the closed door, but didn't hear anything. Very slowly she turned the knob and inched the door open.

At three inches she could get a good look at the table. Rick sat there, flipping through a thick stack of papers and alternately scribbling down notes on a legal pad as he worked his way through a plate of scrambled eggs. Those English guys liked their breakfasts hot and full of cholesterol.

Nobody else was in the room, so she straightened and pushed the door open the rest of the way, closing and latching it behind her. "Good morning, my English muffin," she sang, leaning around him to plant a kiss on his coffee-tasting mouth.

"Good morning."

"Any sign of Larson this morning?"

"Sykes said he ate early. He's probably out patrolling the perimeter."

"Good. Maybe he'll fall in the lake."

He grinned briefly. "You treat criminals better than you do the police."

"Force of habit." She made her way over to the loaded sideboard. "So how many people are coming to dinner tonight?"

"Twenty or so. A few spouses and partners are a bit iffy, but I should know by this afternoon. Sarah will call me with the final count. And yes, we all get the day off tomorrow, so don't worry that I'm keeping them out too late on a weeknight. They can even stay over if they wish."

She frowned as she piled strawberries and a buttered croissant onto her plate, grabbed a chilled Diet Coke, and rejoined him at the table. "You're not going to the office today? You already skipped Saturday. And I thought you were lunching with the PM and some other MPs."

"Oh, very good on the lingo. I'm about to call and reschedule."

"For when, four weeks from now when the exhibit's finished? Do you know how stir-crazy you'll get, staying here every day, all day, for four weeks?"

He looked at her for a moment, a soft scowl on his face. Then he pulled out his phone and flipped it open. "Sarah? Have the helicopter come by for me, will you? And have Wilkins land on the dock, so we don't frighten any tourists." Rick listened for a second, then nodded. "That's fine. Thank you."

"Decided against the car?" Samantha asked offhandedly. "The diamond's in the safe, right?"

"The diamond, once again and for the last time, has nothing to do with any of this. I'm taking the copter because it's faster. And because I like saying it."

She laughed. " 'Send the helicopter' does have a certain ring to it." She popped a strawberry into her mouth. "The day off tomorrow is nifty, but just make sure you let your minions knock off work early today; they'll want to pretty up and they have to drive up here."

"Yes, my lady. I believe several of my minions and their significant others want to thank you in person for making their lives easier."

That actually made her feel good; she knew the impact Rick had on *her* work, but even though Rick said he used the advice she gave him and listened to her ideas, hearing concrete evidence of her contributions was rare. "I rule," she said with a grin.

"Yes, you do."

"And as the queen," she said, popping the tab on her soda, "I suggest you keep that diamond where nobody can see it, much less touch it."

He sighed. "The Nightshade Diamond has nothing to do with anything, and you know it. Bryce Shepherd came calling because he's a thief and you're protecting a gemstone exhibit. My tire blew because there was a nail in the road, and I lost the Blackpool project because I was late arriving for the meeting."

"Connoll and Evangeline believed it was cursed."

"They lived two hundred years ago, Samantha. Don't be . . ." He trailed off.

"What?" she insisted. "Stupid? Ignorant?"

"Superstitious. It's skill, cunning, and persistence that will win the day every time. Not luck." Rick took a last bite of egg and pushed away from the table. "Now, if you'll excuse me, I have to go catch a helicopter." As he walked by, he kissed her on the forehead. "Have a good day. You know how to reach me if anything happens. I can be here in twenty minutes."

She rolled her eyes. *Men.* Rich men, in particular. "Hey," she called to his back as he vanished through the door, "what time will you be home tonight?"

"I'll try for four o'clock. Dinner's set for six."

The exhibit closed at five, which would give her an hour to dodge him, find something appropriate to wear, and steal the diamond out of the safe. If he didn't believe in bad luck, then he could just carry it around with him tonight. Turnabout was fair play, after all.

At nine in the morning, they opened the gates. The crowd was smaller, though still pretty substantial for a Monday in the middle of Devonshire. Apparently the exhibit had been put on some must-see travel websites, because by eleven two busloads of Japanese tourists and one of Americans were parked in the gravel lot.

As Craigson's two riders rounded up a half dozen wanderers trying to make their way onto the sitting room terrace from the lake, though, she began to wonder whether it wasn't just the opportunity of seeing Rick Addison and Rawley Park up close that had prompted all the visits. He was fairly fanatical about his privacy, after all, and had never opened his house to the public before. That would of course change in December when the south wing art gallery opened, but right after the grand opening hopefully she and Rick would be back in Palm Beach. Jamie Craigson could be security *el jefe* by then.

"Larson's on his way in," Craigson said, glancing over his shoulder at her.

She straightened. *Get with it, Sam.* Just because it was daylight and she had her own minions helping her watch the place didn't mean she could drift off like that. One of the garden cameras caught the inspector's backside as he entered the house.

"I could tell him I saw somebody in the woods," the chief guard suggested. "That would get rid of him for an hour or so."

"Don't tempt me, Jamie."

A minute later somebody keyed the door entry code. "What channel are you using on the walkie-talkies?" Larson asked, shoving the door open.

"Hi, there," Samantha returned, swinging around in her chair. "Good crowd for a Monday, don't you think?"

"Stop messing about, Miss Jellicoe. You know I have a radio, so you told everyone to change the security channel. What is it?"

She grimaced at him. "Are you really going to be here for all four weeks?"

"I have another fortnight of holiday leave coming," he returned stiffly. "I'll stay until it's finished, or until I catch my robber—whichever comes first."

"You're a pretty dedicated guy, then," she said grudgingly, "using your vacation to stake out this place."

"My source is a reliable one, whether my superiors want to pay me to be here or not. I'm just doing my job."

"Aren't we all?" she muttered, sending Craigson a reluctant nod.

"Channel eight," Jamie supplied in his Scottish brogue.

"Thank you." Larson turned his radio to the proper channel. "That wasn't so difficult, now, was it? You see, we can cooperate." He left the room again.

"Give him till one o'clock, then switch to channel three," Samantha instructed, standing.

"Certainly. Where're you off to?"

"I'd like to do a walk-through, but that wouldn't go well." Too many people recognized her now, especially here at Addison central. "I'll make sure nobody else is trying to storm the castle."

"I'll beep you if anything changes here."

"Thanks, Jamie."

Tucking her walkie over her belt, she left the room. When Rick had listed the bad-luck occurrences not caused by the Nightshade Diamond, he'd left off Inspector Henry Larson. Her guys knew she was in charge, but if Larson hadn't been present, she would have felt a little more free to add a few more preventive measures to stop Bryce. Tipping off the law before anything actually happened—and might not ever happen—just didn't feel right.

She headed through the central part of the mansion to the sitting room at the back. The terrace doors were open, something Sykes usually did on pleasant days like this one, but with the hordes roaming around outside she wasn't sure that was such a good idea.

Halfway across the room, she slowed. "You know, Bryce," she said aloud, keeping her voice calm and even, "if you want to sneak around somewhere you should lay off the Old Spice aftershave."

"It's not Old Spice," his smooth Irish voice came to her left. "It's the very best a bloke could pinch from Harrod's. Show a bit of respect, will you?"

She faced him as he emerged from behind one of the free-standing display cases Rick had added to house his substantial collection of first-edition books. "Why the hell are you still hanging around here? You know you're never getting into that building."

"Yeah, thanks for leaving the lights on all night. If

that fella of yours had had a taller ladder to hand, I would have had to make a run for it."

Her fella? Dammit, had Rick gone out there again after she fell asleep? That was it; no more sex when there were potential prowlers around for him to stalk. "I was hoping it would rain. Rick hounding you was choice number two."

"Speaking of choice number two," he commented, walking up and slowly reaching out to run his fingers down her arm, "why him?"

"Don't make me smack you in the face," she returned, pulling her hand free from his. "It would ruin your one good asset."

"So you still think I'm pretty. Thanks, Sam. You're lovely as summer days, yourself." He tilted his head, brown eyes gazing at her speculatively. "You know," he said after a moment, "back there in Lord Rawley's wonderland I had me hands on first editions of *Journey to the Center of the Earth* and *20,000 Leagues Under the Sea*. They're worth a fair penny. You probably wouldn't even have missed 'em for weeks."

"Probably not. Once I did, though, I'd hunt you down and get them back."

"That might be fun." He grinned that charming, carefree grin of his—the smile of somebody still in the game, still in top form, and still loving it.

She used to have that same grin, until a couple of months before she'd met Rick. Until she'd begun to realize that eventually somebody was going to have to pay for all of the fun she was having, and that it would be her. "More fun for me than for you. I guarantee it. Leave, Bryce. Hit the exhibit next month."

"I thought about that, but the exhibit's not even the main attraction here anymore, now that I've seen you again. Come on, Sam, we were good together. And not just on the job." He closed in again, brushing his fingers across her cheek. "Do you still make that sound when you come, my girl?"

"Twice as loud, now," she retorted. "Back off. You're cute, but not that cute."

"Ah, you disappoint me. I could have a truck here in twenty minutes, you know. We could empty this house without anybody looking sideways at us. Then we could retire to Cannes or Milan or wherever it is you always wanted to retire to. Just lie on the beach and spend our afternoons picking tourists' pockets for lunch money."

"It was Morocco," she lied, "and now I can go there anytime I want, and have somebody else pay for lunch."

"Is this all a scam, then? You're setting up his lordship for a big fall? I had half a suspicion, but when Etienne got killed during that mess in Palm Beach, I wasn't so sure."

Why was it that her former colleagues and competitors just couldn't believe she'd gone legit? Why didn't any of them believe somebody could just decide to quit the game? Even her dad had made it clear that he expected she would return to the fold. And why could no one believe that she would never double-cross Rick, that she actually loved him, and to a kind of frightening degree?

"Just leave, Bryce," she said again. "I've been going easy on you because we used to be . . . friends."

" 'Friends.' " With that deceptive speed of his, he moved in and planted a kiss on her mouth.

She could have blocked him, but half of her wanted that kiss. Wanted to know if that spark between them still went that deep or not. He was a good kisser, even in stealth mode. His presence did conjure some pretty hair-raising adventures, got her heart pumping and the adrenaline flowing.

"Ya see?" he whispered. "You just think about it, Sam. I'll be about." With another jaunty grin he trotted onto the terrace and down the steps, vanishing around the corner of the house.

Samantha took a deep breath, then went over to close the glass terrace doors and latch them. Now she'd have to do a sweep of the house; while Bryce was considerably more skilled than the average tourist, that didn't mean someone hadn't gotten lucky and wasn't currently looking through her underwear drawer. Hell, Bryce might have been looking through her panties. She looked out over the terrace and the lake beyond again. Why couldn't shit ever just be easy? Simple? Why couldn't—

Her cell phone rang to the James Bond theme. Rick. Jumping a little, she pulled it off her belt and flipped it open. "Hi, stud muffin."

"Does that mean I've been demoted?" his low voice returned.

"Demoted? From what?"

"This morning I was your English muffin."

Get it fucking together, Sam. "I decided that 'stud' is more all-encompassing than 'English.' So technically you've been reinstated."

"Ah. Well, that's good, I suppose. I forgot to tell you, I'm flying in John Stillwell and Tom Donner for this evening. I just called Sykes to have him prepare two more rooms, but I thought you'd want to know before Tom came walking through the front door."

"And I haven't even set eyes on that damned diamond for two days. See, it's wonky after being hidden away for all that time."

"If you hadn't gone legitimate, I would be comforted

to know that I own at least one item you'd never try to steal."

"Ha, ha, funny man. What time are the spy and the Boy Scout getting here?"

"About two o'clock, I would estimate. They're arriving at Heathrow within twenty minutes of one another, so I'm having them share the limo."

"Next time you suggest fishing in Scotland, we're going."

"I'll hold you to that. How's the exhibit?"

"I haven't killed Larson yet, if that's what you're really asking."

"It is. I'll see you in a few hours."

"Okay. Give Tony Blair a kiss for me. He's an attractive man."

"Now who's being oh, so amusing? I love you."

"I love you. Be careful."

"You, too, my lady."

After she hung up the phone she stood in the sitting room for a couple of minutes, trying not to think about anything. Then she went to find the butler. "Sykes?"

"Here, Miss Sam," the scarecrow returned, emerging from the breakfast room.

"For the next couple of weeks, we're going to have to keep the terrace doors closed. Too many tourists walking around the premises."

"My apologies," he said, grimacing. "I hadn't thought. I'll see to—"

"I took care of it." She hesitated. "Rick said there are paintings of Connoll and Evangeline Addison in the portrait gallery. Are they labeled?"

"No. I can show you, if you like."

"Yes, please."

She fell in behind him as he climbed the stairs. Technically she should have asked for Connoll, the Marquis of Rawley, and his marchioness, but that took way too long to say, and she needed to call Craigson and have him send somebody in to help her give the house a quick once-over. If you could give a house with a hundred and ten rooms a quick anything.

The portrait gallery was actually the upper long hallway joining the north and south wings of the house. Tall windows lined one side, while hundreds of portraits, mostly family or notables who'd stayed at Rawley Park, filled the opposite wall. About halfway down the length of the hall, Sykes stopped. "Connoll and Evangeline Addison, Lord and Lady Rawley," he intoned, gesturing.

"Thanks, Sykes. I'll take it from here."

He inclined his head and continued along the hallway, probably to oversee the readying of two additional guest rooms. Samantha waited until he was out of sight, then looked up.

Wow. Rick definitely got his athletic good looks from his great-great. Merry and self-confident blue eyes gazed straight back at her from a very handsome, tall, black-haired man wearing blue and gray Regency-period formal dress. Seated in the chair beside him, a pretty, half-smiling young blonde woman probably eight or nine years his junior wore equally gorgeous clothes, a soft blue silk with lace everywhere.

His left hand covered her right shoulder, and she leaned a little into the embrace, lifting her own hand to touch the back of his. Samantha had read enough faces and postures over the years to recognize two people in love when she saw them.

Automatically her gaze dipped to the bottom of the portrait. It was a Lady Caroline Griffin, the premiere female portraitist of her age, and worth probably a million pounds sterling.

Exquisite as the painting was, for once it was the characters within it that interested her more. They were the ones who'd hidden the Nightshade Diamond. Had it brought them bad luck? Had they disagreed over whether it was cursed or not? Had she put it in his pocket the evening that he had an important dinner party in an attempt to prove that the curse wasn't just stupid superstition?

Whatever had happened, they'd put it someplace they'd hoped no one would ever find it—and more importantly, they'd had what according to Rick had been a very good, loving marriage that had produced three children—and ultimately, Rick Addison, the present Marquis of Rawley.

She returned her gaze to Evangeline. "You'd do it, wouldn't you?" she muttered. "To prove a point?"

Lady Rawley didn't answer, but then if she had, Samantha would have gone and checked herself into the nearest psychiatric hospital. She'd seen what she needed to in the portrait—two very sane-looking people who'd been in love, and who'd believed that the Nightshade Diamond was cursed. Now she wanted Rick to believe it, too, if for nothing else than his own good. And hers, of course.

Chapter 11

Samantha watched the monitor as Ernest and the limousine rolled through the front gates, turning up the drive rather than joining the line to the parking lot.

"I guess your plan for closing the gates and refusing them entry didn't work," Craigson commented.

"You're totally fired," Samantha returned, cuffing him on the shoulder as she got up and left the room.

John Stillwell wasn't so bad; despite the fact that when she'd first met Rick's personal assistant she'd thought he was an intruder and tackled him to the floor, so far he was turning out to be a trustworthy and honest guy. And most importantly, he allowed Rick to spend more time with her. She didn't consider herself particularly clingy or needy—just the opposite, in fact—but she could tell that having backup he trusted left Rick more relaxed.

Donner, though—okay, yes, she trusted him, and she

knew Rick considered Tom to be his best friend. But cripes, he was so . . . superior, and prickly. A Boy Scout. His wife, Katie, was great, and his three kids were fun, but she and Donner would never see eye-to-eye. Maybe it was more fun for both of them that way.

She walked into the huge foyer as Sykes pulled open the front door. "Hey, John," she greeted Rick's personal assistant and second-in-command, stepping forward and holding out her hand. "How was Canada?"

He smiled. "Surprisingly warm. I could have done with fewer jumpers," he returned in his cultured London accent.

While Sykes sent some of his staff out to collect suitcases, Samantha took a breath and faced Tom Donner, attorney-at-law. "Donner."

He eyed her. "Jellicoe."

"How was your flight from Miami?"

"Smooth."

"Too bad." Sykes cleared his throat, and she backed up. "Sykes'll show you to your rooms," she said, flipping the butler a salute and heading back for the security office.

"When's Rick gonna be here?" the tall, blonde former Texan drawled at her back.

She slowed. "In about two hours. You guys probably have time to go see the exhibit, if you want."

"I've been looking forward to that," Stillwell put in with another smile.

"You're not going to have me frisked or strip-searched or anything, are you, Jellicoe?"

Samantha clucked her tongue. "As if." She wished she'd thought of that; it would have been funny.

As she went down the stairs she radioed Hervey, who was manning the door today, that two VIPs would be coming from the house, and to not take them down for being out of the designated visitor area. If it had been just Donner she would have been tempted, but her staff reflected on both her and Rick, and on the exhibit. Another time, maybe.

"They'll still have to go through the metal detectors," Larson's voice came. "No exceptions."

Great. He'd found their new frequency. "Thanks for reminding us, Mr. Assistant Assistant Curator," she shot back. "Keep the line clear for exhibit security."

"This is Danny, north garden," Danny's voice came in almost on top of hers. "I have two females here who were apparently trying to gain access to the house."

She sighed. "AGs?" she asked, using the shorthand for Addison Groupies.

"Affirmative."

"Escort them back to the exhibit area," she returned, ignoring the faint squeal—"Is that Sam Jellicoe?"—behind Danny's voice.

"Hush. I'm talking. Will do, boss."

Rick brought his own set of problems to a security event, but he already knew that, and she'd decided against bringing it up last night. Ah, the perils of being obscenely wealthy and good-looking. Still, if she ever needed ammunition, the girls in the garden might be handy to mention.

As she walked back into the security room, Craigson was chuckling. "What?" she asked.

"Take a look."

He indicated one of the garden monitors. Danny was walking two girls back in the direction of the exhibit. "Jeez, what are they, fifteen?"

"Look closer."

She leaned toward the monitor just as Danny directed

the girls around a hedge. One of them wore a shirt that read "Marry me, Rick," while the other's said "M.I.T.—Mistress-in-Training."

With a snort, she sat back again. "Make me a print of that, will you?"

"Of course."

"At least they decided who would do what. Very organized of them."

A minute or two later Craigson handed her the glossy color photo, and she sat with him, watching the monitors as the girls finally went into the hall. A couple of minutes later Donner and Stillwell followed.

Finally Jamie stretched. "You know, I can watch this," he said. "You could go get gussied up for your dinner."

"Yeah, okay. I'll keep the radio on." Standing again, Sam looked down at the photograph. "Do you think Mrs. Ricky's still here? Maybe I'll just borrow her shirt."

"If you do, *I* want that picture."

"Don't let Larson know I'm not in here. I don't want him getting any ideas about trying to take over security."

With that, she headed back into the main part of the house and on up the stairs to the master bedroom suite. After Bryce's stupid cat toy the night before last she hadn't been sleeping as well, but she was also used to working that way, with nobody ever noticing. A quick shower, though, would be nice. And then a little B&E.

The problem with lifting the Nightshade Diamond wasn't getting it out of the safe; it was that she didn't want to hold on to it once she retrieved it. So she had to time it close enough to Rick's arrival that the curse wouldn't have time to do anything to her before she could slip it into his pocket.

After a quick shower she pulled a red dress out of the wardrobe. It was calf-length and long-sleeved, sleek yet sophisticated. And Rick loved it when she wore red. If she had to go to this dinner, she was going to look good doing it. Just before she pulled it on she wound a band of duct tape on the inside of one sleeve, right below her elbow. Then she slid into the dress.

"Wow."

Surprised, she turned around. Rick stood in the dressing room doorway, leaning against the frame. "You're back early. And high marks on the sneaking."

"Thanks. There wasn't much traffic, up in the sky like I was." He made a flying gesture with his hands.

"Smart-ass."

"Come here and say that."

Samantha frowned. "No way. You smell like helicopter. Take a shower and put on your James Bond tux, and then we'll talk."

"I'm not James Bond."

"You're my James Bond."

Pushing away from the doorframe, he came forward to take her hand and bring it to his lips. For a brief fairy-tale moment, she felt like a princess. Fairy tales, though, weren't for girls with secret Swiss bank accounts and serious unlawful-acquisition issues.

"Very smooth," she murmured. "Shower."

As soon as the water turned on, she hurried into his dressing room. The safe lay in the back corner, one of several he owned, and mostly to protect copies of estate papers in case of fire. Samantha hitched up her hem and knelt in front of it. He had so much security around the mansion that the safe was almost an afterthought.

Glancing over her shoulder, she placed her left palm flat on the front of the metal safe, directly beside the tumbler. With her right hand she spun the tumbler twice, then began a slow turn clockwise, number by number. If she hadn't wanted the safe to remain in usable condition she could have punched the dial, but that was out of the question. Feeling a faint click within the door, she headed back counterclockwise, then went slowly forward again.

At the third click she turned the handle and pulled open the door. "Easy, breezy," she muttered.

Rick also apparently kept some spare cash up here, because she had to move aside a couple thousand pounds, and an equal number of American dollars, before her fingers touched the small velvet bag. Mindful of when she'd tossed the wrong diamond into the lake, she tugged open the strings and looked inside.

"Hello, Nightshade." Before it could work any voodoo on her she closed the bag again, shifted the money back into place, and closed the safe.

She left his dressing room and returned to the main part of the suite, the velvet bag squeezed in her hand. If Rick hadn't been so dismissive about both the bad luck and more importantly her belief in the bad luck, she wouldn't have done it. There was even a small chance that nothing would happen, in which case he would never let her live it down. Then, though, his right to derision would be earned, not just something he handed out because it was an object and he lived in the twenty-first century, and nobody believed anything was cursed anymore.

The shower stopped. Swiftly she stuck the bag up her sleeve, sliding the edge of it under the strip of duct tape. When Rick reappeared with nothing on but a towel, she was seated on the bed fastening her red high-heeled Ferragamos.

"Have you heard anything else from Shepherd?" he asked, heading into his dressing room. "Any more cat toys or anything?"

"Not a thing," she lied. If Rick ever found out that Bryce had kissed her, and that she'd allowed it, all hell would break loose. "You did have somebody call on you here, though."

He leaned out. "I did? Who?"

Samantha picked up the photo that Jamie had printed out for her and crossed to his dressing room. Leaning around the doorway, she handed it in. She felt him take it, and then waited.

"Oh, good God," he muttered.

She laughed. "I'm putting it in the scrapbook."

"You most certainly are not." He paused. "Help me with this, will you?"

Like he wasn't a professional at putting on tuxedos. Straightening, she walked into his dressing room. The towel had been replaced by his trousers, his shirt on but unbuttoned. God, he looked good. He snagged her hand, pulling her off balance in her heels, and swept her into his arms.

"Don't mess up my hair, bub," she said, hoping the tape would hold the bag in place.

"Fine. I'll finish dressing." His gaze still on her face, he slowly stood her upright again. "Are you certain everything's well?"

"I'm sure. Why?"

"I know you don't like attending these dinners," he said after a moment, buttoning up his shirt and then going to work on his bow tie, "but this is more like a family event. You know just about everyone attending, and we have had a very good quarter."

"I don't mind," she stated, helping him with his

jacket. "It's just keeping the cop in the house, the crook outside, and the gems where they are, I guess. My version of multitasking."

"Several tasks most people couldn't begin to handle. Just relax tonight. All you need to do is eat dinner and not tackle anyone."

"No promises," she returned with a grin as he transferred his cell phone and other accoutrements to his tux pockets, "but I'll do my best."

Rick touched her cheek, then leaned down and kissed her softly. "Even your worst is above most peoples' reach."

"You're already getting lucky tonight, Rick. You want the free trip to Maui, too?"

"Is that part of the package?"

"That depends on how close you make me sit to Donner."

Chuckling, he took her hand and headed for the door. "One day I'm going to put the two of you in a room and just let you fight it out."

Surreptitiously Samantha slipped the bag into his left side pocket, then folded the used duct tape with her fingers and dumped it into the trash can as they left the room. Whether she and Donner went toe-to-toe or not, tonight was going to be interesting. Especially for Rick.

He'd been wondering whether moving the dinner party to Rawley Park during the first week of the gem exhibit might be a bad idea, but once Richard saw Samantha in one of the red dresses she bought just because he liked them, he stopped doubting. It was a very, very good idea.

And she'd worn her new diamond necklace, when

she rarely wore any jewelry. He'd learned that several months ago when she'd informed him that she tended not to put on anything that might fall off during a robbery. Other people probably thought she was just modest.

"What are you grinning at?" she asked, as they descended the staircase together.

"Just thinking about later," he improvised. "Apparently I'm getting lucky."

"Like that's a surprise. I'm going to go check in on Harrington for a sec, and see if I can find a way to lock Larson in his room."

He released her hand. "I, ah, invited him to dinner."

Her eyes narrowed. "You what?"

"He's staying here, Sam. I couldn't exclude him."

"Yes, you damn well could have. Forget about getting lucky, your lordship. That's only for the guy who doesn't invite the idiot cop to eat dinner with us."

Frowning, he watched her glide across the foyer to the sound of her heels faintly clicking. High heels were something else she generally avoided while working, but she looked very tasty in them. That was his Samantha, petite, graceful, able to blend in perfectly to fit any occasion, and still standing out to someone who knew what to look for. And packing more punch than an angry rhino when she was mad.

"Hey, Rick," Tom Donner's low drawl came, and he turned around. The attorney appeared from the direction of the garden, a bag bearing the All That Glitters logo in his hand.

"Tom." Rick shook his free hand. "You visited Samantha's exhibit, I see."

Donner glanced down at the bag. "Olivia asked me to bring her home one of the programs."

"Samantha would have given you one."

"Oh, no. Livia said specifically that I had to buy it in order to support the charities getting money for the exhibit."

"Your daughter is a great philanthropist."

"Yeah, for a ten-year-old."

Grinning, Richard patted Tom on the shoulder. "Let me walk you back to your room."

"I don't know." He looked from his polo shirt and jacket to Richard's attire. "You kind of make me look bad right now."

"Do you need a tux?"

"No, I brought mine. I just don't like to fly in it."

The two men headed up the main staircase and for the nearest rooms on the north wing. "Did you find anything out about Bryce Shepherd?" Richard asked once they were well out of Samantha's earshot.

"His file looks a lot like Jellicoe's," Donner returned. "He practically doesn't exist. A possible suspect in a couple of cat burglaries, mostly in Italy, Spain, and here, but that's it."

"Does he work alone?"

The attorney slowed. "Is there any reason in particular you're asking me that question?"

At least Samantha's name hadn't been linked on paper to Shepherd's, or Tom would have been all over the information. "I asked because I want to know if the bloke lurking about the exhibit works with a partner. Is there anything else you'd like to know before you give me the information I asked for?"

"Don't get testy. My question was legit, and you know it. After all, Jellicoe's dead dad showed up in New York a couple of months ago and wanted to work with her. This Shepherd's still alive."

"Tom, I'm not going to ask you ag—"

"A couple of the thefts in the U.K. that might have been his work might have been the work of more than one thief. That's all the file said, and that's all I know. Sheesh."

"Was that so difficult?" Richard asked, not certain whether he was relieved or not.

"After a five-hour plane trip? Yeah. You could have threatened me over the phone."

"You're here for the dinner. The threats were just convenient. Go change. I'll have some champagne out on the sitting room terrace while we wait for everyone."

"And some bourbon, I hope."

"For you, yes."

"Good."

Richard went into the sitting room as two members of his staff took glasses and champagne out to a linen-covered table on the terrace. "Some bourbon for Mr. Donner, too, if you please," he said, taking a seat close to the stone balustrade while the two women lit the lanterns sitting at the center of each of the tables.

As the servers left the terrace, one of the mounted guards hired by Samantha rode by, saluted, and continued on in the direction of the stable. Richard blew out his breath. From the outside, his life looked like a bloody paradise. On the inside, the picture was a little different.

Yes, he'd never been happier. Life with Samantha had a way of altering his perspective on . . . well, on everything. He spent fewer hours working now, and more just enjoying himself. And he could certainly afford private helicopters and airplanes and long weekends in the Caribbean. But while before he'd taken certain things for granted—that his cameras and alarms would keep his possessions safe, that his amusements would be tangled in with the flash of cameras and the hounding by reporters—it was all so much more complicated now.

Previous to Sam, he'd had no idea that a thief could do the things she did. And while he'd discovered and witnessed enough to know that very few others were as skilled as she was, there were a couple of them out there. A few thieves who could match her, catch her, hurt her. Thieves who knew more about her past than he probably ever would. Thieves like Bryce Shepherd.

He shook himself. Tonight was a celebration, not a retrospective on all his worries and nightmares. He checked his watch. His minions, as Samantha called them, would begin arriving within the next twenty minutes or so. Which gave him that time to do something he rarely ever did—nothing.

Sipping the glass of champagne he'd snagged, he looked out over the lake. The swans were close by, ready for their evening feed—though they looked perfectly plump and happy to him. A couple of traveling ducks had joined them, probably having gotten word of a free meal. Richard grinned to himself. Everybody could celebrate tonight.

"Good evening, Mr. Addison."

So much for the relaxing moment of nothing. He steadied his expression before he turned his head. "Inspector. Or I suppose I should ask how you would like to be introduced tonight."

"Henry Larson of the V & A will be fine," the inspector returned. "I don't want *everyone* knowing that I've staked out the exhibit."

"Any leads or further information on who your potential burglar might be?" Richard asked, pasting on his pleasant businessman expression and gesturing at a neighboring chair. This was for Samantha, he told himself. He could talk to an idiot for five minutes for her sake.

"Not a thing. I thought the cat toy might be a clue, but Miss Jellicoe seems convinced that it was some teenagers from the village."

"She's fairly good at figuring those things out."

Larson cleared his throat. "That brings something to mind. May I speak candidly for a moment?"

"Of course."

"I was somewhat surprised that the V & A would grant you the honor of holding the exhibit here. The—"

Richard straightened. "I beg your pardon?"

"No, no, I don't mean to offend. I only meant because of the theft of some of your paintings late last year."

"That was an inside job, as they call it," Richard returned stiffly. "Someone who'd been in my employ for ten years got greedy. And it happened in Florida. Not here."

"Yes, I see. And what about Miss Jellicoe?"

Anger began to creep through Richard's muscles. "What about her?" he asked quietly.

"Well, she is the daughter of a renowned cat burglar. Trusting her with a multimillion-pound collection of gemstones seems somewhat . . . careless."

Richard leaned forward, putting his palms flat on the table. "Where you come from, Mr. Larson, is it customary for a guest to insult his host and hostess?"

"No. I'm just saying, it makes one wonder what—"

"So, Inspector," he interrupted, and took a drink of champagne, "have you been enjoying your stay here?"

"Yes. Yes, I have. You—"

"And do you believe that I could steer your law enforcement career in a direction you might not find entirely agreeable?"

Larson's face reddened. "The—well, I have a job t—"

"With that in mind," Richard continued, ignoring the attempts at an explanation he had no interest in hearing, anyway, "I suggest you exercise a bit more discretion when you speak of the lady of the house."

"Well, you have to admit, she does have a—"

"Given that her father was a very successful thief, Samantha has made it a point to study various security measures and methods. She is an expert in that field, in fact. That is the beginning and the end of your contact with and interest in her. If I hear another word about the possibility of her guilt by association, I will see you ticketing parked cars in Piccadilly. Is that clear?"

"Very clear, sir."

"Good. Why don't you trot down to the security room and make certain that everything's shipshape before my guests arrive?"

The inspector bolted to his feet, his face darkening further and his expression a mixture of mortification, fear, and fury. As soon as he was gone, Richard rose to find Samantha leaning against the sitting room doorframe and gazing out over the lake.

He handed her a glass of champagne and toasted it with his own. "Pleasant fellow, really—once you get to know him."

She snorted. "Christ, Rick, you nearly made me wet *my* pants. You are so cool."

"And don't you forget it."

Chapter 12

Monday, 8:27 p.m.

*Maybe Rick had been right about the Night-*shade Diamond, after all.

He stood at the head of the huge dinner table, everyone rising to their feet in response, and lifted his glass. "To us," he said with his warm smile. "May we have as much success in the next months as we've had in the previous ones."

"To us," everyone echoed, and drank.

Samantha stood at Rick's right elbow, reviewing the evening thus far. He'd nearly gotten into a fight with Larson, which she couldn't classify as bad in any form. He'd greeted each of his guests and their significant others and had remembered everyone's name and relationship—no evil there. And the lobster and steak dinner was fabulous—Jean-Pierre had outdone himself.

They all sat, and Rick reached over to take her hand. "I'm glad I did this here," he said, his smile deepening.

She shifted, uncomfortable at the pure happiness in

those Caribbean-blue eyes. And she'd put a curse in his pocket. Maybe *she* was the evil part of the evening. "This is great," she returned easily. "When do the clowns and the party hats come out?"

"No clowns, but we do have an orchestra and dancing, some spectacular surprise desserts, and some lovely parting gifts, if I do say so myself."

For a bunch of big-money players, his inner circle was a pretty jovial lot. Except for Donner, who admittedly did clean up pretty well. She'd met most of them before, and as formal evenings went, so far it had been pretty stress—and evil—free. "You're a nice guy, to do this."

"You're the one who's been telling me to be nicer," he commented, squeezing her fingers. "And they deserve it."

"You two are going to give me a cavity," Tom Donner said from his seat directly across the table from her.

Samantha thought it was pretty brave of him to sit within kicking range, especially with her in spiked heels, but then he probably knew that she wouldn't want to cause a scene at Rick's party. While she was deciding on the appropriate tone for her reciprocal zinger, John Stillwell, beside her, touched her hand.

"I wanted to tell you, Sam," he said as she faced him, "the exhibit hall is outstanding. The way you designed the lighting to enhance the visual elements of the displays—no wonder Rick wanted you to design his art gallery here."

Now, there was a man who knew how to give a good compliment. "Thanks, John," she said with a warm smile. "The overhead lighting was kind of a last-minute change; I thought we were going to have too much light reflection off the gems, otherwise."

"It's brilliant. The Ashmolean should send someone up here to take a look. They have some reflection problems you could probably help them with."

That could be yet another career for her—lighting designer to the world's greatest museums. "They're welcome to come by, but I think I have enough on my plate."

"Speaking of lighting," Jane Ethridge, Rick's international personnel coordinator, said from beside Donner, "I haven't been able to take my eyes off your necklace all evening, Samantha. Where did you get it?"

Samantha glanced at Rick. If she'd bought it for herself, she wouldn't have hesitated, but this question fell well inside the realm of relationship land, and she couldn't count the number of holes and prickly plants in there.

He smiled. "It's from Cartier, in Paris. When I saw it, I thought it looked exquisite and unusual, which made it perfect for Samantha."

"It is both," Jane agreed. "It's absolutely stunning."

"Thank you," Samantha returned, reaching up a finger to touch it.

"While we're on the subject of precious gems," Rick continued, "you'll never guess what Samantha discovered in an old wall here at the estate."

She sent him another look, this one not as affectionate. If he thought he was going to tease her in public about the damned Nightshade and the curse, if he thought she was trapped here because of her obligations to the exhibit, he had a surprise in store.

"Tell us," Jane urged, the request echoed by the rest of the table.

"It was a diamond necklace, hidden there by my great-great-grandfather, Connoll."

"Are you sure you didn't just stash some loot there

and forget about it, Jellicoe?" Donner muttered, so no one else could hear.

"Ooh, you discovered my secret," she whispered back, smiling brightly at him.

"My goodness! How did that happen?"

"Connoll left a note with it. Apparently it has the reputation for being cursed, and he didn't want to risk any bad luck for himself or his new bride, my great-great-grandmother, Evangeline. Very romantic, really."

Sam relaxed a smidgen. Okay, no curse jokes so far.

"What are you going to do with it now that you've found it again?"

"I'm not certain yet. It's a lovely clear blue diamond, and I'd love to display it, but I'm not willing to curse anything by accident."

His guests laughed.

"I'd love to see it," Emily Hartsridge, the wife of Rick's London administrator, said. "A cursed diamond hidden away in a wall. It does sound very romantic."

Great. Who was supposed to be suffering under the damned curse right now, anyway? If Rick decided to go up to the safe and get the Nightshade, she was up shit creek without a plunger.

When Samantha sent a glance back at him, he was gazing at her. She could guess what he was thinking— was showing off a unique sixteen-million-dollar diamond worth the very good chance of pissing her off? All she could do was look straight back at him and be glad he couldn't read minds. Hers right now was twisting in so many directions it would have made him blow a gasket.

"Perhaps if we have time after dinner," he said. Classic business-guy Rick—noncommittal and polite.

Samantha took a breath as the conversation turned

to the diamond industry in general. One crisis averted. Now all she had to do was pick Rick's pocket, go upstairs, and put the diamond back in his safe before he tried to retrieve it.

"If you don't want it about, I'll leave it in the safe," he said in a low voice, stepping on the tail of her thoughts.

"Why should I care?" she asked flippantly, keeping her voice low. "Just don't expect me to touch it. It's *your* diamond."

"Are you certain?"

"Rick, don't cater to me like I'm some spoiled little kid. If you want to show it off, then show it off."

A muscle in his left cheek jumped, but otherwise his expression stayed cool and composed. "I don't want to fight with you."

"I'm not fighting."

"I'll go and get it after we adjourn to the ballroom, then."

"That's fine."

"Fine."

She looked across the table at Donner, who was at least pretending not to listen. "Do you still need a dentist?"

"No, I think I'm fine now," he returned.

Okay, if she couldn't fight either of them, she was going to make *somebody* uncomfortable. She hated to suffer alone. Henry Larson sat halfway down the table, and while she couldn't hear every word of his conversation, she did make out "museum" and "trusted position." *Aha.* "Mr. Larson," she said in a carrying voice, smiling, "since we're on the subject of diamonds, you should explain the selection process for the ones in the traveling exhibit."

For a second he sent her a look of pure hatred. Amid the encouragement from the others at the table, he began a rambling discussion about carats and diamond mine locations that sounded like stuff he'd overheard during three days of standing in the exhibit hall and listening to the actual V & A employees. *So there.*

As dessert ended, Rick announced that he'd arranged for entertainment in the ballroom. The group began trooping upstairs to the second floor. Thinking fast, Samantha leaned up against Rick as he stopped at the foot of the stairs, digging into his pocket as she did so.

"I'm going to check in with Harrington," she said, stepping back and removing the Nightshade from his pocket in the same motion.

"Does this mean you're not angry any longer?" he inquired, taking her wrist in his fingers.

"I'm not mad."

"Don't be long, then," he returned. "As soon as I get everyone situated, I'm going to get the diamond."

"Like I said," she commented with a half smile, clenching the diamond in her hand, "just don't expect me to touch it. You can give it to Donner, though, if you want. In fact, I recommend it."

"Mm-hm. I won't tell him you said that."

She turned in the direction of the cellar door, but as soon as she was out of the guests' sight she hurried past it to the old set of servants' stairs at the back of the house. Hiking up her skirt, she tore up the steep stairs to the third floor where the master bedroom suite stood. Putting aside the thought that it might have been simpler just to tell Rick he already had the diamond with him, she ran into the bedroom and closed the door behind her.

When she was halfway to Rick's dressing room, high-pitched violins began a staccato screech from her nightstand. The exhibit alarm on her cell phone. Her blood froze.

Oh, so the bad-luck thing worked on her right away. Cursing she grabbed up her walkie-talkie and charged back for the door. It opened as she reached it. And the man standing there wasn't Rick.

"What are you doing here, Larson?" she asked, scowling as she continued forward. "Get out of my bedroom."

Instead he closed the door behind him and locked it. "You are not very nice," he said.

"No, I'm not. And I just got an automated security-breach alarm, so we need to get going. You can tell me how unpleasant I am later."

"It's probably another cat toy."

"Oh, for crying out loud," she snapped, gripping the radio harder. "Move!"

"He said you would be confident to the point of arrogance."

She paused midway to putting a heel through his shiny dress shoe. "What?"

"You heard me."

A different kind of alarm began creeping through her skull and down her spine, fighting with the adrenaline rush of knowing a caper was happening just down the path. "Get out of my way. I'm not asking you again."

"Let's just stay here and chat for a bit, shall we?"

"The alarm went off, Larson. Get that through your skull, will you? I am not going to let you lock me in my bedroom to discuss my manners while somebody robs the exhibit." While Bryce robbed the exhibit, she was sure.

The inspector pulled a pistol from the back of his waistband and cocked it. "You're going to do exactly what I tell you to, Miss Jellicoe."

In an instant, it all clicked into place. He wasn't a bumbling detective, but an accomplice. He wasn't somebody on the lookout for a scapegoat in case of trouble, but somebody ready and willing to make trouble—with a gun. Samantha pressed the walkie's talk button and thumbed it on. "You really think you can keep me here in my own bedroom, Larson?"

Her voice made an odd echoing sound. *Fuck*. He had his radio with him. As her voice subsided he lifted the gun and pointed it at her head. "Put the radio down, Miss Jellicoe."

She complied, dropping it to the floor. "If you're really working with Bryce, you are not going to shoot me," she stated, moving a little closer to the wall, looking to get an angle on him. Whether he knew it or not, this was not the first time someone had pointed a gun at her. Panic meant death, and she was not going to panic.

"Don't move another inch. And he might like you, but he likes a couple million quid in jewels better."

Larson was probably right about that. Bryce did like his loot. And he was going to have a lot of it unless she could get out the damned door. Taking a breath, Samantha took another half step, twisting her foot a little so that her heel slid out from under her. "Damn," she muttered, reaching a hand against the wall to balance herself.

In the same motion she kicked out, slamming her heel into his shoulder. The pistol went off, and the lamp behind her head exploded. Larson fell over, grabbing his shoulder, and she kicked again, straight into his crotch. With a wheeze he rolled into a quivering, gasping ball.

Samantha grabbed the gun, unlocked the door, and ran.

As she flew down the hallway she realized that she still had the Nightshade Diamond clutched in her left hand. *Dammit.* Not having any pockets, she stuffed it into her bra. It had better have already spent its quota of bad luck for the evening—she couldn't take much more.

She rounded the corner to the main staircase—and slammed into Rick as he topped the stairs. "Ouch!"

He grabbed her shoulders. "I heard a gunshot and you on the radio. Are you all right?" he demanded.

"Yeah. Let go."

"Jesus. Just a minute." Gingerly he reached down to take the gun out of her hand. She'd nearly forgotten she held it. "What the bloody hell happened?"

"Larson's a black hat," she returned, shouldering past him. "The rest later."

She heard him thundering down the stairs behind her. If Bryce could help it, he wouldn't be hanging around once the alarm tripped—thanks to Larson, she might have missed him already. That had probably been the plan all along: Have stupid Larson bumble around and get in the way so Bryce could waltz off the estate unopposed.

"Do you have a radio?" she shot over her shoulder as they reached the ground floor and raced across the foyer.

"It's what sent me looking for you."

She reached out as he drew even with her, and he put it into her hand. "Harrington," she panted, "what's the op?"

"I don't know," his tense voice returned. "The cameras went black, then every alarm went off simultaneously. The computers shut the hall down."

Good. Then Bryce was probably still inside. "Don't unlock anything until I get there."

"Roger tha— Bloody . . . The fire alarm just went off. Shit. Sam—"

"Watch the doors!" she yelled into the walkie talkie, charging out of the house and into the garden. Next emergency, she was not wearing damn high heels.

Rick kept pace with her. "The fire alarm releases the doors, doesn't it?" he panted.

"Yep. Dammit. I was supposed to be there by the time anybody figured that out." She cursed Larson again.

At the far edge of the garden she slowed. Every guard on the premises surrounded the exhibit hall, concentrating on the doors at either end. A flash of sympathetic anxiety ran through her. She'd faced security people, but never like this. She wouldn't exactly have called it a career high for Bryce Shepherd.

With a slight frown she radioed Harrington to patch her in to the exhibit hall's internal speaker system. "Attention unauthorized occupant," she said in her most confident voice, trying not to feel stupid since she knew perfectly well who was inside, "the building is surrounded, and the authorities are en route. There is a blue phone on the left side of the entrance door. Pick that up to communicate with me."

Silence.

Come on, Bryce, she urged silently. She'd designed the place as a bring-'em-back-alive thief trap, in case anybody managed to break through her security system. A phone, a remote door release so nobody would have to bust in or out, guns blazing. If he didn't take advantage of what she offered . . . well, it would make him just like her.

She would be checking vents, roof integrity, looking for any opening big enough to squeeze into. Picking up that phone meant giving up, and she wouldn't do that until somebody snapped the handcuffs on her wrists. It was weird to be on this side of things, and easier to relate to what was probably going on inside than with the tense, alert faces she saw around her.

Rick touched her arm, and she jumped. "What?"

"If you aren't comfortable with this, I'll handle it."

"What are you, a mind reader?" she growled, wrenching her arm free. "He broke into my place and messed with my stuff. I don't sympathize. I get pissed. I'm just trying to figure out his next move. Okay?"

"Okay."

Her radio clicked. "Sammi, my love," Bryce's low lilt came, "how'd you get this number? I thought I was unlisted."

Until that moment she hadn't realized that she was disappointed in Bryce, knowing that he was still inside. He was good enough to have pulled this job; he had had half a chance of getting away. "Bryce, the doors are unlocked," she said, knowing everybody with a radio could hear both sides of the conversation.

"Ah, why don't you come on in, then, and we'll have a chat?"

"No bloody way," Rick snarled from beside her. "Wait for the police."

She scowled at him. "This is my gig, remember?" she snapped, lifting the radio again. "Larson tried to put a bullet in me, Bryce. I'm not going in there."

"He wasn't supposed to do that. I only wanted him

to put a bit of a scare into you, keep you occupied while I did my dance."

"Come out, Bryce," she returned. "Don't make the cops wreck my pretty exhibit hall."

No answer.

"What do you think he's up to?" Rick asked, moving closer to her—probably to grab her if she tried to go inside the hall.

"He doesn't want to be tied to the phone. He's still got half a chance of getting out before the cops and weapons arrive, and he's not going to waste it."

She could feel Rick's gaze on her, probably wondering how many times she'd faced this situation herself. "Will he find a way?"

"That depends on what tools he has with him. With a heavy hammer or a crowbar he could probably get out onto the roof. Quiet doesn't matter now."

His gaze lifted to the high, sloped roof of the old stable. Before he could ask anything else, Donner came trotting out from the house. Samantha glanced back in the direction of the garden. Rick's guests were there, watching and muttering among themselves. Great. Just great.

"What's going on?" the attorney asked.

"We're trying to stop a robbery," Rick said shortly.

"Jellicoe, or that Shepherd guy?"

Samantha lifted an eyebrow, shaking herself out of her own distraction. "You told him about Bryce?"

"I asked him to look into it, yes," Rick returned. "We'll save that discussion for later, when we have the one about Larson trying to shoot you."

She looked from the crowd to the building. The longer she stood around waiting for the authorities, the better Bryce's chances were for getting away with a fortune in precious gems. She'd never get another job like this, and Rick would never have the opportunity to contribute his name or fortune to an event like this again. And he loved doing this kind of thing. *Fuck*.

Bending down, she slipped out of her shoes. Rick watched her. "You are not going in there," he repeated.

"Do you really want to have this argument now?" she muttered, turning the volume down on the walkie-talkie and switching back to Harrington's main frequency.

"Yes, I do. Later, you might be dead."

"No. Bryce wouldn't hurt me."

"His friend nearly did."

She actually wasn't that sure, herself, but she knew Shepherd better than anyone else around here did. And she knew he was close to getting out, if he hadn't done so already. "This is my job, Rick."

"No, it's not. Setting up and maintaining security is your job. Not apprehending people who get through your security."

He still didn't get it. "Be here or not when I get back, Rick, but I'm going in. And you can't stop me."

"I could."

Samantha lifted up on her toes to meet his hard gaze. "Are you going to try?"

His jaw clenched. The I'm-in-charge guy in him would hate to relinquish any power, but he had to know what a fight between them over this could do. "Be careful," he finally ground out. "If I hear anything I don't like, I'm going in. And I will shoot him. I have no problem about that at all."

Chapter 13

Monday, 9:39 p.m.

Samantha took a deep breath, sent a last glance back at Rick's angry, concerned face, and pulled open the exhibit hall's main door.

Her mind wanted to take the time to sort out why she was willing to risk her relationship with Rick to walk into trouble, and if and when he would decide he'd had enough of her adrenaline addiction. *Later, Sam*, she told herself sternly. Worrying about her relationship with Rick right now could get her killed.

She went in, stepping quickly to one side so she wouldn't be silhouetted in the doorway, and let the door swing shut on its own. The red emergency lights were on, and the fire sprinklers bolted on the underside of the lowest roof beams sprayed water all over the displays, the walls, and the floor.

In the past she'd never thought twice about making as much of a mess as she wanted while pulling a job. Sometimes the confusion she left behind had even been to her benefit. But at this moment, the mess made her angry.

Instinctively she stayed close to the wall and moved silently as she searched the red dimness. The diamond displays were empty, along with a third of the other precious and semiprecious gem displays. If this was what it felt like to be robbed, she didn't like it. And this stuff technically wasn't even hers.

"Why are you hiding, Sam?" Bryce's voice came. "I thought you wanted to talk, to convince me to give up and walk myself off to prison."

"I asked you to wait, Bryce," she returned, trying to pinpoint his location in the noise and chaos around her. "And I warned you about what would happen if you didn't." She crouched, looking along the floor for feet or legs. Nothing. "Don't blame me for what you've gotten yourself into."

Weight slammed into the back of her shoulders, driving her to the floor. "Of course I blame you, Sam," Bryce breathed into her ear, his arm snaking around her throat. "You're what brought me here in the first place."

Panic flew through her, and she pushed back hard against it. Panic later; think now. "Jeez," she muttered, trying not to wheeze with his body pinning her to the wet floor, "put on some weight there, haven't you, Shepherd?"

"It's all muscle, me girl." He shifted. "Now come up with me slow, or I'll have to get rough. And I'd hate to bloody a face as pretty as yours."

Dammit. She'd let herself get distracted. Putting out her hands for balance, she let Bryce help her to her feet. He wasn't Henry Larson, and he wouldn't get suckered by a stumble and kick.

Once they were both standing, he released her and

took a step backward. "You do look very fine," he murmured, his gaze lingering on the wet front of her dress. "Like when you'd con your way into a house party to scope out where the new Rembrandt was hanging. There's nothing like seeing you on the job, love."

"We worked together on a job once, Bryce," she retorted. "Don't pretend we had some Butch-and-Sundance thing going."

"I think we were more like Bonnie and Clyde—off the clock, at any rate." He smiled his lopsided smile, even more charming with water showering down on him.

"What are you stalling around for?" she asked abruptly, her adrenaline ratcheting up another notch. The cops were on the way, for God's sake.

Since she couldn't imagine Bryce ever calling it quits voluntarily, he had some kind of plan. A plan that seemed to include keeping her there in the hall with him and waiting for the cops to show.

"I'm giving you another chance to come with me," he returned, brushing a straggle of wet hair out of her face. "There are a couple million pounds' worth of gemstones leaving this place with me. Having you on my side would make things a wee bit easier, Sammi."

"Get a clue, will you?" she retorted. "I am not going anywhere with you. Except out that door right now, with you keeping your hands out of your pockets."

"Are you sure?"

"Yes, I'm sure. Stop fucking around before the cops show up and kill you, Bryce."

His grin deepened. "Well, you can't blame a bloke for trying."

Without warning he shoved her backward. She stumbled on the slippery slate floor. As she grabbed a display to right herself, he stood on the next one over and jumped up, grabbing the lowest of the sprinkler pipes and hauling himself onto the beam to which it was attached.

There above the spray from the sprinklers, she spotted the bundle draped over the beam. A police jacket. Of course. Once the cops showed up, he would change out of his wet shirt, climb out through the roof, and just . . . blend in with the white hats. With her gems in his unobtrusive blue shoulder bag.

"Oh, no, you don't," she muttered, running to the wall and planting her foot on the main sprinkler pipe, then scrambling up it to the nearest beam. The dress didn't make things any easier, but she wasn't going to take it off.

"Samantha, if you're not coming with me, then get down," Bryce warned her, snatching up the bundled jacket and straddling the beam.

"After you." Climbing on top of the old wood, she ran along it in her bare feet to the next one and hiked herself up to just below where he sat. He was bigger and bulkier than she was, but she was faster and more agile. A pretty level playing field, really.

He yanked off his wet black T-shirt and pulled on the police jacket. He even had the local patch on the shoulder. His pants were already a pretty close match, especially in the dark. Damn, it was a pretty good plan—and risky, the way she liked them, too.

She hopped from one beam to the next, her skirt flying around her. "Ah, girl, you make me wish I was down on the floor looking up at you," Bryce commented, fastening the last button and standing on the beam again. "Too bad I have somewhere else to be right now."

"You're going to have to miss that appointment," she muttered, reaching out and just brushing the cuff of his pants. Wrapping her fingers into it, she pulled. Hard.

"Shit!" he yelped, as he lost his balance. Scrambling, he went down, grabbing on to the beam with his fingers as he tumbled past it.

Now they were eye-to-eye. The anger in his gaze could have melted the *Titanic* iceberg. "I said you're not going anywhere with those gems," she stated.

He swung his legs forward, catching her in the thigh as she stood there. For a sickening moment she felt herself overbalance. She bent her knees, gripping the top of the beam with her short fingernails, trying to reverse her momentum. Then she pushed off forward.

Reaching out and catching Bryce around the knees, she hung there for a heartbeat before he lost his grip and they both fell. When they hit the floor, her grip on him broke. Samantha rolled to her feet, shoving her skirt back down past her thighs.

"You little bitch!" Bryce bellowed, grabbing her by the front of the dress and shoving again.

The wet silk threads split, and the bosom of her pretty red dress ripped away in his hands—along with the velvet bag stuffed between her breasts. "Give that back," she panted, feeling her neck to make sure that at least the diamonds Rick had given her were still there.

He shouldered her away again. "What's this?" he asked, dropping the scrap of dress and dumping the contents of the bag into his palm. "Good glory, Sammi, love. You've been doing a bit of midnight shopping on your own, haven't you, now?"

"No. It's a family heirloom. Give it to me." She lunged at him, knowing she was handling the situation wrong, but he dodged sideways and twisted away from her.

"Sam, this bauble must be worth a bloody fortune. You sly little cat. You've been holding out on me."

Fucking great. Okay, he wouldn't understand philanthropy or loyalty to Rick, and the more she wanted it back, the more he would want to keep it. "Do you know how long it took me to get that?" she snapped, trying to turn it into her part of the take for this job. Her feet slipped on the wet, debris-strewn floor, and she stumbled a little. "I am not sharing."

"Then neither am I." Bryce sent a roundhouse kick at her. She sidestepped it, then slipped onto her backside when he shoved a display over in her direction.

By the time she got to her feet and out from under everything, he was halfway up to the roof. Still cursing, she climbed after him. Down below, the speakers clicked on again. "This is the police. The building is surrounded. Release Miss Jellicoe and come out with your hands away from your sides."

So now she was a hostage. As she reached the top beam, Bryce slipped out onto the roof through a small hole he'd obviously cut there. Teetering, the ceiling too low for her to stand upright, she hitched herself along the support, reached up, and scrambled out the hole onto the roof after him. This was war, and she was not letting him get away with the Nightshade Diamond. Not for anything.

"Mr. Addison, let us do our job," Lieutenant Thanefield barked, tapping the microphone button on his shoulder to remind his men to be alert.

If they needed to be reminded, they were in the wrong profession. Richard had immediately assessed Thanefield as a fairly competent officer looking to impress the rich man on the block, as it were, and he hadn't seen anything that would cause him to change his opinion.

He ground his fist into his thigh. Not a peep from

Samantha since she'd gone into the exhibit hall. Whatever conversation she might be having with Bryce Shepherd, he didn't like it. However angry it made her,
whatever she threatened, he should never have let her
go in. If anything happened to her—

Another figure limped into sight beneath the bright
surveillance lights. *Larson.*

"Who's in charge here?" the inspector demanded.
The left shoulder of his tuxedo was torn and bloodied,
but the limp favored his groin. Samantha had said that
she'd kicked him, and she didn't play nice when she was
angry.

"I am," Thanefield returned. "Lieutenant Michael
Thanefield. Who are you?"

Larson fumbled into his pocket and pulled out his
badge. "Inspector Henry Larson, Scotland Yard."

Richard touched the outside of his pocket, where Larson's pistol lay hidden. If he pulled it now, they would
probably both end up full of holes. Even so, it was
tempting. Bloody tempting. "Lieutenant, I have reason
to believe that Inspector Larson is an accomplice in
this robbery," he said aloud.

"What grounds do you have for making that kind of
accusation, Mr. Addison?" Thanefield asked.

Richard knew perfectly well that if it had been anybody but him making that statement, he probably would
have been arrested, himself. People didn't go around
disparaging officers of the Yard. "He attempted to shoot
Miss Jell—"

"I'll tell you on what grounds," Larson interrupted.
"Sam Jellicoe is behind the theft. She tried to kill me
earlier." He clutched his arm. "I imagine I'm only here
because she left me for dead."

Richard snorted, attempting to bury his considerable

anger behind cynicism. "She kicked you because you tried to shoot her, Larson. And you should be glad you have an accomplice because if I hadn't had to track him down, I would have gone after you. And I would have made certain you were dead."

"Mr. Addison!"

"This is ridiculous," Larson shot back, patting at his jacket. "I'm not even armed."

"You—"

With a quick flicker, half the security lights went out. He'd been around Samantha long enough to know that someone had blown a charge on the wiring. And he abruptly realized why Samantha had insisted on putting half the lights on a different system.

"I'll sort this out later," Lieutenant Thanefield said, and tapped his radio again. "Enough of this. Gordy, move your team in."

"Roger that."

God. Armed men bursting into an enclosed space with Samantha inside. Every ounce of his overprotective soul wanted to do something to prevent that—but for once he didn't know what he *could* do without making the situation worse. If she got stubborn about it, did her usual refusal-to-cooperate dance that she frequently pulled on him, she could end up dead. If Shepherd hadn't killed her already. That, though, was why he still held on to the gun.

As he watched the first unit move up to the door, he tried to think like Sam, put himself in the head of a first-class cat burglar trapped in a building with police everywhere. Since the lights had just gone out, he was still inside, or at least *very* close by. The dark would have a purpose—to help him get away.

Richard tore his eyes from the exhibit building for a

moment to look around it. With what looked like half a hundred police officers and security guards in the meadow, Shepherd might even already be out of the building, figuring he could escape in the confusion and the half dark. Samantha had several times mentioned the roof, and even that Shepherd had probably been hiding out on it the other night while they tracked down his cat toy.

He looked up—in time to see a faint figure in a red dress drop ten feet to the ground, roll, and come back to her feet. *Christ*.

"Rick!" she yelled.

"I'm here!" he returned, pushing past Thanefield to head for her.

"He's in a cop uniform with wet pants and a blue shoulder bag!"

"Stay where you are, Miss Jellicoe!" Thanefield ordered. "You, too, Mr. Addison. I don't know quite what's going on, but I will figure it out."

An officer grabbed Richard around the shoulders. "You heard him," the man grunted, pulling in the direction of the perimeter behind them. "This is a police matter."

Nobody kept him from Samantha. Moving fast, Richard elbowed the officer in the gut, sweeping a leg around to take him to the ground. As Rick faced the hall again to continue toward Samantha, the downed officer snickered.

"She does have a way of getting under your skin, doesn't she?"

Richard spun around, but Shepherd was already on his feet, running in the direction of the garden. "Oh, no, you don't," he muttered, and charged after him. "Donner! Stop that man!"

Shepherd was clearly in good shape, but Richard was no slouch, himself. At the edge of the garden he launched into a flying tackle, hitting the thief squarely in the back of the legs. They both went down into a tangled heap amid his administrators and business associates.

He got in one good punch before more officers arrived to pull him off. Samantha grabbed his shoulder as they tried to take him to the ground. "Addison's the good guy!" she yelled. "That's Bryce Shepherd. He is not a cop. Look at him, for God's sake!"

Thanefield stepped in, turning Shepherd toward the light left around the hall. "I know all of my men by sight," he said after a moment, "and you're not one of them. Put him in handcuffs."

"I'll take care of that," Inspector Larson put in, stepping into the middle of the crowd. "I've been tracking Mr. Shepherd for several weeks now."

"You are so full of shit, your eyes are brown," Samantha retorted. "They're working together."

"Don't make slanderous accusations you can't prove, Miss Jellicoe," Larson said coldly. "I am the ranking officer here, and this is my case."

"Put a sock in it, Larson," Shepherd said unexpectedly. "You took a shot at my girl. That's against the rules. He's my partner, fellas. Put him in cuffs."

As they slowly began to bring some order to the chaos, Richard took off his tuxedo jacket and put it over Samantha's shoulders. "You're half naked," he said, buttoning the middle two buttons.

"Line of duty," she returned.

"Hurt?"

"Bruised, but no new holes."

"We need to talk."

"Later." Samantha left Richard's side to walk up to

Shepherd. "I warned you that you wouldn't get away with it," she said with a small, clearly regretful smile.

"I'm not in prison yet, me girl," he returned, "and I've got a cop I can rat out as leverage."

She leaned her hands on his hips, went up on her toes, and kissed him. "Stay away from my stuff, Bryce."

"I can't make you any guarantees, love." His gaze turned to Richard, who was doing his best not to kill anyone. "You think you can hold on to her?"

"Bet on it."

"I may just do that. Cheers."

They headed for the police cars scattered across the gravel parking lot, but Richard grabbed Samantha's hand before she could follow. "I think now would be a good time to talk."

"You have guests."

"I think the thousand police cars are keeping them entertained. You kissed him." Anger, jealousy, worry—he couldn't quite put a name to the feeling running through his chest and his gut, but he didn't like it.

"I had to." She swiped wet hair from her face.

"'Had to'?" he repeated, trying to keep his voice low and even. "And why is that, exactly?"

She lifted her hand, dumping the contents into his. "I had this with me. I planted it on you, but nothing happened, and so I took it back to return it to the safe, except then all hell broke loose, and anyway, Bryce got hold of it. I had to get it back."

"You planted it—"

Samantha shot him her quicksilver grin, tired and disheveled as it was. "Once he had it, I knew he wouldn't get away. It's cursed."

Obviously she wasn't going to apologize for trying to see him cursed. Richard frowned, then took her shoulders and pulled her up against him. Leaning his face down, he kissed her hard. The chances she took—and she thought they were exciting. She'd said that the curse hadn't worked on him. Had he had bad luck? The dinner had gone well, but he and Samantha had argued. And then she'd nearly been shot. Bloody hell. Perhaps he wasn't as immune to luck as he'd thought.

"I was worried that you would have all the fun," he murmured against her mouth, lying, kissing her again, wishing he could somehow pull her inside him, hold her safe from the harm she kept seeking out.

"You got to punch somebody," she returned with a low chuckle. "I know how you like that."

"Are you two finished beating bad guys?" Tom Donner's drawl came from a few feet away. Silently he handed Samantha her red shoes.

Christ, he'd nearly forgotten that he was in the middle of hosting a dinner party. "For the moment," he returned, tilting his forehead against Samantha's. "Shall we dance?"

"Only if you stash that diamond somewhere first. I am not going to risk breaking a heel." She held up a shoe.

He wasn't quite ready to admit anything aloud yet, but the more he thought about it, the more he was convinced that Samantha—and his great-great-grandparents—were correct about the Nightshade Diamond. It was cursed. Larson had threatened that Sam might somehow be implicated in any robbery attempt, they'd realized they had a traitor in their midst, she'd been shot at, and he'd been forced to watch her vanish into a building alone with her former lover and fellow thief while armed police surrounded her. "I'll see to it," he said.

"Promise?"

"Promise."

Epilogue

Thursday, 11:47 a.m.

Samantha lifted the access panel and shimmied beneath the display cabinet. Holding a screwdriver in her teeth, she patiently brought the dozen hanging wires together, then clipped them into the connectors and screwed that bundle into the main circuit panel.

"Samantha?"

"Here," she returned, wiggling one foot. "I'll be out in a sec."

She finished tightening everything down and wriggled out again. Rick, hands in his jeans pockets and a canvas bag over one shoulder, looked down at her from beside the display. "How are repairs going?" he asked, offering a hand to pull her to her feet.

"Good." She dusted off her pants as she stood. "I think we'll be ready to open again by Saturday."

"I heard that Armand Montgomery will be returning to help share the supervision duties."

Samantha grinned. "Yep." Thankfully the V & A hadn't blamed her for the fiasco, since Henry Larson had clearly set things up for Bryce. And because of his meddling, she'd made a few additional adjustments, just to keep things interesting for any more prospective thieves.

Rick kicked his toe against hers, a playful, boyish gesture she wasn't used to seeing, but very much enjoyed. *Wow*. He was her guy, all right. "Do you have time for some lunch out on the terrace?" he asked.

"Sure." She set down the screwdriver.

"One thing first." He faced the busy room. "My apologies, but could you give us a moment of privacy?" he asked.

"Rick," she muttered, frowning. "These are my—"

"Your people, and your gig," he finished for her. "I know. Bear with me."

"Fine."

Once they were alone, he took her fingers and drew her up against him. Samantha tangled her fingers into his black hair and kissed him. The security cameras were up and running again, but knowing Craigson had his eye on her was not going to stop her from enjoying one of Rick's liquid sex kisses.

Slowly Rick straightened. "You're not sad about Shepherd?" he asked.

She shrugged. "I don't get why he did this. He had to know that I'd have just about every possible trick in mind when I set things up."

"You like a challenge," he returned, twining his fingers around hers. "Maybe he doesn't know better than to resist one."

"Apparently not."

He glanced toward the nearest camera. "Can you get those shut off for a minute?"

"I'm not having sex in here with you." That just wouldn't be professional. Fun, but not professional.

"It's not for that."

"Fine." She sighed, picking up one of the walkies from a ladder step. "Craigson. Give me some privacy, will you?"

"Don't do anything I wouldn't do," he returned. The cameras' red lights blinked off.

"Okay. Now what?"

Richard kissed her again, lips and teeth and tongue. Then he opened the canvas bag and produced a familiar mahogany box. "Now let's take care of this, shall we?"

Hesitating, she took the box. When she opened it, Connoll Addison's original note was inside, along with a new one. Beneath them both, the velvet bag containing the Nightshade Diamond lay nestled and secure.

"Read it," he urged, taking the box back while she freed his note.

"'To Whom It May Concern,'" she read, glancing up at him. "'You may not believe in curses; I didn't. I do now. Look at the diamond, hold it in your hand, and then put it back. It's brought the Addison family good luck for nearly two hundred years, and I expect that that luck will have lasted up until the moment you made this discovery. Put it back, and the luck will continue. Regards, Richard Addison, Marquis of Rawley.'"

"Sufficient, do you think?" he asked.

Samantha folded the note again and placed it back in the box. "Do you really believe that?"

"I do. And I'm not willing to risk what a curse might do to us in the long run, considering what's happened over the past week." He closed the box, wrapped it in cloth, and headed to the back of the room.

She watched as he climbed up on a stepladder, removed the loose stone, and put the Nightshade Diamond back into its hiding place. "I wonder what the tourists would say if they knew there was an unalarmed sixteen-million-dollar diamond a foot above their heads," she mused.

"They won't know." He stepped down to the floor again and put the stepladder back where it had been.

"So it's our secret."

"Just you and me, Samantha."

She sighed, taking his hand again and leaning against his side. "I still think we could send it to Patricia."

"We are not sending my ex-wife a cursed diamond."

"Okay." Samantha smiled, pulling his face down with her free hand and kissing him again. "I love you, Rick. Thank you for doing that."

"I love you, Samantha. And I hope you realize that most women would not be happy to lose out on possessing a diamond like that."

The diamond was nothing, if it messed with this life that she was becoming increasingly fond of. And this man, who nestled deeper into her heart every day. "I'm not most women."

"Oh, I'm aware of that." Glancing down, he pulled a smaller box from the canvas bag. "Here," he said, handing it to her.

Her heart actually stopped beating. What if . . . what if . . . Samantha took a breath. First things first. And first, she needed to know what was inside the damn velvet-covered box. Resisting the urge to close her eyes, she flipped open the lid. A pair of glittering triangles, tri-tipped in diamonds, winked back at her.

"They go with the necklace," Rick said. "And I had them made into clip earrings, since your ears aren't pierced."

God, he was so proud of himself. She felt pretty good, too, because she hadn't fainted. She leaned up and kissed him again. "Thanks, Brit. They're beautiful."

"You're welcome, Yank. Have I earned your company on a fishing holiday, now?"

She laughed against his mouth. "Oh, you betcha, stud muffin."

＊ ＊

*A*h, summertime. The kids are off from school and underfoot, the temperature may rise to an uncomfortable level, and your body can't believe it's already swimsuit season . . . but fortunately Avon Books has just the solution for the dog days of summer—escape into a sweeping, passion-filled romance.

Embrace the heat with these sizzling Romance Superleaders—so captivating they come with their own warning: You won't be satisfied until you read all four books.

Enjoy!

＊ ＊

Not Quite A Lady
LORETTA CHASE
May 2007

Darius Carsington is the youngest of the Carsington brothers and divides his life into two parts: 1) studying animal behavior, especially mating habits, and 2) imitating these habits. His father challenges him to either bring one of their dilapidated estates back into shape within a year or get married. Having no interest in marriage, Darius moves to the country and—much to his father's despair—quickly begins to put things to rights. But his lifestyle is challenged when he meets the intriguing Lady Charlotte Hayward, a seemingly perfect lady with a past of her own.

"You put your hands on me." Charlotte's face was quite rosy now.

"I may have to do it again," Darius said, "if you continue to blunder about the place, alarming the wildlife."

He had not thought her blue eyes could open any wider but they did. "*Blunder about?*"

"I fear you have disturbed the dragonflies during an extremely delicate process," he said. "They were mating, poor things, and you frightened them out of their wits."

She stared at him. Her mouth opened, but nothing came out.

"Now I understand why none but the hardiest of the livestock remain," he said. "You must have either frightened them all away or permanently impaired their reproductive functions."

"Impaired their— I did *not*. I was . . ." Her gaze fell to the hat he still held. "Give me my hat."

He turned it in his hands and studied it. "This is the most frivolous hat I've ever seen." Perhaps it was and perhaps it wasn't. He had no idea. He never noticed women's clothes except as obstacles to be got out of the way as quickly as possible.

Still, he could see that the thing he held was an absurd bit of froth: a scrap of straw, scraps of lace, ribbons. "What does it do? It cannot keep off the sun or the rain."

"It's a *hat*," she said. "It isn't supposed to do anything."

"Then what do you wear it for?"

"For?" she said. "*For?* It's . . . It's . . ." Her brow knit.

He waited.

She bit her lip and thought hard. "Decoration. Give it back. I must go now."

"What, no 'please'?"

The blue eyes flashed up at him. "No," she said.

"I see I must set the example of manners," he said.

"Give me my hat." She reached for it.

He put the nonsensical headwear behind his back. "I am Darius Carsington," he said. He bowed.

"I don't care," she said.

"Beechwood has been turned over to me," he said.

She turned away. "Never mind. Keep the hat if you want it so much. I've others."

She started to walk away.

That would not do. She was exceedingly pretty.

He followed her. "I collect you live nearby," he said.

"Apparently I do not live far enough away," she said.

"This place has been deserted for years," he said. "Perhaps you were unaware of the recent change."

"Papa told me. I . . . forgot."

"Papa," he said, and his good humor began to fade. "That would be . . . ?"

"Lord Lithby," she said tautly. "We came from London yesterday. The stream is our western border. I always used to come here and . . . But it does not matter."

No, it didn't, not anymore.

Her accents, her dress, her manner, all told Darius this was a lady. He had no objections to ladies. Unlike some, he was not drawn exclusively to women of the lower orders. She seemed a trifle slow-witted and appeared to possess no sense of humor whatsoever, but this didn't signify. Women's brains or lack thereof had never mattered to him. What he wanted from them had nothing to do with their intellect or sense of humor.

What did matter was that the lady had referred to her *father's* property bordering Darius's. Not her husband's.

Ergo, she must be an unmarried daughter of the Marquess of Lithby.

It was odd—not to mention extremely annoying— that Darius had mistaken her. Usually he could spot a virgin at fifty paces. Had he realized this was a maiden, not a matron, he would have set her on her feet and sent her packing immediately. Though he had little use for Society's illogical rules, he drew the line at seducing innocents.

Since seduction was out of the question, he saw no reason to continue the conversation. He had wasted far too much time on her already.

He held out the hat.

With a wary look, she took it.

"I apologize for startling you or getting in your way or whatever I did," he said dismissively. "Certainly you are welcome to traipse about the property as you've always done. It is of no consequence to me. Good day."

Sins of a Duke
SUZANNE ENOCH
June 2007

*Sebastian Griffin, Duke of Melbourne, is not pleased
when the Prince Regent appoints him as cultural liai-
son to a tiny new kingdom. Sebastian is not entirely
convinced that this kingdom is as great as its ruler
claims it is—or if the kingdom actually exists! And
the fact that Princess Josefina intrigues him far more
than he wishes, makes the situation all the more complicated. Reluctant to lose Prinny's favor, but unwilling to allow England to be taken in, Sebastian settles
on the only plan that makes sense: He will seduce the
truth out of "the princess."*

Princess Josefina, a maid, and one of the black-
uniformed men flanking her faced him as he approached. Tonight she wore a rich yellow gown, low
cut enough that the creamy mounds of her breasts
heaved as she drew a breath. God, she was spectacular. Of course that didn't signify anyth—

She slapped him.

Sebastian blinked, clenching his rising hands
against the immediate instinct to retaliate. The blow
stung, but of more concern was the responding
roar from the onlookers in the Elkins ballroom. He

looked directly into her dark brown eyes. "Never do that again," he murmured, curving his lips in a smile that felt more like a snarl.

"My father and your Regent made a very simple request of you," she snapped, no trace of the soft-spoken flirt of this afternoon in either her voice or her expression. "If you are incapable of meeting even such low expectations, I will see you relieved of your duties to Costa Habichuela immediately, before you can do any harm with your incompetence."

It took every ounce of his hard-earned self control to remain standing there, unmoving. No one—*no one*—had ever spoken to him like that. As for hitting him . . . He clenched his jaw. "If you would care to accompany me off the dance floor," he said in a low voice, unable to stop the slight shake of his words, "I believe I can correct your misapprehension."

"*My* misapprehension? I, sir, am a royal princess. You are only a duke. And I am most displeased."

The circle of the audience that surrounded them drew closer, the ranks swelling until it seemed that now people were coming in off the streets to gawk. Sebastian drew a deep breath in through his nose. "Come with me," he repeated, no longer requesting, "and we will resolve our differences in a civilized manner."

"First you will apologize to me," the princess retorted, her chin lifting further.

All he needed to do was turn his back and walk away. The crowd would speculate, rumors would spread, but in the end his reputation and power would win the argument for him. As far as he was concerned, though, that would be cheating. And he wanted the victory here. He wanted *her* apology, *her* surrender, her mouth, her body. Slowly he straightened his fingers. "I apologize for upsetting you, Your Highness. Please join me in the library so we may converse." He reached for her wrist.

The princess drew back, turning her shoulder to him. "I did not give you permission to touch me."

At the moment he wanted to do so much more than touch her wrist. God. It was as though when she hit him, she'd seared his flesh down to the bone. "Then we are at an impasse," he returned, still keeping his voice low and even, not letting anyone see what coursed beneath his skin, "because I am not going to continue this conversation in the middle of a ballroom."

She looked directly into his eyes. Despite his anger, the analytical part of him noted that very few people ever met him straight on. Whatever she saw there, her expression eased a little. "Perhaps then instead of conversing, we should dance."

Dance. He wanted to strangle her, and she wanted to dance. It did admittedly provide the best way out of this with the fewest rumors flying. The rumors it *would* begin, though, he didn't like. Was she aware that she was making this look like some sort of lover's quarrel? He couldn't very well ask her. Instead he turned his head to find Lord Elkins.

"Could you manage us a waltz, Thomas?" he

asked, giving an indulgent smile. "Princess Josefina would like to dance."

"Of course, Your Grace." The viscount waved at the orchestra hanging over the balcony to gawk at the scene below. "Play a waltz!"

Stumbling over one another, the players sat and after one false start, struck up a waltz.

That would solve the yelling, but not the spectacle. "May I?" Sebastian intoned, holding out his hand again.

After a deliberate hesitation, the princess reached out and placed her gloved fingers into his bare ones. "For this dance only."

With her now in his grasp, the urge to show her just who was in command nearly overpowered him. Mentally steeling himself, he slid a hand around her waist, in the same moment sending a glance over his shoulder at Shay. "Dance," he mouthed. Not for all of heaven and earth would he prance about the floor alone.

"Are you going to explain to me why you sent a carriage without bothering to attend me yourself?" Princess Josefina asked.

"Your English is surprisingly good for a foreigner," he said deliberately. "As a native, allow me to give you a little advice. No matter who—"

"I will not—"

"—you may be elsewhere," he continued in a low voice, tightening his grip on her as she tried to pull away, "you should consider that in England you do not strike a nobleman in public."

"For *your* information," she returned in the same

tone, "my English is perfect because until a year ago I *was* English, raised mostly in Jamaica. And I will strike anyone who insults me."

That settled it. She was a lunatic. "You're mad," he said aloud. "I can conceive of no other explanation as to why you would speak to me in such a manner."

She lifted an elegant eyebrow. "If I am the only one who tells you the truth, that does not make me mad. It makes everyone else around you cowards."

The muscles of his jaw were clenched so tightly they ached. "I should—"

"You should what, Melbourne?" she cut in, her gaze unexpectedly lowering to his mouth. "Arguing with me excites you, doesn't it?" She drew a breath closer in his arms. "And there is nothing you can do about it, is there?" she whispered.

Sleepless at Midnight
JACQUIE D'ALESSANDRO
July 2007

Lady Sarah Moorehouse belongs to the Ladies Literary Society of London, a group of young ladies who, rather than read proper novels by Jane Austen, would much rather read books they're not supposed to . . . Mary Shelley's Frankenstein, *for example. During a discussion, the women decide that they, too, would create the perfect man—figuratively, of course. Each is assigned a task, and Sarah's assignment is to pilfer clothing from the host of a country party, the very attractive and very broad-chested Matthew Devonport, Viscount Langston, who catches Lady Sarah in his bedchamber, his shirt in her hands.*

"Daffodil," Matthew murmured. "Very nice. You're as talented with watercolors as you are at drawing."

"Thank you." Again she seemed surprised by his compliment and he wondered why. Surely anyone who looked at these pictures could see they were excellent. "I've painted sketches of several hundred different species."

"Another passion of yours?"

She smiled. "I'm afraid so."

"And what do you do with your sketches? Frame them for display in your home?"

"Oh, no. I keep them in their sketch pads while I add to my collection. Someday I intend to organize the group and see them published into a book on horticulture."

"Indeed? A lofty goal."

"I see no point in aspiring to any other sort."

He shifted his gaze from the sketch and their eyes met. "Why aim for the ground when you can shoot for the stars?" he murmured.

She blinked, then her smile bloomed again. "Exactly," she agreed.

Aware that he was once again staring, he forced his attention back to the sketch pad. He flipped through more pages, studying sketches of unfamiliar plants with unpronounceable Latin titles, along with several flowers he didn't recall the names of, but which he recognized thanks to his hours spent digging holes all around the grounds. One bloom he did recognize was the rose, and he forced himself not to shudder. For some reason the damn things made him sneeze. He avoided them whenever possible.

He flipped another page. And stared. At the detailed sketch of a man. A very naked man. A man who, was . . . not ungenerously formed. A man who, based on the letters printed along the bottom of the page, was named Franklin N. St.—

She gasped and snatched the sketch pad from his hands and closed it. The sound of the pages snapping together seemed to echo in the air between them.

Matthew couldn't decide if he was more amused,

surprised, or intrigued. Certainly he wouldn't have suspected such a drawing from this mousy woman. Clearly there was more to her than met the eye. Could *this* have been what she'd been up to last evening— drawing erotic sketches? Bloody hell, could this Franklin person who'd modeled for her sketch be someone from his own household? There *was* a young man named Frank on the groundskeeping staff . . .

Yet surely not. She'd only just arrived! Still, in the past he'd made his way into the bedchamber of a willing woman the first night of a house party. . . . He tried to recall the man's features, but as best he could remember from his brief look, his face was shadowed and indistinct—the only part that was.

"Friend of yours?" he drawled.

She drew what appeared to be a bracing breath, then hoisted up her chin. "And if he is?"

Well, he had to give her points for standing her ground. "I'd say you'd captured him quite well. Although I'm certain your mama would be shocked."

"On the contrary, I'm certain she'd take no notice at all." She stepped away from him, then glanced in a pointed fashion at the opening in the hedges. "It was lovely chatting with you, my lord, but please don't let me keep you any longer from your morning walk."

"My walk, yes," he murmured, feeling an inexplicable urge to delay his departure. To look at more of her sketches to see if he could discover yet another layer of this woman whose personality, in such a short period of time, had presented such contrasts.

Ridiculous. It was time to leave, to continue with

his mind-clearing walk. "Enjoy your morning, Miss Moorehouse," he said. "I shall see you at dinner this evening." He made a formal bow, a gesture she responded to with a brief curtsy. Then, with a soft whistle to Danforth, Matthew departed the small clearing, with Danforth at his heels, and headed down the path leading toward the stables. Perhaps a ride would help clear his head.

Walking a brisk pace, he reflected on his meeting with Miss Moorehouse and two things occurred to him: First, the woman's in-depth knowledge of horticulture might be of use to him, provided he could glean the information he wanted from her without her realizing his reasons for wanting it—a challenge, given her nosey nature. He'd attempted to get such information from Paul, but while his head gardener knew a great deal about plants, he did not possess a formal education such as Miss Moorehouse clearly did. In having her as a guest, he might have stumbled quite inadvertently upon the key to finding the missing piece to his quest.

And second, the woman very effectively, albeit very politely, dismissed him from his own bloody garden! As if she was a princess and he a lowly footman. He'd not made an issue of it as departing was precisely what he'd wanted to do. Bloody hell. He still couldn't decide if he was more annoyed or intrigued.

Both, he decided. Miss Sarah Moorehouse was one of those annoying spinster women who peered out windows when they should be sleeping, always turned up in spots where you didn't wish them to be, and tended to see and hear things they shouldn't. Yet the dichotomy of her bookish, plain appearance and her erotic nude sketch fascinated him. As did her knowledge of plants. If she could prove to be of some use to him in his quest, well, he'd simply find a way to suffer her company.

For he'd do anything to end his mission and get his life back.

And if, by some chance, she'd followed him into the garden last night, he intended to see to it that she did not do so again.

Twice the Temptation
SUZANNE ENOCH
August 2007

In two connected novellas, Suzanne Enoch will captivate her historical readers with a sparkling romance and mystery about a cursed diamond necklace set in Regency England, then catapult them to contemporary times, where billionaire Richard Addison and reformed thief Samantha Jellicoe will solve the case.

"It occurs to me, Miss Munroe," Connoll said, taking a half step after her, "that you might wish to give me your Christian name."

She paused, looking over her shoulder at him. "And why is that?"

"We have kissed, after all." And he abruptly desired to kiss her again. The rest of his observations had been accurate; he wanted to know whether his impression of her mouth was, as well. Soft lips and a sharp tongue. Fascinating. He wondered whether she knew how few women ever spoke frankly to him.

With what might have been a curse, she reached out to close the morning room door. "We did not kiss, my lord," she returned, her voice clipped as she faced him directly again. "You fell on me, and then you mistakenly mauled me. Do not pretend there was anything mutual about it."

This time he couldn't keep his lips from curving, watching as her gaze dropped to his mouth in response. "So you say. I myself don't entirely recollect."

"I recollect quite clearly. Pray do not mention your . . . error in judgment again, for both of our sakes."

"I'm not convinced it was an error, but very well." He rocked back on his heels. "*If* you tell me your given name."

He couldn't read the expression that crossed her face, but he thought it might be surprise. Men probably threw themselves at her feet and worshipped the hems of her gowns.

"Oh, for heaven's . . ." she sputtered. "Fine. Evangeline."

"Evangeline," he repeated. "Very nice."

"Thank you. I'll tell my mother that you approve of her choice."

Connoll lifted an eyebrow. "You're not precisely a shrinking lily, are you?"

"You accosted me," she retorted, putting her hands on her hips. "I feel no desire to play pretty with you."

"But I like to play."

Her cheeks darkened. "No doubt. I suggest that next time you find someone more willing to reciprocate."

Connoll reached out to fluff the sleeve of her cream-colored muslin with his fingers. "You know,

I find myself rather relieved," he said, wondering how close he was to treading to the edge of disaster and still willing to career along at full speed. "There are women of my acquaintance who would use my . . . misstep of earlier to gain a husband and a title. You only seem to wish to be rid of me."

Evangeline Munroe pursed her lips, an expression he found both amusing and attractive. "You were blind drunk at nearly ten o'clock in the morning. In all honesty, my lord, I do not find that behavior . . . admirable, nor do I wish to associate myself with it on a permanent basis."

"Well, that stung," he admitted, not overly offended. "Suffice it to say that I am not generally tight at mid-morning. Say you'll dance with me tonight at the Graviston soiree, Evangeline. I assume you'll be attending."

"Are you mad? I have no intention of dancing with you." She took a step closer, lifting up on her toes to bring herself nearer to his height. "I have been attempting to convince you to leave since the moment you arrived. Why in God's name would that make you think me willing to dance with you? And I gave you no leave to call me by my given name. I only told you what it was under duress."

"I'll leave, but not until you say you'll dance with me tonight. Or kiss me again, immediately. I leave the choice up to you."

She sputtered. "If I were a man, I would call you out, sir."

"If I were a woman, I would kiss me again."

* * *

"What do you have there?"

"I don't know," Samantha said absently, brushing dust off the top of the box and stepping to the ground. Mahogany, polished and inlaid—and old. Not some child's treasure box.

"Goodness," Montgomery said, looking over her shoulder. "Open it."

She wanted to. Badly. She was in charge of security for this building, after all, so technically she needed to know about everything inside it. Even old, hidden things. Even when they were inside the stable walls of Rick's ancestral property.

And a closed box of all things—she'd spent the last ten months resisting temptation, but nobody could expect her to ignore a box that had literally fallen into her hands. Rick wouldn't.

Taking a deep breath, she opened the lid. A blue diamond the size of a walnut winked at her. Gasping, she snapped the box closed again. *Christ*.

Montgomery gaped. "That—"

"Excuse me for a minute, will you," she stammered, and headed for the door.

The box gripped hard in her hands, she crossed the temporary parking lot they'd put in for the exhibition, opened the low garden gate with her hip, and strode up to the massive house.

A diamond. A *fucking* diamond. That sneak. They'd been dating—hell, living together—since three days after they'd met, and he'd made it clear that he wanted her in his life for the rest of his life. But he also knew that she had an abysmal track record for staying in one place for very long and that she didn't work with partners.

If this was his way of giving her a gift without sending her running for the hills, well, it was pretty clever, really. He knew she liked puzzles—and a hidden box in a secret hole in a wall was a puzzle. But a diamond wasn't just a gift. Diamonds meant something.

"Rick!" she yelled as she reached the main foyer.

"What?" He leaned over the balcony above and behind her. "You didn't kill Montgomery, did you?"

"I like Montgomery."

For a heartbeat she just looked at him. Black hair, deep blue eyes, a professional soccer player's body—and all hers. The smart-ass remark she'd been ready to make about the diamond stuck in her throat.

"What is it?" he repeated in his deep, slightly faded British accent, and descended the stairs. He wore a loose gray T-shirt, and his feet were bare. Mmm, salty goodness.

Still clutching the box in one hand, she walked to the base of the stairs, grabbed his shoulder, and kissed him.

Rick slid his hands around her hips and pulled her closer. She sighed, leaning along his lean, muscular body. Out of the corner of her eye she saw Sykes the butler start through the foyer, see them, and turn around to head back out the way he'd come in.

Pulling away from her an inch or two, Rick tucked a strand of her hair back behind her ear. "What are actly were you and Mr. Montgomery discussing?" he asked. "Not that I'm going to complain about it."

She took another breath, her heart pounding all over again. "I found it, Brit. It's . . . Thank you, but . . . it's too much."

His brow furrowed. "What are you talking about, Yank?"

Samantha moved the box around between them. "This. When did you put it—"

Rick took it from her hands, glanced at her face, then opened it. "Good God," he breathed, lifting the sparkling orb out of the box by its silver chain. "Where did this come fr—"

"You didn't put it there?"

Of course he hadn't. She was an idiot. Did that mean she'd been hoping for a diamond? So much for independent Sam Elizabeth Jellicoe. Great.